THE THRILLING LIBRARY:

VOLUME 3

BY
WHITNEY ELLSWORTH
AND
NORMAN A. DANIELS

THRILLING PUBLICATIONS
2017

TABLE OF

CONTENTS

VII

THE BLACK BAT'S
FLAME TRAIL

CHAPTER I

HELL REACHES UP

PASQUALE MORELLI considered himself a very lucky man. After months of unemployment, he had got, this day, a job on the construction of the new crosstown elevated highway. It would keep him on a payroll for a long time.

And the newly-rented, three-room flat was a bargain, too, because people were moving into tenements that had already been revamped to conform with the new fire laws. This one hadn't. Well, Pasquale would move his little family into one of those other buildings when he got a little money ahead, but right now he was a very lucky man.

The sad thing about it all was the fact that what seemed luck was, in fact, quite the opposite. Pasquale Morelli was doomed to a horrible death—he and his good fat wife and six *bambinos*.

The kids were asleep now, filled with good pasta and plenty of meat balls and hard-crusted bread. Rosa, the good fat wife, slept also. But who could blame Pasquale for sitting up a little late to enjoy a glass or two of vino while he congratulated himself on his good fortune?

When the thing happened, Pasquale had just a moment in which to wonder what was the matter with him. Were his eyes going bad on him, or had he suddenly been taken drunk?

He was facing the door that entered on the kitchen of the fourth floor flat and, suddenly, that door melted before his eyes—melted like a candle! Wood burned, it didn't melt. Even Pasquale Morelli knew that. Yet, this door melted, and a solid wall of flame rolled into the room.

Pasquale's chair crashed over backwards to the floor, and instinct propelled his legs across the kitchen to the rooms beyond, where the seven beings he loved slept peacefully unaware of this strange horror.

But halfway across the room, the rushing flame caught him. He staggered a few steps further, a ghastly human torch, and then melted— melted into the holocaust that had reached up from hell. The devouring

1

tongues of fire swept over him like a wave, eradicating him as quickly and as thoroughly as an ocean comber effaces an image on the sands of a beach. Even his one piercing scream of agony burned to nothingness in his throat.

PATROLMAN O'MALLEY rounded the corner. There bad been nothing amiss on Seventh-sixth Street. Of that, he was certain. But as he turned the corner, he heard a *pufff,* like the sound of a huge sail filling with a sudden wind. Frowning, O'Malley paused. His gaze was drawn upward. The sky was bright. Then, he heard the spiteful crackling of flame, and the pungent odor of burning wood assailed his nostrils.

He stepped back around the corner, and his eyes bulged.

Number 847 East Seventy-sixth Street was a seething cauldron of flame! The five-story building writhed and twisted in its death agony. Where less than one minute before, had been—by the testimony of O'Malley's own eyes—a quietly whole building, was now this hell-hole of horror. No building, even an old wood-lined tenement, could burn so quickly! O'Malley knew that, and yet—

He streaked for the firebox on the far side of the street. His nightstick shattered the glass, and he yanked the hook savagely.

"And come *quick!*" he shouted, as though his voice could carry along the alarm-system.

There was no need to go to the police call-box—plenty of cruisers would come with the fire apparatus. O'Malley raced toward the burning building.

There were people in that building, trapped. He had to do something to get them out. But he knew in his heart that nothing would come alive from that inferno.

He was wrong about that. He heard, above the roar of the flames, a tight scream. Then a body hurtled through the air before his horrified eyes. It was a live thing when it hurled itself from that fourth-story window, but it thudded sickeningly to the pavement beside O'Malley.

A child!

O'Malley cursed—a bitter curse against whatever it was that could let things like this happen to kids. Then he rushed for the front door of the tenement, his arms shielding his face. No use. The blast of heat hurled him backwards, like the blow of a giant fist. O'Malley sat down, hard. His eyes ran water, and his lungs ached. He coughed until he thought the blood-vessels in his neck would burst.

People were running through the streets now, and windows framed questioning faces. Terror-stricken dwellers in nearby buildings began throwing their pathetic belongings from the windows. The Babel of thousands of voices swelled louder than the roaring of the fire.

Apparatus clanged into the narrow street and screeched to hydrants. Rubber-coated men dragged coils of hose from the carts and went to work with the efficiency of machines.

A tower reared itself like a king cobra from a long truck and climbed fifty feet into the air. A hissing stream of water pounded from its high nozzle.

In a matter of seconds, twenty Niagaras converged on their target, but not a man there but knew the effort to save that building was futile. If they could just control it, keep it from spreading to adjacent buildings!

The structures on either side were, luckily, of brick and masonry. Firemen dragged their occupants into the night, and deluged the buildings.

A POLICE riot car sirened its way to the scene. Twenty bluecoats strung lines, pushed back the crowds. Two ambulance orderlies managed to lift the dead child to a stretcher.

Police Commissioner Warner was out of his squad car before the patrolman at the wheel could stop it. Warner found Fire Commissioner Tuthill in the thick of the fight, directing his men by means of a microphone and a loudspeaker mounted on a glistening red car.

Warner tugged at Tuthill's sleeve.

"Bad one, Fred! How'd it start?"

The fire commissioner turned a red face to the Police Department head.

"Don't know. Your boy on the beat says it just naturally went *phfftt!* Here he is now."

Patrolman O'Malley was staggering toward his boss. His eye-lashes and brows were crisped off. His hand went up to the visor of his scorched cap.

"Never mind that," Police Commissioner Warner said, but he was proud, nonetheless, that his men could remember to salute a superior even when they were as distraught as O'Malley apparently was. "What do you know about this blaze, O'Malley?"

O'Malley told him. "...And I swear by all that's holy, Commissioner, the building was okay when I turned that corner! It couldn't have been a minute! And then it was ablaze from top to bottom!"

Warner's brows went up. "Looks as though somebody had the place drenched with kerosene or gasoline," he said to Tuthill.

The Fire Commissioner shook his head.

"I think we'd detect an odor, in that case. Did you smell anything when you passed the place, O'Malley?"

"No, sir. And I'm pretty sure I would have, if there'd been any to smell." He grinned wryly. "I put in a year in the department garage when I first came on the force, and I got to hate the smell of gas!"

Tuthill's mouth set in a firm line. "At any rate, it's arson. Not much question about that! Whoever set this blaze was merciless, diabolical. God grant that the sight of his work may impress him with its horror—and keep him from setting others!"

"Amen!" echoed Warner. But he had scarcely spoken when a fire lieutenant legged up to them.

"Another fire on the West Side, Commissioner!" he said. "A bad one—and it stinks to hell of arson!"

The eyes of Fire Commissioner Tuthill swung to those of Police Commissioner Warner.

"We've a job ahead of us, Warner!"

It was dawn before the two widely separated blazes were put under control, before firemen could search through the still smouldering ruins for the charred fragments of human beings who had perished.

The final tally was seventeen dead!

CHAPTER II

INVITATION TO PERIL

TONY QUINN, former crusading district attorney, sat at breakfast, a morning paper propped on a rack before him. His keen eyes glowered at the horrible news printed there.

"Seventeen!" he muttered. "Seventeen lives snuffed out in two fires! It makes a man's fingers fairly itch to get at the throat of the fiend who's responsible, Silk!"

"Yes, sir."

A grim smile lifted the corners of "Silk" Kirby's mouth. There was something in Tony Quinn's tone that pre-saged action, and his valet-extraordinary liked action. The former confidence man had had plenty of it since the day he joined forces with the man who was later to become—the Black Bat.

The Black Bat

Silk Kirby had been a confidence man for a good many of his lightly carried forty years, but it was his prideful boast that he had never plied his trade against anybody legitimate. His victims were those who had victimized others.

And then, in a lean period, he had attempted his lone burglary. Chance led him to the house of Tony Quinn, then prosecuting attorney. Silk was not the only intruder in Quinn's house that night. The other was a hood sent to murder the district attorney while he slept.

Silk had been instrumental in saving Quinn's life, and there had sprung up between the two men one of those odd, deep friendships that go far beyond the normal association of employer and employee.

Now, as Silk poured fresh coffee into Tony Quinn's cup, there was a sharp stab of the doorbell. Instantly, Silk whisked newspaper and rack from the table. A cloud seemed to pass over Quinn's eyes, remaining there to blunt their keenness to a dead stare. And as Silk moved toward the door, Quinn got to his feet and reached for the rubber-ferruled cane which was always close at hand while he was at home.

When the front door opened to reveal Commissioner Warner and Lieutenant McGrath, Tony Quinn's eyes stared bleakly over their shoulders.

"Commissioner Warner and Lieutenant McGrath," announced Silk, without the slightest facial indication of the humor which this situation always engendered within him.

Quinn's face wrinkled into a smile of welcome. The deep scars around his eyes tightened.

"Hello, Warner. Hello, Lieutenant. Come in, come in!"

He turned, and tripped over a chair. Warner caught him.

"Thanks, Commissioner. Clumsy of me!"

McGrath stared at Quinn, frowning. Sometimes he'd be willing to swear that Quinn could see as well as, if not better than the next fellow. And then he'd take one of these near-headers!

Warner was upset. "Tony," he said, "have you seen the morning papers?" Then he caught himself. "I—I'm sorry, old man. I forgot."

Tony Quinn interrupted him. "That I was blind? No need to apologize, Commissioner. When one's been blind as long as I have, he gets over being sensitive about it. But I'll answer your question. Yes, I've 'seen' the papers—through Silk's eyes. Horrible!" His fists clenched at his sides, and the cords in his neck stood out. "It's at times like this that I feel my handicap most greatly!"

Commissioner Warner laid a hard hand On Quinn's shoulder.

"I understand, Tony."

McGRATH WAS still looking quizzically at the former district attorney.

"I've been thinking," he said, "this is just the sort of thing that might interest—the Black Bat!"

If he was trying to wring some sign from the face of Tony Quinn, McGrath was disappointed. Quinn's granite countenance was immobile.

"I'm getting pretty sick of you, McGrath!" exploded the commissioner. "When are you going to get it through your thick skull that there can be no possible connection between Tony Quinn and the Black Bat?"

"Sorry," murmured the Lieutenant.

"It's quite all right," said Quinn. "As a matter of fact, I consider the lieutenant's suspicions quite an honor. The idea of being the Black Bat myself is a romantic one. I only wish it were true! But I don't suppose you gentlemen have come to chat about the Black Bat."

"No," admitted Warner, "we haven't, though I wouldn't mind seeing him go to work on the perpetrator of last night's crimes! As police commissioner, I have no real right to say that, because the Black Bat, for all his success in hunting down enemies of society, uses extra-legal methods, I'd have to arrest him if I ever had the opportunity!"

Again Tony Quinn smiled. "And with you and Lieutenant McGrath on the job, Commissioner, the Black Bat has more to fear from the law than from its enemies!"

Warner took a cigar from his vest pocket, and bit the end of it savagely.

"When you were district attorney," he said, "you conducted an inquiry into the incomes of various leading citizens of this city."

Quinn nodded. "Yes, Commissioner?"

"That inquiry," Warner went on, "supplied you with evidence enough to indict and convict several so-called pillars of society who were plundering the city on municipal contracts and things of that sort. If I remember correctly, Amos Willard was one of the men you investigated but did not indict."

"True," said Quinn. "Amos Willard was one of my father's closest friends, but his income seemed to merit investigation anyway. I was happy to find that he was absolutely and unquestionably honest."

"You're quite sure of that?"

Quinn drew himself up to his full six feet two.

"I think you know me well enough, Commissioner, to realize that no personal feelings could possibly enter into...."

"Of course, Tony," Warner said. "I'm sorry. But the hell of it is that Amos Willard seems up to his neck in this arson!"

"You're joking!"

"Unfortunately, I'm not. He was the owner of both the tenement properties that burned last night. They were fully insured, and Willard stands to collect an amount far in excess of their actual value in the depressed real estate market of today!"

Tony Quinn's hand fumbled behind him for a chair. He sank into it.

"I'm willing to wager my life on the fact of Willard's honesty! It's incredible!"

"Wait'll you see the next editions of the newspapers," advised McGrath. "The early sheets didn't have time to get the whole story, but when they find the same man owns both those buildings, they'll go to town!"

"Trial by newspapers!" snorted Quinn. "There's too much of that sort of thing! Commissioner, you've come here for my opinion of Amos Willard. My opinion is that he cannot possibly be guilty of such a crime. He's not a young man, nor is he well. I hope you're not going to allow yourselves to be stampeded by a yellow press into arresting him until and unless you have some evidence pointing definitely to his possible guilt."

COMMISSIONER WARNER sounded worried.

"It's easy to say that, Tony, but it's the constant cross of the Police Department to have to listen to the promptings of the press and the public opinion that the press stirs up. But I give you my word that we won't arrest Willard until we have to."

Lieutenant McGrath had strolled to the windows. The shades were drawn against the bright sunlight and McGrath fiddled, apparently idly, with one of those shades. Suddenly, it shot upward on its roller. A bright shaft of piercing light struck Tony Quinn full in the face. Again McGrath was disappointed, for there was no reaction in the eyes of the former D.A. They gazed unblinking into the light.

"Hell!" muttered McGrath.

"What was that?" asked Quinn mildly. "Sounded like a shade going up in a hurry."

Commissioner Warner was angry.

"It was McGrath making a damned fool of himself again! One of these days, McGrath, I'm going to put you back in uniform and on a beat!"

Quinn saw the two to the door, feeling his way carefully before him with the tip of his cane. At the door he reached forth and fumbled for McGrath's hand.

"Good-by, Commissioner," he said, warmly.

McGrath dropped the hand as though it were red hot.

"I'm not the commissioner!" he exploded.

"Sorry," said Quinn. "One of the curses of being blind is that one is forever making embarrassing errors."

The policemen left and Quinn retraced his steps toward the living room. Silk Kirby was already lowering the shade.

"You heard?" asked Quinn.

"Yes, sir." Silk was grinning.

Tony Quinn tossed his cane onto a chair, and rubbed his eyes.

"McGrath almost got me that time, the suspicious rascal! That sunlight hurt plenty! But what do you think of the set-up, Silk?"

Silk shrugged. "I don't know Amos Willard, of course, but sometimes even the most upright of men turn crooked."

"And vice versa, eh?"

Silk winced, grinning ruefully.

"Yes, sir. But to turn to matters slightly less personal, it struck me that Commissioner Warner was handing you a veiled invitation to get into this thing. Of course, he's always suspected, just as McGrath does, that you're the Black Bat."

Quinn downed his coffee.

"Well, Silk, the Black Bat is not one to refuse invitations, however informal they may be."

He strode to the fireplace, reached up beneath the brick front, and depressed a hidden spring. The unit swung easily forward on well-oiled hinges, revealing a small room completely fitted as a crime laboratory. Here, too, hung the habiliments of the Black Bat, and a rack supporting a collection of lethal weapons.

QUINN SLIPPED out of the light gray suit he was wearing, and donned one of sombre black. A wide-brimmed black hat, pulled well down, concealed as well as possible the frightful scars around his eyes. He slipped twin .38 automatics into holsters beneath right and left arms.

"Just for luck," he said. "I don't expect to need guns."

"You're calling on Amos Willard, I suppose?"

Quinn nodded. "And don't look so out of things, Silk. There'll be action enough for all of us before this thing's over, or I'm greatly mistaken. No ordinary firebug set two blazes simultaneously miles apart!"

Quinn bent, and a cleverly concealed trap door swung up from the floor at his touch. An iron-runged ladder led downward into a gloomy tunnel. Quinn stepped into it.

Silk brushed dust from the shoulders of his chief's coat. "You haven't worn it for some time, sir," he said.

Quinn disappeared into the darkness, and the trap door closed noiselessly.

The Black Bat walked again!

CHAPTER III

THE BLACK BAT VS. THE LAW

A **LONG LOW** tunnel was the Black Bat's course to another exit in a small gatehouse at the rear of his estate. This gatehouse faced a quiet street, and, having peered cautiously out to make certain that no passersby observed him, the Black Bat entered into the street.

Further down, a small black coupé of a popular and inconspicuous make stood at the curb. Innocent enough in appearance, the coupé had a suped-up motor, beneath its shabby hood, which was capable of propelling the car at better than one hundred and ten miles per hour. The Black Bat slipped behind the wheel and stepped on the starter.

He drove carefully and slowly through the city, the brim of his hat pulled far over his eyes. There was scarcely a policeman on the force who did not know Tony Quinn by sight, and everyone of them thought him to be blind.

They knew that acid hurled into his eyes by a desperate criminal in a spectacular courtroom fracas had burned all hope of sight from Quinn's eyes. They knew that horrible months of blackout had tested the courage of the former district attorney while he journeyed to the far corners of the earth in search of a specialist who might give him some hope of seeing again. And they knew that the quest had been fruitless.

What they did not know was that new sight had been given Quinn by an obscure midwestern doctor through the agency of a girl, Carol Hastings. It was her father, dying of wounds inflicted by gangdom, who had bequeathed his eyes to Tony Quinn. In return, he had extracted a promise that Quinn would use his regenerated sight in the endless struggle against the underworld.

Quinn had given that promise gladly, and had been keeping it ever since—the Black Bat, extra-legal Nemesis of crime!

The mask of supposed blindness had been a valuable asset to the Black Bat. Nobody would believe that poor Tony Quinn, deprived of his sight, could be anything more than an object of pity. And that suited Quinn to a T. It made possible his acquired role of the Black Bat, and gave him freedom to pursue his relentless offensive against the hordes of evil.

Silk

Ten minutes later, he had threaded his way into the fashionable neighborhood where the apartment of Amos Willard stood. And in front of the building itself, a crowd gathered, a crowd which grew as the minutes passed. The Black Bat could see fists waving in the air, and there were angry shouts from the crowd.

"Murderer!"

"We want Willard! We'll show him justice!"

A cordon of policemen held the crowd from the entrance of the building. There was no mistaking the temper of that mob. Incensed by the tragedy of the night before, they were ready to lynch the likeliest suspect.

The Black Bat guided his car down a side street and stopped. There were, he could see, two patrolmen guarding the service entrance to the building. There would be small chance of slipping past them.

He opened a secret compartment beneath the seat of the coupé, and from it he took a small, almost-round object. He slipped it into the pocket of his jacket. Then he climbed from the car and walked toward the front of the building.

The crowd and the policemen were more interested in each other than in a tall man in black with a wide-brimmed black hat drawn down over his eyes.

He drew the round object from his pocket and flicked a small lever which fitted flush to its surface. Then he bent and rolled the object slowly toward the mass of people.

PRESENTLY A wisp of smoke appeared, and then a veritable cloud. It rolled in thick billows. There were cries of alarm. And then happened what the Black Bat had expected to happen. A cop blew a shrill blast to his whistle, apparently suspecting that this was some trick on the part of the mob to gain entrance to the beleaguered building.

And that whistle blast drew the two patrolmen on the run from their post at the service entrance. They whipped around the corner and passed so close to the Black Bat that one brushed against him.

He slipped around the corner as quickly and as silently as a shadow. A moment later, he was through the rear entrance. In the thick gloom of the interior he paused, briefly. From beneath his coat, he produced a hood, which, slipped over his head, hid the scars and features of his face. A light, oddly-cut cloak he fastened to his shoulders.

And then, moving forward again, he presented the appearance of that nocturnal creature from which he had taken his sobriquet—the Black Bat.

Rubbish and ashcans littered the floor, but the Black Bat stepped easily over all obstacles as though he were capable of seeing as well in the dark as the average man could see in broad daylight.

And, indeed, he was capable of just that! Through the magic skill of the surgeon's fingers, a miracle had been wrought. Subtle alterations in the corneas and lenses of the transplanted optics had given them the quality of being able to pierce the shrouds of darkness.

The service elevator, an automatic affair, was close at hand. The Black Bat entered the small car and pressed the button for the roof, where the penthouse apartment of Amos Willard was situated. As Tony Quinn, the Black Bat had visited there many times in the past.

The car moved steadily and noiselessly upward, but the Black Bat was tense. When the car reached its destination, the door would open automatically. The Black Bat held his finger on the button which would send it down again. The precaution was a lucky one. The car glided to rest, and as the door opened, the Black Bat could see the broad back of another policeman pacing the corridor!

The Black Bat stopped the elevator at the floor below. He stepped cautiously into the corridor and moved silently, on rubber-soled shoes, to a window. Properly speaking, this was the top floor of the building, for the penthouse above was built onto the roof.

Glancing covertly from the window, the Black Bat observed that there was a ledge, and, further along the wall, an outcropping of bricks that might serve as a ladder.

There was great risk attached to such a venture. Not only was there the considerable danger attached to a slip, which would tumble him to a horrible death on the pavement below, but the risk of being seen.

It was the latter danger which gave the Black Bat more pause. But, he reasoned, every interested person in the neighborhood would be in front of the building, where the crowd and the action were to be found. The Black Bat stepped out upon the ledge, with eight stories of space yawning beneath him.

HIS FINGERS gripped the outcropping of bricks. Halfway up, his fingers slipped, clawing at the masonry, and for one awful moment it seemed that he must hurtle down to destruction. Sweat beaded on his forehead and his muscles ached as he clung grimly to the sheer wall. Then, at last, he pulled himself to the open roof.

A swift glance satisfied him that the roof was deserted. The penthouse reared itself clumsily. The Black Bat moved toward a window. It was locked, and the shade drawn.

"The old man must be plenty scared!" the Black Bat told himself. The shouts of the crowd floated up from the street. "Can't say I blame him," he added.

The Black Bat took a small tool from his belt and inserted it between the two sections of the window. A deft twist of his wrist, and the lock slipped free. The window went up without a sound. He stepped through, his keen eyes probing the room beyond.

But there was no one in this room. The Black Bat moved to the door, listened with his ear against the closed panel. No sound came through. His hand turned the knob, but the door did not yield.

The third key he tried fitted the lock, and the door opened. Across the room, Amos Willard sat before his desk, his head cradled in his arms on the polished mahogany. Protruding from under his arms was a copy of a newspaper with glaring headlines, accusing Willard of arson.

There was something so unnaturally natural about Willard's pose that the Black Bat was instantly apprehensive. He was across the room in a single stride, his hand closing over the old man's shoulder.

Willard came upright easily enough, and then slumped down into the chair, his head rolling from side to side. His eyes, open and glazed, stared at the Black Bat. From just left of the center of his chest protruded the hilt of a paper knife, and his shirt front was scarlet.

It was suicide, beyond question. Amos Willard had placed the knife against his chest, its hilt propped on the desk, and had fallen forward on it, in the manner of the ancient Romans. The old man, apparently completely unnerved by the horrible accusations hurled against him, had taken what seemed the easiest way out.

Could it be possible, the Black Bat wondered, that Amos Willard actually *had* been mixed up in the arsons? Perhaps, he had killed himself in horror at his own guilt. Yet, knowing Willard, the Black Bat doubted it. No, Willard's death was simply another to be added to the list of seventeen, and all the murders lay at the door of—whom? The Black Bat meant to find the answer to that riddle.

The Black Bat's eyes swept swiftly over the room. Opposite the desk was a fireplace, and above it a picture which hung in an incredibly straight

Carol

position. To this picture, the Black Bat strode. As he had suspected, it was hinged, and swung outward to reveal a small but well-constructed wall safe.

FROM HIS belt the Black Bat drew an instrument which resembled a doctor's stethoscope. A tiny battery fitted within this instrument gave it great sensitivity. One end of it, he placed upon the door of the safe, just left of the dial. Then his long fingers turned the dial with extreme caution until a faint click conveyed to his ear the information that the lock's first tumbler had fallen.

He repeated this procedure a number of times, reversing the direction after each click.

The safe yielded. The Black Bat scanned its contents industriously. A few items of jewelry and a considerable quantity of currency he ignored completely, concentrating upon letters and papers which might yield some clue. He exhibited particular interest in a small book which the dead man had apparently kept as a sort of informal record of his multifarious deals in business and real estate.

The entries were too numerous to be examined hurriedly, so the Black Bat slipped the book into the inside breast pocket of his coat. Then he closed the safe, locked it, and rubbed the dial with a clean linen handkerchief.

Again the Black Bat gazed pityingly upon the corpse of his father's friend. But now, Amos Willard was beyond human help, and every second the Black Bat lingered here, added to his own peril. At any moment, somebody might enter the apartment.

Swiftly, he retraced his steps, locking both door and window after him, leaving everything as he had found it. He was particularly careful about fingerprints.

Again, he swung over the parapet and dug his toes into the brick ladder, climbing dizzily downward. Unobserved by any eye on his upward journey, he was not so lucky now. From a window across the street, a wheel-chair patient saw the black apparition. For a moment the man could not credit his eyes. Then he wheeled his chair to a telephone and called Police Headquarters.

The man in the wheel-chair was pretty excited. He had read newspaper accounts of the exploits of the Black Bat. And he knew a certain lieutenant named McGrath had a great desire to unmask the Black Bat, and the man in the wheel-chair was curious himself.

Finally, he got McGrath on the wire and told him what he had seen.

"What!" exploded McGrath, and hung up without bothering to thank his informer.

McGrath barked orders. "Get every radio car in that district converging on Amos Willard's apartment!"

"Yes, sir! And do you want a squad car to take you there yourself?"

"You're damned right I want a squad car! But I'm not going *there!* I've got another idea!"

A wild light of triumph gleamed in the eyes of Lieutenant McGrath....

CHAPTER IV

AND DEADLY PERIL

REACHING THE ledge and the window of the floor below, the Black Bat slipped to comparative safety. The elevator was where he had left it. Again in the dark basement, the Black Bat glided toward the door. Rounding the angle of a wall, the light frame of the exit loomed before him, and framed within it were the figures of the two police guards!

From afar came the whining note of a siren, then another. The Black Bat divined the reason for their approach. He had been seen, and an alarm sounded. Soon, the place would be swarming with bluecoats.

There was no time now to seek another avenue of escape. The Black Bat's hands reached for the twin automatics which nestled beneath his armpits. Wraithlike, he glided forward, and hard steel prodded the backs of the officers.

The Black Bat's voice was as cold and hard as the guns he held.

"Step backward, please!"

The deadly tone forced obedience from the guards. They stepped backward into the gloom. The eyes of one angled back over his shoulder to the dim figure in hood and cape.

"The Black Bat!" he cried.

Electrified, the other patrolman whirled, lunging at the dark figure. The masked man could not shoot. Had these been gangsters, his fingers would have closed without compunction upon the triggers of his guns, but policemen, no.

His right arm swung in an upward arc, and the steel barrel of his pistol crashed against the jaw of the nearest patrolman. The man crumpled to the floor. The other was clawing desperately for his own gun, but the Black Bat was upon him like a whirlwind of fury. Again his arm swung, and the clubbed gun thudded against the policeman's skull. There was a sharp *crack*, and the man slid down beside his fellow.

The dark figure bent swiftly. His fingers danced lightly over the heads of his victims and felt for the pulse in the two throats. He sighed with relief. Both men, though unconscious, were not badly injured.

His fingers touched the forehead of each in a last gesture—and came away leaving a mark on each—a small black sticker in the form of a bat, with wings outstretched. The calling card of the Black Bat!

Swiftly now, his hands ripped the hood from his head and the cloak from his shoulders. They disappeared beneath his coat. The man who presently emerged from that door was simply a tall man in sombre black garb, with a black slouch hat pulled down over his eyes.

But the screaming of sirens was closer now. The Black Bat crossed the street to the waiting coupé, slammed his foot down on the starter. The Black Bat threw his car into gear. He had to get back to his home in a hurry!

The Black Bat suspected that Tony Quinn would be having a visitor, and Tony Quinn had better be there to greet him!

Ten minutes later, he was in his own neighborhood. His route took him down the street on which his house faced, and his heart sank as he saw a police squad car drawn up at the door. McGrath had beaten him home!

BUT WHO was that on the sidewalk? The figure of a girl, lying prone. And a large man, evidently extremely annoyed, who bent over her. The Black Bat grinned. There was more than one way to kill a cat—or delay a policeman!

The Black Bat's car turned two corners and stopped. The man in black slid out and walked swiftly down the street. At the gatehouse of Tony Quinn's estate, he paused long enough to glance up and down the street, then disappeared.

He sped through the tunnel. Before the trap door had settled behind him, the Black Bat was peeling off his black garments and exchanging them for the lighter gray. A touch of his finger released the spring, and the fireplace swung open before him.

He could hear excited voices in the entry-hall. The voice of Silk Kirby, and the voice of Lieutenant McGrath.

"You can call a doctor for this dame whenever you get a chance," McGrath was saying, "but right now I want to see Tony Quinn, I tell you!"

And Silk's conciliatory but firm answer. "I'm sorry, Lieutenant, but Mr. Quinn is resting. He left word not to be disturbed. And you can see for yourself that this girl needs attention!"

"I don't care about the girl. I want to see Tony Quinn! Let me past or I'll slug you!"

McGRATH'S VOICE was a bellow of frustration.

Tony Quinn smiled quietly. "Silk! Silk!" he called. "What's all the excitement? Do I hear Lieutenant McGrath?"

McGrath and Silk appeared in the doorway. Quinn's glassy stare went over their heads. McGrath's face was ludicrous. He stared unbelievingly at Tony Quinn.

"Hell!" said McGrath.

"What is it, Lieutenant?" inquired Tony Quinn mildly.

McGrath cleared his throat in embarrassment.

"I was going by and I saw a dame do a nose-dive in front of your house. So I stopped and brought her in. That's all. Mind if I use your phone?"

"Help yourself, Lieutenant."

"There's the young woman of whom the lieutenant spoke, sir," Silk was saying. "She's in the hall. Shall I call a doctor?"

"By all means, Silk, call a doctor. Do we know the young woman?"

"Never saw her in my life, sir," lied Silk glibly.

McGrath slammed down the hook of the telephone. He turned, growling.

"Got away clear, after slugging two of our boys."

"Who?" asked Quinn. "What are you talking about, Lieutenant?"

McGrath stared at Tony Quinn long and hard before he answered.

"I wish I could be *sure* you don't know what I'm talking about! Well, I'm talking about the Black Bat—and I'd give my hopes of promotion and pension just to get my hands on him for two minutes!"

McGrath went slamming out angrily. And no sooner had he left, than the unconscious girl in the hallway—made a miraculous recovery. She got to her feet and smiled warmly at Quinn and Silk.

"Good work, Carol!" applauded Quinn, and took her hands in his. "But how did you think of it?"

Carol Hastings shrugged. "I saw your car was missing, and just as I was nearing the door, along came the squad car and McGrath. Well, I thought I'd better try to delay our friend as much as possible. So I staggered up to him and grabbed his lapels and did a fake faint." She spoke dryly. "But McGrath isn't a very chivalrous soul, is he? He didn't care whether I lived or died!"

Quinn laughed. "He had something more important on his one-track mind. He wanted to prove I wasn't at home, that I was prowling around as the Black Bat."

Carol Hasting looked deeply at Tony Quinn, and there was something deep and age-old in her eyes.

"McGrath has set himself a tough task," she said, "if he expects to outwit the Black Bat!"

Carol wanted to know the reason for the Black Bat's return to action.

"I suppose it has something to do with the fires," she said.

"Yes," nodded Quinn, and proceeded to tell her of the suicide of Amos Willard.

Quinn treated Carol as an absolute equal in the dangerous game he played in the role of the Black Bat. She had earned that equality. In many an adventure she had proved as fearless and as capable as any man. And it was she who had sent Tony Quinn to the one man who could give him back his sight, her father. The bond which held them together was stronger than fused steel.

When Quinn had finished, Carol said, "But it doesn't make sense, Tony! Unless Amos Willard really did have the properties burned for the insurance. And if he was capable of that, you'd hardly expect him to kill himself."

"Exactly," agreed Quinn. I'm convinced that Willard killed himself only because, being old and not able any longer to cope with things, he couldn't stand the thought of the disgrace that would follow the hurling of those false accusations against him. No, somebody else was responsible for those blazes, and the fact that both buildings belonged to Willard may be purely coincidental.

McGrath

"The simplest answer, of course, is that the fires were set by a firebug. But the average firebug sets a blaze so he can watch it, and watch the spectacle of fire apparatus fighting the thing. He wouldn't be likely to set two fires when he could watch only one of them."

"If you want to allow coincidence," Carol offered, "it's just possible that *two* firebugs set *two* blazes on the same night."

Quinn nodded. "Coincidence is a thing that can't ever be overlooked but I'm afraid it had no part in those two fires. You see, the very nature of the fires argues against it. By the evidence of witnesses, those buildings burst completely into flames, apparently spontaneously, and without the use of oil. That isn't the sort of fire that a depraved pyromaniac would set with a pile of refuse and a candle behind a dark staircase."

"Then it's your opinion, said Silk, "that the two fires were the work of one person, or of persons working together. But why, and how, and who? That's what I want to know."

TONY QUINN paced the room.

"Why? For the reason behind all criminal activity—profit. How? By impregnating the buildings with some substance of a horribly destructive nature. I've got an idea about that, which I intend looking into. Who? That'll be the hardest nut to crack."

For a moment he was thoughtful. "You know," he said, "I believe I'm a wicked person at heart. I tell myself that I hate crime and criminals, but I'm really never so happy as when crime and criminals give me an opportunity to work against them with my life-long friends!"

"I think I know what you mean, sir," nodded Silk. "You don't want criminals to operate, but if they do—well, you like to smash 'em!"

"That's about it, I guess. But, speaking of friends, what's become of our good friend Butch?"

Silk Kirby snorted. "The redoubtable Mr. O'Brien, sir, has been chafing at inactivity of late, and in spite of the fact that you furnish him with a living, he has taken a job as sparring partner in a local gymnasium and fight club!"

"Well, I suppose Butch needs some outlet for his brawn and energy," said Quinn. "For the present, at least, let him keep his job. In the meantime, Silk, I want you to lose your own identity. I think your character of the professor would do very nicely. It makes you appear so respectable. You, Carol, will be Silk's daughter, or rather the professor's daughter."

Quinn's aides exhibited their lack of comprehension.

"I want you to rent an apartment in a good midtown neighborhood, and let people think you're moneyed folks from the West," Quinn explained.

Carol and Silk did not question Tony Quinn's motives.

It was enough that he had issued an order. Carol rose.

"When you've become the professor," she said to Silk, "you can pick me up at my apartment."

At the door, she paused and there was deep concern in her eyes as she gazed long at Tony Quinn.

"And you, Tony," she said, "what are *you* going to do?"

"I'm going to read for a while," said Tony Quinn blandly. "Tonight the Black Bat may do a little reconnaissance, but nothing dangerous, my dear Carol, simply a routine matter."

If deadly peril and the danger of sudden death were a routine matter, then Tony Quinn was telling the truth.

CHAPTER V

A BLIND MAN'S WALK

FROM THE black coat, which he had worn on his morning's foray, Tony Quinn procured the small book that contained notes on the business dealings of Amos Willard. He settled himself in a deep chair and began to thumb assiduously through its pages.

The writing was in the small, cramped style, characteristic of methodical and grasping persons. There were figures showing the income on various properties, and notes anent the disposal of properties which did not yield a sufficient interest on capital invested. And some of the entries were in semi-diary form.

One such entry, under a date somewhat more than a year passed, interested Quinn. It read:

> The new legislation requiring the installation of brick fire-wells in existing buildings decreases to a terrible extent the value of some of my tenement properties. God knows, the depression has lowered their value enough as it is, and now I must sell for what the market offers and reconcile myself to taking a heavy loss.

Subsequent entries showed that Willard had indeed begun the liquidation of his tenement properties, and had lost considerably on each investment.

Then, two months after the entry which had first caught Quinn's eye, came this:

> Have had good offers for tenement properties at 847 East 76th Street and 914 West 86th. In fact, the offers are so good that I am inclined to hold on to the properties. If somebody else wants them, there may be a good reason. I'll wait and see.

Quinn whistled thoughtfully. The two buildings mentioned were the very ones which had burned last night under extremely suspicious circumstances! And somebody had wanted to buy those properties from Amos Willard at prices somewhat above the depressed market.

"But old Amos was cagey," Quinn said to himself. "He had a dog-in-the-manger attitude. He didn't want those buildings until somebody else showed a real interest in them, and then he figured he'd take a gamble and hang on to them. And if he'd sold them, he'd probably be alive today!"

Tony Quinn thumbed his way through the tedious pages of the book. The going was tedious, for nothing of interest showed itself for many pages. At last, however, Quinn paused at an entry made scarcely two months before:

> I have sold mortgages on the 76th and 86th Street properties. The face value of the mortgage in each case is $25,000, but in view of the poor market and the fact that the new legislation makes it necessary to spend considerable money upon the buildings to equip them with brick fire-wells before the end of the year, I was forced to sell the mortgages at discounts of forty percent, which brings me only $30,000 for mort-

gages face-valued at $50,000. Still, in consideration of conditions, I may be lucky to salvage even that amount. If, as I suspect, there is any reason for anybody to want these buildings, I may yet turn a good profit. Buyer is the Acme Mortgage-Servicing Company.

Butch

SWIFTLY QUINN

scanned the few remaining pages of the book, and found nothing further. He picked up a telephone book and found the address of the Acme Mortgage-Servicing Company.

The Acme Mortgage-Servicing Company. Was that the answer to the whole affair? Had the two buildings been burned simply for the twenty thousand dollars difference between the face-value and the actual value of those two mortgages? For, naturally, the holder of the mortgages would have first claim against the insurance money. And would this be an end to the entire horrible business of arson for profit?

The Black Bat thought not. That there was some connection between the mortgages and the fires seemed reasonable, but Tony Quinn had an idea that whoever had been responsible for the deaths of seventeen persons would not be satisfied with a comparatively paltry twenty thousand dollars.

Quinn itched to get into the offices of the company, to see if the records would yield him any further information. But he knew that to go there during business hours and to ask for information would be pointless. He must wait until night.

In the meantime, a long afternoon of inactivity stretched before him. He decided to go for a walk. It was well for blind Tony Quinn to be seen picking his way through the streets on a daily constitutional. It served to allay any suspicions in the minds of certain individuals concerning the *bona fide* quality of his affliction.

Quinn called his intentions up the stairs to Silk Kirby who was busily engaged in making the necessary physical and facial alterations to transform him into Professor Kelton.

Quinn slipped a pair of dark glasses over his eyes, and took up the rubber-tipped cane. Opening the front door, he picked his way carefully down the steps. He smiled mentally at a too-innocently loitering man on the far side of the street. The man had plainclothesman written all over him. Apparently, Lieutenant McGrath was interested in knowing all about the comings and goings of the former district attorney.

The man now strolled languidly across the street and took up a position in the center of the sidewalk, directly in the path of the man with the cane. Quinn minced stolidly forward, tap-tapping before him with the cane. And he walked straight into the detective!

There were apologies on both sides. But Quinn felt that he had made an impression on the other. His heel had come down heavily on the plainclothesman's toes!

Slowly, Quinn proceeded. He walked several blocks, finally pausing as though confused on the curb of a busy thoroughfare. The detective was not many paces behind him.

A gentle hand took Quinn's elbow, and a kindly voice said:

"Can't I help you across?"

"Thank you," bowed Tony.

They started across the street. The man who guided Quinn was a dignified elderly gentleman in pince-nez glasses and rich, though somewhat dated, attire. As they reached the far curb, the old gentleman leaned toward him.

"Here we are, Mr. Black Bat!" he murmured.

Tony Quinn's face did not alter its expression, nor did his bleak eyes shift. But his heart lurched within him. Then he breathed a silent sigh.

"Silk, you rascal! Are you trying to scare me to death?" he said, without moving his lips.

THE PROFESSOR chuckled silently. "Had you fooled at that, didn't I!"

And before Quinn could answer, Silk drifted down the street.

A black sedan swung the corner. A blue-jowled man on the right side of the front seat nudged the driver of the car. "Look! Ain't that Tony Quinn, the ex-D.A.?"

"The guy with the cheaters—the blind guy? Yeah, that's Quinn! Wish yuh'd pointed him out while he was crossin' the street. I'd like to give him a little prod with the fender! He sent me up on a tough rap five years ago, and I wouldn't mind settling the score!"

"Yeah," agreed the other. "But what the hell! He got what was comin' to him anyway when Snade blinded him. There ain't any need to worry about Quinn any more!"

"I ain't worryin' about Quinn," the driver said. "The guy I'm worryin' about is the Black Bat! The papers said he left his sticker on them two cops at Willard's place, an' yuh know what that means, don't yuh?"

The blue-jowled man grinned.

"Sure. It means the Black Bat is stickin' his nose in. But the boss is too smart for him. We got nothin' to worry about."

"I ain't so sure," argued the driver. "We do just so many jobs like them two last night, an' the Black Bat'll be goin' to town. An' when he starts goin', so do I—but right in the opposite direction!"

The man in the back seat spoke for the first time. His voice had a strong nasal quality, due, probably, to the fact that his nose was completely flattened.

"Shut up," he said. "What's the matter with you two hombres, anyway? You see a blind guy that used to be D.A., and all of a sudden you start gettin' your wind up about the Black Bat! It don't make sense! They ain't any connection!"

The man with the flat nose would have been very surprised indeed to know that Tony Quinn, blind former district attorney, and the Black Bat were the same person!

CHAPTER VI

FEARLESS BUTCH

OFFICE BOY Tommy Ahern, of the Acme Mortgage-Servicing Company, was feeling pretty good. He'd been trying for a long time to date Helen, the stenographer. And she'd finally said yes, she'd let him take her out to dinner. Tonight! He'd take her to a place where they had a good *table d'hôte* for a buck, and a pretty fair orchestra.

The drinks would be extra. And then maybe he'd take her home in a cab, and if she'd warmed up a bit with the drinks, maybe she wouldn't mind a little necking.

That was going to run into dough, dinners, drinks, cabs. But it'd be worth it. Helen was a swell number. And what the heck, there was always another pay day coming along.

Tommy and Helen said good night to Mr. Hall, and went out. Hall locked the door after them, and repaired to his private office. He dialed a number on the telephone.

Apparently, Hall recognized the voice that answered at the other end of the line.

"Hello, Boss," he said. "This is Hall. Thought I'd better let you know that I had a visit from a flatfoot named McGrath. Yes, he thought there might be something in the fact that the mortgages on both those buildings were bought through this office. Sure, I convinced him that it was just chance. After all, we do a big business in this part of town. The mortgage on almost *any* building might be serviced through this office."

A throaty chuckle came over the wire. It was a chuckle of amusement, yet it somehow sent a chill down Hall's spine. There was something indefinably cold about it—cold and malignant and cruel. And Hall knew that its owner matched the voice.

"This racket is waterproof, Hall," the voice said. "Waterproof and cop-proof. Relax."

Hall replaced the instrument in its cradle. Thoughtfully he opened a drawer of his desk and produced a bottle and a small glass. His hand shook as he poured, and some of the liquor spilled over onto the polished surface of the desk. Hall mopped it up with his handkerchief, cursing softly. Was there any need for his hand to shake just because somebody called the Black Bat had left a couple of stickers on the foreheads of a couple of cops?

Hall chased the drink with another. His hand was steadier now. He even managed a snort of contempt for the legendary nocturnal creature whose very existence struck terror into the underworld. He took his coat and hat and left the office, locking the door after him....

TONY QUINN finished off a lonely but tasty meal in the shining kitchen of his home. The late afternoon sun could not penetrate the drawn blinds, and Quinn found it necessary to switch on a light.

For a few minutes he stood at the sink, his arms plunged to the elbows in sudsy water. Then, suddenly, he laughed until the tears ran from his eyes. There was something ludicrous about the idea of the Black Bat washing dishes, attired in a muslin apron! He wondered what some of his friends—or enemies would say if they could see him now.

"Man's work is from sun to sun, but Woman's work is never done!" he recited—and dropped a priceless porcelain serving dish. By the time he had swept up the pieces he had made a mental resolution to leave his dirty dishes in the sink henceforward.

Quinn proceeded then to the living room, which was by now in total darkness. He lifted a corner of a blind and peered out. Sure enough, the lonely plainclothesman still kept his vigil on the far side of the street.

"I might at least have invited the poor buzzard in for dinner," Tony told himself.

He called a number. Presently a gruff voice answered.

"Hello, Butch," said Quinn. "I hope you didn't start swinging when the bell rang!"

Butch O'Brien's voice was hurt.

"Aw, cut it out, willya, Quinn? I ain't punch drunk, not yet anyway. And you can't blame me for takin' a job as sparring partner if you don't give me enough to keep me busy!"

"I'm not blaming you, Butch," Quinn hastened to say. "But if you're not too tired, could you come over?"

Butch's voice was all eagerness.

"Sure, sure! It there something stirring, Tony?"

"I'll tell you all about it when you get here," Quinn promised. "Use the gatehouse entrance."

"Okay," said Butch. "But look, turn on the lights in that tunnel, will you? I'm not like you, you know. Last time I came through there in the dark I like to have knocked out my brains!"

"If any," said Quinn, and hung up.

He grinned affectionately. You couldn't help loving that hulk of humanity that called itself Butch O'Brien. And you couldn't really blame Butch for taking that sparring partner job, at that. Butch was the sort of chap who had to be doing something, who had to be throwing his fists.

If he couldn't keep himself busy smashing the heads of assorted gangsters, he had to find some other equally legitimate outlet for his pugnacious energies. Otherwise the might pick a fight with the first policeman he encountered, merely for the sake of having a little excitement for himself.

BUTCH HAD first come to the attention of the Black Bat when, in the role of innocent bystander in a bank stickup, he had practically signed his own death warrant by diving at a thug who was about to spray the crowd with a machine gun. The Black Bat had saved his life, and in return for that Butch had contracted to serve with the little band in their private war against crime.

And he was peculiarly suited for such service. A former pugilist of no little ability, he had huge fists that packed the kick of a Missouri mule. His broad face was battered and scarred, and his nose wandered aimlessly. He had practically no neck, his head apparently sitting directly on shoulders which were the despair of manufacturers of ready-made suits.

There may have been some question as to Butch's beauty and mental capacity, but none whatever as to his courage. Butch feared nothing in the world save dinosaurs, and he hardly expected ever to meet one of those.

Quinn depressed the hidden spring in the false fireplace, and entered the little room to the rear. Again, he slipped from his gray house suit, and slipped into the darker garments of the Black Bat. He was adjusting his shoulder holsters when the trap door in the floor swung upward.

The broad face of Butch O'Brien appeared, and then his body squeezed into view. His smile was pleasantly anticipatory.

"The black clothes, eh?" he said. "That means action. And, boy, will I be glad to quit that sissy sparring partner stuff for a real scrap! Who do you want me to bend, Quinn?"

Tony laughed. "Not so fast, Butch! You'll get plenty of chance to 'bend' things before we're through, or I'm greatly mistaken. But tonight, I just want you to keep an eye on the house."

"Aw, Quinn!" Butch's voice was heavy with disappointment.

"Look, Butch," Tony said patiently, "we can't have everything all at once, you know. I've got to go out, and somebody's got to stay here. Carol or Silk may be calling on the private number, and…."

"Oh, so, I'm just a telephone girl!"

Quinn ignored the interruption. "…and it's just possible that our friend McGrath might come busting in here to see if I'm at home."

Butch O'Brien's eyes brightened perceptibly.

"Now you're talking!" he approved. "If McGrath comes here tonight, he'll have to come in a tank to get past me!"

"Even with a tank," said Quinn, "I'd still bet on you!"

He slipped twin automatics into the shoulder holsters beneath the folds of his coat, and pulled the wide-brimmed black hat low over the seared scars about his eyes.

"All right now," he said to Butch. "Into the living room with you."

Butch stepped from the small room. The fireplace swung shut.

"Good luck, Tony," he said.

Alone, now, Quinn extinguished the lights. His hand patted his belt. The folded cape and hood of the Black Bat were there, ready. He sprung the trap door and stepped down into the inky blackness of the tunnel.

A normal man would have had to feel and grope his way through that Stygian gloom, but darkness was no barrier to the strange eyes of the Black Bat.

CHAPTER VII

THE BIG BOSS

B EARING THE official insignia of the city, a limousine stopped before an office building at the corner of Fifth Avenue and 81st Street. The man in the back seat was out before the chauffeur could open the door.

As the car pulled away from the curb, the man entered the building. In the lobby, only two elevators still operated. One was for late workers. The other, as its neat neon sign indicated, "for members of the Sky Club exclusively."

Kenneth Weeks entered the latter car.

At the twelfth floor, the car stopped and Weeks got out. Strains of music from an expensive orchestra smote his ears.

Apparently Kenneth Weeks was well known in the Sky Club. A shapely hatcheck girl in abbreviated skirt came forward to take his things.

"Hello, Mr. Weeks!"

Weeks patted her. "H'lo, Red. Remind me to take you home some night."

Weeks passed on into a low-ceilinged room in which there were tables, an orchestra platform and a dance floor. Eight scantily attired chorus girls were going through a routine in the worst Cuban tradition, while an exotic, dark-haired girl sang and weaved her seductively lissome body in tantalizing gyrations before them.

As Weeks sat down at a table, there was a dark scowl of greeting from the dark-haired girl. His palms went suddenly moist, and his weak mouth grinned loosely back at her.

The number ended and the chorus danced rhythmically off into a dark doorway. Carlotta strode to Weeks' table, swinging her hips as she wove between the obstructions on the way. He half rose as she sat down opposite him.

"You weren't here last night!" she said. "Where were you?"

Weeks spread his hands "Don't start that business, Carlotta. I was tired out, had to sleep. You sleep all day, you know, but I have to work!"

"My poor Kenny!" Carlotta reached across the table and patted his cheek. "How is your pretty bridge coming along?"

"It isn't a bridge. It's an elevated highway. And I hate the damned thing!"

"So does Mr. Legs Landers. Soon they will be tearing down his beautiful Sky Club to make room for your pretty bridge!"

"Where's Landers now?" Weeks asked, yawning.

"In his office, I suppose. Shall I call him?"

Carlotta was looking at him with mischief in her eyes.

"God no!" exclaimed Weeks. "I wouldn't care if I never saw that guy!" He stood up. "I'm going upstairs. Want to come along?"

"Why not? Maybe I bring you luck."

Carlotta walked beside him, her supple body close to his own. Weeks' palms dampened again.

Outside the dining room, they paused before a small door. There was an ivory bell button, and Weeks pressed this a certain number of times. There was a click, and the door yielded. They climbed a flight of carpeted stairs. Halfway up, Weeks paused, took Carlotta into his arms hungrily.

Her snaky arms went about his neck, and her flaming red lips, parted slightly over the gleaming whiteness of her teeth, turned up to his. They stood thus for a moment. Then Carlotta's lips broke free, and she whispered passionately.

"Sometimes your eye looks away from me, my Kenny! Your eye—all right! But your lips, if they look away too, I kill you!"

A CHILL slithered down Weeks' spine. He didn't doubt for a moment that the girl meant what she said.

The floor, on which they emerged, was fitted as a gambling casino.

The drapes and decorations seemed very expensive.

There were only a few people at the elaborate tables. Weeks drifted to a roulette layout. Carlotta stood beside him. "Give me a hundred," Weeks said to the croupier.

The man slid a stack of yellow chips across the table. No money changed hands, but the dealer made a pencilled note on a small pad.

Weeks placed chips on the black, the even, and the center column. His hands were trembling.

"Double O," announced the dealer.

He swept the chips toward him. In fifteen minutes Weeks' chips were gone.

"Give me another hundred, Joe."

Another fifteen minutes, and these chips, too, were gone. Weeks requested another stack. "Sorry, Mr. Weeks," said the croupier.

Weeks moved off, grumbling.

"What is this, Kenny?" Carlotta asked. "You cannot get more chips?"

"A new rule of Landers'! No more than two hundred dollars a night! How can I make any money that way?"

"At least you cannot lose so much."

"Wait here," said Weeks. "I'm going to see Landers."

He disappeared through a door at the far end of the room. Beyond this door was a small vestibule, and another door. Weeks rapped, and entered. A sleek man of average physique sat behind a huge desk. He looked up.

"Hello, Weeks."

"Hello, Landers." Weeks stood irresolute for a moment. "I want you to take that lid off, Landers."

Landers smiled. "Your salary as city engineer is seventy-five hundred a year, isn't it, Weeks? Well, anybody knows that a guy earning that salary can't afford to gamble more than two hundred bucks a night! That's your limit unless you've got cash to lay on the line!"

"Why don't you stop worrying?" Weeks demanded. "You saw some dough starting in your direction last night, didn't you? And I've got a patent pending in Washington that'll make us rich—both of us!"

Landers chuckled mirthlessly.

"By the time the Boss gets his cut, there isn't much left for suckers like us! And if you hadn't been such a fool for gambling, we wouldn't have had to cut anybody else in on the thing!"

"You did the cutting in, not me," Weeks said. "We could've worked the whole racket by ourselves. Why did you have to cut this mysterious Boss of yours in at all?"

LANDERS STUCK his jaw to within a few inches of Weeks' face.

"All right, baby, you've asked, so I'll tell you! I let you get into the bankroll at this place for fifteen thousand dollars! Don't ask me why, because I don't know. I'm supposed to be smart! Well, the Boss told me to get the dough—or your hide! He also told me that if I didn't get the dough, he'd get my hide, too. D'you know what that means, Weeks?"

Landers' forefinger gave an eloquent imitation of a gun-barrel.

The color had drained from Weeks' face. "D'you mean I'd—I'd have been bumped off?"

"Not only you, but me, too! The Boss doesn't get fooled around with very much. There was another guy once, who ran a joint for the Boss and something went wrong. The guy disappeared. Nobody knows what happened to him, but I do. He's standing in a block of cement at the bottom of the river!"

Weeks sank into a chair.

"My God!"

Landers nodded. "That's right. So, my friend, it's a good thing you came up with the little racket we're working now. Even that almost slipped, and it was nip and tuck for a while again. But now, with this invention of yours, it's running okay. Now, is your hide worth cutting the Boss in on it?"

"Who *is* the guy?" queried Weeks.

Landers spread his hands. "I don't know, and that's the truth. Twice a week, I put the receipts, in cash, into a safety deposit box, together with a report. By the time I go again, the last batch is gone, and whatever instructions there are for me are waiting in that box."

Weeks shook his head. "You're a cagey guy, Landers. It all sounds fishy to me. I've got a hunch you're running the whole racket yourself."

Landers shrugged, smiling.

"For example," Weeks went on, "if you do all your business through a safety deposit box, how could you get in touch with the Boss in a hurry if you happened into a jam?"

Landers motioned Weeks to his side of the desk.

"See this drawer?" He pulled it open. "That telephone is a private wire. It connects with the Boss. Want to talk to him?"

"I wouldn't mind, at that!" Weeks reached for the instrument.

For a moment he heard nothing. Then a voice incredibly hard and cold, almost metallic, grated upon his eardrum.

"Hello?"

The single word was a question, inviting Weeks to state his business. The city engineer experienced a chilling sensation at the base of his spine. He had a sudden, overwhelming desire to put down that phone, to rid himself of that cold, interrogating voice. But he mastered the vague sense of panic, and forced himself to speak.

"This is Weeks," he said, and his voice held a note of bravado. "Apparently you and I are by way of being partners, yet I've never seen you, and I don't know who you are. Wouldn't it be a good idea for us to be a trifle more open and above board with each other?"

"No," said the voice flatly. "When I'm ready to make myself known to you, I'll do so. In the meantime, it would be an excellent idea for you to curb your curiosity. I have sometimes found it necessary to take steps about persons who suffered from an overabundance of that quality. I hope it won't be necessary in your case, Weeks! Good-by."

THERE WAS a definite click. Weeks replaced the instrument upon its cradle. He seemed to be glad to be rid of it—as though he had been holding a venomous snake in his moist hand. He faced Landers, frowning very darkly.

"I still can't be sure you're not behind the whole affair, Landers! How do I know you haven't got some thug with a nasty voice sitting at the other end of that phone just to cover up yourself?"

The door opened. A large, florid man stood with his hand on the knob.

"Oh, I'm sorry. Didn't know you were busy, Landers!" He started to go.

Landers got up. "Don't go, Mr. Morley. We were just talking. Have you met Ken Weeks?"

Morley stuck out a huge paw and gripped the hand of the city engineer.

"Seen him around the place once or twice, I think. I won't keep you for more than a second, Landers. I want to do a little gambling, and I'm not very flush. Can you cash me a check, say for five thousand?"

"I guess so, Mr. Morley, if you'll guarantee to drop a little of it at the tables. But you've been running in pretty good luck lately, haven't you?"

"Not bad," admitted the florid man. "Nicked you for about seventeen thousand in the last week, I think."

Kenneth Weeks looked enviously at the big man. He knew him by reputation, of course. "Big Jim" Morley was a Wall Street plunger, and a familiar figure in sporting circles. And with all his dough, he was still able to win seventeen thousand dollars in Landers' Sky Club, while he, Weeks, couldn't win a bet! It didn't seem fair. And, stealing a glance at Landers, Weeks could see that the club's proprietor was worried about losing that kind of money, too.

Morley was writing out a check, and Landers twirled the dial on the heavy safe in the corner.

"I'll be going. Glad to have met you, Mr. Morley," Weeks said.

He went out. He found Carlotta at the bar, still sipping sherry. She pulled him down on a stool beside her.

"Why are you always drinking sherry?" he asked.

For a brief moment, Carlotta pressed against him.

"Because it makes me love you."

"This is a hell of a place to love me," Weeks said, looking around the peopled room.

"I know, but I have a show to do, right now!"

She got up swiftly, and was gone. Weeks gazed after her. His palms were moist.

Allen Hall, the manager of the Acme Mortgage-Servicing Company, got up from his place further down the bar and moved toward the city engineer. He walked unsteadily. He stopped behind Weeks, swaying slightly. Weeks could smell his heavy alcoholic breath even through his own.

"You're drunk," Weeks said, a contemptuous look on his face.

Hall smiled amiably. "Gambling's your vice, whiskey's mine. Makes us even."

"Not quite," said Weeks. "My brain doesn't get foggy. You let anything go wrong in that place of yours, and Landers'll be annoyed."

Hall pondered deeply. "I wonder," he asked himself, "I wonder if I remembered to lock that safe?"

CHAPTER VIII

THE ACME SAFE

HE PEERED cautiously from the door of the gatehouse. The narrow street was deserted. The Black Bat flitted swiftly down the pavement, more like a shadow than any creature of flesh and blood.

The small black coupé was at the curb. The Black Bat slid beneath the wheel and jabbed with his foot at the starter. Turning the corner, the Black Bat switched on the lights, though he had no real need of them.

A ten-minute drive brought the Black Bat into a midtown business section which was as deserted as a graveyard at night. He found the building he sought. Driving once around the block he discovered with satisfaction that an alley serviced the rear of the place.

Back on the street which fronted on the building, the Black Bat parked his coupé. A swift glance down the street showed no living thing afoot, though the window of an all-night restaurant glowed brightly against the gray façade of buildings across the way.

A moment later, he was in the alley, moving silently and invisibly toward the rear entrance of the building.

The door, as he had expected, was locked. From his belt he drew a ring holding several ingenious keys. Connected by a thin wire to a small but powerful battery, any one of these keys need only be of the correct type to slide into a lock. A magnetic current would then draw the tumblers on the cylinder lock inexorably into the proper position, and the key would turn. The Black Bat had yet to encounter a lock that would not yield.

But now, as he inserted the first key, his sharp ears caught the sound of shuffling footsteps beyond the door. The Black Bat withdrew into the shadows. A moment later the door swung open, and a white-thatched watchman exited, carrying a small tin pail. The man locked the door after him, and groped toward the end of the alley.

"That's a break," the Black Bat told himself. "Won't have to worry about the watchman until he's got his coffee at that joint around the corner."

In a matter of moments, the Black Bat was within the building. An index board directed him to the sixth floor. He sped up the dark stairs on rubber-soled feet, and turned down a gloomy corridor. Before a certain door, he paused, and again the keys came from his belt.

The Black Bat stepped into the offices of the Acme Mortgage-Servicing Company, locking the door behind him. The place was in almost total darkness. But the Black Bat needed no lights. The pupils of his eyes dilated like those of a cat, and every object in the room was as clearly defined as though sunlight streamed into the place.

Against the wall was a cabinet-safe. The Black Bat knelt beside it and grasped the handle. To his surprise, it turned. The heavy door swung open.

Within the safe were the usual ledgers, such as any legitimate business would employ for the keeping of its records. The Black Bat set himself to the tiresome task of going through these records methodically, on the off-chance of finding some scrap of information that might put his foot upon the right track.

But in this he was disappointed. There were interminable lists of properties upon which mortgages were held through the Acme Company, but there was nothing to indicate that any of these mortgages were not absolutely regular.

HE SAT back on his heels, the books strewn about him on the floor, and sighed heavily with annoyance. His search had been fruitless. Perhaps there was no connection between the company and those who burned buildings for profit. Perhaps the fact that Amos Willard had mortgaged his properties to this outfit shortly before the burnings was, indeed, coincidence.

The eyes of the Black Bat stared dismally into the empty interior of the safe. He had the sensation of having driven into a dead-end street.

Then his eyes were telegraphing an impression to his brain. Didn't the bottom of the safe seem unnaturally heavy and thick? The Black Bat's knuckles rapped lightly against the steel. It seemed solid enough.

Still the Black Bat's fingers felt about the edges of the safe's bottom where it joined its walls. And there was space enough to accommodate the tip of his nail!

With renewed interest, he probed at the steel. Presently, he lifted and a thin steel sheet came upward in his hands. The safe's bottom was false. Beneath the tray was indeed more solid metal, but in the diametric center there was a flush-fitting plate, perhaps six by ten inches, and in this plate was a lock.

The lock yielded to the Black Bat's magnetic keys and the plate lifted out with the lock. In the cavity thus revealed, lay a reddish fibre envelope, unmarked. His fingers lifted it out and turned it over. The envelope was sealed with hard wax.

The Black Bat studied it thoughtfully. Was there anything in the envelope worth seeing? If he broke the seals, the owner of the envelope would know it had been tampered with. Yet curiosity impelled him strongly. His search thus far had been fruitless, and now, here was this thing, hidden deep in a secret compartment in a strong safe. Perhaps it held the very information he sought.

He debated the advisability of taking the envelope home, and returning with it later in the night.

Then, with a growl of impatience, he ripped through the seals and drew forth the contents of the envelope. What he saw was an ordinary insurance policy. He spread it out and read it, whistling softly. The policy had been issued only three days before, and covered a valuable inventory of drug sundries in a warehouse leased by the Mercy Drug Company at 789 West Eighty-fourth Street.

Another dead-end. Or was it? Anything in the nature of an insurance policy was suspicious these days. Furthermore, what was an insurance policy covering goods stored in a warehouse doing in the safe of the Acme Mortgage-Serving Company?

He again turned to the books of the company. There was no entry for the Mercy Drug Company, nor any record of a mortgage on the warehouse at 789 West Eighty-fourth Street. That was strange. Then there was no reasonable explanation for the existence of such a policy in the Acme safe.

The Black Bat slipped the policy back into the reddish envelope. For a moment, he hesitated. The fact that somebody had opened the envelope would be evident from the broken seals. Why not seal it again in his own fashion and let its owner wonder how it had been accomplished?

THE BLACK BAT moistened a small sticker and placed it on the back of the envelope. It stood out in bold relief against the reddish background—the weird, spread-winged image of a black bat in flight.

In less than a minute, everything had been replaced in the safe. The Black Bat swung shut the heavy door, and this time he locked it.

A clanging sound in the hallway brought him to a tense stop just before he reached the door. He heard a high-pitched voice—probably that of the old watchman.

"Want me to come with you, Mr. Hall?" it asked.

And then a deeper voice, its edge dulled with drink.

"No, no. 'S'all right. I'm okay."

There was the sound of the elevator door closing and the shuffling of uncertain feet in the hallway. The Black Bat crouched behind a desk. The chances were ten to one against the newcomer's coming to this particular office, but there was no point in taking chances.

A moment later, the Black Bat was glad he had paused. A figure, swaying slightly, was silhouetted against the glass panel of the door, and a key grated in the lock. The door opened, and Hall entered. Even in the darkness of the room, the Black Bat could easily distinguish his features.

Hall, he saw, was a large, florid man, with eyes too small and set too closely together. His mouth was loose, and his nose had the pointed, flared-nostril characteristics which bespoke a man shrewd and sly and cunning. His frame was powerful, and the Black Bat suspected that the slight bulge of his coat at the left armpit was caused by the presence of a gun.

Without switching on the lights, Hall proceeded unsteadily toward the safe. As he passed close to the Black Bat, the latter could smell the alcoholic aura which surrounded him.

Hall bent, tugged at the handle of the safe. It did not yield.

" 'S'all right," he murmured. " 'S'locked. Was 'fraid I forgot."

He stood up, turned, and fumbled in his pockets for a cigarette and a match. With some difficulty he ignited the match with his finger nail and applied the flame to the wavering end of his cigarette.

Then, through the light of the match, he saw a dim black figure crouched behind a desk. The match dropped from his fingers and went out. There was a gasping intake of air in his throat, and he choked on the cigarette smoke. His right hand was fumbling for his left armpit.

"The Black Bat!"

His voice was low, but there was a note of hysteria in it.

"Don't reach for that gun!" advised the Black Bat. "Stand still, right where you are, and maybe you won't be hurt."

Hall's hand still crept toward his armpit. The barrel of one of the Black Bat's guns crashed on his forearm. Hall grunted in pain, cowering back against the wall. The Black Bat's fingers reached beneath Hall's coat and lifted the gun from its holster.

"How—how can you see in the dark?" Hall quavered.

"Never mind that. I want to ask you a few questions—and I want straight answers!"

The Black Bat added point to his words by pabbing his automatic into the big man's midriff. Hall trembled violently.

"Look, you've got me all jittery. Let me get a drink. In my desk."

"All right. Have your drink. But remember I can see every move you make. Get going."

Hall stumbled across the large room, and into his private office. The Black Bat was close behind him, his gun ready. Hall fumbled for the bottle and glasses. The amber fluid gurgled out of the bottle.

Hall's mind, cleared of its heavy alcoholic burden by the shock of his encounter with the Black Bat, was working swiftly. If he, Hall, told this guy anything, he'd get himself bumped off surer than hell. The Boss wouldn't quibble over a squealer. On the other hand, what would the Black Bat do to him if he didn't talk? The man in the black mask sounded businesslike, and he could see in the dark—he had the advantage there.

Or could he see in the dark? Maybe that was just a gag.

With a movement incredibly swift in a man of his size, Hall hurled the bottle at the shadowy outline of the Black Bat. Had the Black Bat not been able to see it coming, his skull would have been cracked. He stepped quickly aside, and the bottle thudded against the back of a heavily upholstered divan across the room.

But Hall was following through, hurling his huge bulk in the direction of his shadowing captor. There was a low growl in his throat.

Instinctively, the Black Bat's finger tightened on the trigger of his automatic, but he stopped the pressure before the hammer tripped. A gun would make too much noise.

His free left arm swung in a wide arc. There was a sharp crack as his knuckles collided with the out-thrust jaw of the other. All of the Black Bat's weight, as well as Hall's forward motion, contributed to that blow. Hall hurtled backward, his heels digging for balance.

Straight toward the lighter oblong of a window the big man's body flew. There was the tinkling crash of splintering glass, and Hall catapulted into space, his hands clawing at the empty air. One piercing, agonized scream tore itself from his fear-constricted throat. The ultimate pavement was six stories below....

CHAPTER IX

FLIGHT INTO DARKNESS

SOFTLY, **THE BLACK BAT** cursed. Mischance had taken from him the first concrete opportunity of learning anything of importance. And the crashing glass and that scream of Hall's would bring people to the scene—people and policemen.

The Black Bat slipped into the corridor. This time he did not lock the door behind him. He sped noiselessly down the stairs. At the first floor he paused, listening for the watchman. There was no sound. In another moment he had gained the rear entrance. Twice, now, he had to pause to make use of his magnetic keys, once to make his exit, and again to leave the lock as he had found it.

Close to the shadow of the wall, he drifted through the alley. He peered around the corner to see single figures converging toward the front of the building. It was amazing how, even late at night and in an apparently deserted neighborhood, a crowd could gather.

The Black Bat heard the high-pitched voice of the old watchman.

"Poor fella! Yeah, he was a little drunk, I guess. You can still smell it on him. He musta fell out the window. Poor fella!"

The voice was blotted out by the piercing shriek of a siren.

The Black Bat removed the strangely shaped cloak, and the mask that hid the frightful scars about his eyes. He stowed both articles at his belt, and pulled the brim of his hat low over his face. Then, he stepped around the corner and approached the little crowd.

He was not impelled by curiosity, nor by desire to remain any longer in the neighborhood than was necessary, but he had to pass the crowd to get to the coupé.

The Black Bat had one glimpse of the crushed figure of Hall, and it was not a pretty sight. An involuntary shudder passed over his frame.

All eyes in that little group were riveted in morbid fascination upon the corpse. None took note of the tall man in sombre black. He passed silently down the street, and stepped into the inconspicuous black car which stood beneath the lamppost.

As he threw the car into gear, another car screamed to the curb by the group on the sidewalk. A police car. The Black Bat sighed softly. He drove slowly and unobtrusively. As he neared the end of the block, another police car turned the corner to face him. Its siren wasn't howling.

The driver leaned on his brakes, and the other policeman swung out of the door. He seemed interested in the small black coupé.

"Hold it!" he was yelling to the Black Bat. "Where do you think *you're* going?" And as though to lend weight to his question, he was tugging beneath the skirt of his blouse for the service pistol that nestled there.

The Black Bat recognized the young policeman. He had once been attached to the district attorney's office when Tony Quinn had been the incumbent at that post. There was not one chance in a million that he would fail to recognize the man in the black slouch hat.

Quinn ducked his head close to the steering wheel and jammed his foot down hard on the accelerator. The powerful motor beneath the commonplace hood took hold with amazing eagerness. The car leaped forward like a live thing. In the split-second it took for the cop to get his gun unlimbered, the Black Bat's car was around the corner.

He heard the grinding of the gears of the police car as its driver turned to take up the chase, and, a minute later, the beams of its headlights swung the corner in pursuit.

By that time, the Black Bat had a lead of a couple of hundred yards, and the coupé was picking up speed at every turn of its wheels. The Black Bat switched off his lights.

Sixty—seventy—eighty. The needle of the speedometer crept around the dial. Without a siren, without even the beam of his lights to signal his approach to every intersection, the speed was suicidal. If any other car should exit from one of these side streets—

The Black Bat peered into his rear vision mirror. The police car was gaining upon him, its siren howling like a banshee. That flivver was capable of ninety miles an hour, and apparently the blue-coated driver was willing to open it up. But the Black Bat fed more go-grease to the thirsty cylinders of his own car.

EIGHTY-FIVE— NINETY— ninety-five— a hundred miles an hour! And out of a side street came a lumbering, horse-drawn milk wagon, directly into the path of the hurtling mass of metal!

The Black Bat turned his wheel ever so slightly. A hard wrench at his maniacal speed would send him rolling end over end to destruction against the granite walls of the buildings that lined the way. The coupé ground in a tight *slalom* around the head of the horse. It was so close that the Black Bat could almost feel the animal's terrified breath against his face. Behind him he heard the tortured screeching of the brakes on the police car.

Without slackening his own speed, the Black Bat proceeded for several more blocks. He doubled in complex fashion until the siren sound was dimly distant, and then slowed to normal speed. He had lost track of the streets, and he paused at the next corner to peer up at the sign post. Sixth Avenue and Eighty-eighth Street. Good! He was almost where he wanted to be. He had a desire to look at a warehouse at 789 West 84th Street.

The district in question was largely given over to warehouses and storage plants. An occasional truck stood backed up to a loading platform, taking on or discharging freight. Now and again a truck would rumble down the cobbled streets. Loaders and drivers seemed intent upon their labors. They took no notice of each other, or of the black coupé that moved slowly through the neighborhood.

Number 789 was a low, rambling building of brick, old and weathered. Its rickety loading platform was of wood, and, somehow, the entire structure gave one the impression of being dry and brittle and inflammable in its interior parts.

Two huge trucks stood before the loading platform, their rear doors swung wide. A dozen men worked quietly and efficiently. Half were

Hall catapulted into space, his hands clawing at the air.

engaged in trundling cartons into the dim interior and the other half labored out with cartons of almost identical appearance. Simultaneously, one truck loaded while the other disgorged its contents. And on the front seat of each truck sat a grim-faced man with sharp eyes—sharp eyes that studied the black coupé as it passed.

All this the Black Bat noted on his one turn past the warehouse. He turned right at the corner, and went many blocks out of his way in order to approach the building, this time, from the far street.

On the surface, there hadn't been anything particularly suspicious about the transactions at the warehouse. Yet the Black Bat hadn't liked the looks of those grim-faced men in the cabs of the trucks, and an unloading of cartons identical with those being reloaded seemed strange, too. And then, there was that brand new insurance policy in the safe of the Acme Mortgage-Holding Company—

There were several cars parked before a building on Eighty-third Street, and lights shone from a door labeled "Office." Well, another car wouldn't rouse any suspicions. The Black Bat parked and climbed out from under the wheel of the coupé quickly.

The property, which gave onto the rear of the warehouse, was a lot which served as headquarters for an auto-wrecking firm. A high board fence guarded the rare assortment of junk which littered the place. The Black Bat climbed over it, easily and without undue noise.

He reached the back of the warehouse only to find no entrance there. The gloom-piercing eyes of the Black Bat swept up the blank wall of the building. From the edge of the roof jutted a stone gutter, apparently an integral part of the roof. The metal pipes which had once led water from the gutter to the ground had long since rusted away, but the holes in the gutter still remained.

The Black Bat searched the cluttered junk yard and found a length of thin but stout cable almost as pliable as rope. At one end of this, he fastened a two-inch bolt, also retrieved from the ground. Again he stepped close to the building. His arm swung twice, once to gauge his aim, and the second time for keeps. The bolt soared into the air, its line trailing.

FOR A moment, the Black Bat held his breath. Then he grunted with satisfaction. The bolt fell neatly through the hole in the gutter and plummeted earthward. The Black Bat took a running hitch in the cable, and pulled it taut. He tested his weight on it, ready to spring back if the stone coping gave way. It held.

He paused now to slip on the weird mask which covered his face, and to don the strange cape with the flowing pointed ends. Once again, he grasped the cable in strong hands, and pulled himself swiftly upward.

Had there been any observer endowed with the power to see through darkness, he would have sworn that the figure which now swarmed up the sheer wall of the warehouse could be nothing but a nightmarishly huge version of that nocturnal creature, the bat.

The owner of that name swung onto the roof. A dozen feet away was a flat trap door. Silently he moved toward it, tested it with prying fingers. It lifted easily.

The Black Bat retraced his steps. He untied the cable, threw it to the ground some distance from the wall. He would have to find some other means of leaving the building. He could afford to leave no sign that some one had gained access to the roof.

He listened carefully at the trap door before he lifted it sufficiently to slip through. The upper floor or the warehouse was deserted, but he could hear the men still working on the floor below. The interior of the upper floor was three shades darker than absolute black, but the Black Bat could see clearly enough.

He hung by one hand, while the other let the door gently down until it rested upon his knuckles. Then he dropped. There was a slight clunk as the door fell shut, but the Black Bat made no sound as his feet hit the floor. The warehouse had the dry, musty smell of old wood, and the Black Bat could see that the place was a tinder-box.

There were several rows of huge cartons in the center of the floor. Labels proclaimed these cartons to contain drug staples of the more expensive varieties. The Black Bat supposed that such a quantity of such drugs would be worth a considerable sum of money. Near the far end of the floor was an oblong of light that denoted a stairway, and close to that was the platform of an antiquated elevator.

As he neared the stairway, he suddenly froze to immobility. Steps creaked on the protesting wood of the stairs. Somebody was coming up! And more than one person—two or three.

The Black Bat retreated to the cover of a row of cartons.

Three heads came through the oblong of light, and then the men reached the upper floor of the warehouse. Each carried a box, perhaps a foot square.

One of these men, the Black Bat recognized immediately, was a particularly vicious criminal known as Conal. As district attorney, Tony Quinn had sent him to prison on a manslaughter charge five years before. His companion, the Black Bat did not know. One was a heavy, blue-jowled man. The other was a slim figure, with a completely flattened nose which gave his speech a strong nasal quality.

The man with the nasal voice was talking.

"Come on, you hombres! Are you scared of the dark, or are you expecting to meet the Black Bat?"

The Black Bat smiled.

CHAPTER X

HOLOCAUST!

CONAL WHINED.

"Cut it out, willya?" It gives me the creeps just to think about that guy!" Then, as the flat-nosed man laughed derisively. "You think you're pretty hot stuff, don't you, Berren!"

"I hope the Black Bat *is* in here," Berren was saying. "The joint'd make a pretty funeral pyre for him!"

"Shut up!" said the blue-jowled man. "We got work to do. Where the hell is the light switch?"

"I got it," said Conal.

There was a click and a single bulb glowed to life in the center of the big room. It cast only a vague light, and left wide shadows behind the rows of cartons.

The three men went methodically to work. The lids of the boxes opened to reveal a considerable quantity of a coarse, reddish substance not fine enough to be called powder. This they traced over the floor in a continuous and intricate pattern.

"Run the line to the stairs and be sure it connects with the stuff on the lower floor," Berren ordered. "I gotta get the ribbon set."

The Black Bat watched the proceedings with keen interest. Here were the men, without a doubt, who were responsible for the seventeen deaths of the night before. They received their orders from higher up, of course, for none of the three was sufficiently intelligent to work a large scale plot through to its cunning end. But theirs were the hands that did the actual deviltry!

Hate burned in the breast of the Black Bat—hate for these cold-blooded killers and all others of their kind. Fierce pride burned in him too—pride and thankfulness that he could do something to help clear them from the earth.

He moved cautiously along the shadowed line of cartons as the blue-jowled man approached. But careful as he was, there was a squeak as his foot touched a rotten plank.

Berren looked up, his eyes wide.

"What was that?"

The blue-jowled man grunted.

"A rat, you fool. The place is lousy with 'em."

The Black Bat exhaled silently. Apparently reassured, Berren knelt and produced a long ribbon of gray metallic appearance. One end of this, he placed in a small pile of the reddish substance which connected with the intricate traceries of the same material.

Outside powerful motors roared to life.

"There go the trucks," Conal called. "We're all set. Five minutes gives us plenty time to get around the corner to the car."

Berren twisted off a section of the gray ribbon.

"This thing's too long."

He tossed the discarded portion to the floor. He fished in his pocket. Conal and the blue-jowled man stood over him, watching.

"I hate to think what'd happen to us if anything went wrong with the layout!" Conal breathed tremulously.

"Nothing's going wrong," said Berren. He struck a match and applied the flame to the end of the gray ribbon. Dull red showed, and ate its way slowly along the metallic substance.

"Let's go!"

THEY STARTED toward the stairway. "Just a minute!"

The voice was low and even and deadly. The three arsonists stopped as though transfixed, turning slowly to peer in the direction of the voice.

"The Black Bat!" The words came in a whisper from Berren's throat.

The Black Bat's automatics were leveled.

"Who's behind this? Who gives you your orders?"

The blue-jowled man's eyes were fixed upon the glowing ribbon, and there was horror in his eyes.

"We gotta get outa here!"

"Yeah, take us outa here, and we'll talk!" Berren's voice wheedled.

The Black Bat's eyes flashed.

"How about those people in the tenements last night? Did you give them a chance to get out? No, you'll talk now! Talk or burn!"

The blue-jowled man still gazed at that glowing ribbon. It was shorter now—nearer to the pile of reddish sand.

"I'll talk!" he cried. "I'll talk! Anything, only let us get outa here!"

"All right—talk!"

"Shut up you fool!" Conal hissed. "Talk, and you'll die anyway!"

The corners of the Black Bat's mouth went up in a grim smile. In the pinch, it was Conal, after all, who showed the most nerve.

"All right," said the Black Bat philosophically, "we stay."

His eyes never left the figures before him, but those other three sets of eyes rested upon the ribbon slowly consuming itself. A minute passed, the perspiration stood out upon the foreheads of the three killers.

The mouth of the blue-jowled man sagged open, and his breath hissed through his teeth. Fear glazed his eyes.

"Ribbon must be getting pretty short," the Black Bat observed conversationally. "Any of you birds ready to talk?"

"Stop it!" screamed the blue-jowled man. His voice was tight with hysteria. "Stop it, for God's sake stop it!" He lunged forward, his clawing hands reaching for the Black Bat.

The Black Bat's finger tightened. His automatic coughed. The slug pounded into the other man's shoulder, spun him in a half circle. With a cry of pain, the man slumped to the floor.

With a curse, Conal
fired at the Black Bat.

But the machinery of battle had been set in motion. Berren threw himself forward. Again the Black Bat's pistol spoke, and Berren stopped dead, his face a mask of surprise, before he pitched forward.

Conal leaped behind the wall of cartons. The Black Bat heard a shot, and a leaden pellet sang past his head viciously. He threw himself sideways, and took a snap shot at the light bulb. It went out.

The ribbon of flame glowed brightly red, dangerously near to the pile of combustible powder.

"Better come out, Conal! You can't see him in the dark—and there isn't much time left!"

AGAIN HE darted quickly to one side. It was well that he did, for, with a curse, Conal emptied his pistol in the direction of the voice. The arsonist stood in full view of the Black Bat, as clearly defined in the darkness as he would have been in broad daylight. But the Black Bat hesitated to shoot. It was too easy.

The man with the wounded shoulder was dragging himself painfully across the floor, whimpering in fear. Berren lay quite still, and a rivulet of blood oozed from a neat hole in the center of his forehead.

It was almost ludicrous to see Conal in the blackness of the warehouse, pressing a fresh clip of cartridges into the magazine of his heavy automatic.

The Black Bat stooped, picked up the section of ribbon which Berren had torn from the strip. He shoved it into his pocket. Into another pocket, he dropped a scant handful of the heavy powder from the mound.

Now his foot stepped down on the blazing ribbon, and there was the acrid smell of burning rubber. But the fire crept on, only inches away from the powder.

The Black Bat did not know, for once, what to do. If he kicked the ribbon away from its target, it might easily encounter another line of the reddish substance. If he picked it up and attempted to carry it from the place, a stray spark dripping from it could be equally disastrous.

Conal was moving slowly across the floor, toward the oblong of light that might mean escape from the creature who had already accounted for two of his companions.

The Black Bat streaked toward him. Conal heard the feet on the rotten planks, and turned, his gun blazing. The Black Bat's twin automatics belched their answer. Conal's body shuddered as the slugs took effect, and slumped lazily to the floor.

Besides the Black Bat, only one man still lived in the embattled warehouse. The blue-jowled man still crept painfully toward the stairs. The Black Bat could not bring himself to leave this murderer behind. Besides, in his thoroughly shaken condition, the man might talk.

The Black Bat was beside him, helping the big man to his feet.

"Who's that? Berren? Conal?"

"It's not Berren or Conal," the Black Bat said quietly. "Come, I'll help you out. There's not much time!"

The blue-jowled man's breath sucked into his lungs in a great gasp.

"The Black Bat!"

"Yes. Come on, you fool!"

"No! No!"

The other's voice wailed upward in a terrified crescendo of hysteria. His one good arm closed in a steel-like grip about the Black Bat's neck. His knee jabbed at the Black Bat's groin. For a moment, the Black Bat hovered on the brink of unconsciousness. Pain permeated his body, racking him with hot waves of agony.

The grip about his throat tightened. The other man seemed determined, in his extremity of pain and fear, to take his enemy with him through the portals of Death.

But the Black Bat showed no desire to go on that final journey. Strength flowed slowly back into him and his steel fingers closed upon the throat of his adversary. The man's constricted breath hissed in his ear. At last, the death-grip of the blue-jowled man relaxed, and he lay in an inert heap, his face a blotched purple.

The Black Bat staggered to his feet. And at that moment, there was a puff of white flame where the metal ribbon touched the reddish powder! Fingers of searing flame reached along the floor, melting the rotten wood of the planking into a curtain of flame.

IT CAME on with incredible swiftness, passing over the figure of Berren. The body crisped to a writhing nothingness. No wonder these tenements had gone up in a matter of minutes! No wonder the seventeen had died without a chance to escape the all-engulfing holocaust!

The heat was unbearable. The Black Bat could feel his skin drying in the fire's scorching breath. And in another moment, the flames themselves would be upon him, washing him from life in the space of a single second.

He turned and ran for the stairway. The inferno raced after him, shrieking its rage. It was like a nightmare, in which the sleeper runs from some inexorable "Thing" which cannot be outdistanced.

He swung down the stairs. Flame dripped after him. It was dripping through the ceiling of the lower floor, too, setting up a mad pattern of new fires. He crashed his way through the closely-piled cartons toward the wide, sliding door that was only partially opened. Long tongues of flame licked out hungrily at him.

A last despairing leap took him through the door, and even as he gained the street the entire interior of the warehouse puffed into a seething cauldron of fire in which nothing could survive. A blast of heat hurled after him through the door, and the force of it sent him crashing to the pavement like the blow of a giant fist.

The Black Bat climbed to his feet. His lungs burned, and tears stung his eyes. He gasped great draughts of the clear night air into his lungs.

The street was still deserted. Swiftly the Black Bat tore off his mask and cloak, and pulled the wide brim of the black hat over his scarred eyes. Behind him the warehouse was a writhing mass of fury. He moved away, his long stride carrying him down the fitfully lighted street.

As he neared the corner, a policeman made the turn, coming straight at him with nightstick raised, running full tilt.

The Black Bat had no time for arguments or explanations. His right arm hooked out and his fist caught the policeman flush on the chin. The man hadn't even time enough to look surprised. He went down like a pole-axed steer.

The Black Bat went on, turning the corner. There was a bright red box on a post. He smashed its glass face, yanked at the hook.

Seconds later, he was in the powerful black coupé, driving carefully toward his home. The sky behind him was brightly crimson, and fire apparatus passed him on his way, thundering through the quiet streets.

A grim smile of satisfaction lifted the corners of the Black Bat's mouth. He had not succeeded in wringing any information from the three thugs. He had been unable to save the doomed building. But he had, at least, established beyond question that gangdom—a cruel and organized gangdom—was behind the fires. And in his pockets, he had samples of the horrible ingredients the criminals used in the setting of their fearsome blazes!

If only he hadn't met that cop! He would suspect who the dark-clad stranger was, and the cry of *"Bat"* would be ringing in all the newspapers tomorrow morning. Well, maybe that was all right, too....

CHAPTER XI

RATS AND THERMITE

QUINN ENTERED the gatehouse on his own estate, and hurried through the secret tunnel which connected with the main house. As he lifted the trap door which gave access to the room behind the false fireplace, he was met by the sight of Butch's bulk and a huge fist drawn back in businesslike fashion.

"Oh, it's you!" Butch said almost disappointedly. He sighed. "But some day somebody's going to come through that trap who shouldn't be coming through it, and I'm going to knock him right out from between his ears!"

"Poor chap!" said the Black Bat.

He was standing before the small laboratory table which graced a corner of the small room, and he was pouring a scant handful of reddish grains upon a thick glass slide. From another pocket, he produced a small section of grayish metallic ribbon.

"What's all that?" Butch demanded.

The man in black did not answer at once. He slipped from his sombre garments, and dressed in his gray house clothes.

"When Tony Quinn is at home," he said, "it's not a bad idea for him to be ready to greet visitors."

Again Butch O'Brien pointed to the materials upon the table.

"What's all that stuff?" he asked again.

"That," said Quinn, "is thermite."

Butch's eyes narrowed. "Are you trying to kid me, Quinn? Termites are little ants that eat through wooden buildings."

Quinn nodded. "True. *Thermite* eats through wooden buildings, too—and a lot faster. Watch!"

He placed the metal ribbon so that one end of it touched the reddish pile.

"This ribbon," he explained, "is made of pressed magnesium. As you see, it burns."

He touched the flame of a match to the end of the ribbon, and it glowed into life, creeping toward the glass slide.

"The powder," Tony Quinn continued, "is a mixture of fine aluminum filings and iron oxide, which is merely ordinary iron rust. But I suspect that this particular mixture contains still another ingredient, an ingredient of terrible power. Watch!"

The glowing ribbon burned to the pile. There was a *pufff,* and a blinding flash of sustained flame. Butch's arms went up before his eyes.

The white heat ate through the glass, liquefying it, and the molten glass, in turn, ate at the porcelain table-top. The sound of sharp cracklings filled the room. Heat shimmered the air.

At last, the light and the heat subsided. Slide and tabletop were utterly ruined. Butch stared at the wreckage. His voice, when he spoke, was a mixture of awe and respect.

"That's some stuff, Quinn!"

"Pretty effective, isn't it! Welders use thermite industrially, and, like most good industrial products, it can be corrupted into inhuman usage. Munitions makers load it into incendiary bombs, and now we've seen what firebugs can do with it, too! But as I said before, Butch, this is the most potent thermite I've ever seen. There's some extra ingredient in it that gives it an effect so devastating that I shudder to think of it!"

Butch was staring at him, wide-eyed.

"And this is the stuff they used in those burnings last night? If I could just make those rats sit in a pile of this stuff themselves!" His gestures suggested that he would take much pleasure in such a sight.

"Three of them did just that tonight, Butch," Quinn said quietly. "And it isn't a pleasant sight even for people you hate, believe me!"

TONY QUINN outlined his night's adventures. Butch listened avidly, his small, honest eyes aglow with excitement.

"You should have taken me with you, Tony!" he said when Quinn had finished. "Between us we coulda dragged those three monkeys outa the warehouse and sat on 'em until they talked!"

Quinn smiled. "Perhaps you're right, Butch. I'm willing to admit that you're a handy man in a pinch."

"Yeah," Butch said disgustedly, biting the end off a cigar. "I'm a handy guy in a pinch, so what am I doing when the pinch happens? I'm playing telephone girl, waiting for calls that don't come!" And does even Lieutenant McGrath come to the door looking for trouble? He doesn't! It ain't fair, Quinn!"

Tony Quinn was laughing aloud. With considerable annoyance, Butch lighted his cigar and puffed furiously. Quinn sniffed the blue smoke.

"What on earth do you do to those cigars of yours, Butch? They smell like moth balls."

"Camphor," explained Butch. "I like a cool smoke, see, so I put the cigars in a humidor with camphor for a few days." His face darkened. "But don't change the subject, Quinn! How come I play telephone girl when there's work to be done?"

"Don't get excited, Butch. I've got a job for you—tonight."

Butch beamed hopefully.

"Tonight? Good! Do I get to smash anybody?"

"I hope it won't be necessary." Quinn scribbled on a piece of paper, his photographic memory reproducing in his brain a page in one of the books of the Acme Mortgage-Servicing Company. "Here are two addresses and the names of two people. One is a young man, the other is a woman. I want you to bring them here, but you'll have to blindfold them, of course, before you bring them in through the tunnel."

Butch groaned. "Getting the guy is all right. I'll bring him back on foot or over my shoulder. But how can I go ringing a dame's doorbell at three o'clock in the morning?"

"That's easy. Turn on your fatal charm."

"Cut it out, Quinn. You know I ain't any ladies' man!"

Tony Quinn shrugged. "You wanted something to do, and I gave you something. Of course, if you think that you can't do it…."

"Okay," grumbled Butch. "Okay, I'll do it!"

At this point, the trap door moved upward, and the dignified head and shoulders of Professor Kelton appeared. Butch dove at the stranger, his fingers seeking the throat. Quinn managed, with some difficulty, to drag him free.

"Your disguise is too good, Silk," he said.

Silk nursed his throat gingerly, climbing into the room. The grinning face of Carol followed.

"Well, doggone!" muttered Butch. "I didn't know it was you two!"

Silk glowered at him. "Remind me never to wear a disguise again without getting your okay!"

"Sure," said Butch.

Tony Quinn and the girl went into the living room.

"Well, Pop and I rented us a nice apartment on the Drive. What do we do now?" Carol asked.

Quinn's eyes narrowed.

"Better get some rest, for one thing," said Quinn. "Tomorrow's another day."

SILK AND Butch came in.

"Incidentally," Silk said, "there's a big warehouse fire on the West Side. Wonder if there's any connection between that and last night's fires?"

In a few words Quinn told them of his night's adventures. With frowning, thoughtful eyes, Carol and Silk looked from each other to their fearless chief.

"And what d'you think I'm supposed to do?" Butch demanded. "I'm supposed to kidnap a guy and a dame in the middle of the blasted night—right now!"

"But I want those two people!" Quinn said. "The entire success of our fight against this vicious ring of arsonists may well depend upon their being brought here tonight! Still, I suppose I can do it myself!"

He moved toward the room behind the fireplace. Tonight, his nerves were more jangled than he ever remembered their being before. The harrowing experience in the flaming warehouse had left him spent and exhausted.

It was Carol who took charge. She caught at Quinn's arm, and there was an imploring look in her eyes.

"Tony, you know any one of us would do anything you asked! But Butch is right, don't you see that? If he starts trying to take a girl from her home in the dead of night, the girl will yell for the police. It's a job for a woman, Tony. I'll go with him and see that nothing happens."

Tony Quinn smiled down at her, and his hard eyes softened. His hand closed on the hand which lay on his arm.

"Thanks, Carol. You're right—as usual."

Carol turned to Silk.

"Make some coffee, strong coffee. All right, Butch my boy, let's be going."

Together the huge, homely man and the slim, lovely girl walked into the secret room, and a moment later they had disappeared through the door in the floor.

CHAPTER XII

AN INTERRUPTED MARRIAGE

DRAINING THE cup, Tony Quinn drank great mouthfuls of steaming coffee laced with brandy. Fatigue drained from his body, and a sense of well-being stole over him.

"That's mighty good coffee, Silk," he complimented.

Silk nodded. "Ought to be! Costs you better than a dollar a cup!"

"What are you talking about?"

"That's right. The brandy is Napoleon, 1814 version. Costs fifty bucks a bottle."

"Nothing's too good for us, eh, Silk?"

"For you, sir; I don't pull that particular cork for anybody but you."

"You show remarkable restraint, Silk." Tony Quinn drained his cup.

Silk carried the tray to the kitchen. When he returned, Quinn was sitting before a large desk, on the top of which was spread a map of the city. Silk peered over his shoulder.

Quinn had made three red pencil marks upon the map.

"The three fires, eh?" suggested Silk.

Quinn nodded. "The first two netted somebody twenty thousand dollars. The third—the warehouse fire tonight—is really big-time. Silk, everything in that warehouse was phony. They insured an inventory of valuable drugs, then moved the stuff out and substituted junk."

"Who did?" demanded Silk.

"The Mercy Drug Company," said Quinn. "But I've a hunch they won't be collecting any insurance on that little job! You see, it's going to seem funny when three bodies are found in the smoking ruins of that warehouse. It's also going to seem funny to have a cop say that somebody who might have been the Black Bat came out of that blazing building and smacked him.

"The insurance company will not pay the claim unless some of those little details can be explained by the policy holder, the Mercy Drug Company. And I'll bet you that Napoleon brandy against a bottle of soda pop that the Mercy Drug Company won't even *file* the claim!"

"You mean, sir," asked Silk, "that the Mercy Drug Company will already have ceased to exist?"

"That's what I think."

"If that's the case," Silk said, "what we've managed to do so far will have been worthwhile. Perhaps, if the crooks find that they can't profit from their crimes, they'll be less likely to perpetrate any others."

Tony Quinn shook his head sadly.

"Considering your own early career, Silk, you show a remarkable lack of insight into the criminal mind. You should know that nothing heightens the avarice of a criminal so much as to see one of his carefully planned crimes go amiss. I'm afraid there will be more trouble than ever, now."

"And in the meantime," complained Silk, "I'm dressed up to represent a guy named Kelton, and I have an apartment on the Drive, and I don't know what it's all about. Would you mind explaining?"

"Not at all," said Quinn. "You're just establishing yourself as a good, solid citizen, and when the proper moment arrives, you're going into the real estate business."

"The real estate business? Are you crazy?"

"Probably," admitted Quinn. There was, suddenly, the sound of screaming tires in the street. "Hand me my cane and my dark glasses, will you, Silk? We're going to have visitors, or at any rate a visitor."

Silk did as he was requested. Quinn slipped the opaque lenses over his scarred eyes. "Now get into the secret room and keep the others quiet when they arrive!" he said.

There was a sharp stab at the doorbell.

"How did you know?" Silk demanded.

Quinn smiled. "When you're blind, your other faculties become more acute. For example, you get to realize that a car which screams to a stop from fifty miles an hour is usually a police car, and when it stops in front of your house, you imagine that perhaps you are about to have a caller. Of course, you can follow the same line of reasoning even if you *aren't* blind. Now beat it while I let McGrath in!"

QUINN WATCHED until the fireplace had swung shut behind Silk, then *tap-tapped* to the front door. He called cautiously through the panel.

"Who's there?"

He heard, first, a deep groan, and then an unmistakable voice.

"Okay, Quinn, open up!"

Quinn threw the bolt.

"Oh, Lieutenant McGrath! Come in, Lieutenant."

The detective entered. He glared suspiciously about the hall, and through the wide arch into the adjoining living room.

"Up pretty late, aren't you, Mr. Quinn?"

Quinn was leading the way. His shoulder thudded against the door frame.

"Late? To tell you the truth, Lieutenant, I have no idea what time it is. My man's not here tonight, and I've been reading."

"Reading? Did you say reading?" There, was an unholy glint in McGrath's eyes, and a grin of long-awaited satisfaction suffused his bulldog countenance. "How can a blind man read?"

Quinn's hand fumbled for the desktop. "Braille, Lieutenant. You read through your fingertips. Fascinating." He held a book in McGrath's general direction, "Care to try your hand at it?"

"No, thanks!" McGrath helped himself to a perfecto from the humidor on Quinn's desk. He sniffed at it, then, apparently well satisfied as to its quality, he bit off a section of the end and placed the remainder of the cigar in his vest pocket.

"There was another fire tonight," he said at last.

"Really?" said Quinn politely, concern in his voice.

"Arson," said McGrath. "A warehouse with a valuable inventory of drugs. They've found two bodies already, and there may be more."

"Good heavens, I hope not!" said Quinn. "A horrible business, Lieutenant, a horrible business!"

"Yes. And there was a young cop named Mahoney slugged by somebody he said was all dressed in black."

"That would be the Black Bat, I suppose."

"It would indeed. The young cop that was slugged is my nephew on my sister's side. A fine lad, and as brave as they come, but he hasn't stopped shakin' yet! Now, what I want to know is, what would the Black Bat be doin' at that fire?"

"I wouldn't know."

"I'm thinkin' maybe he set it."

Quinn shrugged. "That's a possibility, of course, but it doesn't shape up with the Black Bat's activities in the past, does it? Usually he's on the side of the law, in spite of his methods."

McGrath seemed to ignore that.

"Earlier in the night, a guy named Hall fell out a window and got killed. He was drunk," he said.

"Too bad. Unfortunate dissipation. But what's the connection, Lieutenant?"

McGrath sighed heavily. "None, I'm afraid. Unless *you* can tell me something, Quinn!"

Quinn smiled tolerantly. "How long is it since you've taken a vacation, Lieutenant? Seven years? You really ought to drift off someplace and let the hallucinations blow out of your brain!"

McGrath bristled. "Hallucinations, is it? Well, one of these fine days I'm going to see those hallucinations turn solid, and on that day there will be weeping and gnashing of teeth, and it won't be me who's doin' the weeping and gnashing! Does *that* make sense, Quinn?"

"No," said Quinn, "it doesn't." McGrath started for the door. "But you're welcome to that cigar!" Quinn added.

McGRATH STOPPED, glaring at him. Then he jammed his derby over his ears and slammed out of the house.

The fireplace swung open. The little room behind it looked like the subway at rush hour. In addition to Tony Quinn's three aides, there were a boy and girl whom he had never seen before. Both were blindfolded, and the boy's face was almost as white as the handkerchief that covered his eyes. The girl had the advantage of makeup.

"Almost we didn't get 'em!" said Butch. "The guy wasn't at the address you gave us, so we went to the girl's place. And what d'you think? They were just leaving!"

"Leaving for where?" Quinn asked.

Tommy Ahern spoke through tight lips. "None of your damn business! And tell this gorilla to take the blindfolds off of us!"

"Be quiet, Tommy!" the girl named Helen said. "This girl said we wouldn't be harmed, and I trust her. I don't know what it's all about, but we have nothing to hide." She faced in Quinn's direction. "I can't see you, but I like your voice. Tommy and I were going to rent a car and go upstate and get married, tonight. That's all there is to it."

Quinn smiled. "That seems a perfectly respectable thing to do. Look, Tommy, how much money do you earn?"

"Sixteen bucks a week," the boy said sullenly. "But Helen earns twenty. We'll get along. Anyway, what business is it of yours?"

"None," admitted Quinn. "But how would you like it if your wife didn't have to work?"

"I'd like that fine," said Tommy. "But that'll come later."

"It'll come right now," Tony Quinn corrected him. "Helen quits her job, and I pay you the extra twenty bucks every week—make it twenty-five."

"What's the hitch?"

"No hitch at all. Helen quits her job, and the young lady who brought you here takes it over in her name. That's all"

"No good. Even if it's on the level, the boss'd know the difference. He's made plenty passes at Helen, the rat!"

"He won't be making passes at anybody else, ever," said Quinn. "He's dead."

The girl gasped. "Dead? How...."

"That doesn't matter," Quinn said. "The important thing is that he's dead, and that he richly deserved to die. Listen, Helen, you say that you trust the young woman who brought you here, and you've also been kind enough to say that you like my voice. All I can tell you is that we're honest people and that your late boss wasn't. We need your help, and the only way you can help is to accept the proposition I've just made you. What d'you say?"

"I say all right," Helen said. "And that goes for Tommy, too—or I won't marry him!"

"Okay, okay," Tommy said.

TONY QUINN opened his billfold, extracted a crisp note which boasted the figure one and two ciphers in each corner. This he folded and slipped into the palm of Tommy Ahern. "That's a wedding present," he said. "And as you'll need someone to stand up with you, the people who brought you here will drive you to a preacher, and, incidentally, make all the necessary arrangements for the rest of our little deal. Good luck!"

The party of four disappeared into the dark tunnel.

Silk sighed. "There goes the best daughter a man ever had!" he said.

"Carol's a very clever girl," Quinn pointed out. "I see no reason why she shouldn't be able to be Helen Scott of the Acme Mortgage-Servicing Company and the daughter of Professor Kelton at one and the same time. At any rate, my professor friend, you'd better be getting back to your little nest on the Drive."

Silk scribbled on a small piece of paper. "That's the address," he said, "and the telephone number of the building. Good night, Chief. You'd better get some rest!"

"Good night, Silk. Yes, I'll get some sleep."

Silk stepped from the room, and the fireplace swung shut behind him. Tony Quinn sat down before the large desk, but the "blind" former district attorney did not take up the book of Braille. He poured, instead, over a map of the city on which were three red pencil marks. Quinn had a crazy idea that those marks represented the beginnings of a pattern—a definite, diabolical pattern that might yet furnish an answer to the why of the fires, and to the, as yet, unknown fiends who set them.

CHAPTER XIII

PAROLE JUMPER

UNFORTUNATELY, TONY QUINN was wrong about the Mercy Drug Company. They not only filed a claim for Insurance on the warehouse full of drugs—they actually collected. Three bodies had been found in the ruins, and although two of these bodies were burned beyond hope of identification, the third was named as one Rudolf Berren. The identification was established by means of dental work done recently by a local dentist.

"Imagine the unmitigated gall of it!" Quinn said to Carol. "They claim that Berren was their watchman, and that he lost his life in combat with arsonists who also died in the fire. Therefore, they have a reasonable premise upon which to base their claim.

"Not only that, but the insurance company is also mulcted on a ten thousand dollar policy on Berren's life, which could not be payable if it could be established that he lost his life in a criminal undertaking!"

"And the beneficiary of the life policy was Berren's brother?" asked Carol.

Quinn nodded. "And the brother sailed for South America the day the policy was paid, said he'd always wanted to go there! Of course, it's perfectly obvious how that was managed. Whoever's behind this thing has got it figured to pay him a profit of some sort no matter what happens. You can bet that the brother who left for South America didn't leave with ten thousand dollars in his jeans. He's lucky if he was allowed to keep half of it."

"Pretty idea, isn't it?" Carol said.

"Very nice. And there was the same story in the case of Hall. He falls out of a window and gets himself killed, and there's a $15,000 policy on his life, payable to his estate. His estate goes to his wife, who's a miserable, frightened little woman. She won't say a thing to a soul, but do you suppose for a minute that part of that dough isn't being handed over to somebody else?"

"And how about the Mercy Drug Company?" Carol wanted to know.

"Small jobbing outfit," said Quinn, "and in business for twenty years. The owner is a man named Halley. I sat on the edge of his bed for two hours last night, and though he was scared stiff he wouldn't slip an inch. Said he'd taken a loss on a valuable inventory of drugs, and that was all there was to it."

"Too bad you hadn't taken the policy from the Acme safe when you were there," Carol said. "That would have made it a little tougher for them to collect."

QUINN WAS studying the map of the city again. He looked up, shaking his head.

"No, let them collect their insurance. Give 'em enough rope and they'll hang themselves. But the touch I like is the fact that they hadn't any insurance on the warehouse itself. That makes it look good. And, as a matter of fact, they probably couldn't *get* any insurance on the old rats' nest. It was on the verge of collapse anyway.

"They still have the land, and the land alone is worth as much as the land with the warehouse on it."

"Who's the owner?"

"Man named Curland. Insignificant little guy who's sorry he lost his tenant for the warehouse. Our friend, professor Kelton, is calling on him just about this time, with an eye to buying the property."

"What on earth for?" demanded Carol.

Quinn grinned broadly. "Principally because our friend Professor Kelton was getting a bad case of armchairitis. He was beginning to demand a little action." The former D.A.'s face grew more serious. "Too,

I've a hunch—just a silly little hunch, mind you—that something might happen if Silk manages to buy that property."

"Even a hunch is better than nothing," Carol sighed. "I've been working in the offices of the Acme Company for a week now, and all I do all day is listen to Tommy Ahern telling me how happy he and Helen are! The man who took over Hall's job is about as communicative as a fish."

"Yes. Our plodding genius, Butch O'Brien, has been doing detective work on Acme's Mr. Dunbar, you know, and all he can find out is that Dunbar comes from San Francisco. And Dunbar admits that himself!"

Carol paced the room, her high heels clicking across the parquet.

"We're not getting any place, Tony Quinn."

Quinn was up and across the room to her side.

"Sure we are! We know the Acme Company's crooked, and that's something. We've got you planted there, and I have confidence enough in you to know that you'll catch the first wrong ball they pitch. On top of that, Silk's buying a building from a guy who's mixed up somehow in this thing. And if you want another tip, it might interest you to know that I've developed quite an interest in maps!"

Carol smiled up at him quizzically, and for a moment she put here head against the soft sleeve of his coat.

"Tony," she said affectionately, "you're a nut! What have maps to do with it?"

"Quite a bit, I think. But it's like studying the map of a battlefield. It doesn't make sense until you've figured out the terrain, and until you know where your enemy has his forces drawn up. When you know all that, you can begin to stick pins in the map, and move up your infantry and your heavy artillery."

They both turned as the fireplace swung outward to admit Silk Kirby in his role of the Professor. The Professor's dignified countenance was strangely animated. The old gentleman seemed excited.

"I've bought that land!" he exclaimed. "I told Curland I was interested in housing, and wanted to build a model tenement. The price is twenty-five thousand dollars for the land, and Curland contracts to remove the wreckage of the warehouse!"

"Very good," said Quinn. "But that in itself isn't enough to make you as excited as a Mexican jumping bean, Silk. What else?"

"You won't believe me. It's too good."

"Let's hear it anyway. We'll give you the benefit of the doubt."

"Well, Curland seemed impressed by my interest in building model tenements for the poor, said he thought it was a very nice idea, indeed. Then he suggested that it must take a good deal of money for that sort of thing, and if I wasn't too well-heeled with liquid capital, he thought he could put me in touch with an outfit that put out money on mortgage on very good terms considering the bad state of the mortgage market."

"And that outfit, I suppose," Carol said, "would be the company for which I now work."

"That's right, the Acme Mortgage-Servicing Company! Can you tie that?"

"Not easily," admitted Quinn. "When do you see them?"

"Tomorrow morning."

"Good. With you and Carol both sitting in their offices, we ought to go to town!"

BUTCH CAME through the fireplace. Tony Quinn said, "I'm thinking of putting a revolving door there."

Butch was haggard. There were dark circles beneath his eyes, and his clothes were rumpled. He sank heavily into the nearest chair, glowering at the others.

"Those airplanes," he complained, "are no good for sleeping. Sixteen hours to San Francisco, and another sixteen back again! And eight hours hunting all over that burg looking for information about a guy named Dunbar. Anyway, I got the information. The guy's a parole jumper, and his real name's Jones, believe it or not!"

"Why, if you say so, I'll believe it, Butch," said Quinn. "And the information is very interesting. It gives us a nice lead pipe to swing over his head if necessary, and if it isn't necessary, we can always ship him back to the California authorities, anyway."

"Good," said Butch. "How's about lending a guy a bed for the night, Quinn? I'm too tired to even get to my own place."

"You're welcome to stay," said Quinn, "but you aren't going to do any sleeping. You've got to read some scientific material, and you've got to learn it!" He ignored the horrible groans which arose from the deep chest of Butch O'Brien.

"Yes, before morning you have to be at least a half-expert on matters explosive and incendiary, for bright and early you go out to meet a man named Kenneth Weeks, who happens to be city engineer."

Quinn took a newspaper clipping from his desk.

"This was in tonight's paper."

The others grouped together and read the clipping:

WAR DEPARTMENT CLAIMS PATENT

Washington, Mar. 5.—The United States War Department today, appropriated a patent filed by the city engineer of a large Eastern city. It was understood that the formula was for material to be used in incendiary bombs of a nature far more destructive than anything hitherto conceived.

The Secretary of War announced that because of the horrible efficiency of the formula, it would not be used by the armed forces at this time, but would be filed in the vaults of the department. It is understood that the inventor, being a reserve officer, is technically an employee of the Government, which make the Government's step in taking over the patent entirely legal.

"But the large Eastern city it speaks of could be any large Eastern city," Silk said.

"But this is the only large Eastern city where there have been fires that burned buildings as buildings have never before been burned," Quinn pointed out.

"Let's pose a hypothetical case—suppose a man cooks up a formula that he figures will make the most terrific incendiary bombs in the world. Inasmuch as incendiary bombs are intended to burn buildings, how would our man better test the practicability of his formula than by actually *burning* some buildings with it?"

Silk and Carol seemed to be weighing the possibilities.

"It sounds very reasonable to me, Quinn!" Butch said. "Where's all this scientific stuff you want me to learn? The sooner I get my hands on the guy that's been roastin' people alive, the better I'll like it!"

Quinn produced an encyclopedia, together with several learned tomes dealing with combustibles. Book markers were carefully inserted at the proper places.

"Sit down and go to work," he invited Butch, "but remember this—I want you to get all this stuff in your head, but I want you to get it all twisted and hind foremost, so that anybody to whom you talked about it would consider you crazy."

"Huh!" Silk said. "That's no trick for Butch!"

Butch glared at Silk from red-rimmed eyes. "All I got to say, Professor Kelton, is that it's very lucky for you that I'm too doggoned tired to get up and smack you for that crack!"

CHAPTER XIV

HIGHWAY BATTLE

PROMPTLY AT ten o'clock the next morning, Professor Kelton entered the offices of the Acme Mortgage-Servicing Company with Leonard Curland, owner of the burned warehouse.

Carol Hastings, maintaining the identity of Helen Scott, stenographer, looked up without recognition.

Curland was looking at her.

"Are you Miss Scott?" he asked.

"Yes," said Carol.

"I'm sorry, I didn't recognize you at first," said Curland. "But then, I've met you only once before."

Carol smiled. "It's quite all right, Mr. Curland. Did you wish to see Mr. Dunbar?"

She escorted the two visitors into Dunbar's private sanctum, then withdrew discreetly, closing the door after her.

Curland introduced Professor Kelton to Dunbar.

"If you're not too busy, Mr. Dunbar," he suggested, "why don't we step downstairs to a restaurant for our little talk? I came away without breakfast this morning, and I could stand a cup of coffee."

There was a signal in his look that told Dunbar that what he said was more an order than a suggestion.

The three men left the office.

Over a white tablecloth they talked. Curland explained to Dunbar that Professor Kelton was interested in building model tenements, but that in order to accomplish his plans on an adequate scale, it would be necessary for him to mortgage each property he acquired before he could go on to buy the next.

Dunbar nodded gravely. He considered Professor Kelton's plan an extremely worthy one. Acme would be very happy to coöperate with him to the limit of its resources. Of course, in the present state of the mortgage market, they would be forced to ask for a bonus on any mortgage placed. For example, if Professor Kelton intended to build a fifty thousand dollar tenement on the property he had acquired for twenty-five thousand, Acme could give him a—well, say thirty-five thousand dollar mortgage on the place, but the company would require a thirty percent bonus on the transaction.

"In other words," said the Professor, "the mortgage would have a face value of thirty-five thousand dollars, but I would receive slightly less than twenty-five thousand in actual cash." He sighed.

"It seems like a lot, but I've come to the time of life where I'm more interested in doing a little good in the world than I am in my personal fortune. We can probably do business, Mr. Dunbar." He rose. "As soon as my architect has plans for the new building, I'll contact you."

The Professor left the restaurant.

"What was the idea of bringing us down here?" Dunbar demanded.

"Because I didn't like your stenographer," said Curland.

"Didn't like her? Personally, I thought she was quite a tasty dish!"

Curland glowered. "I'm not speaking of her physical attractions, Dunbar. The point is, she's not the Miss Scott who used to work for Hall! Oh, she's enough like her to be her sister, but there's one thing about her that doesn't match. Miss Scott's eyes were blue—and this dame's eyes are brown!"

"Then...."

"That's right! She's a ringer! A spy!"

BUTCH O'BRIEN climbed the scaffolding that surrounded the first stages of construction on the new Crosstown Elevated Highway. He was still tired, and his head buzzed with an accumulation of technical knowledge—or misknowledge. For two hours Tony Quinn had been coaching him in the intricacies of science.

A laborer pointed out the city engineer.

As the huge bulk of Butch approached him, Weeks looked up apprehensively from the blueprint which he held before him. Butch noted that the blueprint shook and that the city engineer's mouth twitched in a face that was pasty white.

Butch introduced himself. "...and I fool around with chemistry quite a bit now that I can't fight any more." He grinned a vacuous grin. "Guess I'm a little what they call punch-drunk." Then his face grew ardently serious. "But it don't affect my thinking any. Look, Mr. Weeks, you got a big job in this new highway, and you're gonna have to use a lot of rivets unless you use this invention of mine."

Weeks relaxed somewhat. This man was quite evidently a crank, but probably a harmless one.

"What's on your mind?" he asked.

Butch plunged into his explanation.

"Well, this invention of mine makes it possible to do away with rivets. You weld the joints instead, see? You take a mixture of aluminum filings and iron oxide, and you put it on the joint you wanta weld, see? Then you ignite it with magnesium, and it makes the hottest heat you ever saw! *Fooof!* like that—and the joint's welded, see?"

Weeks was looking at him narrowly. Butch's countenance was suffused with nothing more subtle than an apparently avid desire to make the city engineer appreciate the magnitude of his discovery.

Weeks smiled tolerantly. "It's a good idea," he admitted. "The only trouble is that your formula has been in general commercial use for a good many years. The stuff is called thermite."

Butch's face was as long as his arm. He seemed to be on the verge of weeping.

"Honest, Mr. Weeks? Then I suppose all my work has been for nothing!" He shrugged philosophically, "But I guess that's one of the hazards of scientific life!"

"I'm afraid it is."

Butch looked at the city engineer, and the small eyes took on an almost doglike respect.

"You're pretty smart, Mr. Weeks. Maybe I really could do something worthwhile some day if I could work with a man like you! Could I, Mr. Weeks? Could you let me work for you?"

"I'm afraid not."

Butch's face grew even longer. Weeks couldn't help feeling sorry for him, in a way. The approach had been good, even clever, but Weeks wasn't a complete dope!

Three very large men approached. Muscles bulged beneath their work shirts. They all looked grim. The largest of them stepped close to Weeks. "Look, Mr. Weeks, we're the Kelly brothers to talk to you about the discharge of Al Kelly yesterday."

Weeks' face twitched. "I don't care to talk about Kelly's discharge! I do the hiring and firing on this job, and that's final! You can take your complaint about your brother and...."

"Oh, yeah?"

The large man's hand reached forth and grasped the front of Weeks' wind-breaker. His other arm pulled back.

But before it could lash out, Butch went into action! All fatigue vanished from his body, and his tired eyes brightened at the prospect of bodily combat. His hamlike fist swung in a short arc and crashed against the jaw of the other.

THE MAN'S hold on Weeks' coat relaxed. He exhaled wheezily and dropped to the planking. Butch grinned delightedly.

But the other two members of the family committee closed in. One of them threw a haymaker which Butch ducked easily, but the maneuver gave the second man time to get in a good hard right to the side of Butch's head. Butch's brain rattled in his skull like a skeleton on a tin roof in a windstorm. But Butch didn't necessarily need a brain in order to fight—he could do very well on pure instinct.

His left flashed through the air and collided with the midriff of his nearest adversary. The man folded as neatly as a jackknife, and when his head came forward it met the devastating piston of Butch's right. He staggered backward and sat down hard, his eyes glassy.

The only remaining gladiator grew weary. He had seen his two brothers rendered *hors de combat* in astonishingly short order. Moreover, he had heard the horrid sounds of Butch's knuckles against vital bone-structures. Pride would not allow him to retreat, however, so he concentrated on defending himself as best he could.

He harbored no illusions concerning his ability to whip the wavy-nosed man who now bore down upon him. His only hope was that the battle might end as quickly and as painlessly as possible.

Butch was quite willing to coöperate on that point. He measured his man, then drove out with a trip-hammer right that caught the Kelly brother flush on the correct portion of his jaw. The man went down, smiling very blissfully.

Butch turned to the engineer. "What were you saying, Mr. Weeks?"

Weeks looked incredulously upon the three fallen knights, and then upon their vanquisher, who was blowing now upon his knuckles.

"I was saying," said Weeks, "that I can give you a job, but not as an inventor! How'd you like to be my bodyguard?"

Butch considered. "Well, a job's a job. I'll take it."

When Kenneth Weeks entered the large Sky Club that evening, Butch was with him. Carlotta was going through her routine, and when she had finished the turn, she swayed to their table. Butch sat between Weeks and Carlotta, glowering suspiciously at the girl. Carlotta seemed somewhat annoyed.

"Kenny, who is this man?" she demanded.

Weeks smiled. "He's my new bodyguard." Then, to Butch, "Why don't you run along to the bar and have a drink, Butch? This lady doesn't want to kill me—yet!"

Butch left.

"A bodyguard?" Carlotta repeated. "Why do you need a bodyguard, my Kenny?"

"Because there are likely to be people who'd like to bump me off. You see, a little invention of mine that promised to bring some nice returns has gone sour, and some of my partners are likely to be annoyed about it."

"And this—this 'Butch,' he will protect you?"

"I'll say he will! And why? Because it's to his own interest to keep me alive—because I'm the only guy in the world outside of the United States War Department who knows a certain formula that every government in the world would give its eye-teeth to possess! If this guy who calls himself Butch O'Brien hopes to get the formula for whatever foreign power he represents, he's got to see to it that nothing happens to yours truly!"

Carlotta's eyes gleamed. "It is all very exciting, my Kenny! But if you have some secret which governments would pay to possess, why do you not sell it to them?"

Weeks shook his head slowly. "No, Carlotta. I may be a lot of things I shouldn't be, but I'm no traitor!" He smiled sardonically. "Where else but in the United States of America could some of these things be got away with?"

"I do not understand, Kenny."

"You don't have to. And you can also keep your mouth strictly shut about what I've said about Butch!"

Meanwhile, completely unaware that the glamorous mantle of espionage had been thrown over his wide shoulders, Butch sat placidly at the bar and sipped a glass of celery tonic.

CHAPTER XV

THE MENACING VOICE

WORRIED, TONY QUINN glanced at his watch. At the close of each day, Carol had been reporting to him. But it was now past nine o'clock at night, and he had had no word from her. It was not like Carol.

He dialed a number. Presently, he heard the voice of Tommy Ahern.

"When did you last see Miss Scott?" Quinn demanded.

Tommy recognized the voice. "Who's this, Mr. No-name? Glad you called. This is the first chance I've had to thank you in person for that nice wedding present!"

"Never mind that! Answer my question!"

"Sure. She was in the office when I left at five o'clock."

"Who else was there?"

"The boss, Dunbar, and a guy named Curland. Anything wrong?"

"I hope not. Thanks."

Quinn hung up, chewing his knuckles thoughtfully. For the hundredth time, he considered calling Acme, and for the hundredth time he rejected the thought. If Carol were there, and alone, she would have called him. If anything was amiss, what could be gained by phoning?

Quinn strode quickly to the fireplace. A moment later he was in the secret room beyond, donning the sombre clothing of the Black Bat. He slid the bolts of the two automatics to make certain they were loaded and in working order, and slipped the weapons into the holsters beneath his armpits.

The Black Bat crossed the living room swiftly, and peered from a darkened window in the hall. He smiled grimly. Across the street one of McGrath's plainclothesmen still paced innocently.

The Black Bat opened the door of a closet and threw the switch on a small metal box.

The box contained a rheostatic mechanism which operated in conjunction with an electric clock. At a certain hour, this mechanism would cause the living room lights to be extinguished, and a dim nightlight would glow in the hall. After a short interval, lights would appear on the upper floor, first in bedrooms, and then in bathrooms.

At length, all lights but the one in the hall would be out. Any interested observer outside the house might reasonably assume that a blind man's valet had at last got his master and himself to bed, and that the occupants of the house were pursuing an extremely normal course of existence.

The Black Bat piloted the small coupé as swiftly as he dared through the streets of the city.

Having visited the offices of the Acme Company before, he was familiar with the terrain. He parked beneath the same lamppost on the deserted street, and gazed upward. There were lights on the sixth floor, but he could not be certain that they were in the offices he planned to visit.

He drifted silently around the corner and into the alley. Again the lock yielded to his ministrations, and he drifted ghostlike up the dark stairwell. A black mask covered his face, and a strangely-shaped cloak hung from his shoulders.

The Black Bat moved down the corridor of the sixth floor on rubber-soled shoes. Light glowed through the glass panel of the door to the Acme offices, making a square of light in the otherwise pitch-black hallway. The Black Bat stooped, pressed his ear against the door. He could hear voices.

"There's no use beating around the bush!" a man's voice was grating. "You're not Helen Scott—and I want to know who you are and why you're here under that name!"

THEN, EVERY nerve tensed in the body of the Black Bat! The voice he heard was that of Carol, incredibly weary.

"I don't know what I can tell you. You've just got some sort of crazy notion in your heads and there's nothing I can do about it!"

The Black Bat's first impulse was to break through that door, smash anybody who stood between him and the girl. But caution stayed him. It was evident that Carol had not been harmed, and so long as the men in that office with her kept talking, there was the chance that they might say something that would be of interest to the ears of the Black Bat. With an effort, he remained where he was.

Another male voice drifted through the panel.

"What's the point in arguing any longer, Dunbar? Let's take her to the house. Maybe the sea air'll make her talk better."

There was a sharp edge of menace in the voice.

"Okay, sister," the Black Bat heard Dunbar say, "let's get going. And while we're in the elevator and on the way to the car, just remember that I've got a rod in my pocket, and that it'll be pointing at you all the while!"

The Black Bat steeled himself for action. When they came through the doorway into the dark hall, he would have the advantage of sight over them. It would be an easy matter to rescue Carol.

But would she *want* to be rescued? The thought struck him like a thunderbolt! One of the men had spoken of a place known as the House. With the possibility of being led to the very lair of the murderous gang, would Carol want to trade the opportunity for her own immediate personal safety? Knowing the girl as he did, the Black Bat thought not. If he could in some way let her know that he was here, that he would be following close behind!

The lights in the office went off, and the door opened. There was no light now, but the Black Bat could see every feature and detail of the three people who came through that door.

"That little bulb at the far end of the corridor is the elevator. Walk toward it," Curland said.

Swiftly, the Black Bat's hand darted for his armpit and came forth with a .38 automatic.

Carol, like her two companions, could see nothing. The darkness pressed in upon her like the shrouds of doom. She shivered involuntarily. For a brief moment, she had the impulse to run, to try to elude the gun she knew was trained in her direction, to find a stairway which might lead her to the street.

But she knew such a break would be dangerous in the extreme, and she had no wish to die while the riddle was yet unsolved. She had a strong desire to see the place called the House.

And then, a cry started from her throat and she had to bite her lip to keep from giving it utterance. Something cold and hard and metallic thrust itself into her hand, and her fingers closed upon it.

Had the Black Bat not been tense and troubled, the expression upon Carol's face as she clasped the automatic might have caused him to smile. It was a ludicrous admixture of surprise, relief—and amusement. Yes, even amusement over the fact that the Black Bat could be so close to the abductors without their being in the least aware of his presence!

He watched her slip the pistol into her bag. A .38 was a pretty big gun for a woman's pocketbook, but Carol luckily had a preference for bags of a copious nature.

The entire transaction was completed in so short a space of time that the party of three did not so much as pause on their groping way toward the elevator!

WHILE THE others waited for the car, the Black Bat slid into the stairwell and ran swiftly down. He let himself out the back entrance. He was behind the wheel of the black coupé before Carol and the two men exited from the front door of the building.

He saw them cross the street, walk toward a long sedan which stood at the curb further down. Carol was hustled into the back seat, and one of the men got in beside her. The other man climbed behind the wheel. The Black Bat allowed the sedan to get a block under way before he set his own car in motion.

Block after block he kept that same respectful distance. He could not afford to let the others know that they were being followed, though he knew that Carol would use her very capable brain and cover as much of the back window as possible to minimize the efficacy of the sedan's rear vision mirror.

The way led directly crosstown. In the midtown traffic, the Black Bat found it difficult to keep the other car in view without getting too close or losing it completely. He breathed more easily again as they entered the quieter streets of the East Side.

Still the sedan ploughed straight East, past First Avenue and into the teeming freight district. It turned left into Avenue C, and streaked northward. The Black Bat turned the corner and saw his quarry still in view and still a block ahead of him.

A fast freight pounded southward on glistening tracks that paralleled the avenue. The Black Bat saw a red lantern swinging in a swift arc in the center of the roadway. The sedan passed it. The Black Bat slammed his foot down on the gas pedal. The powerful coupé leaped forward.

But it was too late! The fast freight-engine shrieked to a stop, and its impenetrable string of cars stretched out in a wide curve behind it, completely blocking the street! The Black Bat jammed on his brakes and swung the wheel over hard. The coupé's tires screamed their protest. The left front fender scraped raspingly along the side of a freight car. The man with the lantern was yelling.

The Black Bat turned the coupé in swift jerks, and roared up the side street. At the next intersection he turned north. Three blocks further on he swung back to Avenue C. The blocking freight train now lay to the rear of him, but the sedan was no longer in sight!

He cursed himself bitterly. Somehow he had let that car escape him, bearing with it the person most precious to him of all the people in the world! The man who had never experienced fear for himself now felt an overpowering sense of panic for the safety of a slip of a brown-haired girl. He had been a fool to let them leave that office. If anything now happened to Carol, the blame would rest upon him, and it was a blame that he thought he could not bear.

Then confidence oozed slowly back into his frame. Carol was a smart girl, and a plucky one. And she had a .38 pistol in her handbag....

THE SEDAN crossed the river bridge and left the city behind. Carol made mental notes of the route they followed. After some time, the houses thinned out.

"Okay, sister," Curland said, "down on the floor. From now on you travel blind."

Carol slid to the floor, and Curland spread a robe over her.

It would be almost ridiculously easy, she thought, to take the gun from her bag and blast her way to freedom. They had searched that bag for firearms before they left the office, and could now have no suspicion that she was armed. A quick shot would finish Curland, and the hard muzzle of the gun against the back of Dunbar's neck would make him reasonable enough.

Still, she made no effort to escape. She knew that the Black Bat was following, though she had not been able to risk a reassuring look from the rear window of the car. But she had seen the familiar black coupé at the curb as she climbed into the sedan. And the gun in her handbag would be as valuable as an ace-in-the-hole later as now.

Carol Hastings wanted to see the House, and she wanted to lead the Black Bat to it. Therefore, she stifled uncomplainingly beneath the musty folds of the blanket.

At last the car stopped. Dunbar got out of the driver's seat and tied a handkerchief around Carol's eyes.

"Okay—get out!"

She could hear the soft rolling of surf upon a sandy beach, and the odor of salt was in her nostrils. Apparently the House faced the broad sweep of the Atlantic, a shoreline virtually deserted at this season of the year.

Carol was led up some steps, and through a door. Presently, she heard a voice as cold as wintered steel.

"What's this? We don't go in for week-end parties here, you know."

Dunbar's voice was respectful as he answered.

"This girl's a snooper, Boss. She was in the office posing as the girl who used to work for Hall. She won't talk, so we thought we'd better bring her here."

"You did right," the cold voice said. "If she knows anything, we can find ways to make her talk." He paused. "Ways to make her talk about, perhaps—the Black Bat!"

Carol's expression did not change, and the voice went on.

"On the other hand, if she knows nothing, it is merely her misfortune to have got in the way."

There was something so deadly in the voice that a shiver danced the length of Carol's spine. Her left hand gripped the handbag. She thought she would like to see the face behind that voice, see the man who gave the orders to this murderous gang.

Her free hand darted to the handkerchief about her eyes, but before her fingers could pluck it free a fist lashed against the side of her head. Everything went dizzily black.

When Carol recovered consciousness, she was in a small upstairs room with the windows barred. She got painfully to her feet and staggered to the door. It was locked. Then, suddenly, apprehensively, her eyes darted about the room.

The handbag and the gun were—missing!

CHAPTER XVI

McGRATH OUTWITTED

G RAVELY, THE BLACK BAT turned the coupé homeward. Perhaps there would be some further word from Silk, or from Butch. Butch had found a moment to call Tony Quinn earlier in the day to inform him that he had become Kenneth Weeks' bodyguard. Silk had also called to tell of his conversation with Dunbar and Curland— the very men who had abducted Carol! If they had made a later appointment with the Professor, it might be that the Black Bat could again get within striking distance of them!

He switched on the forbidden shortwave radio beneath the dashboard of the car. The nasal, metallic voice of the police announcer came in. Routine stuff. Car so-and-so return to your station, car such-and-such go to such a point—a drunk annoying pedestrians.

The Black Bat reached for the switch again, but just as he was about to cut the voice from the air it blared out with the more electrifying— "Attention all cars!"

The Black Bat listened—"Attention all cars! Tenement fire at six-sixteen East Seventy-seventh! Large crowd gathering! Proceed at once!"

The black coupé turned, and hammered for 616 East 77th Street. In five minutes, the Black Bat slid the car to the curb a block away from the tortuous flames that marked the death of another building—and heaven knows how many people!

He pulled the brim of his hat low over his scarred eyes, and the upturned collar of a black topcoat hid most of the remainder of his face from view. He stepped out of the car and moved with the gathering crowd toward the fire lines.

Powerful streams from a score of hoses hurled themselves hissing into the maelstrom of fire, but it was apparent that there could be no hope for the building. Other nozzles jetted their drenching spume over adjoining structures. If that fire got out of hand, spread to other properties, there was no telling where the conflagration would cease.

Two white-coated ambulance surgeons bent over huddled forms upon the sidewalk. The Black Bat moved closer. One of the internes stood up, and a shudder seemed to pass over his body. He turned to the policeman who stood grimly by.

"No use," he said. "They got the fire in their lungs! And God knows how many other poor wretches are cooking in that hell!"

This blaze was just as typical as the three which had preceded it. The tenement had burst spontaneously into all-enveloping flames—flames from which no living thing could hope to emerge alive.

The Black Bat listened to those around him, and to the cadence of the crowd as a whole. The sustained murmur of many voices struck a note of horror and hate—horror at what had happened, and hate against those who had perpetrated this fresh outrage.

For a week the yellow press had been screaming for vengeance, and the lust had spread to the populace of the tenement neighborhoods.

The Black Bat was certain that if the criminals could be delivered into the hands of this growling mob, they would be torn literally to bloody bits. And he thought that such a fate would not be too horrible a one to be visited upon them.

And it was these same fiends in whose hands the fate of Carol now lay! The thought sickened him, brought beads of cold perspiration to his forehead. If they were capable of the mass murder of innocent tenement dwellers, what mercy would they show a single girl, particularly if they considered that girl a menace to their evil plannings? The Black Bat breathed a silent prayer that the .38 automatic in the girl's bag might shield her from harm.

Lieutenant McGrath brushed past the Black Bat, so close that their shoulders touched. He stepped over the rope which held back the crowd, and paused beside another police officer in plain clothes.

"Come on, Engle, we're going to see a man. I had a check made, and I've got the name and address of the owner of this building. There may be nothing to it, but I want to see him!"

THE TWO detectives climbed back over the rope and burrowed their way through the masses of people. The Black Bat followed. He had been wishing violently that he knew the owner, or ostensible owner of the property, for that person might be forced into revealing those higher up in the complicated criminal structure, might even be coerced into telling the location of the place known as the House. And in the House was Carol!

McGrath and his men climbed into a police squad car. The uniformed policeman at the wheel set it in motion. The Black Bat sprinted for the coupé, spinning people like tenpins from his path, headless of the shouts that were hurled at him. The car was in gear and rolling forward even before he had closed the door.

He was not worried about following the police car too closely. He was well aware of the fact that the police are not in the habit of being tailed, and therefore do not expect to be.

The squad car proceeded north for perhaps twenty blocks and turned into a street lined with brownstone-front houses of almost identical appearance. It slowed, and ultimately stopped before one of these houses. McGrath and the other detective got out and began looking closely at the dim house numbers. The uniformed driver remained at the wheel.

The Black Bat stopped his own car a half block away. He alighted and drifted casually down the street. As he passed the squad car, McGrath and his man were already at the door of the house they sought. The Black Bat continued unobtrusively on his way.

Almost at the end of the street, he came to an apartment house. There was a cellar entrance, and he surmised that this entrance would give him access to the back yard and the other yards with which it connected. He ducked as swiftly and as silently as a shadow into the gloom of the cellarway.

There, he paused for a moment to don the mask and cloak. He loosened the one remaining automatic in its holster beneath his left armpit. Then he moved sure-footedly through the inky blackness of the cellar, his lips set in a hard, grim smile.

The immediate intention of the Black Bat was to kidnap a witness from the very hands of the police! It was a risky business, especially when McGrath was one of the policemen involved, but no more risky than the adventure into which Carol Hastings had allowed herself to be drawn.

The Black Bat moved through the dim back yards. There were fences separating most of the areas, and these he vaulted easily and silently. He counted each house upon the way.

At the thirteenth house he stopped. Thirteen. Was there any significance in the number? Was this some sort of warning from the god of chance that the luck of the Black Bat was running out? Would this prove to be the occasion upon which the Black Bat would engage McGrath in a battle of wits once too often? If anything were to happen to him, it would leave Carol at the mercy of those who held her, for he was the only person who so much as knew of her abduction.

"Rot!" he told himself. "You're shying at shadows!"

The door which gave onto the ground floor of the house was no match for the Black Bat's magnetic keys. In less than thirty seconds, he was inside, moving cautiously toward the front of the place. The floor on which he found himself contained only kitchen, serving pantry and dining room. The living and sleeping rooms were on the floors above.

HE LISTENED at the stairs. He heard the voices of the two detectives, and the whining voice of a third man.

"How could I know the place was burning? I have no telephone!" the thin voice was saying.

And McGrath's sarcastic voice:

"And I suppose you have no insurance on that place that's burnin'! Come along, now, get into your clothes. I want you to see the fire, and I may want to take you to Headquarters!"

"Wait here," said the man in his whining voice. "I'll go upstairs and dress."

"We'll go along," McGrath said. "I lost a smart guy once on that gag. That was back in 1909, and it isn't due to happen again until nineteen seventy-nine!"

There were sounds of three pairs of feet climbing a flight of stairs. And as they went a floor higher, so did the Black Bat. Again, he listened. He could hear the whiny-voiced man complaining bitterly about honest people being routed from their beds in the middle of the night by overbearing policemen.

It would be humorous, the Black Bat thought, if this man really were an honest man. It would make these efforts on the part of McGrath and the Black Bat pretty ludicrous!

The stairs to the bedroom floor were dim, lighted only by a dull nightlight. The Black Bat moved slowly upward. His feet seemed to know instinctively which boards would creak, and these he avoided. Presently, he was directly beneath the nightlight, which hung on its own wire from a wall bracket.

From his pocket, the Black Bat drew a knife. His thumb flicked open the razor-edged blade. He reached for the wire of the light, bent it into a loop. He inserted the blade in the loop, and exerted pressure. There was a flash as the wire shorted, and a shower of blue sparks from the fused steel of the knife-blade.

One sharp jolt of electricity jerked through the Black Bat's body, and then every light in the place went out.

He heard McGrath's explosive. "What the hell!" and the other detective's, "It's all right, I've got my hand on his shoulder. Are you dressed, you?"

The whiny-voiced man was.

"Okay," said McGrath, "down the stairs with you, and no funny business! It still doesn't seem like pure chance that would blow a fuse just at a time like this!"

The heavy footsteps approached, and then, through the darkness, the Black Bat could see the three men. The whiny-voiced man was small, he noted with satisfaction. That would make him easier to get away with.

The Black Bat backed silently down the stairs while the others clattered stumblingly on their way. At the parlor floor, he stopped again, and his right hand reached for the automatic. As the two policemen and their prisoner reached the last step, the Black Bat spoke, and his voice was low and even and deadly—if somewhat out of character.

"All right, coppers!" he snarled. "Stand still and don't reach!" McGrath's hand crept toward his pocket, and the barrel of the Black Bat's .38 crashed on his forearm. "I said don't reach!"

It was almost funny to see the three sets of eyes trying to bore through the darkness. He reached out and drew the little man from between the two officers.

"Okay, coppers," he said, "turn left and march!"

McGrath and the other plainclothesman were both old-timers. They knew the futility of battling against odds. Better to wait for a new break than try to make a good one from a bad!

THE BLACK BAT herded the policemen into a closet and locked the door on them. But just before doing so, he dropped a small article into the loose pocket of McGrath's coat. It would be a pity to have a brush with the great McGrath and not leave the mark of the Black Bat somewhere on his person!

"Who are you?" the whiny voice was asking. "You must be new to the mob—but good work anyway! And how the hell do you see in the dark?"

"Never mind that!" said the Black Bat. "Start down for the front basement entrance!"

He could see the little man picking his way carefully down the dark stairs. The Black Bat opened the front door to the merest crack. From his pocket he produced a round object such as he had found useful on the occasion of his entry into Amos Willard's apartment. He flicked the small lever that fitted flush with its surface, and placed the round object upon the floor of the hall. Then he ran for the stairs, hurrying his man before him.

In the car, the uniformed policeman was wondering what was keeping the two plainclothesmen. When the lights had gone out, he had expected them to emerge almost immediately. But now, glancing at the door at the top of the high stoop, he saw thick clouds of smoke pouring out. With a curse, he was out of the car.

From his vantage point at the door on the basement floor, the Black Bat saw the young patrolman legging it for the stoop. He opened the basement door and took the arm of the whiny-voiced man.

"Let's go!" he growled.

In the comparative light of the street, the man looked at his deliverer, stopped dead in his tracks.

"The Black Bat!" he cried.

"The same! But let's go anyway!"

He dragged the little man protestingly after him. For a moment he paused to lift the hood of the police car and yank at the wire beneath. Then the Black Bat and his trembling captive legged it toward the coupé farther down the street.

By the time the police came out of that house and started slinging ineffectual lead in the general direction of the two fugitives, the black coupé was rolling smoothly on its way. One of the fugitives was jubilant. The other was the most unhappy man imaginable.

"Please," he begged, "please take me back to them cops!"

CHAPTER XVII

THE MYSTERY OF CARLOTTA

LAZILY, **BUTCH O'BRIEN** sipped his fourth successive celery tonic at the bar of the Sky Club. But across the rim of the glass, his eyes watched Kenneth Weeks in conversation with the dancer, Carlotta.

At last, the couple rose and walked toward the door which gave access to the stairs leading to the gambling room on the upper floor. Butch slid from the bar stool and followed. He noted that the glance which Carlotta now bestowed upon him lacked some of its earlier enmity. The glance held, rather, a subtle quality of respect. Butch wondered why.

Weeks went directly to a roulette table, and started play with his usual hundred-dollar stack of chips, Butch stood beside Carlotta, watching him toss the chips expertly onto the layout. Presently, Butch became aware of a beefy person attempting to get close enough to the table to watch the play. Butch moved over a few inches.

"Thanks," said Big Jim Morley.

He grinned at Butch in friendly fashion.

"That's okay," said Butch.

After a minute or so, Morley spoke again.

"You don't play?" he asked.

Butch shook his bead. "Nope. I just watch."

The wheel spun. The little ivory ball clicked into a slot, and the croupier pushed a pile of chips toward Weeks. Weeks' eyes were bright, and his nostrils flared with excitement. Butch almost felt sorry for him. It was always rather pathetic to view the excitement of a confirmed gambler while the goddess of chance was smiling her temporary smile upon him. For Weeks, nothing existed except the roulette wheel, the croupier and himself.

There was a low, sharp exclamation of pain from Carlotta. She lunged sideways, rubbing one bare shoulder with her other hand.

Big Jim Morley was extremely apologetic.

"I'm terribly sorry! I'm afraid I let my cigar touch your arm. I hope you'll forgive me!"

Carlotta was glaring at him, and anger smoldered in her dark eyes. She seemed to be debating whether the burn had been purely accidental.

"It's all right," she said at last.

Morley was smiling.

"I'm glad you're not angry," he said. "And to show you I'm truly sorry, I'd like to buy you a drink, if I may."

"No thank you," said Carlotta. "I am with Mr. Weeks."

Her voice was almost prim, and primness was the last thing one would expect to encounter in Carlotta.

Morley laughed quietly. "He doesn't even *know* you're with him! Come on, have a drink with me."

Somehow, Butch was between Morley and the girl, and Morley had been forced unobtrusively back a few steps. "Let's let it go at that," said Butch softly.

Morley's brows went up. "Just where do you fit into the picture, my meddling friend?"

"I take care of Weeks, is all," Butch said.

"And that includes taking care of his women?" asked Morley.

Butch shrugged. "I've never had any orders to that effect, but I've never had any orders to the opposite effect, either. So, in the meantime, I just protect his interests!"

Morley was smiling broadly.

"Good! Fine! That's the sort of loyalty I like to see! I can see that Weeks has nothing to worry about with you on the job!"

He fished a thick roll of bills from his pocket and peeled off a twenty. This he handed to Butch.

"For your trouble," he said.

Butch tore the bill into tiny pieces, and stuffed the fragments into Morley's breast pocket.

"Some night, when you haven't anything to do," he said, "you might put those pieces together again."

MORLEY WAS still smiling. For a long moment he looked at Butch. Then he turned and walked off, leaving the place.

Weeks was doing all right. Within a half hour he was seven hundred dollars ahead. He was flushed with excitement.

"Lady Luck's done an about-face!" he said to Carlotta. "This is the first night in God-knows-when that the numbers have come up for me!"

But Butch was still staring covertly at Carlotta. He was wondering whether or not it had been his own imagination that had seen some significance in a look Carlotta had thrown to the croupier, and in the almost imperceptible nod which the croupier returned.

"And I'm going to push the old luck while it holds!" Weeks was saying to the girl. "I'm going to have a crack at one of the higher limit tables."

Carlotta gave his arm a fond squeeze.

"All right, my Kenny. I must go down and change for my next show, and when it is over, I will come up again."

The girl moved off, swaying her hips. Weeks moved to another roulette table at which the play was for higher stakes. Butch was close behind him, but his eyes followed Carlotta until the door closed after her.

"Five hundred," Weeks said to the dealer, and, as the man's brows went up, "Don't worry, I'm playing for cash tonight!"

He slid a little pile of currency across the table. A moment later he was completely engrossed by his gambling.

Butch drifted unobtrusively away. Weeks wouldn't know or care where he was, and Butch had a yen to follow the dark-haired dancer. There was nothing personal or romantic connected with his interest in her. He just wanted to see what she did and said when she wasn't in the company of Kenneth Weeks.

Downstairs, Butch's eyes swept the club for Carlotta. She was not in sight. Probably doing exactly what she said she was going to do, changing her costume for the next show. Butch circled the room, now filled with a dancing, drinking, noisy crowd. The orchestra was giving out, with great blasts from the brass section.

At the door which served as entrance and exit for the members of the floor-show, he paused. Then, he stepped through. The trumpet player winked at him lasciviously, and Butch winked back. Apparently, it was not forbidden for an occasional patron to enter the dressing rooms.

Inside, Butch lowered his eyes modestly as a sketchily-attired chorus girl stepped from a side room into the hall. She looked at him.

"Well, what d'you want, Tall and Handsome?" she demanded.

"I'm looking for Carlotta," Butch admitted, his eyes still averted.

The girl snorted. "That high-falutin' Spanish dame is too fancy to use the same dressing room as the rest of us!" The girl's thumb jerked. "Try the door at the end."

"Thanks," said Butch.

The door indicated, he saw, had a small star upon it. He knocked. He didn't know exactly what he was going to say if she answered, but it was Butch's practice to act first and worry about the conversation afterwards.

There was no answer. He tried again, then cautiously turned the knob. Butch's small eyes took in the contents of the tiny dressing room, but Carlotta was not part of the contents.

HE LEFT the dressing rooms and strolled again around the edge of the supper room. Where in hell had Carlotta gone to? She had said she was going to change for her next show, but she wasn't changing. Why did she have to lie to her boy friend about a simple thing like that? The natural assumption was that she was doing a little two-timing.

Butch remembered the swift glance that had passed between Carlotta and the croupier at the roulette layout. If she had the prerogative of telling the dealers when a customer should and should not win, it was natural to assume that she was on a highly friendly footing with the management of the place. What, then, could be more natural than for her to be making a report of some kind to the establishment's manager?

Butch sidled toward the door marked "private." For a moment, he stood with his back to it, his hand turning the knob. For a man of his bulk, Butch went through the door in a manner most unostentatious.

He found himself in a small alcove, on the far side of which was another door. He placed his ear against the panel of this door. From within came the unmistakably Latin voice of Carlotta, and because there was no answering voice, Butch assumed that she was talking over the telephone. The only trouble was that he couldn't quite catch what she was saying.

A more cautious man would have cursed his luck, and let it go at that. But Butch was not overburdened with caution. His present desire was to hear what Carlotta was saying, and the only way to accomplish that was to open the door.

CHAPTER XVIII

DEATH AND
A LOST HOPE

E **LUSIVE CARLOTTA** was behind the desk in Legs Landers' office. She had a French phone in her hand. Another phone rested quietly in its cradle upon the desk. Why two phones, Butch wondered. But he cleared his brain of empty wonderings to concentrate upon what the dark-haired girl was saying.

"Yes, Landers is out. I thought you would like to know that Weeks has a bodyguard now." Carlotta paused to snort impatiently. "No, not an ordinary bodyguard. Weeks says the man is a spy, a real international spy, who wants to get the formula for the incendiary stuff! And Weeks is too much of an American to sell such a secret to a foreign government! Is that not funny?"

A bee was buzzing in Butch's head.

"She means me!" he told himself. "They think I'm a spy!"

The idea was so amusing that Butch could scarcely restrain the guffaw that rose in his throat to strangle him.

Apparently Carlotta was being given detailed instructions by whoever held the other end of the wire, for she was listening intently.

"Yes... yes... yes... I understand," she said. "Good-by."

Butch closed the door quickly but silently. In a single stride, he was across the foyer and out the other door. When Carlotta came out he was wandering aimlessly about the supper room. Carlotta went directly to the other end of the room, and disappeared into the dressing quarters.

Butch found a pay-telephone and dropped a nickel into the slot. He dialed an unlisted number which connected by direct wire with the home of Tony Quinn....

The Black Bat piloted his small car by a devious route until he had almost gained the gatehouse. Then, he pulled to the curb and stopped.

The little man on the seat beside him was still whimpering with fear.

"Let me go! You got no right to do this to me! Let me go, I say!"

His hand pressed on the door handle.

"No use," said the Black Bat. "I took the precaution to lock it." He half turned in his seat, facing the small man. "You've got one more chance to talk. Who do you take your orders from?"

"I don't know what you're talking about!" the man whined.

The Black Bat opened the car's glove compartment and drew forth a roll of two-inch adhesive tape. The tape made a ripping sound as he jerked it from the spool.

The little man's eyes widened. "What are you going to do?"

The Black Bat ignored the question.

"There's a house somewhere at the shore. I want to know where that house is. Either you're going to tell me, or you're not going to do any talking at all. You're not going to do any seeing, either. What'll it be! Quick! We can't stay here forever!"

The captive's mouth hung open, and has breath came in rasping jerks from his constricted throat. The pupils of his eyes were dilated, staring at the inexorable black presence beside him. His voice was a thin, reedy murmur.

"He'd kill me if I told you!"

The Black Bat reached forth one hand and gripped the man's shirt, shaking him as a terrier might shake a rat.

"Talk, damn you!"

The little man's lean fingers clawed ineffectually at the steel clamp at his throat.

"I'll talk—I'll talk!"

The Black Bat's grip relaxed ever so slightly.

The little man tried to moisten dry lips with a tongue equally as dry.

"The House is…. The House is at…."

The words gurgled to nothingness. His breath hissed from his lungs, and the little man slumped into himself. His eyes stared glassily.

Swiftly, the Black Bat's hand darted beneath the other's coat, and thence to the thin wrist. Had he literally scared the man to death? A faint pulse reassured him, but the pulse was weak and uneven. The captive had suffered a heart attack, there was no doubt about it.

THE BLACK BAT, who only a moment before had hated this miserable creature along with all denizens of the underworld, now became solicitous in the extreme. He must not let him die! He must make him recover sufficiently to finish the sentence he had started to utter. He must keep that faint heart beat alive in the sack of bones, for locked behind the little man's lips was the secret of the whereabouts of the House—and Carol Hastings.

The dark coupé rolled several blocks further on its way. The Black Bat parked it nearer to the gatehouse entrance than was his general practice. He couldn't go the whole length of a block with a body slung over his shoulder like a sack of grain.

He lifted the unconscious man from the car and flitted into the door of the gatehouse with the easy burden. Through the pitch darkness of the tunnel, the Black Bat moved with sure steps. Halfway through the tunnel, he stopped before an iron-grilled door. Beyond the door was a cell-like room, furnished simply with great care to cleanliness.

It had been constructed a long time ago against any occasion upon which it might be convenient to harbor a guest without either the rest of the world or the guest himself knowing a great deal about his whereabouts. The room had never before been occupied.

The Black Bat lowered his burden to the iron bed which stood against the wall. He loosened the man's clothing, and rubbed his wrists and face vigorously. At length, he was rewarded by a more discernible heart action, and by a return of color to the patient's face.

Yet, the man did not return to consciousness. He seemed to be embarking upon the early stages of a long, restful sleep. His captor watched him with annoyance and impatience. There was no help for it. He'd simply have to wait until the little man's condition improved sufficiently to make further questioning possible.

A red light blinked in the tunnel, signaling a call on the private telephone in the small room behind the fireplace. The Black Bat bestowed one more glance at his guest, then left the cell. Moments later, he was through the trap door and into the secret room. He lifted the telephone from its cradle.

Butch's voice drifted across the wire. Tony Quinn listened attentively as the former pugilist made his report.

"Good work, Butch!" he said at last. "The idea of their thinking you're a spy isn't as silly as it seems to you. Your cue is to play that angle for all it's worth, if you get a chance. Besides that you've proved beyond a doubt that Weeks is the man who filed the patent for the incendiary bombs. Whoever the girl talked to over that telephone knows about the formula, too, and will probably make an attempt to do business with you if you can struggle along on that spy angle. Butch, the man on the other end of that wire is the man we want—I'm sure of it! And we've got to find out who he is and *where* he is in a hurry, because he's got Carol!"

He could hear the explosive exclamation from Butch's mouth.

"Carol? My God, Quinn!"

"Exactly. I'm working on a visitor who may be able to give me a lead in that direction, but if you get information first, get in touch with me. I'll stay by the phone as long as I can."

The Black Bat's voice was crisp and businesslike, but Butch could sense the overtone of deep concern.

Quinn hung up, and stepped down again into the darkness of the tunnel. His strange eyes pierced the thick gloom as though it did not exist. The rubber-soled shoes made no sound on the stone flooring.

HALFWAY DOWN the tunnel, he turned to enter the cell-like room, and paused at once. The sight which greeted his eyes was both surprising and, somehow, amusing.

The bed was vacant, and its late occupant now stood against the far wall, his eyes straining against the complete darkness. And in the little man's hands, raised high over his head, was the only piece of portable furniture in the place, a steel chair.

It was apparently his intention to await the return of his captor and to crush his skull with one blow of that heavy chair. Somebody would pay well, no doubt, for the death of the Black Bat! Well enough, even, to inculcate murder into the heart of so miserable a specimen as this skinny little man.

Yet the Black Bat could not help but admire the other's histrionic ability—and the heart attack must have been pure acting.

He spoke quietly, but the little man all but jumped to the ceiling.

"Put it down," said the Black Bat.

The wide eyes of the pallid face stared in the direction of the voice. For a moment a sort of bravado shone in those eyes.

"You're bluffing," he said hoarsely. "You can't see me any more than I can see you!"

"You've just taken one step forward on your left foot," was the answer. "Now I'm telling you to stand still and put down that chair!"

The look of bravado washed off the little man's face, to be replaced by an expression of superstitious horror. His mouth worked dryly before he could force himself to speak again, and now his voice was scarcely audible.

"What sort of Thing are you?" he breathed. "No living man has eyes that could see through this darkness!"

With a hoarse cry the little man hurled the chair with the desperation of panic. The Black Bat stepped easily aside and the chair tangled in the door of the cell. But the prisoner hurled himself forward, too, his bony fingers clawing wildly at the air.

The Black Bat made no effort to step aside this time, and the other crashed into him. There was an hysterical, gurgling note in the man's throat, and his whole body seemed to shrink as though it had come into contact with something unnatural. The clawing fingers scurried up the Black Bat's chest and clamped on his throat. And there was more strength in those fingers than might have been expected in so small a man.

The Black Bat could, of course, hurl the little man away from him with one thrust of his powerful arm, but he could take no chances on disabling his opponent. Instead, he closed his own hands about the man's throat and exerted pressure. When the little chap had had enough, he would relax and be reasonable.

But the little chap apparently had no intention of relaxing. He had quite evidently given himself up, and was determined to accomplish but one thing—to take the Black Bat with him on the one-way journey into the unknown. His fingers bit deeper.

The Black Bat knew that he was the stronger of the two, and that in any ordinary combat the little man would be of little more annoyance than a mosquito. He also knew, however, that psychopathics are sometimes imbued with a strength far above the norm, and his present antagonist was unquestionably frightened to the point of insanity. The Black Bat relaxed his own stranglehold and, placing his hands against the other's chest, catapulted the little man across the room.

The man's left leg collided with the leg of the iron bed, and the thin body pinwheeled over backwards. There was a flat, sickening thud as his head struck the stone floor, and almost at once a trickle of blood showed darkly.

Swiftly the Black Bat bent. This time there was no heart beat, no pulse. He turned the light figure over. The back of the skull was split.

The little man was dead—and with him all present hope of discovering the whereabouts of the mysterious House—of Carol!

CHAPTER XIX

PREDICAMENT EXTRAORDINARY

IMPERTURBABLY PLAYING the role of Professor Kelton, Silk Kirby sat in his pleasant apartment on the Drive playing his one hundred and eighth game of solitaire Canfield.

With a disgusted grunt he scattered the cards to the four corners of the room. He crossed to a table which held a telephone, and called Tony Quinn's private number.

He had been calling the number at intervals all through the evening, and there had been no answer. That in itself was disquieting. Quinn and the others of his little band were out in the world doing something, while he sat about listening to the hardening of his arteries.

Silk held the phone for a long time, and was on the verge of hanging up when the crisp voice of Tony Quinn floated to him across the miles.

"Yes?"

"This is Professor Kelton. I've been trying to get you all evening."

Quinn quickly told him of the events of the evening, ending with the news that Carol was in the hands of the enemy.

Silk experienced a strange tightness, a coldness about his heart, and his hand gripped the instrument until the knuckles showed white through the taut skin.

"Isn't there anything I can do, sir?"

"I'm afraid not. Butch may turn up a clue. I thought I'd be able to do something myself, but now all I've got on my hands is a dead man!"

"What are you going to do with him, sir?"

"I'm going to present him to somebody, and let that somebody worry about what to do with him! In the meantime, Silk, hold your fort."

There was a click, and the line went dead. Silk replaced the instrument in its cradle and started to pick up the scattered cards.

The house telephone rang, and Silk was informed that there was a Mr. Dunbar in the lobby.

"Send him up!" said Silk, a happy gleam in his eyes.

A surge or jubilation went through him. Dunbar was one of the men who had abducted Carol. Therefore, he must know Carol's whereabouts! Silk was determined to discover where she was being held, and to free her from the grip of the murderers.

Professor Kelton opened the door to Paul Dunbar.

"I hardly expected to be seeing you so soon again, Mr. Dunbar."

Dunbar declined a cigar and sank into a deep chair.

"I'm sorry to disturb you at such an hour, Professor, but I've got a deal in which I think you might be interested, and it has to be made quickly, if at all."

Silk smiled inwardly. The crooks must be getting worried if they wanted to liquidate their holdings in so much of a hurry.

"Of course," Dunbar went on, "we can arrange mortgages on the properties for you, so that your cash outlay will not have to be too great—"

"At the usual discounts, I suppose?"

Dunbar nodded curtly. "I realize that the deal doesn't seem the best in the world for you, Professor Kelton, because of course the face value of the mortgages won't represent the cash they'll bring you. On the other hand, if you intend building model tenements on the sites of the present properties, the increased values will more than offset your original paper loss.

"And on top of that, you've said yourself that you're more interested in the philanthropic than in the personal financial angle."

"He's making it all sound very fine and upright, even almost reasonable," thought Silk.

"That's correct, Mr. Dunbar, entirely correct," he said. "What little good we can do in this world, you know—" Professor Kelton spread his hands significantly.

"Naturally," agreed Dunbar, "I feel that the least Acme can do is to coöperate with you to the fullest possible extent!"

"Thank you, sir. I appreciate your helpfulness. If you can supply me with the addresses and descriptions of the properties, I can go over the information tonight, and tomorrow I'll call at your office and you can show me the actual buildings."

Dunbar drew a thin sheaf of papers from his breast pocket, tossed them on the table.

"These will locate and describe the properties, but I'm afraid any business meetings we may have in the future will have to take place here, or across the dinner table in some public place. You see, we've closed our offices."

The surprise which showed on the countenance of Professor Kelton was not entirely fictitious.

"Closing your office? Why on earth?"

Dunbar shrugged. "The usual reason. We're not making much money. We've liquidated as far as possible, and the little we still have doesn't warrant maintaining an expensive suite of offices."

"I see." Professor Kelton looked thoughtful. "It always grieves me to hear of a business ceasing to exist—people losing their positions, landlords losing tenants, telephone companies losing subscribers. It widens out, you see."

"True," admitted Dunbar sadly.

"Take your little office staff, for example," Professor Kelton pursued. "What will become of them?"

He watched the other's face closely.

Dunbar sighed, and his expression was one of interested concern.

"I hope they'll be able to find new positions. They're both efficient workers, and to tide them over for the present, I gave them each a month's salary upon dismissal."

"Very generous of you," said the Professor. Then, as though a sudden thought had struck him, "As a matter of fact, if I'm to go into business on a rather large scale, I shall be needing a staff myself. If you could give me their addresses...."

"I don't happen to have their addresses with me," Dunbar said easily, "but I'll look them up before we meet tomorrow. I needn't tell you how pleased I am that you're interested in taking over my former staff." He rose. "Well, it's quite late. I must be getting along. If you'll look over the papers and try to reach a decision tonight, we may be able to close the deal tomorrow. I'll get in touch with you."

AT THE door, Dunbar paused. "Oh yes, I'd suggest that you make arrangements to consummate the deal in cash, Professor Kelton."

"In cash? Isn't that a bit unusual?"

"Very. But you see, we've closed our books, made out our tax report, and all that sort of thing. We'd like to keep the transaction as simple as possible. However, if you have any objections...."

"None! None at all!" Professor Kelton hastened to say. "So long as the deeds are in order, I have no objection to dealing in cash."

The door closed after Dunbar, and immediately Silk gave visible indication of the mental turmoil he had been undergoing for the past few minutes. He paced the length of the room, wondering if any man had ever been called upon to make a decision like the one which now confronted him—and to make it so quickly.

Dunbar had given him a list of addresses which he knew were of vital importance. He had a hunch that Tony Quinn would want to waste no time in plotting those addresses on the map of the city which covered the top of his desk. He had to get those addresses to Quinn—and yet, he had to follow Dunbar. He had to get some inkling of where Carol was being held!

He seized the house telephone.

"Has Mr. Dunbar come out of the elevator yet?"

"He's just stepped into the lobby at this moment, sir."

"Good!" said Silk. "Ask him to step upstairs again, please."

Silk hung up and reached for the outside phone. He called Tony Quinn's private number, but, as he had feared, there was no answer.

"Out getting rid of a stiff!" Silk groaned.

He had only a moment before Dunbar would again be at the door. He grabbed a pencil and a piece of paper, and jotted furiously. Next he addressed an envelope. He was just sealing the paper into the envelope when Dunbar's knock sounded.

Silk slipped the envelope into his pocket and went to the door. He greeted Dunbar with a bland, apologetic smile.

"Sorry to have brought you up again on a wild goose chase, Dunbar. There was something about one of those papers that I didn't understand at first glance. Very stupid of me, but I think I've got it straight now. I'll ride down with you. Got a letter I want to drop at the desk."

They said another good night in the lobby of the apartment, and Dunbar went out. Silk crossed to the desk and gave the clerk the envelope he had lately addressed.

"Call a messenger," he instructed, "and have him deliver this. Tell him he's to wait on that doorstep all night if necessary, ringing the doorbell every five minutes."

"But, sir," the clerk said, "if there's nobody at home when he first rings. What...."

"Don't argue," said Silk. "Just do as you're told!"

Professor Kelton legged it up the street with an agility and speed surprising in a man of his apparent age. At the corner was a taxicab stand, and into the foremost hack the Professor climbed.

"In a moment," he told the driver, "I believe there will be a car appearing at the next corner, headed east. When it passes the corner," Silk told the cabby, "I want you to follow it unobtrusively, and at a safe distance."

"Look," said the driver. "There's always somethin' fishy about that 'follow-that-other-car' gag. I ain't gonna do it."

Silk sighed. "People are always arguing with me tonight!" He reached a hand into his trousers pocket, and it came forth with a ten-dollar bill. He handed the note to the driver. "Would that make any difference?"

"Yes, *sir!* Exactly ten dollars worth!"

"Okay, get going. There's your car!"

The taxi rolled....

WHEN BUTCH returned to the gambling room, he found that most of Weeks' seven hundred dollars profit from the other table had disappeared in the more expensive game. Just as though he had been standing behind his employer all the while, he tapped his arm.

"Look, Weeks, why don't you take what's left of that dough and get back to the other game?" he asked.

Weeks turned bloodshot eyes upon him.

"And why don't you mind your own business?" he snapped.

"I'm your bodyguard, ain't I?" Butch demanded. "Well, then, when I bodyguard I do a complete job, including the bankroll. The dealer at that other table's got kinder eyes than this guy. Come on."

Weeks complied, more out of amusement than for any other reason. And when he had picked up some of his lost profits at the lower-priced table he turned to Butch with a grin.

"Maybe you're a hunch, Butch!" Weeks said.

"Sure," said Butch.

Carlotta weaved her way toward them, looking gorgeous in her darkly brittle way, and attired in a silver fox cloak that looked as though it cost more than her salary. She had done her last show of the evening and was apparently ready to leave the place.

She hooked an arm through Weeks' and smiled through lowered lashes at Butch.

"Kenny is going to take me away from here," she told the big man coyly, "so you will have the rest of the evening to yourself."

"When it's gone two o'clock in the morning," Butch said, "there ain't much of the evening left, strictly speaking. Besides, where Weeks goes, I go."

Carlotta looked extremely pained.

"Everywhere?" she asked. Then, to Weeks:

"How can that be so, my Kenny?"

Weeks looked down at her, grinning.

"Don't worry, Carlotta. I'll give him the rest of the 'evening' off, as you suggested."

Butch shrugged. "It's your funeral, Weeks."

Weeks shuddered. "I don't like your choice of words. Anyway, I'm safe enough with Carlotta. She doesn't want to kill me—yet!"

Butch didn't like the laugh that came from Carlotta's red gash of a mouth. If he were Weeks, he wouldn't be too sure about her!

"You staying here?" Weeks asked him.

Butch nodded. "For a few minutes."

Weeks and Carlotta left. Butch went down with them as far as the lower floor, and sat at the bar for a few minutes.

He lighted a cigar and sipped another glass of celery tonic.

The bartender sniffed. "I don't like to be fresh, mister, but that's an awful smellin' rope you're smokin'. What is it, anyway?"

BUTCH EXHALED a huge cloud of blue smoke.

"Camphor," he stated. "I soak 'em in camphor for a few days before I smoke 'em. Makes 'em cool and nice."

"It may make 'em cool," corrected the bartender, "but it certainly don't make 'em nice!"

Butch moved haughtily away from the bar and sat at a small table near the door marked private. The supper room was dim, and few people remained at the tables. The orchestra had put away their instruments and departed for the night. But Butch intended to remain until he could get into that private office without being too obtrusive about it, and have a look a round. He particularly wanted to have a look at the private telephone over which Carlotta had spoken.

A waiter handed the check to a beefy man who seemed to be host to a large table of people at the far end of the room. The beefy man questioned the check. There was a quiet argument, and then a noisier one. Finally the beefy man rose unsteadily from his seat and threw a wild swing at the waiter. Other waiters closed in efficiently, as they always seem to do in night club emergencies. The beefy man and his party were eased from the place. The show provided a brief but interesting spectacle, and all present watched it to its conclusion.

When the excitement was over, and the customers returned to their drinks, Butch was no longer seated at the small table near the private door. He had passed quickly and quietly through that door into the office of Mr. Legs Landers.

CHAPTER XX

VISIT FROM A CORPSE

MORBID TENSION held the Black Bat as he drove through the silent city street with a dead man as his only company. Luckily, the man was small, and his body fitted neatly into the confined space of the luggage compartment.

It was the Black Bat's intention to leave his grisly companion in the apartment of Kenneth Weeks. The idea held its element of grim humor, for Butch had told him that Weeks was in a generally jittery condition. But it was not the humor of the situation which activated him.

He reasoned that Weeks would be thrown into a very paroxysm of panic when he came home to his flat to find a dead man already occupying it. Weeks would have to find some way of disposing of the body, and it wouldn't be easy for a man not versed in the methods of the underworld. For, in spite of his present criminal activities, Weeks was not a professional gangster. He would have to call in help from his partners, and the Black Bat was desirous of making personal contact with some of that crew.

The apartment building in which Weeks lived was neither pretentious nor squalid. It was simply average. There was a front door, and another door which led to the basement. The Black Bat chose the latter.

He parked the coupé directly opposite the door and stepped to the sidewalk. He glanced upward, scanning the rows of windows. There was not a light in the building.

Swiftly, he unlocked the luggage compartment and drew forth the body. He held the small form close to his own and, in one stride, was across the walk and into the cellarway.

Four dumbwaiters, he saw, serviced the various apartments. The third of these listed, among others—K. Weeks, Apt. 305.

That would be on the third floor. The Black Bat put his head in at the shaft and looked upward. He drew easily at the rope, and the dumbwaiter slid silently to the bottom of the dark shaft.

A half dozen milk bottles came out of the box, and were replaced by a dead man.

The Black Bat squeezed through the narrow aperture and leaned his weight upon the proper rope. The counterbalance had not been designed to offset such a weight, so the pulling was hard, but, one hand over the other, he managed to draw the box upward until he faced the small door that must let upon the kitchen of Week's apartment.

Retaining a grip upon the rope with one hand, the Black Bat produced a thin, flat sliver of steel, pliable and exceedingly strong. It was almost too easy. The door was held only by a pressure-clasp, and it yielded easily to the steel sliver.

Lifting his deceased companion from the dumbwaiter, the Black Bat found a small fireplace in the living room. Drawn up to face it was a deep divan, a cozy spot for cozy moments. It was in this divan that the Black Bat deposited the small man's body.

AND NOW, from beyond that door, he heard the soft sounds of feet. Quickly, he retreated to his sanctuary in the dumbwaiter. Perched there, and with the door slightly opened, he commanded a view of the living room.

The entry door opened, and Weeks and Carlotta entered the apartment.

"Fine thing!" Weeks was saying. "They close all the bars and make a man go home to get a drink!" Then he paused and folded his arms about the dark-haired girl. "But home isn't such a bad place sometimes, after all!"

For a moment, Carlotta contributed to the embrace, then she pushed Weeks gently away from her, laughing softly at him.

"We were to have a drink, my Kenny," she reminded him.

"Okay. Park yourself while I rustle up the mixings."

Weeks crossed to a folding bar in the far corner of the room. Carlotta strolled toward the fireplace, her hips swinging. The room was dim, lighted by only a single lamp. She slipped before the divan, preparatory to sitting in it—and then she froze, her eyes widening.

The sound she uttered was not, strictly speaking, a scream. It was not loud, nor was it piercing. But it held the ultimate note of horror.

Weeks swung. "What is it?"

Carlotta was leaning against the mantel, and her long forefinger pointed fixedly at the grisly sight before her. Her eyes stared, and the dead eyes of the small man stared unblinkingly back at her.

In a moment, Weeks was beside Carlotta, and he, too, stared down at the grim sight.

"My God!" he whispered. "It's Ware—and he's dead as hell!"

The Black Bat could see Weeks beginning to tremble. Then the city engineer's face hardened.

"What kind of a joke is this!" he gritted. "And what the hell am I going to do with it?"

He bent, looked more closely at the dead man. In the center of the corpse's forehead was a small black sticker in the form of a bat with wings outspread.

Weeks staggered backwards as though he had been struck.

"The Black Bat!" he muttered, and his voice was edged sharply with terror.

Then, by some superhuman effort, he pulled himself together. He reached for the telephone, and dialed furiously.

"What are you going to do?" demanded Carlotta. "Call the police?"

"Police, hell!" grunted Weeks. "I'm calling Legs Landers. He ought to know how to get rid of a stiff!"

In the dumbwaiter the Black Bat settled down for a wait....

WHEN BUTCH first entered Landers' office, he went directly to the desk. There was only one telephone visible. Therefore the one over which Carlotta had spoken must be hidden in the desk. He found it in the lower right-hand drawer. Characteristically, he lifted the instrument from its cradle, and listened.

Presently a voice drifted across the wire—a voice incredibly cold and hard that even the imperturbable Butch was shivered by the single word,

"Hello...."

Butch hung up quietly. He had nothing to say to the owner of that voice—at least at present. But he remembered the voice, and some day he hoped to meet its possessor in person. For Butch knew intuitively that that man would be the one responsible for the present activities of the Black Bat and his little band of crime-busters!

He looked systematically through the office. At length, the opening of the other door warned him of someone's approach. Butch looked swiftly for a haven. A closet offered itself, and Butch accepted the offer.

HE WAS scarcely within it, and the door closed after him, then somebody entered. Butch could hear his steps crossing the room, and the creaking of the swivel chair as he sat down at the desk. Then came the sound of the desk drawer opening, and presently, a one-sided conversation.

"I don't know what you mean," Landers was saying. "I just got in. This is the first time I've called you this evening." There was a pause, then, "Yeah, must have been a crossed wire. Anyway, Boss, I did what you wanted me to do. I watched to see if that Professor Kelton was strictly on the level. He isn't.

"When Dunbar left Kelton's apartment, Kelton followed him. It won't do him any good, and it makes the plans for tomorrow night that much better! Kelton's either a cop or an aide of the Black Bat's. But whichever he is, it won't do him much good when he's burned to a cinder!"

In the closet, Butch's big frame tightened. So they were going to murder Silk, were they? Maybe Silk and Butch had their little arguments, their little differences of opinion, but nobody was going to harm Silk Kirby, not while Butch O'Brien was still able to crack one gangster's head against that of another!

But he remained quietly in his closet, and Landers hung up the phone. Almost immediately, however, the ordinary phone upon the desk rang sharply. Landers answered, listened briefly.

"All right, don't tell everything you know over a telephone, you fool!" Another pause. "All right, Weeks, I'll be over. Where's that big lug of a bodyguard of yours, anyway? Here, you say? No, he must have left before I got back. Yeah, I'll be over!"

Legs Landers left his office hurriedly. Butch came out of the closet, chuckling quietly. He had an idea concerning the reason for Weeks' call to Landers. The Black Bat must have planted his dead man on Weeks, and Weeks needed help in getting rid of his unwelcome guest!

Butch slipped into the supper room. There was a man sitting at the small table which Butch had vacated a few minutes before. Butch had never seen the man before, but the stranger was motioning to him to sit down. Butch complied.

"You really should be careful about snooping around other people's private offices," said Leonard Curland.

Butch bristled. "Look, I don't know who you are, but...."

His huge fists bunched up, and he glowered at Curland.

"Take it easy," Curland said hastily. "I understand you're acting as bodyguard for Kenneth Weeks."

"What about it?" Butch asked.

"Just this—I know you're not a bodyguard by trade. But I think I do know your real occupation."

For fully thirty seconds, the two men looked into each other's eyes.

"All right," Butch said, "talk. I'll listen."

"Weeks has something that you'd like to get," Curland said, "that a number of people would like to get. But you won't get it from Weeks.

He's a strange mixture of weakling and patriot. But I believe I can put you in touch with a party who is also able, and more willing to sell the information you want."

Butch was acting the part of a sinister international plotter with an aplomb which would have been the envy of more *bona fide* members of the profession. His eyes narrowed to mere slits, and he studied Curland.

"How do I know you're reliable?" he asked.

Curland shrugged. "In your—er—work, can you *ever* know?"

Butch leaned closer. "What's the price?"

Curland rose. "If you're interested, and care to come with me...."

BUTCH ALSO rose. Together he and Curland left the Sky Club. At the curb was a sedan, and at its wheel was a hard-eyed man who reached behind him to open the car's back door. At Curland's invitation, Butch stepped in. Curland followed. The car rolled down the street.

For perhaps a half hour, the car rolled smoothly on its way. Curland and Butch spoke politely but inconsequentially of such matters as the weather.

At length, with the city behind them and only an occasional house facing their route, Curland produced a large handkerchief.

"You understand the necessity for this, of course," Curland said apologetically.

"Of course," agreed Butch.

He submitted to the blindfold.

"I should have your gun, too," Curland pointed out.

Butch laid a restraining paw upon the other's reaching arm.

"Wait a minute. The blindfold's okay, but I'd just as soon keep the gun, if you don't mind. I don't know you, nor where you're taking me. I'm showing my good faith by going with you at all, so you ought to be willing to show good faith on your side by letting me keep my gun."

The driver of the car spoke for the first time.

"The guy's right, Curland. We're friends, not enemies. Let him keep his rod!"

Curland subsided and Butch breathed a silent sigh of relief.

The car turned and slowed, and Butch could hear the crunching of gravel beneath the wheels. Then the sedan stopped, and Butch was being helped to the ground.

From the barred window of her upstairs room, Carol could get a partial view of the arrival. Her eyes strained through the darkness. There was something definitely familiar about the width and gait of one of the dusky figures below. It seems to Carol that that figure had a cloth of some kind over its eyes, which would seem to denote that its wearer was not an habitue of the House.

Yes, she was almost sure that the new arrival was Butch O'Brien, and, even if he had come here as a prisoner like herself, the very presence of the huge ham-fisted man gave the girl a feeling of imminent security which she had not felt in many long, hopeless hours.

Yet her most persistent anxiety revolved about the question of the whereabouts of the Black Bat. And Silk Kirby, Professor Kelton, where was he?

Had Carol been able to see Professor Kelton at that moment, she would have laughed in spite of her many misgivings. The Professor had followed Paul Dunbar to a highly respectable hotel, where Dunbar had gone to his room and, presumably, to bed. The Professor had returned to his lonely apartment on the Drive, where he had had no luck in reaching Tony Quinn on the private number. He had then sat down to his interminable solitaire. And his language, muttered at the four walls and the fifty-two cards, was most unprofessional.

CHAPTER XXI

TREASON AMONG THIEVES

NOT DIRECTLY, but Legs Landers did go to the apartment of Kenneth Weeks. But first he detoured to a questionable boarding house known affectionately to gangdom as "Mother Martin's Place." Here he interrupted a poker game, taking away with him two capable-looking thugs who answered respectively to the cognomens of Push-face and Wheezy.

En route to Weeks' place, Landers explained the reason for their trip, and the time was thus taken up with a discussion as to the best method of disposing of the body of the late Mr. Ware.

"I don't care a damn what you do with it," Weeks said when they arrived, "but get it out of here!"

"Sure," said Push-face. "Me an' Wheezy'll take care of it."

The two thugs left, bearing their macabre masquerader. Weeks sank into a chair.

From his point of vantage in the dumbwaiter, the Black Bat had witnessed the little drama. The Bat prepared to make himself known to his adversaries. He loosened the twin .38s in their holsters.

Then Carlotta herself solved the question of her presence.

"I am going home," she announced. "I am sorry, but I cannot stay longer in this room. I will get a taxi at the corner."

A moment more and she was gone.

"I'm sick of it, Landers!" Weeks said. "Everything's going wrong. The Black Bat is in on this thing, and you know what that means. Look what's happened so far. Hall is dead, and Berren and Conal and Peters died in that warehouse blaze, and tonight—Ware. The Bat got all of 'em, Landers! Maybe I'm next!"

Landers was grinning at Weeks, but there wasn't much mirth in his smile.

"Maybe so," he agreed. "It sure looks like he's got you tied up with this thing. Me, now, I'm lucky. He doesn't know about me!"

The Black Bat smiled grimly. "That," he thought, is what *you* think!"

"Look, Landers," Weeks said. "I'm on the spot. Did it ever occur to you that I'm the guy that's responsible for the whole set-up? If it wasn't for me, there wouldn't have *been* any racket!"

"If it wasn't for you, there wouldn't have *needed* to be any racket!"

Weeks waved his hand despairingly.

"That's beside the point. There *is* a racket, and it's a damned good one—a damned sight better from a financial point of view than the legitimate racket we started out to work. But what I'm getting at is—what is there in it for me after the Boss gets through? For that matter, what is there in it for *you?*"

"Not much," Landers admitted.

Weeks glared suspiciously at his companion. "Unless you're the big Boss yourself! I'm still not sure you're not!"

Landers shrugged.

"If you're not," Weeks pursued, "it puts you in the same class with me. D'you know why the big Boss won't let us know who he is? Because he wants a couple of patsies to hang the whole thing on if anything goes wrong! We wouldn't even be in a position to turn state's evidence and try to make a deal for ourselves!"

Landers was thoughtful. For a long time he said nothing.

"I told you I didn't know who the Boss is, Weeks," he said slowly. "But I've got a sort of idea who he is. There's a lot of sense in what you've been saying. As I see it, the only solution is for you and me to stand strictly together. Sometimes that safety deposit box gets very full of cash—very full indeed. If I can ever make sure about the guy I think is the big Boss, there'll be enough to make you and me both rich—if anything should happen to the Boss."

Weeks stuck out his hand.

"Too bad the Boss won't be alive to spend it."

LANDERS TOOK the proffered hand, and they shook.

A voice, low and level and commanding, said:

"Hold that pose."

The two men turned slowly, stared at the black apparition which confronted them, a blue-black and businesslike automatic in each unwavering hand.

"The Black Bat!" Landers muttered at last.

The Black Bat bowed. "I've been considerably interested by your conversation."

Weeks found his voice.

"What do you want of us?"

The Black Bat's shoulders shrugged. The twin automatics waved significantly.

"Of course, I should kill you."

Legs Landers was staring hard at him. "Who *are* you, anyway?"

"Who am I?" the Black Bat repeated. "Suppose I were to tell you that I'm—the Boss!"

Landers' eyes glittered, and the Black Bat saw that he could not be taken in thus. But Weeks, who had no inkling of the Boss' real identity and had only once heard the cold, cruel voice of that mysterious personage, took the Black Bat's rhetorical remark for gospel.

With a smothered cry of mingled fear and rage, he hurled himself forward. If the black-garbed visitor were indeed the Boss, it was a case of kill or be killed!

The merest pressure of the Black Bat's finger would have blasted Weeks to eternity. But he did not yet want to eliminate Landers and Weeks from the dangerous game they were playing.

Landers thought he knew the identity of the Boss, and that was a piece of knowledge which the Black Bat coveted. Too, a criminal organization torn by internecine strife was already half beaten.

The Black Bat's right arm moved with the swiftness and accuracy of a bolt of man-made lightning. The hard steel of the gun barrel cracked against Weeks' jaw, and the man crumpled.

But Landers had taken advantage of the split-second in which Weeks' body was between himself and the Black Bat. Landers skirted around like a ball-carrying halfback on an end run, and flung himself upon the Black Bat's back with the force of a panther.

Landers was not a small man, nor was he soft. And he had grown up in the catch-as-catch-can tradition of street brawling toughs. The Black Bat sensed that in Landers he had met an adversary worthy of his note.

Landers' hard right arm went beneath his chin in a devastating stranglehold, and the room spun before the Black Bat's eyes. Again he might have disposed of his adversary by the simple expedient of reversing one of his guns and blowing Landers' head from his shoulders, and yet again he held from that course. Landers seemed to have divined this unwillingness on the part of the Black Bat to indulge in gunplay, and was staking his life on it.

The very fact that he held a gun in each hand hampered the effectiveness of the Bat's fists, which he needed badly to tear that choking arm from his wind-pipe.

He tossed the gun from his left hand. It plumped into an overstuffed chair. His freed fingers gripped at Landers' right wrist, digging into the artery there, but the encircling arm did not relax its hold.

Landers' eyes were glued hungrily upon the gun lying so temptingly in the chair across the room. Foolishly he had come unarmed, but if he could reach that weapon—

Slowly, every muscle tense and aching, he forced the Black Bat in that direction, only, in the next moment, to be forced backwards himself. Yet he gained ground.

SUDDENLY, THE BLACK BAT insinuated his right foot between Landers' legs, and hooked his toes around the other's right ankle. His left hand reached over and back, and his fingers gripped the corded back of Landers' neck. Then, with every remaining ounce of his strength, he crouched low, kicked out with his right foot, and at the same time tugged mightily at his adversary's head.

Landers rolled up and over the Black Bat's head like a pinwheel. Almost simultaneously, the butt of the .38 cracked hollowly upon Landers' skull, and the Black Bat eased the unconscious man to the floor.

The Black Bat knelt, and swiftly ran through the pockets of Weeks and Landers. He found only one thing which interested him, and that was a small key in Landers' vest pocket. One side of this key was inscribed with the numbers 5-8-4, and the reverse side bore the legend "Savall Safety Deposit Company."

He returned the key to its resting place in Landers' pocket.

From the bedroom, he procured a set of sheets, which he tore into narrow strips. First he gagged both men, then proceeded to truss them. He was careful to tie the knots so they would appear businesslike, yet be capable of solution after a certain amount of industrious effort on the parts of the victims. Let Landers and Weeks escape. Let them believe that the Black Bat was not the formidable antagonist they had thought him. Let them even have a feeling of contempt for him. Then, in the ultimate moment of cracking down, the Black Bat would disillusion them.

He left the apartment as he had entered it, via the dumbwaiter. A moment later he was in the black coupé, driving toward the building which housed the vaults of the Savall Safety Deposit Company.

Even the Black Bat had no idea nor intention of attempting to invade the vaults of the company. Case-hardened steel defenses and inviolable time-locks made such a task insurmountable, and the Black Bat was not presently interested in the contents of box 584 anyway. What he *was* interested in was simply the record books of the Savall Company. Box 584, he knew, would be listed under two names. One of those names would be Landers—but it was the other name, and address, which he was particularly anxious to uncover.

The offices he planned to visit were on the ground floor of a large office building, and had their vault deep in the foundations of the structure. Overalled janitors and charwomen moved through the building on their nightly rounds. One man industriously polished the brass entrance doors. He turned, hearing a tentative "Pardon me," and saw a black-garbed man who wore a wide-brimmed black hat far down over his eyes.

"I'm looking for a neighbor of mine," said the black-garbed man. "His wife has been taken sick, and he's needed at home."

"What's his name?"

"Nelson."

The name came easily to the mouth of the man in black.

The janitor shook his head. "Don't know him. But there's quite a few of 'em works here. If his wife is sick, I guess it'd be all right for you to go in an' look for him." He produced a key and unlocked the heavy alarm-lock.

"Thanks," said the Black Bat. "Thanks very much."

He passed through the door and into the gloom of the lobby. Leading off the lobby was a door to the offices of the Savall Safety Deposit Company, and the door was open!

The Black Bat slipped through the door and proceeded unerringly through the darkness to a row of cabinets at the rear of the floor. There he paused to look once again at the janitor. The man still plied his mop.

FROM HIS belt, the Black Bat drew the small ring of keys. The first cabinet which he opened contained a variety of ledgers, but nothing, the Bat saw at a glance, which would interest him. The second cabinet was equally as unproductive. But in the third he found that which he sought, a ledger with the single gilt-embossed word "Clients" on its binding. He drew it forth and turned the pages carefully. Each box-number was listed, and presently the Black Bat's finger stopped at number 584.

Two names were entered under that number, indicating that the box was held jointly. The first name was Arthur Brown, and the address was one on Fifth Avenue. The name, the Black Bat realized, was fictitious, but the address was that of the Sky Club. The other name, listed as William Hanley, was doubtless also fictitious, but the address that followed it was one on Seaview Boulevard!

The Black Bat whistled silently, and exultation surged over him. Seaview Boulevard! Dunbar and Curland had spoken of the House being near the ocean when they had left the Acme offices with Carol as their prisoner. And Seaview Boulevard ran directly beside the wide sweep of the Atlantic for many miles! At last the Black Bat knew the location of the House—and it was there that Carol was held captive! He replaced the ledger and closed the cabinet door quietly. Then he turned and slipped out the way he had come.

A moment later the Black Bat was behind the wheel of the coupé and it was gathering speed, headed east toward the ocean and Seaview Boulevard!

CHAPTER XXII

PRELUDE TO HELL

JUST AS soon as they entered the House, Curland removed the blindfold from Butch's eyes. Butch found himself in a spacious, comfortably furnished drawing room. Also in the room were Curland

and the driver of the car, and still another ugly looking man whom Butch had not seen before. The latter stood near the room's one entrance.

"The person who wishes to see you," Curland said, "will be down presently."

Curland ordered the two thugs from the room. They left sullenly.

"I can make all the arrangements short of the actual price-setting," Curland said, "We have a copy of the formula which is in the vaults of the United States War Department. We're willing to sell that copy—if the price is right."

Butch fidgeted in his chair. All this silly talk, and what he really wanted to know was whether Carol was in this house?

He said, sparring, "How do I know you won't sell the same formula to others?"

Curland smiled. "You don't. You'll have to take our word on that. And even if we sold the formula to every other—to every other interested party in the world, could your employers still afford to be without it?"

"Have you sold the formula to any other—*person*—yet?" queried Butch.

For a moment Curland studied him. "I'll be frank. No, we haven't."

Butch sighed with silent relief. Thus far the world was safe from the newest war-scourge. "I would suggest," he said, "that you refrain from doing so. I believe I can offer a price large enough to make it worth your while to withhold the formula from any other bidders."

Butch was rather proud of that speech.

Upstairs, Carol had been debating the advisability of making her presence known to Butch, if the man who had been brought to the house were indeed Butch.

But before she could make any plans, a key turned in the lock, and the door of her prison swung open. A burly, evil-faced fellow stepped through and stood menacingly before her. Behind him two others entered the room very quickly.

One was an attractive dark-haired girl with swaying hips and deep black eyes that harbored cruelty. The other was a large, florid man, who had the appearance of a man used to giving orders—and having them obeyed. Now, however, he spoke not at all. It was the dark-haired girl, Carlotta, who did the talking.

She stared now at Carol with the antagonism of one beautiful woman for another.

"Have you had time yet to decide whether or not you will tell us why you were spying upon us, who, for example, is the Black Bat?"

Carol did not answer. Carlotta turned her head, nodded slightly to the two thugs. They left the room, but returned almost immediately with a common armchair of the dining room variety, together with a squarish metal box and a coil of wire. They placed the chair against one wall of the room, and the two men became busy over the wire and the metal box.

Carol watched the proceedings with mingled interest and apprehension.

"You are interested, no?" said Carlotta. "Perhaps we should explain to you what we have here. This"—she touched the metal box with the toe of her slipper—"is a contrivance which steps up the electricity from the house current. This electric chair of ours will not kill, or, at least, it will not kill at once. But perhaps, after the current has been running through your body for a few minutes, you will talk."

AT A signal from the florid man, each of the thugs took one of Carol's arms and literally lifted her into the chair. She did not struggle, for she knew it would be useless, and she knew that she would have need of her strength. Straps fixed her wrists and ankles to the arms and legs of the chair.

At last the others stood back.

"You have still time in which to change your mind," Carlotta said. "Who is the Black Bat?"

Carol's eyes stared into the other woman's levelly, and her voice was as level as her gaze.

"I don't know what you're talking about!"

At a signal from Carlotta, one of the thugs touched a rheostat on the transformer. Carol's body tensed as the first shock coursed through her body. The current danced up her spine, seeming to shower into sparks in her brain, setting her teeth chattering.

The rheostat was moved up another notch. An added surge of power washed over her. Every nerve fibre in her body was fraying. The faces before her swam in her vision. The current was just sufficient to hold her suspended in an abyss of horror which stretched below and beyond her to a terrible infinity.

She knew what would happen. Sooner or later she would crack, her mind flogged into acquiescence. She would answer anything, any question, to be freed of the awful nerve torture which assailed her.

If only she could scream, she thought dully. If she could open her mouth and let forth all the pent-up noise within her, it might give her new strength. Her head went back, and her mouth opened wide.

The shattering cry which issued from Carol's agonized throat was not a simple scream. It was a name—a name which rose, unbidden, from the depths of her subconscious.

"Butch!"

Downstairs, the owner of that voice stiffened in his chair. The cry which reached his ears could have come from but one person, Carol Hastings!

Deep rage shook Butch's frame. His face was livid. His shoulder and neck muscles strained against his clothes.

His lips curled back from his teeth in an animal snarl. He started to rise from his chair.

"Stay where you are!" Curland was saying.

"That's me she's callin', see? Outa my way, rat!"

Curland was on his feet, his eyes widening, his right hand darting toward his left armpit. But Butch O'Brien bore down upon him like a juggernaut. The powerful right arm drew back, then lashed out with the devastating power of a steam-turbine.

All the world's hatred of evil was in that punch. The hamlike fist crashed full into Curland's face. There was the sound of crunching bone, of teeth snapping at their roots. Curland toppled heavily backwards to the floor, his jaw splintered, his mouth poring blood.

In a stride, Butch was across the room to the door and out into the hallway, headed for the stairs, his hand groping for his gun. As he started upward, a man showed himself at the head of the stairs. In his hand a .45 coughed death. The heavy slugs tore past Butch.

Then his own heavy automatic was belching flame and lead. The man at the top of the stairs spun in a half circle and plunged downwards, his body crashing on the stairs. Butch pounded on up the steps.

Another gunman loomed before him. This time Butch's .45 expended only a single bullet. It caught the man in the mathematical center of his forehead.

BUTCH WAS in the upper hall. To his right a door slammed, and he heard a key turn in the lock.

"Butch!"

Again the cry assailed him. With a bellow of rage he threw himself against the closed door. There was a crash from within, and something ripped through the door a scant inch from his head. Tiny splinters dug into his face and neck. Again he hurled his weight against the door. The two hundred and twenty pound battering-ram tore the door from its hinges.

For one fleeting instant Butch saw Carol slumped in the chair, and then something hard and heavy thudded against his skull as he went through the doorway. He toppled heavily to the floor, joining Carol in the infinite reaches of oblivion.

Carlotta dropped the monkey wrench. She turned to the florid man.

"So, Jeemy, even Mr. Butch O'Brien is a part of the Black Bat's organization!"

Carlotta left the room. In less than a minute, she was back. She came close to the florid man.

"Dirks and Arnold are dead, Jeemy," she said, "and Curland is unconscious downstairs." For a moment she was thoughtful. "The Black Bat has keeled of seven of us so far, Jeemy. Who will be next? You? Me?"

The man took Carlotta into his arms and held her close.

"There won't be any more of it, Carlotta. After tomorrow, there'll be just you and I, Carlotta. Every one that has died has meant one less to share in our profits. And there'll be two hundred thousand in cash from that phony Professor, all for us!"

"But if you know the Professor is a phony why do you think he will have two hundred thousand dollars in cash?"

"Because he isn't aware of the fact that we know he's a phony! He supplied Dunbar with bank references and they're one hundred percent. Whatever his game is he's got the dough to back up his masquerade, and apparently he's perfectly willing to spend it if he thinks he's getting anywhere on this case!

"Unfortunately for him, he's not going to get anywhere but dead! He'll roast in one of those buildings he's buying, and we'll plant plenty of evidence to indicate that he was behind the whole business and got caught in a boomerang blaze of his own setting! Not bad, eh?

"And speaking of being dead, it wouldn't be a bad idea if Weeks and Landers and Dunbar were to die too!"

Carlotta smiled. "And then there would be just us."

"Yes, just us. A ship to South America and a life of luxury. And the bomb formula can be marketed just as readily in South America as here!"

"Where is the formula now?"

"In three places, Carlotta. One copy is in the vaults of the United States War Department, another is in my safety deposit box and the third is in the mind of Kenneth Weeks! That's a good reason in itself for the elimination of Weeks!"

"Just one more day!" Carlotta said dreamily. Then she faced the more practical aspects of the present. "But what are we to do now?"

"Burn this place. With our gang almost annihilated, we couldn't cope with the Black Bat now, even if we did get his identity from this girl. No, the best thing to do is follow our plan and clear out. There's enough of the stuff in the cellar to do the job and leave enough for tomorrow's work too."

Carlotta motioned toward the unconscious forms of Butch and Carol.

"What about them?" she questioned the florid man.

"Remove all identification from their bodies, and leave them here, of course. Yes, and Curland too. He's out, and he's no good to us anyway with a busted head. Push-face and Wheezy will catch up with us at the other place. These two, with Weeks and Landers and Dunbar, will be enough to take care of tomorrow's work.

"Push-face and Wheezy are just ordinary hoods. We can pay them off in peanuts without denting our bankroll. Weeks and Landers and Dunbar we won't need to pay off at all."

THE FIRST streaks of approaching dawn serrated the blackness of the sky. And, as the light grew, Carlotta and the florid man were extremely busy. The man carried foot-square zinc boxes from the cellar to a sedan whose rear floorboards lifted to reveal a commodious secret receptacle for them.

Carlotta, meanwhile, traced intricate patterns of a coarse, reddish powder through the place. Both finished their work at precisely the same time.

Once more, they visited the three unconscious figures. None showed signs of any early recovery. Carlotta and the florid man then repaired to the attic.

In the center of the floor was a small pile of the same powdery substance which trailed its serpentine way throughout the House. A length of grayish metallic ribbon extended from the pile.

The man struck a match, applied it to the free end of the metal ribbon. There was a dull red glow.

"Five minutes," he said simply. He and Carlotta walked leisurely down the stairs, through the front door, and into the sedan. In slightly less than one minute from the time of the ignition of the metal fuse, the sedan was two blocks away.

One hundred and eighty seconds later, a small black coupé stopped before the House. A figure in solid black stepped from it, and advanced toward the door. In his hands were twin .38 automatics. Apparently, the man in black was here for a purpose, and was in a hurry to accomplish it, whatever the dangers presented by a frontal attack.

The door opened to his touch. Cautiously the Black Bat entered, guns ready. None barred his way. Beneath the black mask, his brows furrowed. Had he found the House only to have its occupants, foe and friend alike, gone?

The living room showed him the unconscious form of Curland, battered and bloody.

That mashed face seemed to bear a trade mark with which the Black Bat was familiar—the imprint of the fist of Butch O'Brien!

The Bat turned, made for the hall and the stairs. And as his foot touched the first step, he heard, far above him, a muffled *pooof!*

He had heard that same sound before, and he knew it was the first note in a seething symphony of searing flame—a prelude to hell!

CHAPTER XXIII

THE WINGS OF FLAME

VICIOUSLY, THE heat reached down at him from above like the fetid breath of some horrid monster, choking him, hammering at his eyeballs. But the Black Bat took the stairs three at a time.

The ceiling of the upper floor was already starting to drip fire—that devastating liquid fire that melted everything with which it came in contact. Smoke swirled down from the attic in blinding eddies.

To the right, the Black Bat saw a battered door, and on the floor of the fume-filled room beyond, a huge, huddled figure. Butch! The Black Bat was through the door in a leap.

Then another figure—the figure of a girl, strapped into a grotesque parody of an electric-chair. Carol! A silent prayer of thanksgiving flooded the heart of the Black Bat, for he could see that the girl lived!

Carol's head moved lazily on her shoulders, and her eyes were trying to open. The Black Bat was tearing the straps from her arms and legs, and his voice was calling her back from the dim depths of darkness:

"Carol! Carol! It's Tony!"

A shudder passed over her slim young body, and her eyes looked upon him.

"Tony! Thank God!"

"Quick! We haven't an instant to lose!" He was helping the girl to her feet.

"I'm all right," she said. "Get Butch!"

The Black Bat bent, threw the weight of the huge man over his shoulder like a bag of feathers.

"Don't wait for me!" he told Carol. "Get out of the house!"

But she would not leave him. Together they worked their way toward the stairs. Little pools of fire burned evilly on the floor, and they picked their way carefully. Drops of searing flame lobbed from the ceiling. And now new traceries of fire appeared, dancing about them like mad demons of hate.

Down the stairs they went, feeling through the denseness of the smoke. The force of the heat pushed at their backs. The hungry, angry flames raced after them, greedy tongues licking out at the escaping meal.

In the lower hall, the Black Bat paused. From the living room came a piercing scream—a scream of mingled pain and horror. A man with a bloody face crawled toward him across the floor. And then the man stopped, and a new horror froze his face.

"The Black Bat!" he hissed through mashed and broken lips.

Curland! And as much as the Black Bat hated him for all he represented, he could not bring himself to leave him in the holocaust.

The Black Bat turned away and ran for the front door. A moment later he was outside, loading the huge form of Butch into the coupé. Then he turned, started again for the blazing building.

"Tony, don't! You can't go back in there!"

"I've got to, Carol!"

He was racing toward the doorway that poured a solid stream of smoke into the open. As he neared it, there was a deep-throated roar and the House burst into a solid mass of all-consuming flame.

The Black Bat staggered backwards. And from the inferno came one long, agonized scream of pure horror—a scream that terminated suddenly on a high, piercing note, almost as though the sound had been cut with a knife.

The Black Bat climbed into the coupé, and threw it into gear. Beside him was Carol, and beyond her, Butch. The big man was stirring painfully. Driving with one hand, the Black Bat removed the mask that covered his face. The wide brim of the black hat served almost as well.

THIRTY MINUTES later the three were in the living room of the home of Tony Quinn. Butch was shaking the grogginess from his head like a huge setter divesting itself of water.

The doorbell rang. Tony Quinn tapped his way to the door with his rubber-ferruled cane. A sleepy messenger boy held out an envelope.

"Why," he asked plaintively, "couldn't you have answered the bell sooner? I been here all night with this message!"

The boy left, examining a ten dollar bill with patent disbelief.

Quinn was back in the living room, tearing open the envelope. Butch and Carol watched as he drew forth the one scribbled sheet. It contained, simply, five addresses, but Quinn knew its significance as well as if Silk had enclosed a long letter of explanation.

"They've made a deal with Professor Kelton," Quinn told the others. "They're scared, and they're unloading."

"And I'll tell you something else they're doing," Butch volunteered. "They're plannin' on burning the Prof in one of the buildings after they get the dough from him!"

Carol gasped. "Then they know Silk is working against them?"

Butch nodded. "I heard Landers talkin' it over with the Boss. I heard that guy's voice myself, and I was lookin' forward to meetin' him!"

His huge fists clenched into tight balls.

"I saw him," said Carol. "And I've seen the man's pictures in the paper, too, but I can't place him."

Tony Quinn was across the room, bent over a desk upon which was spread a map of the city.

"I can go you both one better," he said. "I know who the Boss is, and I know his name. And if I knew where he was at this moment, I'd feel a lot better!"

"You know who he is? Who?"

Quinn shook his head. "Not yet. Tonight will end the whole affair, I'm sure. Then I'll tell you who he is—or, I hope, who he was—and I'll also tell you a story about a map!"

The face of a desk clock upon the table glowed dimly red, signaling that some one was calling on the private phone in the room behind the fireplace.

"That'll be Silk," said Quinn. "But we can't answer it!"

"Can't answer it?"

Quinn shook his head grimly. "If they suspect Silk, they've probably managed to tap his phone wires. And we can't afford to have any of that crew listening in on us. No, I'm afraid Silk'll have to walk into danger without knowing what faces him! It's simply up to us to be on hand at the right place at the right time!"

IT WAS late evening before Dunbar arrived at the apartment of Professor Kelton. He was all apologies.

"Sorry I couldn't make it sooner, Professor. Been busy as the proverbial bee all day."

"That's more than I've been," Silk thought. "It's all right, Mr. Dunbar," Silk said, "though I must admit I've been a little nervous with all this cash on my hands all day." He nodded toward a small black bag on a chair. "Two hundred thousand dollars in cash. If the buildings live up to your prospectus, I see no reason why we shouldn't be able to consummate our deal at once."

Dunbar's eye glowed. "And there's no reason why we shouldn't look at the buildings tonight," he added.

"Do you have a gun?" the Professor asked. "I hate to leave the money here in the apartment, and I dislike carrying it at night, unarmed."

Silk's last remark was not entirely true, for beneath his left arm nestled a very businesslike .38.

"It so happens that I do have a gun," Dunbar said. "I've been carrying rather large sums lately myself, in the course of liquidating our business, you know."

Silk held out the black bag.

"Would you mind?"

"Not at all." Dunbar's hand closed around the handle of the bag. "And now, shall we go?"

"Of course."

The two men left the apartment.

SILK HOPED fervently that the Black Bat would put in an appearance this night. All day he had tried to reach Tony Quinn on the private telephone, and without success. It wasn't particularly reassuring. Perhaps the Black Bat had been disposed of. Perhaps Carol and the huge Butch also had been snatched from the fight.

If such were the case, Silk Kirby was now alone in the struggle. The odds against him, he knew, were long. Once it became necessary for him to show his hand, he could expect no mercy. But if defeat and death were stacked in the cards for him, Silk was determined to play his losing hand to the last chip.

Before the building a car waited. At the wheel was Legs Landers. Silk and Dunbar climbed into the back seat. The car completed the loop around the Drive, and headed east on the next street. As it turned into the next avenue, two other cars started from the curb a block away.

One of these cars was a black coupé, and in it was a man wearing sombre black clothes and a wide-brimmed black hat that shadowed grim scars about his eyes. In the other car were a large man and a small girl.

At 83rd Street, Dunbar's car turned east again. Landers had been giving considerable attention to his rear vision mirror. It seemed to him that two particular cars were trailing him. But now he sighed with relief. Instead of turning the corner after him, the two cars had continued straight on.

What he did not know was that the black car pulled to the curb as soon as it had passed the corner. The other car drew beside it for a moment.

"Only one of the houses on Silk's list is on 83rd Street," the Black Bat said softly through the window. "We'll give them a chance to get into the place before we catch up. If, by any chance, they're really headed for one of the other places, we can catch 'em anyway. We know that car, and we know the other addresses."

Presently, the two cars moved again, very slowly now. They turned down 81st Street to Eighth Avenue, then doubled north again to 83rd. A dozen doors from 783 West 83rd Street they stopped again, but this time both cars pulled to the curb. Dunbar's car was parked a hundred feet in front of them, and it was empty. Bumper to bumper with Dunbar's car was another, roomier sedan.

The black-garbed man was on the sidewalk. Butch got out of his car. Carol started to follow him.

"You're staying in the car, Carol!" the Black Bat reminded her. "We settled that some time ago!"

There was authority in his voice, and Carol heeded. She got back into the car.

"Be careful!" she begged.

The tenement at Number 783 was a fire trap of a place if ever one existed. And now, it was almost devoid of tenants. There were names in only three of the dilapidated mailboxes in the dingy vestibule.

The Black Bat spoke softly. "Butch, I want you to get those three families out of the building! Tell them their lives depend on it! Give them money, tell them to get new quarters. And if they won't get out quietly, throw them out!"

Suddenly, Carlotta whirled and the gun barked.

"Sure," said Butch. "But it's likely to be a little noisy. Ain't that likely to interfere with your progress?"

"Butch, in a few minutes this place is going to be so noisy that a boiler factory would seem quiet by comparison! Get going!"

Butch pushed through the door. For a moment the Black Bat paused, drawing a mask over his eyes, and a strangely shaped cloak over his shoulders. Then he flitted through the interior hallway through thick gloom to the very rear of the building. And as he went, he noted thin streams of a coarse, reddish powder traced in intricate patterns over the floor and up the stairs. The tinder-box had been opened, and the priming was ready. It needed only the spark!

At the rear, he climbed nimbly out upon a fire-escape, and ran aloft as easily as a sailor in the rigging of a ship. At each floor he paused to look in through dark windows.

On the fifth floor, he found what he sought. Through the window he looked in upon a dimly-lighted room. And in the room was being enacted a grim drama!

CHAPTER XXIV

FLAMING DEATH

KNOWING WELL enough what he was up against, Silk Kirby, in the role of Professor Kelton, stood with his hands upraised. Facing him was a large, florid man, who held a gun.

"We're obliged for the money, Professor," the florid man was saying in a mocking voice as hard and as cold as steel. He motioned to a white-faced man who stood nearby. "All right, Weeks, tie him up!"

Legs Landers pinioned the Professor's arm, and Weeks bound him securely. A dark-haired girl stuffed a cloth into the Professor's mouth. His trussed body was lowered to the floor. And this floor, too, was traced with the reddish powder.

The florid man spoke to Dunbar.

"You've attended to everything?"

Dunbar nodded. "Everything. The deeds of this and the other buildings have been made over to Kelton, and he's paid us. A nice, clean-cut business deal. When the properties burn, what simpler deduction could anybody make than that he lost his own life setting incendiary blazes in his own buildings?"

The florid man put his gun back in his pocket. Then, in a perfect example of timing, Landers and Weeks drew their own guns.

"All right," Landers hissed. "Just stand still. Weeks and I are taking over!"

The florid man gaped.

"Put down those guns, you fools!"

Landers shook his head. "Too bad you got so short of help that you had to show yourself, Boss! Push-face and Wheezy didn't even show up, did they? Know why? Because Weeks and I paid 'em off and got rid of 'em! Now you can burn with the Professor!"

Carlotta stood silent. Weeks turned to her. "Okay, Carlotta, get that black bag and we'll get out of here!"

Carlotta turned her back upon Weeks and Landers and walked toward Dunbar and the beefy man. Her hand opened her bag surreptitiously and came forth with a short-snouted pistol.

Then, suddenly, she whirled, and the gun barked. Weeks sank to his knees. There was a look of unbelief on his face, and his head shook in negation. He was dead before his head hit the floor.

The sudden unexpected turn had taken Landers quite by surprise. His gun hung useless for a moment in his hand. And that moment was enough to seal his fate. Dunbar turncoated. His hand came up with a .45. Its roar filled the room like something solid. The slug ripped into Landers' face. Landers' body thudded upon that of his ally.

"Good work, Dunbar!" the beefy man gritted. "For that you can have your life!"

Carlotta took up the black bag.

"Now!" she said.

And at that moment, the window glass crashed and a black figure stepped into the room. Two guns covered the room. His voice was crisp, authoritative.

"Stand still, all of you! Get your hands up!"

For a moment, those in the room stood transfixed. From the floor, the eyes of Professor Kelton grinned up at the Black Bat.

Carlotta walked slowly toward him. There was a strange smile on her face, and her eyes stared into his narrowly.

"Back!" ordered the Black Bat. "Back, or I shoot!"

The girl's slow progress did not cease.

"Even the Black Bat would not shoot a woman!" she said mockingly.

NOW SHE was directly between the Black Bat and the florid man, gambling her very life on the truth of the statement she had just made. And her bluff worked. The Black Bat could not quite—quite exert the pressure that would have sent a slug chewing into the beautiful, lithe body before him.

And with the girl as a willing shield, the florid man acted. There was a gun in his hand now, but he made no attempt to fire it at the Black Bat. Instead, he fired a single quick shot into a small pile of the coarse reddish powder at the far side of the room!

At once, there was a blinding flash, and one huge billow of smoke filled the room.

"Now!" cried Carlotta.

The Black Bat could hear the thud of something being thrown to the floor, and then the steps of the enemy running from the room. The twin .38s barked, and the Black Bat heard a scream of pain. Dunbar

Carol paused beside the fireplace.

reeled backwards into the room, fell against him, but he was already dead.

With fire racing through the room, the Black Bat could think only of Silk now. Swiftly he bent, drew a knife. The blade cut through Silk's bonds. Weaponless, Silk reached for the gun which the florid man had hurled to the floor.

"Let's go!" he cried excitedly.

Together, the Black Bat and his trusted aide dashed down the stairs. Below them they could hear the clomping, running feet of their quarry.

The fire tightened its grip upon the doomed house. The heat beat upon the backs of Silk and the Black Bat as they ran for their lives.

Down three flights more, and at last the door. Behind them the tenement was a seething, churning, howling mass of red flame.

Butch was on the sidewalk, struggling with a screaming group of immigrants.

"I got 'em out!" he yelled triumphantly. "I told 'em I set the fire, an' then I ran!"

The roomy sedan was roaring away from the curb, and Carol stood on the sidewalk emptying her pistol at it as calmly as though she were engaged in practice on a range.

But is was the gun in Silk's hand that did the trick—the gun which had been thrown down by the florid man. Its chambers were loaded with tracer-bullets, incendiaries. It was one of those bullets which had started the blaze. And now Silk was emptying it after the fleeing sedan.

One of those white-streaked slugs ripped into the lower part of the sedan's rear. There was a flame as the gasoline ignited. Still the occupants of the car might escape—

But there was still a case or two of the incendiary material in the false bottom beneath the rear floorboards of the sedan. The flash was all-engulfing. Where a moment before had been a car was now only a solid mass of flame coasting with awful precision toward a light-post. The crash sent showers of sparks mushrooming high into the air. The car and post were nothing but a twisted, horrible mass of molten metal, white-hot in the darkness.

The Black Bat put an arm about Carol's shoulder. She was trembling.

"It's over," he said softly. "And it was no more than they've done to others, you know!"

He turned toward his own car. "All right, Butch!" he called. "Time to get going!"

The screaming sirens of approaching police cars and fire apparatus were drawing nearer. Two cars moved swiftly away from the scene.

BACK AT the house, Tony Quinn and his three aides gathered about a table in the living room. On the table was spread a map of the city. Tony pointed out a series of red pencil marks.

"As you can see," he said, "the red marks follow a definite directional pattern. Each of those marks represents either a burned building or a building which was slated to be burned. There was a definite reason for those fires being in a straight line."

Tony drew a line on the map. It formed an X with the line connecting the red marks which designated the burned buildings.

"Do you know what that line represents?" he asked.

"Yes, sir," Silk put in. "It represents the route of the new crosstown elevated highway which is now being constructed."

Carol's eyes were flashing with comprehension. "Now I'm beginning to see! The elevated highway could very well have taken another route—a route passing over the red marks!"

"Exactly," nodded Quinn. "The moment there were three fires in a straight line, I began to wonder why. Then the papers came out with the story about a certain city engineer who had invented a formula for incendiary bombs. Weeks seemed a logical choice for that dubious honor, for he was city engineer in a city which was having some extremely strange fires."

"Look," said Butch, "I hate to seem thick, but would you mind starting at the beginning with Weeks and following through on just how much he had to do with the whole business?"

"As a matter of fact," Quinn said, "Weeks had everything to do with it. He wasn't the Boss, of course. But if it hadn't been for Weeks' weakness for gambling, a great many people who are dead might still be alive at this moment.

"Weeks was a gambler, and a bad one. He was unlucky. He owed a lot of money to Landers' Sky Club, and he couldn't pay up. Landers' secret Boss was sore, and no doubt Weeks was told he'd be killed if he didn't produce the money. He was panicky."

"So he had to let Landers and the Boss in on the genteel little racket he'd doped out about the new highway," Carol said.

Tony Quinn looked at the girl with admiration.

"I see you've got it figured out, Carol. And you're right.

"Weeks, as city engineer, drew up the plans for the proposed elevated highway, and he intended to get some friends to go in with him on what was almost a legitimate racket—a plan to buy up property along the proposed route before the route was officially announced and approved. And if the properties were acquired cheaply enough, a neat profit might have been turned in condemnation awards from the city.

"And then, when it was a choice of paying his gambling debts or being liquidated, Weeks offered the proposition to Landers and the Boss. They'd have to put up some more money to buy the properties, of course, but they'd make a profit, and it was the only way they could get the money Weeks owed the Sky Club's tables.

"They went for the deal, and Weeks breathed easier for a while. He submitted his plans for the highway, but the city fathers turned down the route.

"Weeks and his playmates were left with a lot of real estate that wasn't worth even as much as they'd paid for it, because the new legislation requiring fireproof firewalls in tenements had been passed in the meantime."

Butch was chuckling.

"As Butch has guessed, Weeks must have been scared blue. So he gave them the formula. It made beautiful fires that left no tangible clues and offered a neat solution as to what should be done with a lot of worthless buildings—buildings which, incidentally, were still insured under old policies of higher value than the actual worth of the properties."

"And the Acme company," Carol said, "was simply a cover-up."

"Right. The Acme Company had always been a respectable outfit. The Boss bought it up through a dummy, and at an easy price. While Acme conducted its part of the dirty business, it was also engaged in liquidating its legitimate business.

"The Boss was also clever enough to coerce old-time outfits like the Mercy Drug Company into cooperating on insurance blazes. They had the warehouse fire that was supposed to have destroyed a valuable inventory of drugs, and which was really only cartons filled with junk."

"And that guy Berren that they said was watchman in the warehouse," Butch said. "They even collected insurance on him! It looks like pretty nearly anything that happened figured to give them a profit!"

Tony Quinn nodded gravely. "That's the way they had it figured."

"But, Tony, who was the Boss?" Carol said.

"The Boss," said Quinn, "was a man known in sporting circles as Big Jim Morley...."

"Wait a minute!" Butch interrupted. "I'm sorry, Quinn, but I'm afraid you're wrong about that. It couldn't have been Morley, because I saw him and Carlotta at the club, and they didn't know each other."

"Naturally they wouldn't recognize each other at the Sky Club," Tony explained patiently. "Morley had Carlotta planted there to watch Landers, and she threw herself at Weeks' head so she could keep her eye on him, too. The Boss wanted to be sure Weeks wouldn't skip town, and he knew Weeks wouldn't do anything or go anyplace without talking about it to the girl with whom he was so infatuated. But Morley was really the big moment in Carlotta's life."

"But how, sir," Silk asked, "how did you know that Morley was the Boss?"

"I didn't know for sure until I saw him, but I was wondering about him. You see, when I was district attorney, there was a case involving the murder of a night club owner who was the front for a man we believed to be Big Jim Morley, just as Landers was fronting for Morley in ownership of the Sky Club. The man disappeared, and though we were certain he'd been murdered, his body was never found.

"Hence, we had no case against Morley even had we been able to establish that he was the actual owner of the club, and that the missing man had held back on some of the receipts. Now, normally there isn't any reason for an owner to keep his identity a secret, particularly from the man who's fronting for him, and as the two cases seemed to parallel in that respect, I wonder if it couldn't be Morley who was behind Landers in the role of the Boss."

"And that's all," said Carol softly.

"Yes, that's all." For a full half minute the little group was silent. Then Silk spoke.

"I think, sir, that a time like this might be a suitable one for all hands to enjoy a short one from your private bottle of Napoleon brandy."

QUINN SLAPPED Silk Kirby soundly on the back.

"By all means!"

From the street came the sound of shrieking brakes.

Silk sighed. "I'm afraid it will be necessary for Butch and Miss Carol to repair to the room behind the fireplace for the present. And here, sir, are your dark glasses and your cane. Apparently, we are about to receive a call from Lieutenant McGrath."

"How do you know McGrath's comin' here?" Butch demanded.

Silk bent a patient eye upon the large man.

"When a car shrieks to a stop from fifty miles an hour," he said, "you may be reasonably certain it's a police car, and if it stops at this door, you may be even surer that it contains Lieutenant McGrath!"

Then, turning, Silk favored his employer with a broad wink.

"You'd better delay that Napoleon brandy for a while, Silk," Quinn said. "I feel almost good enough to give McGrath a taste of it—almost, but not quite!

"And Butch! Before you go through that fireplace, slip a couple of those cigars of yours into my humidor, will you? I think I'd enjoy seeing McGrath work on one of those!"

Carol paused before the fireplace. Her eyes lingered on the man she loved.

"And me, Tony Quinn? Have you any orders for me?"

Quinn's features softened as he returned her gaze. "Orders for you, Carol? Yes. Remind me, won't you, to tell you how wonderful I think you are—sometime when these two birds aren't around, you know...."

And this time, a wink passed between Silk Kirby and Butch O'Brien.

THE BLACK BAT'S TRIUMPH

CHAPTER I

HUNCHBACK KILLERS

IT WAS well after midnight and a slashing rain pounded against the windows of Grant Hollis' exclusive mansion. Inside, a fire on the hearth flickered cheerfully and Hollis himself was sprawled out in an easy chair nearby. A man of about fifty, he seemed at home among the trophies of the hunts which hung from the walls. Grizzly bear from Alaska, a leopard from African jungles, a massive elk head, a wild boar from India.

Grant Hollis had traveled during his lifetime and he had met countless surprises, but none quite so stupendous as that which occupied his brain at the present moment.

He didn't hear the rain, but it was certainly a night when no one would expect weird-looking creatures to be stalking about. Yet, if someone with a good pair of eyes had been watching the rear of the Hollis home, he would have seen two eerie-looking beings dart from one drenched bush to another, always keeping well in the dark.

A profile of them would have shown that they were both, amazingly enough, hunchbacks. They wore wide-brimmed hats from which the rain poured off in rivulets. Their faces were masked by black scarfs which were drawn tightly around their heads, leaving only their crafty eyes in view.

One of them signaled his companion to remain hidden. Then he stalked closer to the house, clambered up on a small portico and side-stepped carefully until he could look through the French windows. His gloved hand stretched out and tried the latch. The window was locked.

He dug into a pocket, found a slender instrument and inserted this so gently that the man inside the room had no inkling of the doom that was approaching. The gentle click was hushed by the lashing torrent of rain. From the darkness came the second hunchback, drawing a gun as he approached.

Hollis felt the cold draft against the back of his head and also noticed that the sound of the rain was stronger than ever now. He arose abruptly and turned toward the French door.

Then he stopped. His eyes narrowed, his lips set in a hard line. Hollis was no coward. Even the two eerie creatures who faced him with drawn guns only made his heart beat a little faster.

"Burglars, eh," he said coldly. "Well, what do you want?"

"Sit down," one of the men ordered gruffly. "Use your head and you won't get hurt. Try one trick and we'll blow your ears off."

HOLLIS BACKED away slowly, avoided two or three chairs and finally reached a swivel chair behind his desk. If he was going to be tied up, he wanted to be strapped to that particular chair. Hollis' mind was working fast. He noticed that both intruders were hunchbacks and he coolly reasoned that it was almost too coincidental for two burglars to be so afflicted. In the first place it made marked men of them both.

They used silken tie-backs from the portières to bind him and they did a remarkably good job of it. They didn't gag him. Then one of the burglars let the muzzle of his gun rest against Hollis' temple.

"Just give us the combination of the wall safe, brother, and tell us where it's hidden, too."

Hollis gave the number and indicated where they might find the safe. He watched them open it, loot the contents and fill a small satin sack with convertible bonds, cash and jewels.

The total take was probably ten thousand dollars, all covered by insurance. Hollis made no mistake of trying to yell for help. Something told him these men were born killers, without an iota of mercy in their grotesque makeups.

"There must be more than this around," one of the men said. "Let's search the whole place. Make sure that baby can't get loose first."

Hollis could have informed them that their work of tying him up was perfect. But they tested his bonds anyway, to their satisfaction, and both of them started a tour of the first floor to search for more loot. They returned, after several minutes, carrying some precious keepsakes which Hollis had obtained on his travels. He winced as these were dumped into the satin sack.

Then both men headed for the second floor. They seemed so certain of themselves that Hollis realized this was no chance job. These two men knew that there were no servants in the house this night and that Hollis was the only occupant. This robbery had been carefully planned.

He heard their footsteps in the hallway of the second floor and Hollis waited no longer.

He turned the swivel chair until his hands could reach a top drawer. He pulled this open very quietly and revealed a telephone inside. Scrupulously neat, Hollis hated to litter the top of his desk with a phone. He had had this one installed in the drawer. He leaned forward, pulling the chair off the floor to do so, and picked up a pencil with his teeth. Then he sat back, maneuvered the chair again, and finally managed to get the pencil into the dialing slots.

He had already removed the instrument from its cradle and supported it against the side of the drawer. It was painful work, for the bonds were tight and he had to strain against them, cutting off the blood supply to his extremities:

He dialed the last number and heard a voice answer: "Police Headquarters."

"Give me Commissioner Warner— quickly," Hollis whispered.

He heard a click and then Police Commissioner Warner's voice came over the wire.

"This is Grant Hollis," the burglar victim whispered. "There are two armed thieves in my home. Send help,

The hunchbacked men stalked into the living room.

but send it quietly. They don't know I phoned and your men can surround the house and nab them as they get away. Hurry!"

"Sending radio cars with muted sirens," Warner advised. "Hang on, Hollis. Help will be there within four or five minutes."

GRANT HOLLIS let go with a long sigh of relief. Then he heard the men coming downstairs again and he closed the desk drawer all but a bare inch or two. When they strode into the room again, he was sitting erect in the chair and eyeing them with open contempt.

"You're being a smart guy," one hunchback said. "Now, have you got any more dough hanging around—or jewelry? Hell, mister, you're covered by insurance. You might as well make things easy for us so we'll go easy on you. You got nothing to lose so...."

Suddenly both intruders stopped dead, as though some invisible sign had come to them. They didn't move for fully half a minute. Then one of them ground out a curse.

"So you warned the cops, eh? They're sending help, are they? Well, mister, that means lights out for you."

The second hunchback hurried to the davenport, picked up a thick pillow and thrust his gun into its depths. Hollis' eyes grew wide in horror as he watched this killer approach and press the pillow against his head. He could feel the muzzle of the gun through its thickness and knew what they intended to do—shoot through the pillow to mask the roar of the weapon. Hollis strained forward horribly.

"It's murder! They'll burn you for this, you fools! You can get clear if you hurry."

"We still got two minutes before them radio cars get here," one of the men snarled. "They'll find you croaked. And maybe you understand, it ain't just because you got in touch with the cops that we're doing this. You had it coming anyway. So long—sap."

Hollis screamed one word:

"Garland!"

Then the gun exploded. Hollis didn't hear the roar of the weapon for the bullet had already shattered his senses before the thunder of the weapon could blast his eardrums. The killer backed away, flung the pillow on the floor. His teammate grabbed up several ornaments which he threw into the satin sack. He swung this over his back and both men raced for the door.

They vaulted the low railing and headed out across the estate. Head-lights from a police radio car swerved around the corner and encompassed them in their glare. A gun cracked. Both hunchbacks whirled, raised their own weapons and threw a hail of leaden death straight at the radio car.

A MAN screamed. The door of the police car opened. One uniformed patrolman jumped out and leveled his gun. He fired two shots before a chunk of remarkably well aimed lead pounded into his chest. He wilted and fell into the rain-swollen gutter.

For a few seconds, there was a grim silence. Then a police whistle shrilled and barked orders called for a rapid advance on the killers.

Lieutenant McGrath, short, stocky, bald-headed and rain-drenched was in charge of the police cordon. He issued his orders and then hurried into the house. He grimaced at what he found tied to that swivel chair. His eyes spotted the partly open desk drawer and the phone it contained. He picked up the instrument and discovered that Commissioner Warner was still on the wire.

"Hollis is dead, sir," McGrath reported. "Shot through the head by some rotten, cold-blooded murderers while he was tied in this chair. But we'll get 'em. I've got plenty of men thrown around the whole block and Sergeant Wolfe is giving orders over the two-way radio set in his car. Radio cars will converge from every direction. We had a look at the two guys—both hunchbacks. Yes, I said hunchbacks. Two of our men wounded, one pretty bad."

McGrath hung up and darted back out into the rain to give more directions. But half an hour later, he discovered that the pair of killers had eluded the cordon of police and escaped. He spent another half an hour searching the house and found nothing. Fingerprint men dusted likely spots and discovered no significant prints.

McGrath began to get the idea that the murderers were as clever as they were ruthless. His only chance now was to check on what was missing and have all the pawnshops and fences watched.

Then two of Hollis' servants returned. After they recovered from the shock of seeing their employer dead, they talked. McGrath began making a list of what was missing.

"About twelve grand all told," he figured aloud.

CHAPTER II

THE BLIND CANNOT HELP

EARLY THE next evening Police Commissioner Warner stopped his car in front of a large house, shielded from the street by tall, regal trees and cleverly cultivated bushes.

There was a neat brass nameplate fastened to the gate. It read:

Warner opened the gate, walked up a path and stepped on the porch. He rang the bell and the door was quickly opened by a slender, almost bald-headed man whose eyes flashed over Warner suspiciously. Norton Kirby, better known as Silk, was Tony Quinn's butler, valet and general all-around man. He had once been in active conflict with the law and he regarded all law officers with a remnant of his old animosity.

"Good evening, Silk," the commissioner said affably. "Tony's home, I hope."

Silk flashed a smile that was genuine. He liked this democratic, jovial police commandant.

"Yes, sir, and I rather think he'll be glad to know you're here, sir. A blind man finds life boring, you know,"

Warner nodded and walked into the spacious library. He could see the back of a big, comfortable chair and a column of pipe smoke rising slowly above it. A mellow voice greeted him.

"Come in, Commissioner. I'm delighted to have company."

Warner pulled up a chair and for a moment or two gazed in silence at the man who sat before the fireplace. He saw a well built person, clad in rumpled tweeds and a smoking jacket. He held a well heeled pipe between his teeth and he looked into the blazing fireplace without the least tremor in his eyes.

Flames meant nothing to this man, for his eyes held the stark deadness of the totally blind. His face, just below the eyes, was horribly scarred and the scars gleamed in the firelight until Commissioner Warner grimaced at the sight of them.

He knew how Tony Quinn had become blind. Once Quinn had been a determined, resolute district attorney, fighting crime tooth and nail. Then, one day in open court, gangsters had endeavored to destroy evidence with acid, Quinn had interfered and the acid was flung into his face. It had seared deeply and the best eye doctors in the world had pronounced Tony Quinn as a hopeless case.

His resignation was automatic and he had become a recluse. Independently wealthy, he managed to exist very comfortably, but his sightless eyes and his face constantly held the bitterness of a man defeated early in life.

Commissioner Warner helped himself to a pipeful of Quinn's aromatic tobacco, lit up and leaned back in his chair.

"Tony, I'm up against another stone wall. I like to come here and talk these cases over with you. The legal background you have helps me tremendously at times and I know I can trust you. Of course, you read of the murder of Grant Hollis last night?"

Quinn nodded. "Silk read it to me from the newspapers. Hollis was a good man. I hope you land the devils who murdered him. But what makes this case so important? All I gathered was that he tried to get word to you and they killed him for it. They simply robbed his house. Nothing out of the ordinary there."

"But you're wrong," Warner said tensely. "Hollis phoned me. I sent radio cars out under orders to go quietly and surround the house. There was an open connection between my phone and Hollis'. I heard the two burglars talking. And then, suddenly, I heard them tell him I'd been warned and that radio cars were on the way. If Hollis was right, there was no possibility of their knowing this had happened. Yet they did—even to how much time they had before the radio cars would get there.

"I heard one of them tell Hollis that he was being killed partly because he had warned the police, but mostly because of something else. He didn't say what. Then Hollis yelled one word and I couldn't have been mistaken about it either.

"He called out the word—'Garland.' I've checked on all of Hollis' friends and I can find no one with that name. Our records show no crooks with that name either."

TONY QUINN puffed slowly on his pipe.

"And there is something else, Commissioner. I can tell by the inflection in your voice. Blind men rely on their remaining senses, you know, and my ears are especially good."

"You don't have to remind me of that," Warner said. "I've seen concrete examples of it. Yes, you're right, Tony. There is something else.

"Ninety minutes ago, the same murderers appeared at the home of Robert Kilpatrick, the financier. They tied him up, looted his home and then one of his servants returned unexpectedly. He happened to look in the window before he entered the house, saw his master tied up and promptly went to the nearest phone and called Headquarters.

"When my men arrived, Kilpatrick was murdered, the killers gone and seven thousand dollars in gems, cash and trinkets missing. Now, those men left very abruptly, without finishing the job of looting certain silver services which Kilpatrick owned. They were warned somehow that the police were on the way. How in heaven's name could they have known in both instances?"

"How do you know it was the same pair of killers?" Quinn asked quietly.

On the surface he betrayed no emotion at all, but inwardly he was seething. There was something mysterious about these murders and the way the pair of killers were warned of danger. Behind them must be a brilliant mind, a brainy man who directed his agents and kept them from capture.

"That's easy," Warner answered. "In both cases the killers were seen. They were similarly dressed and both men were—hunchbacks. And that's not all. Five other homes were robbed tonight. In two cases the burglars were seen. They were hunchbacks."

Quinn pursed his lips and whistled softly.

"It does sound interesting. Of course, they left no clues. But Commissioner, what can I do to help you? I'm blind! Helpless as a ten-minute-old kitten. But don't bother to answer. I know the reason. You kindly seek me out to give me something to think about.

"I have been able to offer a few suggestions in past cases, mainly because I have nothing to do but brood on them. This one is different. It calls for some conclusive action and I—well, I'm not capable of that."

"Yes, I know." Warner puffed serenely on his pipe. "This is one of the cases I'd like to see the Black Bat get his teeth into. Don't sit there chuckling at me. I know Lieutenant McGrath is positive you are the Black Bat. I know you suspect I think the same thing. Maybe I do and maybe I don't. That makes no difference.

"I'm merely venturing a hope, remote perhaps. But even though the Black Bat uses methods that aren't exactly in line with the laws of this State, there are times when that kind of action is called for.

"Damn it, Tony, if I were sure you were the Black Bat, I'd tell you to go ahead and handle it your own way. I'm not sure. I only hope, and that's forlorn, too, because how on earth could you be the Black Bat? I know of all the examinations you've had. Every doctor has pronounced you hopelessly and completely blind. Lieutenant McGrath has checked with them until they're sick of seeing him."

QUINN THREW back his head and laughed out loud.

"Poor McGrath. Time and again he's tried to trick me. I couldn't see him, but I could feel it. Once, he lit a match and held it so close to my eyes that he almost burned the tip of my nose.

"No, Commissioner, you're wrong. As you have said, I couldn't be the Black Bat even though I'd sell my soul to be in his shoes—or, shall I say, his wings. How about a drink?"

Warner got up. "No thanks. I need a bottle of aspirin tablets much more than alcohol. Thanks anyway, Tony. I'm going to have a last look at the homes of both murdered men. Then I'll withdraw the guards I've placed there. No use maintaining them when there isn't a speck of a clue. Thanks again."

Silk watched the commissioner until he drove away. Then he hurried into the library and hastily drew the window shades. Tony Quinn hadn't moved, but his face had changed. Those dead eyes sparkled with life now.

"He was trying to trip you up that time, sir," Silk said.

"No, Silk. Warner suspects I'm the Black Bat, but he can't prove it any more than Lieutenant McGrath can. Still, Warner would like to have the Black Bat take a hand in this case. He made his story interesting enough, too, because if I did happen to be the Black Bat, then I'd go for it in a big way—which is exactly what I'm doing.

"Those murders may be part of a crime ring, but I don't think so. They were too coolly and deliberately staged. Remember, in five other robberies no one was killed. Hollis and Kilpatrick were not murdered simply because the police were on their way. The killers would have wanted every second possible to make good their escape. Staying long enough to commit murder is proof they intended to do this all along.

"What I'd like to know is, how in the world they found out the police were coming? And why hunchbacked killers? Men crippled that way are usually sickly and weak. Very few of them are cut out to be ruthless killers or even burglars. Silk, if Warner wanted to get the Black Bat interested in this case, he certainly succeeded. Phone Butch and Carol. Have them come over, at once. We're starting in while the trail is hot."

Silk nodded eagerly.

He was more than willing to put his sharp wits to the task of outthinking murderers. Silk had once been a confidence man and then a burglar. He had saved Quinn's life by risking his own liberty to do so. From that moment on, he had become Quinn's devoted friend and ally.

As he dialed a number which would connect him with Carol Baldwin, he thought back to the dark days when Tony Quinn really had been blind. Then she had come, blonde and lovely, to provide the one means of restoring his sight. Her father had been a law officer and dying from a bandit's bullet. He bequeathed his eyes to Tony Quinn so that the fight against crime could go on.

A skillful and little-known country surgeon had performed the operation and Tony Quinn saw once more. The operation had been kept extremely secret.

Besides Carol and Silk, only one other person knew that Tony Quinn could see and that he was the Black Bat. This man was Jack O'Leary, better known as "Butch" because of his massive size. He wasn't a fast thinker, but he was faithful, and when the Black Bat needed brawn. Butch really proved his worth.

THIRTY MINUTES later, the four of them were gathered in the privacy of Tony Quinn's laboratory, concealed cleverly behind the walls of his study. Here, every scientific device used in fighting crime, was at Quinn's fingertips. Volumes on crime psychology, toxicology, microscopic analysis and all the equipment necessary to put their theories into active use.

Quinn sat beside Carol and held one of her hands between his own. Something more than friendship had grown up between these two. But now, everyone was tense as Quinn spoke.

"We've got to strike hard and fast. Silk, you'll have to be my liaison officer for the present. Sorry, but you remain here to receive and broadcast my orders if I need help. Carol, you'll begin an investigation immediately of Grant Hollis and Robert Kilpatrick.

"Delve into their lives, consult people who can give you a line on their friends and enemies, their finances, who would benefit by their deaths. Just keep away from their homes because I'm going there myself. Commissioner Warner very kindly presented the Black Bat with an open invitation to check both houses for clues. He told me he was withdrawing all guards. Then check on the other five victims. Get their names from the newspapers."

"How about me, Boss?" Butch's rumbling voice broke in. "Don't I get to sock somebody on the nose?"

"Maybe," Quinn grinned. "In fact, I'll almost guarantee it. However, for the present, you circulate around in the underworld resorts. See if you can get a line on a pair of hunchbacked crooks who are very friendly with each other. Listen to what's being said about these two murders and—keep out of trouble."

Quinn raised a trap door set in the floor. Butch went down a ladder and made his way along a tunnel until he reached a garden house at the further end of Tony Quinn's estate. He slipped out to the street and disappeared. This means of entrance and exit was worth a hundred times the work Quinn, Silk and Butch had put in to fashion it.

Quinn opened a locker and took out some neatly folded black pieces of cloth. Carol smiled at him, turned around and faced the wall while Quinn slipped out of his tweeds and smoking jacket. He donned black trousers, a black silk shirt, black crepe shoes, black gloves that fitted as tightly as if they were made of rubber.

Finally, he drew a hood over his head. It concealed his face, masking the hideous scars from the burning acid. A cloak formed the rest of his regalia. It was a peculiar cloak for it was ribbed, like the wings of a bat and, when he extended his arms, he looked for all the world like one of those nocturnal mammals in full flight.

The clicking of the mechanism of two heavy forty-five calibre automatics brought Carol around to face him again. She walked to his side, grasped his arm lightly and looked into his eyes. "Tony, I know you have to do this. Only, please be careful. I—I don't know what I'd do if anything happened to you. Really, I don't."

He patted her cheek and smiled. "They've tried every device known to erase me from the face of the earth, darling. I'm still alive and I'll stay that way. Now, the Black Bat is taking flight. Remember to contact Silk every fifteen minutes. I may need all the help I can get."

The Black Bat slipped down the ladder and vanished.

If the underworld could have witnessed this scene, the men who comprised it would have shuddered and sought their various rat holes. They all knew and dreaded the Black Bat.

CHAPTER III

DEATH TRAP

L **OGAN, VALET** to the late Grant Hollis, didn't like it when the police guard was abruptly withdrawn. All the other servants had quit in a body and he was alone in this big house which violent death had visited so recently. He was nervous and ill at ease. What if those two hunchbacked killers should come back? What chance would he have?

He got up and poured himself a drink. His hands shook badly and he sat down again, jumping at every creak emitted by the massive house. Then Logan didn't jump—he just sat frozen. Even the powerful whiskey trickling down his throat didn't make him wince. There was a hand resting on his shoulder.

"No need to be alarmed," a voice said quietly. "I'm not here to harm you, Logan. Get up and have a look at me."

Logan arose very slowly. His eyes grew wide and round when he saw the sombre figure of the Black Bat standing behind the chair. Logan had never seen the Black Bat before, but he had heard of him and there was something about those piercing eyes that shone from behind the mask which reassured him.

"Y-yes, sir," he gulped. "You're the Black Bat. I—I'll do anything I can to help you."

"Fine," the sombre figure said. "Now tell me about everything that was stolen. Not the money or jewels, but other things, personal articles and curios."

Logan pointed at the mantelpiece.

"There were four articles there used merely as ornaments. They weren't worth a great deal. One was a vase, another a statuette, a small hand-colored portrait on a small easel and a lacquered jewel box which the master picked up in northern Africa some years ago. All told, these things were worth perhaps fifty dollars apiece."

The Black Bat moved back suddenly extinguished all the lights in the room.

"Hollis was quite a sportsman, eh Logan? That boar's head, where did he bag that?"

Logan's jaw dropped. "Why, how can you see it in this darkness? The—the master shot that beast in Bahawal, a little independent state somewhere between India and Tibet. That happened two or three years ago, sir. But I still can't imagine how you could possibly see in this darkness."

The Black Bat's lips curled into a smile. Many other persons had wondered the same thing and only the Black Bat and his three associates knew the answer.

When the operation on Tony Quinn's eyes had been completed, he had developed a super-sensitive sight which enabled him to see almost as clearly in darkness as in the brightest light. Even colors assumed their appropriate hue to his eyes. Other details made him something of a superman, too. The months of blindness had developed his hearing and his sense of touch to an astonishing degree.

"Sorry we have to continue our little talk in darkness, Logan, but if anyone should happen to look in the windows—well, I wouldn't want to be seen. Now describe those articles that were on the mantelpiece."

LOGAN WISHED his whiskey glass wasn't empty.

"There was nothing outstanding about them, sir. Yet, now that I think about it, the master seemed very excited the day before he was murdered. He was in this very room when he shouted something, grabbed his hat and ran out to his car. Not long after, he phoned me, said he was at his office and that he was dining out. Now about the articles that were stolen—as I told you, they were not of particular importance or value."

"So Hollis went to his office in a rush." The Black Bat's remark came out of the darkness. "Logan, did Hollis know this Roland Kilpatrick who was murdered a few hours ago?"

Logan frowned and the Black Bat's eyes penetrated the gloom to see that facial contortion.

He sighed, then spoke.

"Well, sir, it really was very odd about Mr. Kilpatrick. They did not know one another, yet Mr. Kilpatrick came here early this afternoon to offer his condolences. He practically forced himself into the house, sir, and went directly to this room where we're standing now. He looked around and then hurried out."

Logan waited for more questions and none came. He tried to figure out where the black figure was standing, but the darkness was too complete. Two minutes went by and Logan's wobbly nerves let go.

"Say something, sir. I—I don't like this darkness. I—I can't stand it. I'll tell you more about the things that were stolen. Shall I?"

There was no answer. With a choked cry, Logan sped toward the nearest lamp and turned it on. There was no one in the room.

"Vanished! Without making a sound," Logan gasped. "I'm glad he isn't on my trail."

The Black Bat had slipped out the door as quietly as a ghost. Kilpatrick's residence was only about ten blocks away. He vaulted a hedge, crossed the sidewalk like a blob of shadow and climbed into a cheap coupé which he had parked conveniently near the Hollis place.

As he drove toward Kilpatrick's, his agile mind went over details. Kilpatrick hadn't come to Hollis' home to offer any condolences. He had paid that visit merely to satisfy his curiosity about something. What?

If the two men were not acquainted, how could Kilpatrick know that Hollis owned something of interest? And what had made Hollis cry out and rush directly to his offices on the top floor of the big downtown building which bore his name? More and more the Black Bat realized that while this case looked like the work of crude burglars, there was something else that lay behind it.

The Kilpatrick home was the equal of the Hollis mansion. It lay in the center of a huge estate and the entire first floor was lit up. The Black Bat parked his coupé, invaded the estate and hurried toward the rear of the house.

He crouched below a window, risked a quick look into an empty room and then repeated that operation until he discovered the study in which a gray-haired man sat behind a desk and studied reams of documents stacked before him.

The Black Bat knew this man. He was an attorney, a good one, too, who had two specialties as far apart as the poles. He was an expert on estates and one of the shrewdest criminal attorneys in the country. Jay Fenner was anything but a fool.

THE BLACK BAT looked up toward the second floor. A window beckoned invitingly. He climbed a tree, crawled out on a thick limb and a moment later stood inside a bedroom. He stepped into the hallway outside and listened. There wasn't a sound in the big house. Apparently Jay Fenner was the only person present.

The Black Bat crept down the staircase, drew a gun and moved silently into the room until he stood directly in front of the desk where Jay Fenner was at work. The attorney sensed more than saw his visitor. He looked up, gave a startled exclamation and jumped to his feet. His chair went catapulting backwards.

"Sorry to have alarmed you," the Black Bat said quietly. "Please pick up your chair and sit down again, Mr. Fenner. Pardon the gun I'm holding. It's merely to indicate that I hold the upper hand."

Fenner recovered his wits quickly. He stood the chair on its legs and sat down again.

"The Black Bat!" he exclaimed. "So you've taken an interest in this case. Why? It's nothing but a cheap robbery and murder."

The Black Bat disregarded the question. He indicated the papers strewn on the desk with a wave of his gun.

"Have you discovered anything interesting among Kilpatrick's papers, Fenner? Who inherits his money, by the way?"

"His cousin, James Downing, gets everything. You know Downing, the polo player and big game hunter?"

"I know Downing," the Black Bat replied. "Have you a list of the things stolen from this house?"

Fenner looked up at the piercing eyes that gleamed from behind the mask. He shivered and decided he'd never laugh derisively again when one of his crook clients brought up the name of this Nemesis of crime. He fumbled among the papers and found what he wanted.

"Jewelry worth three thousand, two thousand in cash and three more in negotiable bonds. A neat haul! There were a few other things taken, too, inconsequential objects. A book end, for instance. They only stole one and left the other. An enameled humidor, worth about five dollars, a small desk clock.

"Looks to me as though the robbers merely swept everything off Kilpatrick's desk into a sack of some kind. They were inhuman devils! Did you know they tortured Kilpatrick before they put a bullet through his skull? Burned his fingers in a ghastly fashion."

The Black Bat's eyes flicked over the spacious room. It was more of a trophy room than a study.

LIKE HOLLIS, Kilpatrick had been a renowned big game hunter. The usual array of heads lined the walls. One trophy especially intrigued the Bat. It was a cobra, stuffed by an expert taxidermist and mounted in a coil. There was a brass plaque below the exhibit. The Black Bat read the words even though he stood too far away for the average man's eyes to have made out the lettering:

1939—Bahawal Cobra

The Black Bat bowed toward Attorney Fenner.

"Thank you. The cooperation was even better than I'd hoped to get from a criminal attorney whose clients are my enemies."

Fenner laughed. "I do it for money. I don't class the rats I serve as friends."

As Fenner finished talking, the lights went out. He muttered a curse, but he didn't arise to put them back on until fully five minutes had elapsed.

"Damn impudent devil," he muttered to himself. "If I only had a gun—"

Fenner made a sudden decision. He reached for the phone and dialed rapidly.

"Hello, Downing," he said. "Fenner speaking. I have some news for you. The Black Bat was here. He wormed information out of me that connects you with this case. He may be on his way to see you.

"Get a gun, hide it well and if you get a chance, shoot him. What? Well why not? The man's a crook, isn't he? He's wanted by the police. And Downing, I happen to know that the underworld has a standing offer of fifty thousand dollars for the man who knocks him off. So that interests you, does it? Good, we'll split and—shoot straight and fast."

CHAPTER IV

GUN FLAME

THE NIGHT watchman in the Hollis Building rang his clock at the far end of the top-floor corridor. He passed by an office labeled with Grant Hollis' name and marked private. The watchman shivered. He didn't like to be near things which were associated with violent death—not even in an empty office.

He passed a darkened office door, had no idea that it opened after he had gone by. His first inkling of danger came with violent force.

Something struck him a tremendous blow on the skull. He reeled a few steps, sagged against the wall. As he slipped toward the floor, he wondered if he was already dead and descending into the depths. There were four—no, five weird-looking creatures converging on him. They were all clad in black, with wide-brimmed hats pulled low and black scarfs drawn around their faces. And—they were all hunchbacked.

One of the hunchbacks bent over him. Evil eyes glittered. A glistening knife was raised high. It came down in an arc that proved the wielder was no novice at murder. The watchman didn't see anything after that. A man with a blade piercing his heart never does.

"Hurry," one of the hunchbacked men muttered. "Drag that watchman into one of the offices and wipe up the blood. Matt, go to work on the door of Hollis' office. Mac, roll the tank of gas up here. Don't make any more noise than necessary. I'll put in the watchman's rings for him. Get going!"

Each of the hunchbacked men seemed to know exactly what his share of the work consisted of. An oxy-acetylene torch assembly was rolled out of a freight elevator. The hunchback called Matt had the office door open and the tank was quickly rolled inside.

Flashlights with taped lenses allowing only a small crack of light to filter through, searched the room and finally rested on a huge, modern safe. One of the intruders pulled down the scarf around his face a little, donned blue glasses and got the torch going.

Outside in the corridors, near the elevator shaft, two more hunchbacked men stood guard with drawn guns. Neither of them heard nor saw an office door open twenty feet down the corridor. If any trouble turned up, it would come from either the elevators or the stairway. The offices on this floor were all empty. One of the guards glanced to his left. He blinked and started to raise his gun.

"The Black Bat!" he yelled in a hoarse scream.

His gun barked and it was echoed by the roar of a forty-five automatic in the Black Bat's fist. The second guard began shouting for help and running madly toward the stairway.

Just before he reached it, he paused long enough to take a pot shot at the sinister being who stood in the center of the corridor. The bullet only hit the ceiling, for as his finger compressed the trigger, the Black Bat's gun blazed again and the hunchbacked man's hand became a bloody pulp.

He screamed in pain, tripped and went rolling down the stairs.

THE DOOR of Grant Hollis' office opened and three men ran out. The Black Bat faced them with guns ready. Three pairs of arms shot high.

"Stay exactly as you are," the Black Bat warned. "Your friends were foolish and suffered for it. Take sidesteps until you come to the end of the corridor, then turn around and face the wall."

The men began moving as commanded. The sombre figure watched them intently. He didn't expect to win this bout so easily and he sensed that there was still a terrific amount of danger in the building. His keen eyes saw the faces of the three hunchbacks change.

He kept one gun pointed at them, half turned around and saw two more of the weird beings rushing toward him. He fired twice. One of the men went down, clawing at his shoulder. The other swerved and beat a hasty retreat.

But there were more of them! Hollis' office gave forth two others and three more came up the stairway.

"It's the Black Bat!" one of the men at the head of the stairs yelled. "Get him! Gun him out! He can't get away now. We've got every exit covered."

The Black Bat's guns blazed and he leaped forward in a fierce attack. It sent the men in the hallway scurrying toward the stairwell for protection. But the others, who were lined up against the wall, swung into action now.

A bullet struck the tile wall behind the Black Bat, ricocheted dangerously close and made him realize there were too many for one man to handle. His lunge had carried him directly in front of the office door through which he had gained entrance. He backed toward it—and then he was gone.

One of the hunchbacked men gave a shout of triumph.

"He's cornered. One of you guys tell Mac to hurry with that safe. Somebody will report this shooting in a minute, but before we leave, the Black Bat is going to find out what our lead tastes like. Cover this office. I'll shoot the lock away and when the door opens, throw plenty of lead around—and fast."

The killer edged his way along, back against the wall, until he was close to the door through which the Black Bat had vanished. He aimed his gun and fired three quick shots. The lock flew into pieces. He gave a quick jump past the door, kicking it wide open as he did so. Inside was nothing but darkness and no flaming gun muzzles gave away the presence of the Black Bat.

"Okay," the hunchback growled elatedly. "He's got to be inside. Hiding maybe, until we show our hand. We're thirty-three stories above the ground. The only way out of this office is through the window, and unless the Bat can really fly, he's still inside. Get set, we're going to take him."

The man who had assumed leadership of the killers waved his gun and charged through the door.

Nothing happened. The leader found a switch and turned on the lights. He surveyed the small office with his mouth agape. There were no other doors. The window was tightly closed—and there was no sign of the Black Bat.

"But he went in here," the hunchback exclaimed. "We all saw him. Maybe he had a rope ladder and he went to the roof."

The window was hurriedly opened and no rope dangled outside. The hunchback peered straight down to the street and shivered. He raised his eyes and looked over the tops of the buildings far below, as if he expected to see the wings of the Black Bat outlined against the night sky.

HE CLOSED the window with a bang, growled a curse and kicked a chair savagely.

"Okay, you guys," he snarled. "Search every damned office on the floor. Make it snappy because the cops may head for this place any second. Find the Black Bat, hear me? Find him and fill his hide full of holes. I'm going back and see how Mac made out."

The hunchback watched his men deploy and start searching the offices. He walked briskly toward Hollis' private quarters, but he kept looking over his shoulder every step or two.

Damn the Black Bat! He could materialize out of nowhere and vanish as completely as a puff of steam. At any moment, the sombre figure might step before him with spitting guns. The crook shivered, stuffed a hand into his coat pocket and pulled out a grenade.

He had hesitated using this before because of the tremendous racket it would make, but if the Black Bat showed now, he'd pull the pin and let him have it. He thrust his finger through the ring and kept the grenade half hidden behind him.

He heard the reassuring hiss of Mac's torch and he stepped boldly into the office. Something drilled against his left side. He froze. Mac, kneeling before the safe, was working fast while sweat poured down his face and his eyes, behind the colored glasses, were abject in terror.

The hunchback leader risked a glance toward his left and he shuddered. The Black Bat had materialized again.

"Just stand very quiet," the dark shadow warned, "until your friend gets through opening the safe. I'm greatly interested to know what Hollis hid there and why you men want it."

The hunchback's warped mind decided on a bold gesture. The Black Bat hadn't noticed the grenade. He began slipping the pin out very slowly. The safe dial dropped to the floor with a thud. Mac glanced over his shoulder and the Black Bat gestured with his gun, Mac pulled the heavy door wide open.

"Walk forward!" the Black Bat ordered the hunchback. "Remove whatever you were after from that safe."

The only light in the room was the bluish flame of the oxy-acetylene torch which Mac held in a shaking hand. The hunchback leader yanked the pin free and snapped the grenade into a far corner of the office. Then he gave a wild shout, pushed the Black Bat violently and darted out the door, slamming it shut after him.

The Black Bat's eyes flicked across the room in the direction of the thud which the grenade had made. He saw it rolling slowly toward the wall.

"Save yourself!" he yelled at Mac. "It's a grenade!"

He made a dive toward Hollis' heavy steel desk, grabbed the edge of it and turned the heavy piece of furniture over on top of himself. Mac gave a scream of terror and headed for the door.

Then the grenade let go. The explosion rocked the whole upper part of the building. The office walls collapsed, the window was blown completely out.

Mac, caught in the full devastating force of the explosion, died instantly. Heavy chunks of plaster fell on top of the steel desk. There was no movement beneath it.

In the corridor outside, the hunchback leader gave a shout of triumph and headed toward the office.

"If that didn't get him, nothing ever will," he gloated. "This is one time the Black Bat was up against a guy with brains. I...."

HE STOPPED talking and seemed to be listening intently.

"Inside with you," he ordered his men. "Never mind anything but the safe. Get the stuff out of it and work fast. A hundred radio cars are coming this way and we've got to get clear."

They opened the door and even the callous hunchback leader shuddered at the appalling ruin within. He saw Mac's limp body spread out on the floor, stepped over it and went directly to the safe.

He fumbled around inside for a moment, drew out something and stuffed it into his pocket. Then he glanced toward the further end of the room. Hollis' desk was turned over and he could see a pair of legs sticking out beneath it.

"Take a look, boys, at what's left of the Black Bat!" he exulted. "Now get out of here. I'd like to see who was behind that mask, but the cops are entering the building now. We take the freight elevator, shoot straight down and if any cops are in the cellar, give it to them."

CHAPTER V

PLUNGE TO ETERNITY

ALL THE men started racing down the corridor with their leader streaking well ahead. One man, the last to leave the wrecked office, didn't see Mac's corpse in time. He tripped and fell flat on his face. The force of the impact with the floor stunned him and when he raised his head again, he realized that he had been trapped. Several patrolmen, drawn guns ready, were racing along the corridor.

The crook rose hastily and looked around for some exit. His eyes swept toward the toppled desk. Those two feet were no longer in evidence. He felt a cool breeze and automatically turned to look at the window. It was wide open and a rope swayed before his startled gaze. There was no other way out for him.

He ran to the window, grabbed the rope and went over the sill. He didn't dare look down into space as deep as eternity. He hauled himself up slowly, praying that the police wouldn't notice the rope dangling by the window.

He was nearly at the top. But this man lived an easy life. His hardest work for years, had been wielding a blackjack at some helpless victim's skull. His muscles were getting tired. He began to slip and a wail of anguish came from his lips. Then a soft voice called down to him from the rooftop.

"Hang on. I'll haul you up."

He knew that voice could belong to but one person—the Black Bat. But even facing that ominous figure was better than falling thirty-odd stories to a hideous death below. His fingers fastened frantically to the rope. Then he felt himself being pulled slowly upward. Strong hands seized his shoulders and lifted him onto the roof. He flopped there, unable to move, his brain spinning, his senses outraged by this encounter with death.

The Black Bat threw the rope on the roof and rushed over to the edge. He peered down. There were radio cars closing in from every direction. He was as completely trapped as he had been in Hollis' office when the hunchback leader hurled the grenade.

His lips compressed themselves into a tight line. At any moment, a horde of patrolmen would come up on the roof.

The hunchback, whom the Black Bat had rescued, was on his knees now and reaching for his gun. Thoughts of the fifty thousand dollars reward for the Black Bat's death dulled his puny brain. It didn't occur to him that he was in the same deadly trap as his intended victim and that the police were bound to get him.

He leveled the gun, but his hand shook badly from the strain he had placed on his muscles. He squeezed the trigger and missed by more than a foot. The Black Bat whirled. His own guns came up. The crook gave a screech of terror and threw his weapon away. He raised his hands, sobbing surrender.

THE BLACK BAT had no time either to question or examine the hunchback. That single shot would draw every patrolman in the building to the roof. He scooped up the rope that he had used to lower himself into Hollis' office and to haul himself back to the roof again. It was provided with a strong hook.

He ran to the rear of the building, fastened the hook in place and then swore softly as he saw the hunchback trying to find his gun in the darkness again. The Black Bat could have shot him down, but he didn't even reach for his guns. Those weapons spoke only in self-defense.

With a wailing cry,
the figure of the Bat
hurtled through space.

A moment later, four patrolmen barged out on the roof. More followed. One of them pointed. Near the edge of the roof was a stooped figure, clad in black and he seemed to be wearing a cape that billowed out.

"The Black Bat!" one of the men yelled. "Take him! Alive!"

They started forward. The figure was trapped completely. He raised a gun. It lanced flame and one patrolman slumped against a pipe and slid to the roof. The others held guns ready and now they didn't hesitate. The guns roared.

The black-clad figure straightened up, staggered back a step and hit the low cement parapet. He swayed and then pitched over the side. A long, wailing cry trailed after him. One of the patrolmen turned away, covering his eyes.

"That was the Black Bat," he said slowly. "What if he was a little on the wrong side of the law? He never hurt a cop yet and he helped us plenty."

"Yeah," another patrolman said. "But we had to do it. I guess he'd rather have gone out this way than be unmasked. Here comes Lieutenant McGrath. Will he be happy—the big lug!"

McGrath listened to the excited story of the patrolmen. He walked over to the edge of the roof and looked down. When he turned around, his face was harsh, but his eyes were moist.

"No question but it was the Black Bat?" he asked.

"How could there be?" one man challenged. "We saw him clearly enough. All dressed in black with something that looked like a cape. Sure it was the Bat."

McGrath gulped. He couldn't face his own men. Now that it had come and the Black Bat was really dead things seemed different. The Black Bat's taunts, his stickers in the form of a bat plastered everywhere he appeared on the scene of a crime, all seemed inconsequential. McGrath almost felt as though he had lost a friend who could never be replaced.

"Well," he said finally, "we'll go down and see who he is. Not that I have any doubts. Then I'll go over and tell Tony Quinn's man what happened. Damn it, why couldn't you mugs have grabbed him?"

McGrath didn't wait for an answer. He reached the street, ran around the huge building to its rear court and found a number of men there. He looked for signs of the corpse and found none.

"Where is it?" McGrath demanded. Fierce excitement gripped him. "Where's the Black Bat's body?"

"Black Bat?" someone said in an awed voice. "Gosh, Lieutenant, there wasn't any corpse here. We thought we heard somebody yell and then there was a thud like a body makes when it hits the cement, but, see for yourself, there's nothing here."

McGRATH SHRUGGED. "Then some of his pals must have been with him. I always suspected he didn't work alone. They carried the body away. Well, I'm on my way."

McGrath reached his car, piled in and drove quickly to Tony Quinn's home. He parked, but he didn't get out of the car right away. Once he dabbed at the corner of his eyes with his handkerchief and then he blew his nose lustily. Best to get it over with, he decided. But telling Silk of his master's death was no different to McGrath than announcing a similar tragedy to a widow and family of nine kids. He walked slowly up the path, rang the bell and slowly removed his hat as Silk opened the door.

"It's you, is it?" Silk barked.

"It's me," McGrath said. "Silk, I've got bad news for you. I know I've been tough on you and Quinn. I know I swore never to rest until the Black Bat was in a cell or dead. Now I wish I hadn't said those things. You see...."

"What are you jabbering about?" Silk asked. "Say, McGrath, are you sure you feel all right?"

McGrath nodded. "Fine thanks. I mean—oh, damn it, Silk, Quinn is...."

A voice from inside the house reached McGrath clearly.

"Silk, if that's Lieutenant McGrath's voice I hear, let him in. Why must you two argue all the time?"

Lieutenant McGrath's jaw fell, his mouth opened wide. He gulped and stumbled into the house. He stepped across the study, looking at the man who sat in his accustomed chair in front of the fireplace, as though he were seeing a ghost.

"Are you here, Lieutenant?" Quinn asked. "You're walking oddly. What's wrong?"

McGrath sat down on the edge of a chair as if he wanted to get up and run. He licked his lips, twirled his derby and tried to talk. Only a wheezing sound came from his lips. Someone touched him and he jumped nervously.

"Skittish as a cat," Silk grunted. "It's just me—with a drink. You look as though you need one."

McGrath took the glass, gulped its contents and felt better. He leaned forward.

"Quinn, I apologize. I'm sorry for all the trouble I ever put you to, because now I know you are not the Black Bat. The Bat is dead! He fell off the edge of a roof thirty-some stories above the ground. His body is missing, but no man could live after a fall of that kind!"

Quinn's face grew serious. "Are you certain, Lieutenant? The Black Bat dead! Why, it's hardly believable. I thought nothing on earth could kill that man."

"Neither did I," McGrath said. "But I also thought you were the Bat, which goes to show how great fools men can be. Well, I apologize once more, Quinn."

HE STRETCHED out his hand, but Quinn's sightless eyes never flickered. McGrath looked slightly abashed, dropped his proffered hand and turned away.

"Oh, Lieutenant," Quinn said, "what is new on those hunchback killings? Commissioner Warner told me what happened to Hollis and Kilpatrick and I'm interested."

"Not sure," McGrath grunted. "Two more men were robbed and by hunchbacked crooks, too, but they weren't killed. I think some bunch of crooks is cashing in on the publicity and disguising themselves like hunchbacks. Elmer White and Ed Johnson were the new robbery victims and they were both so damned scared they couldn't remember much about anything that happened. See you later, Quinn."

He left the house, got back into his car and started the motor. He was still thinking of that figure which had plunged to a grisly death. He'd have to do something about locating the corpse, but he decided he wouldn't tackle the proposition too belligerently. The least he could do for the Black Bat was to let his true identity remain secret.

McGrath reached for the gear shift on the wheel. There was something foreign to his touch there. He peered down and his face went alternately white and crimson. He threw back his head and bellowed a series of curses. Then he shook his fist at Quinn's house, jammed his hat down and dropped his voice to a monotone.

Plastered on the surface of the gear shift was one of the Black Bat's stickers!

As McGrath drove away, a bulky form moved from behind the protection of a tree. Butch O'Leary's shoulders were shaking, his eyes running with tears of laughter.

CHAPTER VI

ORDERS FOR ACTION

BACK IN Tony Quinn's library, things moved serenely. Silk puttered around. Quinn stared straight ahead with those dull, blank eyes of his. Once, when Silk passed close by, Quinn spoke.

"Don't draw the shades yet. McGrath may come back. I'd have given a lot to see his face when he spotted that sticker."

Finally Quinn rose, yawned and stretched his arms. It was well after midnight. Using his cane, he tapped his way across the room. Silk began extinguishing lights. Five minutes later, Quinn crossed the room again, this time with the sure footedness of a cat. Darkness meant nothing to him. He touched a switch and paneling swung open. He stepped into his laboratory, waited a moment until Silk joined him and then, as the panel closed, Butch's roar of laughter filled the small room.

"Honest, boss, McGrath was so mad the windows in his car rattled at the way he cursed. Boy, oh boy, I never seen a man so mad in my life."

Carol held Tony Quinn's hand tightly.

"I was there, darling, in the crowd watching that building. We saw someone fall off the roof and I—I was so certain it was you. Oh, Tony, I thought I'd faint or shriek your name. I don't know what prevented me from giving the whole show away."

Quinn smiled tenderly at her.

"I do. It's called courage. The man who tumbled off the roof was one of the hunchbacked killers. Some of his pals must have whisked his body away so he wouldn't be identified. I killed or wounded a couple of them and they were taken away, too. Perhaps the gang is composed of well known criminals and unmasking one may reveal the whole set-up.

"I slid down my little rope to three stories below the top floor. I opened a window, slipped into the office and phoned Silk to get things ready. Then, after the police were either all on the roof or on the top floor, I used a private elevator, reached the cellar and got away. Fortunately, the coupé was parked nearby."

"What did you discover?" Silk asked.

"What's it all about, sir?"

Quinn shook his head slowly from side to side.

"I don't know, yet. In fact, I haven't even a suspicion. They are after something of great value. Hollis had one of the things they wanted. He must have discovered he was the owner of it, because he rushed to his office at night and put something in his big safe. It looks as though he didn't trust his wall safe at home.

"That means the hunchbacks who murdered Hollis only *thought* they had gotten what they came for. When they discovered it was missing, they traced back on Hollis' movements, went to his offices and broke open the safe. I heard them take whatever it was out, but I couldn't do a thing.

"If I'd so much as taken a deep breath, they would have filled me full of holes. I was badly stunned by the force of an exploding grenade, too, so I just had to lie there and let them get away with it."

Butch scratched the back of his neck.

"I asked a million questions, Boss. Nobody seems to know anything about these hunchbacked guys. They must be new in town."

"And you, Carol?" Quinn asked. "Did you discover anything about Hollis or Kilpatrick?"

"Not much. Hollis and Kilpatrick were both ardent hunters. They used to spend whole seasons in Africa and India. But I'm sure neither of them knew one another, except casually. They were financially independent, honest and noted for their philanthropies.

"Hollis' sister gets his estate. Kilpatrick's goes to some rooting-tooting playboy who spends all his time falling off polo ponies and into heart balm suits. I saw him, and I wasn't impressed. To me, Jim Downing looks like a two-legged, white-skinned edition of a skunk."

Quinn lit his pipe and puffed slowly on it.

"All of which adds up to nothing. Now there have been two more of those robberies by hunchbacked men, making a total of nine breaks. Fortunately, this time, the victims were not murdered. Why? If I knew the answer to that, I'd have a slim lead. Why should two men die and the others permitted to live?

"And those hunchbacked outfits, that's what they are—outfits! There must be a significant reason why those killers operate in such grotesque disguises. Silk, hand me my regalia. The night is still young. I'm going to find out about Elmer White and Ed Johnson, the latest victims of the gang's terror."

CAROL GASPED and half rose.

"Tony, did you say Elmer White and Ed Johnson? Wait, just a second." She fumbled in her purse, drew out a small notebook and rapidly consulted it. "Tony, I knew those names were familiar. Listen to this!

"Grant Hollis and Robert Kilpatrick donated several valuable specimens of jungle life to a museum. I went there to see if I could get a line on them. I happened to notice that several other people had donated similar specimens. Elmer White and Ed Johnson were among them."

Quinn whirled around. "And the others, the five victims who were robbed after the murders?"

"They were not among the donors," Carol answered. "But if the four I mentioned are significant, we can tie them up with certain dates. They and three other men donated the most recent specimens. The other three are Geoffrey Thomas, the broker, Dr. Hugo Norden, the surgeon, and Alex Pierce, the jeweler. All of their specimens came from somewhere in India."

Quinn faced Silk. "It's time for you to get busy. Adopt a simple disguise. Find out all you can about those three men. Get into their homes, even if you have to act like a burglar to do it. Examine everything in their trophy rooms. That means book ends, vases, statuettes, pictures, keepsakes, anything.

"Butch, you cover Silk in case he gets into a jam, Carol, you stay by the phone as contact agent.

"There is no time to lose! The hunchbacked killers may strike again, and if Carol's hunch is right, Thomas, Dr. Norden or Alex Pierce will be the next victims."

Silk hurried away to don a disguise. His thin face and bald head were especially adapted for the purpose. In twenty minutes, not even Lieutenant McGrath's scrutiny would have detected any similarity between Silk Kirby and the man who slipped out of Quinn's house.

Silk now wore a black wig. He had darkened his skin, made his cheeks puffier and his nose broader. He dropped his usual very erect posture and assumed a slouching walk. He hailed a taxi, looked around before he got in and saw Butch behind the wheel of a sedan half a block away. Silk felt considerably relieved. Butch was a handy man to have around if serious trouble started.

Inside the laboratory, Quinn had donned his regalia and was sliding bullets into the firing chamber of his twin guns. He thrust these into their holsters, stepped over in front of Carol and placed both hands on her slender shoulders.

"Carol," he said quietly, "some day we'll find time to think of just ourselves. I know how you feel because I feel the same way. But so long as there is crime and violence abroad, we've a job to do, if for no other reason than to honor and respect the memory of your father who gave me back my sight."

"Yes, Tony," she said and her eyes were wide and honest. "And I'm not afraid. Good luck! I'll go back to my apartment now and wait for further orders."

SHE HELD open the trap door and he vanished into it. The cheap little coupé was parked nearby. Quinn didn't wear the Black Bat's hood, nor the cape. They would have attracted too much attention. Instead, he had donned a floppy-brimmed hat worn well down over his eyes to conceal the scars which would have given away his identity to the newest rookie on the police force.

Oddly enough, his course took him in the direction of Police Commissioner Warner's home. He drove by, noticed that a nightlight had been left burning in the hall and that the garage doors were open. The Black Bat parked his car well out of sight. Twenty minutes went by and then Warner's car turned into the drive. He rolled to a stop in the garage, got out and shut off the lights. Then Warner's hand darted toward his hip pocket.

"No need for a gun, Commissioner," a calm voice said in the inky darkness. "This is the Black Bat!"

Warner couldn't see the Black Bat, but he recognized the voice.

"I'm glad you came to see me," Warner said. "Things have been happening. How much do you know about the case so far and how did you evade Lieutenant McGrath at the Hollis Building?"

The Black Bat chuckled.

"McGrath will have to figure that out. About these hunchback killers, I know very little. That's why I'm here. You said things happened. What?"

"Two more robberies," Warner sighed. "Thank heaven no one was killed. I'm firmly convinced these men are a cleverly organized, masterly led group of criminals intent on looting the richest families in the city. Tonight, they robbed Elmer White and Ed Johnson."

"And in every case the loot included not only cash and gems, but odds and ends, like book ends, statuettes, tobacco jars and other knick-knacks?" the Black Bat asked gently.

"Yes, every case," the commissioner groaned. "Two of the families, robbed soon after the murders, even lost silverplate. Now what kind of an organized gang bothers with that stuff? It's more trouble to hock than it's worth."

"Did you," the Black Bat's voice came out of the darkness," know the five families who were robbed immediately after the killings? Was any member of those various families known to be a big game hunter?"

"Big game hunter?" Warner asked in a puzzled tone. "What has that to do with it? No, I don't think they were. But wait, the two most recent victims—White and Johnson—they are known as sportsmen. Why did you ask that? Is there some connection?"

There was no answer. Warner waited a moment, turned on the lights of his car and then shook his head slowly. The Black Bat was gone! Warner sat down on the running board of his car.

"He's as badly stumped as we are. This is one case in which the Black Bat is bound to fail. Not the barest clue and, for once, I think Lieutenant McGrath is right. The first two victims of the gang were murdered simply as an example to others—that the hunchbacked gang was not to be opposed. Hollis' dying words that I heard over the phone, meant nothing—were just the incoherent shouts of a man who knew he was going to die."

Warner walked slowly toward the door of his house. He was badly worried. There were bound to be repercussions soon. The victims of the gang were all wealthy, influential people and they had a right to squawk. Orthodox methods of running down the gang were useless. Warner found himself praying that the Black Bat would get a lead and wade into that outfit with blazing guns. Warner didn't very often countenance violence nor the wanton breaking of the law, but those hopes still persisted.

CHAPTER VII

DEATH WILL BE THERE

S ILK, IN his disguise, attracted no attention as he walked down the quiet, elm-lined street where Geoffrey Thomas had his home. Silk ambled by the place and noticed there were no lights burning. That made his task just a little easier.

To carry out the Black Bat's instructions, he would have to perform some high class burglary, invade the house and search it. Silk knew that the Black Bat was working on theory alone, but that was enough for Silk. Those theories of his usually seemed to bear fruit.

Silk decided on a bold course. He walked up on the front porch and rang the bell.

When the butler or servant would arrive, he was ready to ask some logical question about the neighborhood, to keep the servant so busy that he wouldn't notice Silk's manipulation of the door lock. Then, after the household settled down again for the night, he'd merely open the door at his leisure, walk in and have a look. There would be no trace of an intruder then.

Silk heard two-toned chimes peal somewhere deep in the house, but no one came in answer to his ring, even after three or four minutes went by. Silk took a flashlight from his pocket, walked softly to a window and sprayed the light into a room. The furniture was covered with protective cloths, the rugs rolled. Geoffrey Thomas and his family were apparently not in town.

Silk grinned now for his task had become comparatively simple. He examined the lock, tested several master keys which he carried and finally he stepped into the reception hall. He closed the door behind him, masked the ray of his light with the palm of his hand and walked into the spacious living room.

There was an ornamental desk in one corner and mail was stacked high on it. He consulted post marks and discovered that Thomas must have been away for over three weeks. Apparently he was on a trip and didn't have his mail forwarded, leaving it for some servant to put away. There was a box, about ten inches square, placed alongside the mail. Silk picked it up.

Then his eyes happened to rest on the desk drawers. They were all open and their contents had been hastily pried into. Silk gulped. The hunchbacked burglars had beaten him to it. He glanced at the package he held, saw that it was addressed to Geoffrey Thomas and that it carried some odd-looking stamps. There was a return address in the corner and he tried to make out the small letters.

He heard a stealthy sound behind him, as though someone were brushing against the covered furniture. Silk turned his head quickly, raised the box he held and hurled it straight at the two men who were ready to pounce upon him.

In one quick second, he saw that they were hunchbacked, their faces were well covered by black scarfs and they had guns drawn. He reasoned that they wouldn't shoot except as a last resort for any undue noise in this neighborhood would attract police in droves.

THE TWO men ducked the flying missile and Silk whirled. He streaked toward the front hall. Two shadowy forms seemed to rise up out of nowhere. Silk didn't stop. He merely lowered his head and changed his flight into a lunging charge. He hit one of the shadowy forms a terrific blow and sent the man back on his heels. The second figure swung a gun butt and missed Silk's head by a fraction of an inch. Then Silk was sprinting across the hallway toward the door.

Silhouetted against the windows on either side of the exit, were two more of the hunchbacked men. Silk skidded to a stop, turned and headed for the stairway. His only chance now lay in creating enough of a rumpus to give Butch warning that he was in trouble.

Silk managed to reach the top of the stairs with two of the hunchbacked killers trying to grab his ankles. There was a huge ornamental vase on a pedestal set against the balustrade on the second-floor landing. Silk gave it a vigorous shove and the heavy object crashed against the bare floor below. It made a terrific racket.

He veered to the left and shot through a doorway into a bedroom. He slammed the door in the face of a cursing killer, and shot the bolt home. Then he turned on his flash and took stock of his predicament. He groaned, because now he noticed that he had virtually trapped himself. When he glanced out of the window, he saw two more of the weird killers lurking outside in the darkness.

Someone was already trying the door and a harsh voice gave orders. Silk berated himself for not taking along a gun. Yet he had expected nothing like this and if he ran into any trouble, he didn't want to be armed. Silk usually depended on his own smooth ways to get himself out of a jam.

Silk picked up a chair and sent it hurtling through the window. That made noise enough. Butch was bound to hear it. Everything depended on him now and Silk fervently prayed that he wouldn't attempt to clean up this mob of killers alone. Now he had to use his wits and try to bluff it out. Silk moved toward the door.

"I give up," he said in a gruff, sullen tone. "I ain't heeled so don't start shootin'. I'll open the door."

He turned the key and was hurled back by the force of two men who catapulted into the room. A pair of guns prodded Silk's ribs. He kept his hands stretched high and he gaped at the men who surrounded him. Then he let a bitter laugh escape his lips.

"Imagine it," he groaned. "I figured you guys owned this joint or were servants or something. Instead you're in the same boat I am—a bunch of crooks. Why didn't you sing out?"

"Quiet, you," one of the men snapped. "The rumpus you raised may draw the cops and if they come, you won't be here to meet them—on your feet."

SILK GULPED. He had a vague idea he wasn't fooling these men. Five minutes went by and then he heard someone running up the stairs. It was another of the hunchbacks.

"Okay, boys, nobody heard the window bust. Everything is under control. What'll we do with this bird?"

"Hold him and find out who he is," another of the partially masked and grotesque-looking men snapped. He turned to Silk and fastened steely fingers around his throat.

"Talk, you rat. You were trying to warn somebody, a plant outside. No burglar would have gone to all the trouble of busting a big vase and a window. What were you looking for? Who sent you here?"

Silk couldn't answer because those crushing fingers prevented him from even taking a breath. The fingers relented a trifle.

"F-for anythin' worth takin'," Silk managed hoarsely. "Say, what's the idea of gettin' so damn high hat? You're a bunch of crooks same as me. I ain't done nothin' to you lugs."

The hunchback who seemed to be in command of the others, stepped back a pace and turned the ray of a flashlight full on Silk. He studied him in silence for a moment.

"I wonder if this bird is just a second-story mug. He looks stupid enough to be, but you never can tell. Maybe he works for the Black Bat. There are ways of finding out. Tie his wrists behind his back. Somebody get the car ready. We'll go out the back way."

Silk placidly allowed them to bind his wrists. Just so long as he could stall, that was all that might be necessary. Butch hadn't blasted his way into the house yet so he must have used his head for once and gone to warn the Black Bat.

They led Silk down the stairs watching him narrowly every second. He was pushed out the back door and the house. No wonder he hadn't noticed any signs of intruders. Their getaway car had been boldly housed in the garage.

Silk climbed into the back seat. He noticed that while he had observed eight hunchbacked men in and around the house, only six got into the big car. He wondered where the other two had gone.

Then he noticed another significant thing. One of the hunchbacked men carried a satin sack and it contained an article just about the same size and shape of the package Silk had been examining when they burst in on him.

The car pulled out of the driveway, without headlights and slowly, so as to arouse no attention. Its powerful motor made a minimum of noise. The driver turned left and Silk had a momentary glimpse of Butch's car parked near the curb. It was empty and his heart rose in elation. Butch had gotten himself clear. Now if he was only close by to take up the pursuit.

They headed for the outskirts. Two of the hunchbacks held a whispered consultation. One of them exposed a gun.

"How about telling us who you are, sucker?" he snapped. "How come you were in that house and who sent you there?"

"Like I said," Silk protested weakly, "I was doin' a job on the place. Only I picked it wrong because there wasn't anythin' worth swipin'."

THE GUN racked across his face, drew blood and made Silk wince in pain. The weapon was slowly being raised again. The next blow would knock him cold and there was nothing he could do to prevent it.

"When you wake up," the hunchback snarled, "you'll remember this sock and then maybe you'll talk—or get some more of the same treatment."

Silk tried to roll away from the blow, but he was cramped between the bulky forms of his captors with no room to move. The gun barrel slammed against the top of his skull and he folded up.

He awoke as he was being dragged across a cinder path. He opened his eyes and saw that he was being taken into what seemed to be an isolated farmhouse. A run-down place with boarded-up windows and no lights. He could hear night insects chirping and never once the noise of passing cars. He shuddered despite himself. This was complete isolation where anything could happen.

Someone unlocked the front door. Silk was dragged through, for he still pretended to be unconscious. They threw him into a chair and someone slapped him smartly across the face. He feigned coming out of a coma. The eerie-looking man who led this pack applied a match to a lamp. Then he flipped the still lighted match at Silk's face.

"Still going to give us that phony yarn about being a second-story guy and working alone? Don't bother to say yes, because I know you'll be lying. You had a pal, didn't you? A big bruiser of a guy who was parked down the street from the Geoffrey Thomas place. He hid when we passed by, but he came out fast enough and followed us here—the big dope. Listen, stupid, for the last time—who sent you to that house and why?"

Silk shook his head stubbornly, although his rising hopes had been dashed to pieces. They knew that Butch had followed them here. They'd set a trap for him and Butch didn't possess the brains to avoid it.

"Kind of a tight-lipped guy, ain't you?" the hunchbacked leader snarled. "We'll take that out of you damned soon. I got one more question to ask. If you don't answer it right, it's curtains. Do you work for the Black Bat?"

"Who? Me?" Silk put the proper amount of outraged surprise in his voice. "The Black Bat! Say I'd earn fifty grand if I could put a bullet through his back. Not me! Say, you guys don't work for him, do you?"

Two of the men laughed. Their leader silenced them with a wave of his hand.

"You're pretty smart, pal. Maybe you don't work for the Bat, but we're going to find out. He'll go through hell and high water to save his friends so he won't mind coming here to save you. Only you won't be here and—Death will."

CHAPTER VIII

GHOSTLY COMMAND

PARKING WITHIN easy sight of Geoffrey Thomas' house, Butch watched Silk enter. Minutes went by. Then Butch heard a muffled crash and sat erect. A couple of minutes later a window crashed and Butch vaulted out of the car. He headed toward the house, curling his big fingers into mighty fists as he did so.

There was a high hedge running around the estate, but as he passed the break which permitted the driveway to go through, he came to an abrupt halt and dropped to his knees. He had caught a glimpse of two hunchbacked men lurking in the darkness behind the house.

"Silk's in trouble," Butch told himself grimly, "and I can't do anythin' about it because the Black Bat says I gotta report what happens before I wade in."

Minutes crawled by. Once Butch saw one of the hunchbacked men step out on the sidewalk, look around hastily and then duck back out

The hunchbacks dragged Silk and Butch toward the barge.

of sight. At last, something happened. He heard a garage door open and then a car starter whirred. Tires grated on cement and a big sedan slipped out of the driveway.

Butch didn't see Silk inside, but he was certain he must be there. The big man merged with the darkness and waited until the car was well down the street. Then he darted toward his own car, got it into motion and started as careful a pursuit as he could manage.

He drove without lights and allowed the car he trailed to remain well ahead.

When they headed out into the country, he was certain that Silk must be a prisoner. The chase was easy, too easy—although Butch never thought of that. His mind was centered on one thing—to keep the car in sight, learn its ultimate destination and phone the news in to Carol.

He braked the car suddenly and stopped. He slipped out, ran forward with an amazing speed for a man so big. The sedan he followed had turned off the highway and rolled along a narrow country lane. It topped

a grade and vanished. Butch topped that grade too and dropped flat. In the glare of the sedan's headlights, he saw two men drag Silk out and pull him toward the house.

Butch's jaw clamped shut hard and a low growl emanated from his lips. They weren't treating Silk too gently and he seemed to he unconscious. He wouldn't be the only one with a busted head once Butch returned from reporting this information.

He hurried back to the highway and sent his car streaking eastward. He recalled that they had passed through a small town on their way here. On the outskirts of the village, he saw beckoning lights. A lunchwagon was open. He parked beside another big car, entered the lunchroom and went directly to the phone booth.

BUTCH, INTENT on his important mission, didn't notice two men enter right behind him. One ordered coffee. The other sauntered up toward the booth as though to wait for Butch to finish his call.

The lone counterman, busy getting the coffee, didn't see the man press his ear against the thin paneling of the booth and then raise his hand in a signal to his companion. Butch had a notebook listing Carol's phone number and he consulted it briefly. Then he had Carol on the wire.

"Listen close," he said, "I ain't got much time. Silk is in trouble. They got him in a farmhouse at the end of a lane that runs off Highway Sixty-seven. You pass through Flaggsport, watch your mileage and just five and six-tenths miles after you pass the sign that says 'Come Again' is the lane. Got it?"

"Got it, Butch. Go back and see if you can help Silk."

"I'll go back and bust a few heads," Butch growled.

He hung up, stuffed his notebook back in his pocket and opened the booth door. There were two men waiting for him, on either side of the booth. He caught the glimpse of a gun, shown for his express benefit. Then one of the men wound an arm around his shoulders.

"If it ain't our old pal. Say, this is great. We got a car outside. Take you any place you want to go."

Butch opened his mouth to argue and a gun jabbed his ribs. His arms were gripped and he was led out of the lunch cart.

"In the car," one of the thugs told Butch. "You're a big lug, but we got a nice little chunk of lead that will whittle you down to our size."

Butch got into the car, waiting and hoping for the slightest relaxation of vigilance so that he could wrap his hands around the necks of these men and smash their skulls together. That chance never came. After the car was well away from the town, the man beside him poked his gun under Butch's nose.

"Let's see that notebook from which you took the phone number, sap. Give, hear me?"

Butch brought out the notebook, because there was nothing else he could do.

The thug flipped the pages and found Carol's number.

"So this is your pal's phone number, huh? Swell. We'll give him a ring later on in case he don't show up at the joint where we're taking you. If he does, you'll have to phone hell to reach him again."

The car rolled at a fast speed back to the isolated farmhouse. Covered by two guns, Butch walked into the place and was immediately surrounded by a squad of hunchbacked killers. They pounced on him.

Two minutes later he was firmly tied and able to move only by hopping across the floor. Butch was forced into another room. He saw Silk seated and well guarded. Butch let go with an audible groan. Silk merely looked at him as though he were a complete stranger.

THE LEADER of the hunchbacked men eyed them malevolently. He stepped up to Silk and struck him across the mouth with the back of his hand.

"So you are just a plain crook, huh? How come then, that this big gorilla followed us here and then made a phone call to a third party, huh? Well, you know what this means."

He shouted a command and all the occupants of the house assembled before him.

"These two"—he indicated Silk and Butch with a wave of his gun— "are to be taken to the barge. Get both cars out and we'll start as soon as we finish setting a nice little reception for their friend. Haul up the stiff, one of you guys. We'll arrange one swell party for the guy who'll come to save these chumps."

Two men carried a corpse up from the cellar. It was thrust into a chair, tied in place and Silk's coat placed over its shoulders. The hunchbacked leader surveyed the set-up critically.

"Perfect. Everything is set. Let's go!"

Silk and Butch were dragged to their feet and propelled out of the house. The hunchback leader remained behind for a few moments and when he emerged, he carefully closed the door behind him. Silk, standing beside Butch, gave him a nudge with his elbow. Immediately both of them began struggling furiously.

A gun butt crashed down on Silk's head and he dropped flat. He seemed to be writhing in the path, but in reality he was digging up the cinders as much as possible. Butch, straining against the ropes that bound him, shook off two savage pistol butt blows to the head, gave a howl of rage and lowered his head. He butted the nearest man in the stomach, doubled him up in a spasm of agony and then turned to tackle another.

The hunchback leader drew a blackjack from his pocket, maneuvered himself behind Butch and crashed it down. Butch passed out without a whimper. They were hastily loaded into separate cars and driven away. When they recovered consciousness later, Silk sniffed the odor of the river. Loose boards of an old pier rattled under the automobile tires. The cars stopped.

There was a dirty-looking barge tied up at the pier. Butch was thrown into it bodily and Silk followed. The killers scrambled down a rope ladder. A tug, with steam up, began pulling the barge away.

Silk and Butch were taken through a concealed door in the side of the hold. They found themselves in a cramped room and encompassed by pitch darkness as the door closed.

"We're in a mess," Silk said loudly. "These crazy guys seem to think we got a friend who'll help us. That's a laugh."

"No, it ain't," Butch whispered. "It's bad, Silk. Awful bad. They heard me phone Carol. They even got her number and they'll trace it. Don't look so good for her either."

Both men subsided into silence. There wasn't much to say and it was dangerous to speak. They could feel the barge moving rapidly and heading into midstream.

"Looks like we feed the fish," Silk said finally. "Try those ropes again, Butch. You always bragged no rope could hold you."

Butch strained against his bonds until the muscles in his neck stood out like iron bands.

"Yeah," Butch relaxed, "but I never met these kind of ropes before. No use."

A DOOR, facing them, opened and the hunchback leader entered. His eyes, above the black scarf, glittered evilly. Three of his men filled the doorway to watch. The hunchback drew a knife, held it near his hip and slowly advanced toward his victims.

"Here it comes, suckers," he said. "This is where we part company—for good. We got plenty of old scrap iron on deck to weigh you down with. You'll never come up again."

Silk took a long breath and steeled himself against the searing slice of the knife. It came forward slowly, for this hunchback had an overwhelming amount of sadism in his makeup. He would draw out the agony as long as possible. The knife touched Silk's throat and he felt a tiny rivulet of blood run down his neck.

It was too late now—even for the Black Bat's interference. Silk's life was numbered in seconds.

Then, very abruptly, the hunchback withdrew the knife. He was looking over Silk's head as if some mysterious presence had suddenly appeared. He put the knife away reluctantly and backed up a pace.

"Changed my mind," he muttered. "It's just possible you guys work for the Black Bat. We got to keep you alive until we're sure he's done for. He's slippery and may get out of the little trap we set, so the fishes will have to wait."

The door closed and Butch gave vent to a long drawn out sigh of relief. Silk was frowning deeply.

"Butch, did you see that? He was ready to slit my throat and something stopped him—something we couldn't see. Those words that hunchback spoke were not his own. He was merely repeating what someone else had just told him."

Butch gulped noisily. "You mean ghosts?"

"I don't know," Silk answered slowly. "I can't figure it out. Those hunchbacks are under the orders of someone they fear. A certain party was right. There is a guiding mind. Butch, try those ropes again. Keep trying. I'll see if I can wiggle over beside you and reach the knots. We've got to work fast. Once Carol transmits your message, it may be too late to prevent that trap from being sprung."

CHAPTER IX

BLACK BAT RESCUE

WEALTHY ALEX Pierce was a man of about forty, but he looked ten years younger. Slim and neatly dressed, he possessed a professional air that never left him. He was pacing the floor of his living room nervously. His hair was rumpled and a cold cigar rolled between his teeth. Finally, he walked over to his desk and sat down. There were eyes watching him. Outside the house, four hunchbacked killers were crouched below two windows. One of them raised his hand in a signal. They all crept softly toward the front of the house, stole up on the porch without making a sound and flattened themselves against the wall close to the doorway. Then one pressed the bell.

Pierce arose abruptly, flung his cigar into the waste-basket and hurried to answer the bell. He opened the door, saw no one and made a bad mistake. He stepped out on the porch. Instantly a hand was clapped across his mouth and his arms were pulled savagely into a position from which there was no possibility of extricating himself. Strong-muscled arms dragged him back into the house and the door was gently closed.

The hunchbacked killers flung Pierce into a chair and one of them pointed a gun at his temple.

"Don't move, sucker," he rasped, "unless you want to feel a slug bust you wide open."

Pierce licked his lips and remained rigid as a corpse. He watched the hunchbacked killers search his desk and take several jewel cases. These were dropped into a satin sack. Another of the thieves located the wall safe. Pierce gave the combination after the gun was pressed hard against his head.

They opened the safe and looted it. Then they picked up a cigarette box on his desk, appropriated that and selected a large ornamental cigarette lighter. Pierce watched a small paper weight, in the form of an Oriental idol, get dumped into the sack.

The quartette of crooks seemed to have completed their work. Two of them started for the front door. At that moment, every light in the house winked out. Then an eerie form with outflung wings like a bat, darted across the hall and into the big living room. A gun blazed. The new invader had two weapons in his fists and both of them opened fire simultaneously.

One of the hunchbacked killers gave a wild yell and slid into a heap on the floor. Two of the others streaked for a window at the rear of the room, shooting to cover their own retreat. Alex Pierce half rose from his chair. The hunchback beside him brought down the butt of his gun in a vicious, murderous blow. Pierce moaned and tumbled out of the chair.

The hunchback jumped over his form and raced through the darkened room in the wake of his two pals.

One of the men scooped up a foot rest and hurled it through the window. Then each of the killers dived into the protection of the night outside the house. Bullets struck dangerously close, for the man in the house was shooting fast. Then the night swallowed up the three men.

When the lights were turned on again, Alex Pierce was just opening his eyes. He saw a hooded and caped figure bending over him and he drew away in horror.

"Don't be afraid," the man said quietly. "I'm not one of those hunchbacks. I'm the Black Bat!"

Pierce sat up and rubbed his head.

"Thank heaven you came in time. They were going to kill me. I'm sure of it. How did you know they were here?"

THE BLACK BAT laughed. "I didn't. I came to pay you a little visit, which must be cut short because someone will have reported the shots. I saw what was going on, took the liberty of opening your front door and messing up the house with bullets. Sorry, but I did nail one of the killers. While I examine him I'll ask you a few questions. Answering them may help me run down these crooks."

The Black Bat moved to the hunchback sprawled on the floor. The man was dead. The Black Bat stripped away the scarf which concealed the killer's face and revealed a thin, pimply-faced little rat of a man. But the Black Bat didn't stop with that. He lifted the corpse and stripped off the man's coat. Something fell to the floor with a hollow sound. He picked up a papier-mâché hump.

"Fake," the Black Bat exulted. "I was certain that members of this gang couldn't all be hunchbacks. Perhaps they wear these outfits as a sort of grisly uniform. Now Mr. Pierce, what did they take from you?"

Pierce was on his feet, wavering a little and mopping some of the blood out of his hair.

"I'm not sure. There were some jewels in the safe and about two hundred dollars in cash in my desk. I know they took that. Then—why, look at my desk! They stole half a dozen practically worthless objects. My cigarette case, a paper weight...."

The distant wail of a siren warned the Black Bat that he had little time left. He approached Pierce and the eyes glittering behind that mask were very serious.

"Mr. Pierce, this is a strange question but it must be answered. Did you ever do any big game hunting in Bahawal, India?"

Pierce gaped for a moment.

"Why, yes—yes I did, about a year ago. My trophies are in a room upstairs. What in the world has that to do with this?"

"Perhaps nothing." The Black Bat stepped close to the dead man again and pasted a Black Bat sticker on his forehead. "I'll brand the corpse to let the police know I killed him. Then they won't hold you. And now, I'm following in the tracks of the hunchbacks. I can hear police cars stopping at the curb already. Good night, Mr. Pierce."

As the Black Bat spoke, he walked briskly toward the door and the light switch. Suddenly the room was plunged into darkness. Pierce thought he felt something pass very close to him. Then police pounded on the front door. He opened it and Lieutenant McGrath, leading a squad of detectives, swarmed into the house with drawn guns.

"I'm glad you came," Pierce managed to talk after half a minute. "There—there's a dead man in my living room. One of the hunchbacked murderers. They robbed me, possibly fractured my skull. I need a doctor."

McGrath shouldered Pierce aside, headed into the living room and stopped to turn on lights. He walked over to where the corpse lay, took one look and let out a yell.

"Why didn't you tell me the Black Bat was here? Outside, men. Scour the neighborhood. Broadcast an alarm for the Black Bat. He can't be far away. Now, Pierce, what happened here?"

"The Black Bat came. He asked me a lot of questions. He prevented four of those devils from killing me. The Black Bat began shooting and this—this man fell dead. But it was self-defense. They were shooting too. You can see bullet holes in the walls. The Black Bat had to kill this man."

"Yeah," McGrath looked down at the dead man. "Yeah, he always has to kill 'em and the mugs who fall by his gun are always rats, like Lewis here. We been hunting this weasel for weeks.

"Well, we got a lead about these hunchbacks at last. Phony too, huh? Fake humps to make 'em seem more vicious, I suppose. Okay, Mr. Pierce, you'll have to make a statement about this, but that sticker on Lewis' cheek proves the Black Bat did the job. You got nothing to worry about."

BEFORE McGRATH was inside the living room, the Black Bat had reached his car. When orders went out to create a dragnet, he was far beyond its scope, riding along sedately so as to attract no attention.

The nose of his car was pointed homeward. It was about time for Silk and Butch to report. Also, with McGrath on the war path it might be well if he was at home in the event that the doughty detective-lieutenant decided to check up on Tony Quinn.

Moments later, the Black Bat slipped through the gate, crossed the lawn to the garden house and made certain he was unobserved. He raised the cleverly hidden trap door, started to slide down the ladder and paused.

Ordinary eyes might have noticed the small slip of paper tacked to the under side of the door, but ordinary eyes would never have been able to read it in this darkness. The Black Bat did and his face went grim beneath the hood. It said:

> S. and B. in trouble. S. taken to house at end of lane off highway 67. The turn is exactly five and six-tenths of a mile beyond the south line of Flaggsport. B. called a second time and asked me to meet him. Good luck!

The Black Bat read the last line again and his heart missed a beat. Butch had phoned a second time asking Carol to meet him? But Butch wouldn't have done that, not when Silk was in trouble. He'd have dusted straight back to the house where Silk was held. The Black Bat knew exactly how Butch's mind worked.

"Someone else phoned Carol. They're getting close to me, to Tony Quinn," he muttered. "She may be in danger, too, and I can't help her. My only lead is this farmhouse."

He closed the trap door softly and darted back to where he had parked his car. This time, he sent it racing madly toward the outskirts. Now he cared nothing for interference from the police. His friends were in deadly peril. They depended on him alone to get them out. The Black Bat's foot was like a ton of steel on the gas pedal.

CHAPTER X

DEATH DEFERRED

O UTSIDE OF Flaggsport the Black Bat looked for the town line, found it and also saw the 'Good-by' sign swinging gently in the early morning breeze. He checked his speedometer, leaned on the gas pedal again and went racing off into the night.

He covered the five-odd miles in less than that many minutes, braked savagely and spotted the lane. He turned the car off the road, concealed it under low branches of a big oak and climbed out. He checked his guns as he raced toward the crest of a slope. He slowed up as he reached it, saw the solitary farmhouse nestled in a small valley and made a half circle of the place so that his attack would come from the rear.

There was a weak light burning on the first floor, but no other signs of life. The Black Bat observed the place intently from the protection of high grass and then he darted like the wind across the cleared space, reached the back door and stood very quiet, listening. Nothing stirred within.

He went around to the front of the house with a heavy heart. He had no way of knowing how long it was since Butch phoned in the news of Silk's capture. Both of them might be dead inside, or they may have been taken to some other hideout.

He glanced at the cinder path and then knelt hastily. He saw the tracks indicating that one man had been dragged toward the house. He crept forward a little and saw signs of a terrific struggle. Had that taken place as the prisoners were led into the house, or when they were being taken away? The Black Bat's super-sensitive eyes traveled off the cinder path to the softer dirt at its shoulders. There he saw Butch's huge shoe tracks imbedded clearly. The toes pointed away from the house. They had been taken away then.

Yet, even if they were no longer prisoners inside, the Black Bat's only chance to rescue them lay there. He had to find some clue. There was sheer desperation in his movements now.

He found the front door ajar about a quarter of an inch. He gave it a shove and discovered that it was an exceptionally heavy door. Something hit the floor with a clang. He looked down. It was a thin bar of metal which had held the door open. The Black Bat sensed that this was some kind of a trap. Gun in hand, he stood there.

He raised his head and looked into the house. Then his spirits dropped to a new low. There was a long corridor running through the house. At the far end, he could see a sinister object seated in a chair. It was a man, either dead or unconscious and—that man wore the coat which Silk had donned as part of his disguise.

The Black Bat stepped into the hallway and let go of the door. It closed with a clanging sound, but he paid no attention to this for he was rushing along toward the last room in the house. He reached it, stopped beside the man in the chair and raised his head. Then he emitted a sigh of relief. It was a corpse all right, a badly crushed and battered cadaver—but it was not Silk! The Black Bat had an idea this was the man who had tumbled off the roof of the Hollis Building.

THE BAT tensed. There was a low hissing sound from somewhere nearby. It sounded like gas being forced by high compression from a tank. He whirled around and things began to spin. There was no odor, but whatever that gas was, it had a sinister potency. The Black Bat found that he was reeling and staggering along.

Then a sudden wave of horror struck him. Hardly realizing it, he discovered that he had fallen and was trying to climb to his knees. Every muscle and nerve seemed utterly paralyzed. He summoned all the strength he possessed, but even that wasn't enough. The Black Bat slowly sank to the floor. He wasn't unconscious, but that stage was rapidly approaching.

Then he heard a pounding noise, and at first he thought it was his own heart. But the wrench of wood being parted by some instrument indicated that help was coming. The Black Bat couldn't move, but his eyes were open and they still functioned. He could see through the darkness. He watched one of the heavily boarded windows being opened. Just a little air—a little cool, life-giving air would save him. Sweat poured down his face, soaked his clothing.

A dark blob of shadow filled the window for a moment. Then the person in whom the Black Bat placed hopes for his life, straightened up. He was very short and inclined to be pudgy. He wore his hat low over his forehead and his coat collar was turned up. And—a curved knife glittered in his hand.

The Black Bat wondered why he couldn't see this man's face. Then he noticed that the newcomer held a handkerchief against his nose and mouth. He knew about this gas then. Was he coming in to finish the job? The knife hand raised high. The man crept forward confidently.

Then the Black Bat saw no more. Merciful unconsciousness gripped him. His last thought was that everything was ended now. Yet it wasn't, for the intruder lowered the blade a moment later, knelt beside the Black Bat and uttered a sharp cry. Without wasting another second, he slipped an arm under the unconscious figure's waist, hoisted him up and slung him over one shoulder. The man was small but apparently very strong, for he carried the Black Bat easily.

He went straight toward the window he had forced open, slid the Black Bat's body through it and then exited himself. Outside, in the darkness, he again picked up his burden and carried him twenty yards from the house where grass and shrubbery was thickest.

He laid the Black Bat down gently, straightened the Bat's arms and legs and then bent over the unconscious form of the hooded man. His face was a study in conflicting emotions as he reached out to remove the hood and reveal the identity of the Black Bat....

CAROL BALDWIN, in the security of her little apartment, slowly hung up the phone after Butch had called. She didn't know where to contact the Black Bat nor when he would find an opportunity to call her. He might even return home first, and Silk needed help badly. Carol didn't hesitate any longer. She hastily wrote a note outlining Silk's predicament and the location of the hideout. She was pulling a jaunty little hat when the phone rang again.

She answered it eagerly, hoping to hear Tony Quinn's voice. Instead it seemed to be Butch again and he was very excited.

"Something else just turned up. It's necessary that you meet me at once. Go to the corner of First Street and Millbrook Avenue. Dark and quiet there. Expect you in thirty minutes."

Before she could answer, he hung up. Carol added a postscript, tucked the note in her purse, left the apartment and slipped around to the side of Tony Quinn's estate. She fastened the note on the under side of the trap door, returned to the street and walked briskly away. She took a cab several blocks from there and gave directions which took her to within a quarter of a mile of the rendezvous.

But something inside Carol seemed to be warning her, a sixth sense that repeated over and over again to be careful. She tried to recall the second phone conversation word for word. 'Necessary that you meet me at once.' That didn't sound like Butch. The voice seemed to have been his, but not the words. He had either read a prepared dialogue to her or—someone must have imitated his voice.

Yet she wasn't certain and at this stage she couldn't afford to take a chance in not keeping the appointment. The corner was dark and dismal—a perfect spot for a murder or a kidnaping. Carol was anything but a coward, yet she felt a terrific urge to cut and run for it. Then a reassuring sight met her eyes. A patrolman, nightstick swinging to match his stride, came sauntering up the street. Carol waited until he approached and began eyeing her suspiciously.

"Officer," she said, "someone is following me. I'm nursemaid for Mrs. Loring's two children and I'm afraid they may force me to let them in the house so they can kidnap the children. There have been threats, you know."

The patrolman nodded briskly, for Carol had basic material to her bluff. There had been threats against the wealthy Loring family and they did live only a matter of a few blocks away.

"Where are they?" the patrolman asked. "How many were there?"

"Two, I think," Carol said.

The cop's face went grim and he loosened the gun in its holster. "Okay, lady, you keep on walking home just like nothing happened. I'll trail along. Dugan, the cop on the next beat, is due here in a minute or two. We'll handle the tough guys if they start anything."

Carol glanced at her wrist-watch. It lacked about four minutes of the half hour allotted her. She nodded to the patrolman and began walking very slowly toward the corner. She heard a car rolling down the street and its headlights were out. Carol reached the corner and stood there. The car pulled up and two men jumped out. They separated to cut off any possibility of retreat on her part.

A gun roared. One of the men stopped abruptly. His left leg buckled under him and he went down to the pavement, drawing a gun as he did so. He managed to lift the weapon, but he never pulled the trigger. Two service pistols went into action. The wounded man simply dropped flat. The other wheeled and raced back toward the car. Bullets slammed into the machine. One flattened a tire, another perforated the gas tank. Two patrolmen came up warily.

The second crook and the driver surrendered, protesting wildly as to their innocence. One of the patrolmen searched the men and found them armed.

"Innocent, are you?" he growled. "My eye! There will be radio cars here in a minute. Dugan, keep watch on these punks while I see how bad the other one is."

"Okay," Dugan said and he kept looking around. "Now ain't it just like a girl to get scared and run away. Oh well, we know where to find her and these buckaroos will get a nice stretch anyhow for traveling heeled."

CHAPTER XI

STYMIED

CAROL HAD ducked hastily when the shooting began. She watched the arrival of two radio cars. Then a detective cruiser howled up and the prisoners were taken away. She didn't wait any longer. By cutting through a yard, she reached the parallel street, spent ten precious minutes trying to spot a taxi and Finally hailed one. She had herself driven past Flaggsport and she paid off the driver near the lane Butch had described.

Carol ran along the lane, stumbling and almost falling several times, for the rutted, stony road was never meant to be traveled in high heels. She topped the ridge and spotted the house in the valley. It was dark and sinister-looking, reminding her more of a tomb than a residence.

Her heart more than kept pace with her running steps. She knew that Silk was, or had been there. Probably Butch was a prisoner in the place, also. It was even possible that Tony might have been taken. Carol unlatched her purse and removed a small Twenty-five calibre automatic. She pumped a bullet into position, released the safety catch and kept on going.

Then suddenly, she veered off the lane and crouched in the tall grass. Someone was coming out of the house through a window. In one brief instant, she had a glimpse of the Black Bat's hooded head and his ribbed cape. Her heart sank, for the Black Bat was being forced through the window head first and he appeared to be dead.

She checked the impulse to rush to his side when another figure scrambled out of the window. She saw this man lift the Black Bat and carry him away from the house. Carol moved forward carefully. From a vantage point on the side of a hill, she could watch, in the graying dawn, all of the unknown man's actions. She saw him lay the Black Bat down gently and then reach up for the hood.

Carol raised her gun skyward and yanked the trigger. The little automatic made a flat report that wouldn't have been heard very far, but the unknown man heard it. He straightened up, jumped over the Black Bat's prostrate form and began running madly toward the forest growth behind the farm.

Carol rushed down to where the Black Bat lay. She dropped to her knees beside him and held her breath as she lifted one limp wrist and placed her fingertips gently against the pulse. He was alive! His eyelids were moving.

She raised the Black Bat's head, and when he recovered consciousness, he blinked at her as though he saw a ghost.

"It's all right, darling," she told him. "Everything is all right. Are you badly hurt? Shall I get you a doctor?"

The Black Bat sat erect and pressed both gloved hands to his temples. He managed a wan smile.

"Just an asphyxiating gas. Soon as the world stops spinning like a top, I'll be all right. I... Carol, how did you get here? Did you see a small man with a big hat? He was in the house, ready to knife me."

"The little man carried you out here, darling," Carol told him.

A WAVE of relief passed through her. When the Bat asked questions, there wasn't much danger of his having been badly hurt.

"He was going to unmask you," she continued, "but I fired a shot into the air and frightened him off."

"Silk and Butch?" the Bat queried. "And you, Carol? You really did write that note I found pinned to the trap door? I thought someone might have guessed the identity of the Black Bat because that note lured me into one of the neatest traps I've ever seen."

"I wrote the note," Carol explained. "Butch phoned me and described this place. Then another call came and I suspected it was a trap for me. I was right. It's getting light. We'd better go back."

"With Silk and Butch in trouble?" the Black Bat asked. "No, Carol. We've got to find them. Help me up. I'm going back in that house to look for clues. There must be something to give us a lead. You go back to the highway. The coupé is parked under a big tree just north of the lane. Drive it here."

He was wobbly on his feet for a few minutes, but he soon had another window ripped away so that there was cross-ventilation to air the house. Then he climbed through a window, lit a lamp and found the gas cylinder. Its contents were exhausted. He also located the mechanics of the trap. The door of the house had been made extra heavy and a spring closed and locked it after he had entered. The closing door also operated the mechanism which had turned on the valve of the gas cylinder.

He examined the corpse still seated in the chair, but the dead man offered no clues. He started a complete search of the house. A closet caught his eye. Inside, he discovered several articles of clothing. A slicker, an oil skin hat and knee-high boots. He appropriated these.

Carol had the coupé waiting. They drove back to the city fast. They made their way, unobserved, into the estate, used the tunnel and reached the laboratory.

Quinn sent Carol into the kitchen to make coffee. Without removing his sombre clothing he set to work at once. He scraped some white spots off the slicker and put them through a simple test. Then he studied the hat intently and finally tackled the pair of boots. Carol brought a light breakfast into the lab and Quinn ate hastily and told her of his findings at the same time.

"The slicker was coated with residue from sea water. Both the hat and coat are those of a sea man. The boots were literally embedded with pieces of copper drillings. There was some rope strands fastened to the instep, too, the kind of hemp that is used for tow lines at sea.

"Carol, there's one answer to this. At least one member of the hunchback gang works aboard a barge. That barge was recently loaded with copper drillings and that shouldn't be hard to trace. The copper shows no signs of oxidation so it must have been carried via the barge from some big factory direct to a freighter, probably intended for trans-ocean voyage to Europe. Copper is an important commodity over there right now."

HE TURNED to finish the breakfast. "But how can you be sure Silk and Butch are on the barge?" Carol asked.

"Because it's the very best spot in the world to hide them. Their captors must have guessed they were my agents, which means they won't be killed immediately. They'll be hostages until the gang can land the Black Bat.

"Our job now is to locate a barge which was recently filled with a cargo of copper drillings. That's your work, my dear. I can't do it, not in broad daylight, and we can't afford to waste one minute's time. I know how tired you must be, but...."

"What's being tired compared to being a prisoner in the hands of those men?" Carol interrupted. "Tell me how to go about it and I'm on my way."

Tony Quinn gave her detailed instructions and after she left, he changed to his tweeds and smoking jacket. He spent ten minutes tapping his way along the path beside his house, simply to show himself and arouse no suspicions. But windows in the house were wide open so he could hear the phone in case Carol called.

Two hours, the longest Tony Quinn had ever known, dragged by and still no word. Every passing minute meant that Silk and Butch were that much closer to death. Yet Tony Quinn displayed none of the anxiety that was running rampant in his brain. He made several complete circles around his house. Once, a police car rolled by and the siren wailed softly in a salute. Every cop in town knew Tony Quinn and respected him as a man who had suffered more than death to carry on a fight against those who broke the law.

Finally he returned to the house, closed all the windows and resumed his usual chair in front of the fireplace. He tried to force the worry out of his mind by thinking over all the details of this bizarre case. Two murders so far, and why? How did it happen that Hollis and Kilpatrick were ruthlessly killed and the other victims permitted to live? How were these victims linked? By the fact that some of them had, in the past, been big game hunters?

Why were cheap, unimportant articles like book ends, cigarette boxes and statuettes stolen? How did those hunchbacked killers know when to strike and when to run for it? What had Hollis meant by that one word, Garland? Was it the name of a man? Certainly he couldn't have been talking of flowers, not with death staring him in the face. And the mysterious individual who had rescued the Black Bat! Quinn's brain couldn't sort the facts, yet. Perhaps Silk had uncovered something. If only Carol would call!

Tony Quinn wasn't used to inactivity when his two friends were in danger, but for one of the few times in his life he was completely stymied. His pretended blindness became a barrier which he was unable to hurdle. Yet there had to be some way of rescuing Silk and Butch.

THE DOORBELL buzzed. Quinn almost started up in alarm. Above all things he didn't want a visitor now. But there was nothing to do but tap his way across the room, open the door and stand there with his blank eyes staring straight over—Police Commissioner Warner's head.

"Why, Tony," Warner said. "I thought Silk would be here to let me in. You don't look very well to me. Is anything wrong?"

Tony Quinn laughed.

"I'm as fit as a blind man can be, Commissioner. I'm very glad you stopped by. Silk is downtown doing some shopping. There's nothing new on those hunchbacked murder cases, is there?"

Warner took Quinn's arm and piloted him back to his chair in front of the fireplace. He sat down too, sighed and crossed his legs.

"Another robbery. Alex Pierce, the jeweler, this time. Fortunately for Pierce, the Black Bat showed up in time to save his life."

Through Quinn's mind ran the thoughts of a worried man. The Black Bat had saved Pierce but could he rescue his own two aides? Carol might phone at any minute. Immediate action might be demanded, and here, of all people, sat the police commissioner.

"I hope you don't mind my dropping in like this, Tony," Warner said. "I know you're a lonesome man and company does you good. I like to come here for a more selfish reason however. I can relax and forget about murders and robberies and hunchbacks. Or, if I have a mind to, discuss the cases with you."

"You're welcome at any time." Quinn smiled although he'd never felt less like smiling since the day when acid had been dashed into his eyes. Again and again he realized how each elapsing minute made Silk and Butch's peril greater. They might even be dead by now. And Carol? Why didn't she call? Had she fallen into some neatly laid trap too? Was this the beginning of the end for the Black Bat? Without his three friends, the Black Bat would find it hard to operate.

Warner tamped tobacco into his pipe, lit it and leaned back with a long sigh of comfort. Quinn realized he might be here for hours and there was no possible way to get him out. He might plead he wasn't feeling well, but he knew Warner well enough to realize the man would then stay at least until Quinn's valet got back.

Then the telephone buzzed and Quinn sat erect with a startled ejaculation. Warner got up and pushed his chair back.

"No, please," Quinn said, "I'll answer it. You forget, Commissioner, that even a blind man becomes accustomed to the layout of his own home. I can find my way about easily."

Warner sat down again and Quinn headed toward the phone on the small desk near the door. His mind was working furiously. He couldn't talk to Carol here and it could be no one but her. Suddenly he tripped over a small ornamental urn on the floor. He throw out both hands and came crashing down on the table. The telephone crashed to the floor with Quinn on top of it. Quinn's hands seized the wires and jerked them out of the instrument. Warner came rushing over to help him up. Quinn had an abashed grin on his face.

"Silk must have stuck that darned vase there by mistake. He always tells me when he moves anything. Will you pick up the phone for me?"

Warner glanced at the instrument.

"Sorry, but you ruined it, Tony." Quinn headed for the hallway. "There's another one upstairs. No, don't come with me. Unless I keep going on as usual I'm apt to become too frightened to move about my own house. Please, Commissioner, go back and enjoy your pipe. I can manage very nicely."

QUINN'S CANE tapped the way along the stairs. He stepped into a small room on the second floor, closed the door and sprang for the telephone. If only Carol hadn't hung up. She was still on the wire but extremely worried.

"Sorry I couldn't answer right away," Quinn said. "Warner is downstairs and I had to do some fast thinking so he wouldn't hear me talk. What's up?"

"I pretended to be a reporter, as you suggested," Carol said. "I asked a lot of questions around the waterfronts about scrap metal being shipped to Europe and—I found what you are looking for. A barge, named the Timothy Three, hauled a load of copper drillings yesterday. Last night, after midnight, the barge suddenly moved off, towed by a tug. It went up the river and it's now tied up at an old pier near the end of Carmody Street. I'll meet you there."

"No," Quinn countered. "I can't get rid of Warner but I have an idea. I've been thinking of a way of getting out with Warner around here. You phone the Reliable Yacht Company, give them my name and say I want a small yacht moored at that pier as quickly as possible. They base several of their demonstrators at a yacht club only a mile further up the river. I'll have to work in broad daylight and I'll need your help badly. Now listen carefully. Do just exactly this...."

Carol listened intently and laughed musically at the sheer audacity of the Black Bat's plan. Quinn hung up and made his slow way downstairs again.

"A salesman," he told Warner with a smile. "But not the ordinary kind. This one wants to sell me a yacht. He's got one tied up at a pier uptown. I've been thinking seriously about buying one so that I can get out in the air more. Have to wait until Silk returns so he can take me there."

"Why wait?" Warner said quickly. "My car is outside and you know I'm something of an authority on boats. I'll be more than glad to take you there."

CHAPTER XII

DAYLIGHT RESCUE

DRIVING TONY QUINN uptown, Warner finally brought the car to a stop at the end of the pier. He helped Quinn out and the blind man stood quietly waiting for Warner to make the next move. A trim little yacht was tied up but Quinn's blank eyes gave no indication that he saw it—nor the dirty-looking barge that was floating only a matter of yards away. One man sat in a chair on the after-deck smoking a pipe, but watching Warner and Quinn very closely.

"Trim looking little craft," Warner approved. "Shall we go on board?"

"Might as well," Quinn said. "The salesman will drag us on board anyhow. See if you can raise him, Commissioner. I'll wait here for you."

Warner nodded, hurried toward the end of the pier and walked up the short gangplank to the yacht. He shook hands with a dapper-looking man who came out to meet him. Then Warner turned and called:

"I'll be after you in a minute, Tony. I..."

Warner suddenly stopped shouting. A woman's voice was yelling somewhere, yelling with the frenzy of grim terror. Warner and the salesman rushed to the starboard rail. Far out, past midstream, they saw a girl standing in a rowboat and waving her arms madly.

"Tony," Warner called. "Someone is in trouble. We're going to run this craft out to the rescue. Wait right where you are."

Quinn waved his cane in acknowledgment, tapped his way back to the car and climbed into the rear seat. He noticed that the guard on the barge had suddenly vanished. It was more than probable that he had recognized Commissioner Warner and gone below to give the alarm.

Quinn didn't relax once he got back in the car. Rather, he took a quick look around, thankful that this part of the river was so deserted. He hastily removed his coat, put on the Black Bat's cape, slid a pair of dark trousers over his own tweeds and then donned the hood. He opened the door of the car, slipped out and ducked behind a run-down watch-man's shack.

Certain that he was unobserved, he raced straight toward the barge. The Black Bat moved fast. Everything depended on swiftness of motion now. Without a pause he leaped off the edge of the pier and onto the deck of the barge. He headed toward a companionway and darted behind it when he heard someone coming up.

Two men appeared and while they exhibited no guns openly, the Black Bat could see the outline of the weapons thrust into their back pockets. He drew his own guns, reversed one of them and crept forward. One man walked over to the rail and watched the yacht maneuvering closer to the girl in the rowboat. The other remained close by the spot where the Black Bat was hidden. This man had no warning of danger for the Black Bat worked very quietly. He stepped up behind his victim and slammed the gun butt down hard. As the man wilted, he caught him, lifted him off the deck and deposited him behind the companionway out of sight of his friend.

The other crook turned around, saw that his mate had vanished and cursed softly as he made his way across the narrow deck. Then a gun jabbed against his ribs.

"Keep your hands by your sides and don't make a sound," a low voice warned. "How many others are below?"

"T-two," the remaining crook managed. "Wh-what's the idea?"

HE DIDN'T speak further because a thudding gun butt dispatched him into a world of complete blankness. Then the Black Bat darted down the companionway ladder and gave a grunt at what he found below.

This was certainly no common garden variety of barge. The hold, into which cargo was dumped, looked big, but the builder of the craft had contrived to save plenty of room below. There were even two small cabins.

A man with a broken nose and a sour expression on his face backed out of one cabin. Backed out and into the hands of the Black Bat. A palm clapped across his mouth to check the cry of surprise. The gun drilled against his side gave notice that this was no picnic.

"Into the other cabin," the Black Bat ordered softly. "One word or move and I'll let you have it."

The crook gulped and obeyed. He had one glimpse of the masked man who had captured him and that had almost as much effect as the gun.

"The Black Bat!" he said hoarsely.

"Inside," the Bat answered. "Fast!"

He closed the cabin door quietly, forced his prisoner to remove a necktie and belt and then used these to tie the man up tightly. He left him lying on a narrow bunk.

"I'll be back," he said tensely, "if I hear the slightest noise out of you."

He stepped into the dark corridor, approached the second cabin and tried the latch. The door wasn't locked. He pushed it open a notch. His eyes lighted up for Silk and Butch were there, both cruelly tied up and haggard from lack of sleep and food. One man guarded them. He heard the latch rattle, turned on his heel and fired. The Black Bat's guns blasted a split second later and the killer doubled up.

The Black Bat drew a knife, cut Silk free first and talked fast as he did so.

"No time to answer questions. I'm with Commissioner Warner. It was the only way I could get here. Cut Butch loose. Then both of you get away from here as fast as possible."

The Black Bat hurried on deck, darted across it and leaped back to the pier. He saw the yacht heeling over preparatory to its return to shore. The rowboat was in now and the girl who had been in it, stood beside Warner. The police commissioner came down the gangplank in a big rush.

"Tony," he called out. "Tony, what the devil happened? We heard shots." He opened the rear door of the car. Tony Quinn sat there, his cane between his knees, an excited expression on his face.

"I heard shots, too. They seemed to come from down the river a bit. Oh, curse the luck. I'm blind and I can't do a thing."

"We'd better get down there," Warner slid behind the wheel. "Your yacht will have to wait."

Warner spent twenty minutes cruising up and down the waterfront without getting much success.

"Hopeless," he told Quinn. "Couldn't have amounted to much anyhow or we'd have heard more excitement. Want to go back to the yacht now, Tony?"

Quinn shook his head. "I don't think so. Anyway, what's the good of me going on board? You tell me all about it and that will make up my mind. By the way, what was going on? Was someone in difficulty on the river?"

"A fool girl who went for a row, and when she stopped to smear a little rouge on her lips, the oars dropped into the water. I didn't even ask her name and you can rest assured I didn't introduce myself. I'm not looking for publicity of any kind. Not now, with this gang of hunchbacked killers on the loose. Well, let's go back. I'm sorry it all turned out to be such a fiasco. Wish I could find out who fired those shots."

He stopped in the driveway beside Quinn's home. A door opened and Silk, immaculate and smiling, helped Quinn out of the car. He nodded to the commissioner.

"How was the boat, sir?" he asked eagerly. "Did you buy it?"

Quinn's face was deathly white, but he managed a smile.

"Not yet. Help me in, Silk. I—feel a bit dizzy. Too much excitement, I guess."

WARNER JUMPED out of the car and took Quinn's other arm. They put him in a chair and Warner went for a glass of water. Quinn took it gratefully.

Silk escorted Warner to the door. When he returned, Quinn had pulled down the shades and was stripping off his coat. Beneath it, his left shoulder was matted with blood.

"That gunman winged me," he smiled wanly, "I kept the robe and hood wadded against the wound as much as I could so the blood wouldn't leak through. Is Butch all right and Carol?"

"Butch is in the laboratory, sir." Silk was helping to bare the wound. "I'll get water and antiseptics, sir."

Silk cleansed the wound very carefully.

"A bad nick, sir, but the bullet isn't there, luckily. I haven't thanked you yet for saving my life. They'd have murdered us tonight. Steady now, sir. This will sting a little."

Quinn winced as the powerful antiseptic cleansed the wound. He felt better after it was bandaged.

"Have a look around," he ordered Silk. "Then we'll adjourn to the laboratory."

Carol detected the stiffness of Quinn's arm the moment he entered the lab. He quieted her fears and grinned at her damp and bedraggled clothing.

"A perfect act," he said with a chuckle. "Warner fell for it as I knew he would. It gave me time enough to reach Silk and Butch."

Butch had a bad bruise alongside his right cheek and he kept rubbing it. There was some concentrated hatred in his eyes.

"Just promise me a crack at them birds," he grumbled. "Just one juicy crack at 'em, and I won't ask anythin' else as long as I live."

"You'll have it, I hope," Quinn said. "Now to business. Silk, did you carry out your assignment before they seized you?"

SILK NODDED. "I did, sir. I broke into Geoffrey Thomas' house and found that he was out of town and has been for weeks. His mail was stacked up and—listen to this— There was a package on his desk with some peculiar-looking postage stamps on it. I didn't have time to read the return address, but those hunchbacked crooks took that package and nothing else. Maybe they'd searched the place before I arrived, but I'm sure they stole that package."

Quinn's eyes lighted up. "Our first clue. Silk, in the library is a treatise on stamp collecting. Go through the volume and see if you can pick out pictures of the stamps you saw. Take all the time you need and be absolutely sure of yourself."

Silk hurried out. Carol was stuffing Quinn's pipe full of tobacco. She handed it to him and applied a match while she talked.

"Tony, that strange man who saved you from being killed in the farmhouse. Who could he be? He was no more than five feet one or two. Why did he save you and then try to see who you were?"

"I don't know why he saved my life," Quinn answered thoughtfully. "Raising the hood to observe my identity was a perfectly natural thing for him to do, however. He'll turn up again. We're sure of one thing— the hunchbacked killers are not really deformed. Their apparent afflictions are fakes and they are known to the police as crooks and killers.

"We have suspects, but nothing really to pin them down with. Jay Fenner, the attorney, is crafty enough to deal his cards from the bottom of the deck. Then there is Jim Downing, Kilpatrick's nephew. From all reports he'd be quite capable of turning crooked if there was a nickel of profit in it for him. That stranger who rescued me has possibilities too. I have a feeling our main clue is connected with big game hunters and I'm going to run it down as soon as we're all rested."

"Perhaps," Carol suggested, "they knew one another better than we think and during one of their expeditions they ran across something worth a great deal of money. Don't you think that's possible?"

"Yes," Quinn admitted slowly. "But improbable, because it's practically a proven fact that these men did not know one another very well. If your theory is right, our list of suspects is considerably longer for one of those men may be killing off the others so he can have the loot all to himself. It's a mess, and so far we've taken the brunt of everything. That band of murderers has had us on the run. From now on, we'll take the offensive. Butch, go back to your room and get some rest. Carol, you'll have to remain here until we can find you another apartment. Those crooks can trace that phone number and I don't want you in any danger. We'll rest until tonight and then—there'll be some action."

CHAPTER XIII

DR. NORDEN'S MYSTERIOUS ACTIONS

QUINN SAT alone in his study that night until Police Commissioner Warner came at nine, excited and worried.

"More of the hunchback mob's rotten work," he said before he sat down. "Within the last three hours four different homes have been invaded. Jewels, money and knick-knacks taken. Damn it, Tony, haven't you got some theory about all this?"

Quinn's fingertips beat a tattoo on the arms of his chair. He turned his head toward Warner and those blank eyes seemed to be looking about three feet to the commissioner's left.

"I have been giving this a lot of thought, Commissioner. I had a theory, yes. It revolves about the fact that there must be something in common between the victims. But what you've just told me now seems to explode such an idea. Several men might be related by some one thing, but as the list of victims grows, I'm beginning to doubt it. Why don't you assemble some of the men originally victimized? Edward Johnson, Elmer White, perhaps the cousin and heir of the murdered Kilpatrick."

Warner nodded glumly. "I thought of that, but these men don't even know one another so far as I can find out. However, I'll take your suggestion and have them at Kilpatrick's house tonight, at about eleven o'clock."

Warner stroked his chin for a moment and then he went on.

"If only there was some way of letting the Black Bat know of the meeting. I've an idea he'd know the exact questions to ask."

Tony Quinn's smile was enigmatic. "It's said the Black Bat usually knows everything that goes on. He might be there, Commissioner. I wouldn't mind going along myself except that I'd be in the way. And, of course, I couldn't help with any questions because the whole affair is as dark as my blindness, so far as I am concerned. Did you, by any chance, hear more about the shooting near the river this morning?"

Warner nodded. "Just another headache for the department. A corpse with a couple of bullets through its heart was picked out of the river a couple of hours ago. We identified the man as a cheap little gutter rat and the time of his death was affixed as approximately that which corresponds to the moment we heard the shooting. The girl I helped rescue disappeared, too."

"Rather ungrateful of her," Quinn said. "Well, I wish there was something I could do. You know, Commissioner, it does me a great deal of good having you come here and discuss these cases with me. I know I rarely have much to offer in the way of a solution, but it gives me something to take up my time. Have you ever considered the old, old theory that the murders of Hollis and Kilpatrick may have been committed so certain heirs could come into their money?"

"Considered it?" Warner grunted. "I've run it to the ground. Hollis' heirs are out of the question, but Kilpatrick left his estate to a pretty shabby heir, a young fellow named Jim Downing. He's already managed to get an advance from the executors, moved into Kilpatrick's home and made himself quite comfortable. I rather think I'll call the meeting there, to see how Downing reacts to it."

"Good idea," Quinn said. "Let me know how it comes out."

Warner arose slowly. "I'll do that, Tony, and"—he uttered a little laugh, "if you should happen to meet the Black Bat, you might tell him what's going on." Quinn used his cane to reach Warner's side and he walked with him to the front door.

"Always hinting, aren't you, Commissioner?" he chuckled. "Pretty soon you'll be as bad as Lieutenant McGrath."

WARNER'S HAND closed around Quinn's in a firm shake.

"The Bat's methods aren't exactly criteria to hold up before members of the police department, but everyone has to admit they get results. Sometimes I even wish he were on my payroll."

For ten minutes after Warner departed, Tony Quinn sat in his study smoking a pipe. Silk bustled around. Finally Quinn gave softly spoken orders and Silk drew the shades. Quinn walked briskly over to the hidden entrance to his laboratory, opened it and stepped inside. Silk was immediately behind him. Carol and Butch were playing rummy and with a rather stupendous score in Carol's favor.

"Warner just paid me a visit," Quinn explained with a smile. "I convinced him that some of the victims should be assembled in one place. Warner hopes the Black Bat will be there—and that's what's going to happen.

"However, there is one man who should logically be next on the gang's list. I'm speaking of Dr. Hugo Norden. Like six of the other victims, he is a big game hunter and a traveler. It's the only thing that ties these men up. Therefore, I'm going to have a look at the eminent doctor and perhaps question him, if I get the chance.

"From there I'll go to Kilpatrick's home. That's where Warner is bringing those men together. There's nothing for any of you to do at the moment, but don't think I'm neglecting you. Sooner or later I'll need your help, and next time, Butch, perhaps we'll find an opportunity to let you use those hams of fists."

"I'll be waitin'," Butch declared, "and hopin'. Just say the word."

Silk got out Quinn's regalia and helped him put it on. Then the Black Bat was off once more.

He reached the vicinity of Dr. Hugo Norden's residence and decided that before he interviewed the doctor, he'd try to observe him and get a line on his characteristics. From a dark spot, the Black Bat observed Norden's silhouette pass several times the windows of one room. He drew closer until he could raise his head and peer inside. The shades were drawn, but the window he selected was open an inch and the interior could easily be observed.

Dr. Norden was a man of about fifty-five with white-edged vest, professional glasses hanging from a silken loop and a neatly trimmed Vandyke beard. Norden was a specialist with a very good practice and he was also a wealthy man. The Black Bat saw him open a desk drawer, take out an opened envelope and scan the contents rapidly as though he'd read the words several times before.

THEN NORDEN rose with determination in every movement. He walked over to the fireplace, struck a match and applied the flame to the edge of the letter. He threw it into the fireplace, and, when the flames leaped high, he placed the envelope on top of the letter. He watched them burn before he returned to his desk.

He opened another drawer, using a key to unlock it. There was a small fireproof box inside. He opened this and removed an object which the Black Bat couldn't distinguish. He thrust this into his vest pocket, walked into the hallway and put on his coat and hat. Three minutes later he was backing his car out of the garage.

The Black Bat waited until he was certain Norden wouldn't come back. Then he simply raised the already partly open window, climbed into the room and went immediately to the fireplace. One corner of the envelope hadn't completely burned and he could distinguish the postage stamp it bore. The Black Bat searched the house to guard against interruptions by servants, but he discovered that they were all out.

He drew his gun, walked over to the window and wrapped heavy velvet drapes around the butt of the weapon. With one blow he shattered the pane. Working fast, he extricated two large chunks of glass, returned to the fireplace and gently transferred the ashes onto one piece of glass. He placed the second on top of it, pressing the ashes down firmly. He tied these together.

The Black Bat returned to his laboratory. There, with Silk, Butch and Carol looking over his shoulder, he set about examining the ashes. The postage stamp was easy to make out. Silk saw it and gave a cry of astonishment.

"That's the same kind of a stamp as appeared on the package those hunchbacks took from Geoffrey Thomas' house. I'm positive of it."

"Great!" the Black Bat said. "It's from one of those small, independent states in India, Bring the stamp catalogue. We'll check it quickly now."

They pored through the fat volume. Silk's finger pointed to a stamp. "That's it!"

"State of Bahawal," the Black Bat said slowly. "In India. We've got something here. I paid especial attention to the trophies some of the victims brought back from their hunting expeditions. Each one must have visited India and the regions near Bahawal because they shot animals native to that section. The link holds. We were right!

"Unless this is pure coincidence, the other victims of the gang were nothing but blinds, to give the impression that no one clique of people were involved as victims."

"But what are they after?" Carol asked. "And why should they murder one man, torture and murder another, and then not harm the rest of them? If they have something the gang wants, all of them should have been killed, not just Hollis and Kilpatrick."

"I've thought of that, too," the Black Bat admitted slowly. "It puzzles me, but there's an answer somewhere. There has to be! Perhaps I'll find it when I question the men Warner is assembling. That's our next move and I'm on my way."

"How about us?" Butch asked. "Don't we get to do nothin'?"

"Have patience. Before tonight is over, you'll probably enjoy pushing in a few faces. For the present it's a one man job."

CHAPTER XIV

THE VANISHED MEN

U **PON THE** stroke of eleven, Police Commissioner Warner arrived at the home of the late Robert Kilpatrick with his police chauffeur. The heir and new owner let him in. Jim Downing wasn't particularly gracious about it.

"What's the idea of using my home for a precinct police station? Why didn't you have these men go to your office, Commissioner? I don't like it, I tell you."

"Who cares," Warner challenged, "what you like or don't like. Two men have been murdered. Almost ten homes robbed. A band of the most desperate killers I've ever known is on the loose and you refuse to coöperate. I don't mind telling you it makes your actions seem suspicious. Now take me to the others and less talk about the whole affair or the next time I see you it will be in a police station."

Downing grumbled something uncomplimentary under his breath, but he led the way to a spacious living room. Warner recognized the men seated awkwardly around the room. There was Elmer White, owner of a chain grocery company and very wealthy. Ed Johnson, a manufacturer, sucked on a cold, ragged cigar. Alex Pierce, the jeweler, regarded Commissioner Warner with open animosity. He got to his feet and cleared his throat importantly.

"So it isn't all a hoax," he said. "Now that you're here I'll tell you what I think of your methods. In the first place, I don't like detectives coming to my home and demanding that I meet you in this house. In the second place I don't...."

"Quiet," Warner barked. "I'll do the talking. There's a reason for disturbing you gentlemen. It concerns you. My duty is to prevent crime and to check it if it does get started. It's my opinion that the hunchbacked killers may pay you another visit. And next time, you'll be in the same boat with Hollis and Kilpatrick. Now will you all relax and listen to me? I've a few questions to ask."

"Ask away," Elmer White shrugged. "I'll do all I can to help."

"A very commendable attitude, Mr. White," a quiet voice spoke from the further end of the room.

All eyes turned in that direction. The Black Bat was slowly advancing toward them. He held a pair of guns. Jim Downing gave a squeal of terror, but he didn't move. The others were visibly affected by the arrival of this eerie crime fighter. Warner cleared his throat and stepped forward a pace.

"What do you want?" he demanded hotly. He had to put on an act for the benefit of this audience. "How did you know we were here?"

The Black Bat's lips curved into a smile.

"I've been watching some of you gentlemen. When I found that you were all headed for this house, I decided it might be to my advantage to put in an appearance. You, Commissioner, will kindly remove the gun from your pocket and place it very carefully on top of the mantelpiece. I shouldn't want to shoot you."

Warner obeyed docilely and then returned to the little group of astounded men. The Black Bat came closer, put one gun away and drew a straight-backed chair toward him. He straddled this and waved his automatic.

"Please make yourselves more comfortable. Answer my questions and you'll discover that by doing so, you'll be helping yourselves. First of all, Mr. White, when were you in Bahawal last?"

WHITE GAPED for a moment.

"Why, two years ago. I was a guest of the Rajah."

"So was I," Johnson interposed. "Now that I think of it, he mentioned that he knew you, Mr. White. Then"—Johnson's face lighted up—"you must have received news from the Rajah lately. Wait! I'm beginning to see things more clearly. Hollis and Kilpatrick also know the Rajah. There are a couple of other local men who were his guests, too. Mr. White, have you heard from the Rajah?"

White answered tensely. "Yes—yes I have. Three days ago. A package came, containing a small statuette of some god of India. A letter followed. The Rajah asked me to keep the statuette for him, that he'd be in the United States soon and he'd explain everything."

"Exactly what happened to me," Johnson said excitedly. "My package contained a tiny temple in which incense is burned."

"Wait," the Black Bat broke in. "Before you go any further, let me ask this. Were those two objects among the bric-a-brac stolen by the hunchbacked men?"

"Yes!" White and Johnson replied simultaneously.

The man tumbled forward as a bullet crashed into him.

"I never thought much about it because the temple he sent me wasn't a particularly valuable piece of property," White went on.

The Black Bat rose. "Now think carefully, you two. While you were house guests of the Rajah, did he ever mention anything called a garland?"

"Garland?" White shot out of his chair. "What a fool I've been. Yes! Yes! The Garland! I even saw it and…."

There was a single shot, the sound of breaking glass and the horrible impact of a bullet against human flesh and bone. White spun around like a top, hit the chair with his thigh and then slumped to the floor.

There was an ugly bullet hole through his skull. White had never known what hit him.

The Black Bat's second gun appeared as if by magic. Both weapons blared twice, aimed directly at the window through which the murder shot had been fired. Then hell broke loose. Windows were caved in. Doors opened and a horde of hunchbacked men invaded the house. The Black Bat's gun came down, fired and the electric light switch across the room was smashed by the slug. The house was plunged into complete darkness.

"Duck!" the Black Bat yelled. "Everybody down—out of range."

He whirled toward the living room door and pumped a couple of shots toward it. The flashes of his gun gave away his location and he had to move fast after he pulled the trigger. The hunchbacked men were shooting back and some of their slugs came unhealthily close. Warner had made a leap toward the mantelpiece and his gun at the instant the light winked out. His weapon went into action also, but there were too many of the killers.

Edward Johnson, cowering behind a big chair, felt a light touch on his shoulder. Before he could yell in horror and surprise, the Black Bat's voice whispered an order.

"Watch the window directly in front of you. When I open it, run across the room and dive through. Dive, do you hear? If you attempt to crawl through, they'll kill you. Alex Pierce made it. So can you! Ready?"

"R-ready," Johnson whispered.

THE BLACK BAT stepped away a few paces. He saw in the darkness clearly and counted eight hunchbacked killers. There would be more outside, but with Elmer White dead and Alex Pierce safely out of the house, their only objective could now be Johnson. Jim Downing couldn't possibly know very much about the case.

The Black Bat fired point-blank at two of the killers. He also noticed that they traveled always in pairs. He broke up one team, for his aim was true. As they began shooting in the direction of his gun flares, the Black Bat leaped toward the window he had indicated to Johnson.

He slid it wide and pulled the curtains aside. Then he pumped a couple of more bullets in the general direction of the killers. Johnson caught his signal, held his head low and went streaking across the room. He launched himself through the air and sailed through the window in a perfect dive. No shots came from outside and the Black Bat breathed again in relief.

Warner had emptied his gun and was frantically trying to reload it. There was no sign of Jim Downing. The Black Bat's weapons only held a couple of more bullets apiece and he knew better than to stand and fight it out with his enemy outnumbering him so tremendously. He reached Warner's side. "The window! I'll hold them back." Warner nodded and made his way to safety. The Black Bat held his two guns rigidly beside his hips. Four of the killers were trying to penetrate the darkness at the far end of the room. Two were on the floor, groaning in pain. Two others guarded the door.

The Black Bat launched a violent attack at these latter two. He blazed them aside with lead, slammed an empty gun against the face of the one nearest him and streaked into the hallway. He reached the front door, opened it and slammed it shut again.

But he didn't go out. Instead he went racing lightly up the stairs to the second floor. He took refuge in one of the bedrooms, ran over to the window and looked out.

He muttered a low curse and hastily reloaded his guns. Two more of the hunchbacks were standing near the garage and a third man had his back against that small building, with his hands stretched high. The Black Bat recognized him as clearly as though the sun shone on him. It was Lieutenant McGrath and he was at the mercy of those men.

The Black Bat raised a window gently, slid out to a slanting roof over the back porch. He whizzed down the incline, off it, and landed lightly on the grass. He was up in a second. The two men who held McGrath at bay, whirled on him.

The Black Bat's guns blazed as fast as he could pull the trigger. One of the killers doubled up. The other gave a shriek of terror and raced away into the night. In a moment, the Bat was at McGrath's side, pressing one of his automatics into the detective's fist.

"I'm trusting you to do the right thing," he hissed. "There are half a dozen of those killers still inside. Warner is at the front. You take the north side and I'll cover the rear and the south."

"All right," McGrath agreed. "But this is only a truce. Soon as it's over, I'll stick you up with your own gun. You're no better than those hunchbacked murderers inside."

The Black Bat thumped him on the back so hard that McGrath almost lost his balance. As they took their stations, four of the killers emerged from the house to look for the Black Bat. They split in pairs, as usual. But then, the Black Bat saw an amazing thing happen.

ALL FOUR of them stopped suddenly and remained transfixed for a moment. Then, as one man, they rushed back to the house. The Black Bat waited five minutes and no sound came from within. Warner prowled toward the rear of the house and McGrath came from the other direction.

"What the devil happened?" McGrath growled. "They went back inside. I think we ought to go after them."

"Wait," Warner ordered crisply. "There's help coming. A radio car crew heard the shots and I sent them for more men. Here they are now. This is one time the crooks pulled a boner. We've got the place surrounded. I'm giving orders that no man is to try and stop you, Bat. Just for this one time, mind. I could drop handcuffs on your wrists right now if I chose, but you did save my life at the risk of your own."

They headed for the house. A score of patrolmen responded to the alarm and they all closed in. McGrath and Warner opened the front door, guns ready. Eight men entered behind them. They searched warily, but in vain. After half an hour they gave up. There wasn't a soul in the house except themselves. Even the dead and wounded crooks were gone.

"How could it happen?" McGrath raged. "And where's the Black Bat?"

"And how did you happen to come here?" Warner parried. "I didn't give you orders to follow me."

McGrath looked a little sheepish, but he defended himself stoutly.

"I figured maybe the Black Bat would show up. Anyway, you've got to admit I used my head. That is, until two of those devils shoved guns under my nose. Know what they intended to do? Shake me down, riddle me with lead—until the Bat showed up."

"They got away, somehow," Warner groaned. "Nothing more we can do here. Four of you men go to Edward Johnson's house and guard him. He got clear. Anybody seen Jim Downing?"

Nobody had. While the police cars left the scene and patrolmen dispersed the crowd that had assembled outside the house, Lieutenant McGrath went prowling again. He was forced to work in darkness for the lights were still out and the two hunchbacks who had captured him had taken his flashlight.

A hand tapped him on the shoulder. He swiveled around, gun extended. He could see no one. Then, steely fingers closed around his gun wrist and the weapon was taken from him.

"It's only me," the Black Bat's voice announced. "I happen to need that gun, Lieutenant, and you might decide to call the truce off, now that the killers have escaped."

McGrath's chin stuck out.

"Okay, the truce is off. I know you saved my life, but that's neither here nor there."

"Most unappreciative," the Black Bat laughed quietly. "Now I'm afraid we're finished here. I can tell you this—watch Edward Johnson. They may try to kill him next, or Alex Pierce. And look for Jim Downing. He vanished as completely as the crooks."

There was a swishing sound near an open window. McGrath headed for a more orthodox exit, the front door. Two minutes later, he was driving off. But McGrath had been skillfully duped. The Black Bat was still in the house and well hidden behind the thick drapes hanging on each side of the window.

The hunchbacked killers had tricked Warner and McGrath, but the Black Bat didn't give up so easily.

When six or eight men went into a house, they had to come out again and detection was certain if they tried to escape. Therefore, they must still be here. The only answer was a secret room of some kind. Had Jim Downing known of it and taken refuge there, too?

CHAPTER XV

ESCAPE FROM DOOM

FOR A period of ten minutes the Black Bat maintained his vigil with every sense attuned for the first signs of the killers. Now, at least, he had some semblance of an idea as to what they were after. A mysterious garland, the property of a wealthy Nabob of India. The Black Bat knew the fabulous fortunes some of these potentates wrapped up in some small articles which particularly suited their fancy. He quietly reloaded both his pistols as he waited.

Then he heard soft footsteps on the floor above. Someone was coming down the stairs on a mission of surveillance. It was one of the hunchbacked killers with a gun in his hand. He searched the first floor, peered through the windows.

Then the others came. There were seven of them on their feet. One was carried between two of his companions. Another walked with a limp and was obviously in great pain. Now the Black Bat could distinguish the leader by his size and shape. He was pudgy and not very tall, but he walked with the grace of a panther.

The leader stepped aside at the back door and watched his men file out to vanish in the darkness. He stopped the last man.

"Back upstairs and be sure that secret door is closed tight. We may have to use it again some day. I'll meet you outside."

The last man hurried back. Before he was at the top of the stairs the Black Bat was after him. He watched the hunchback enter a normal looking bedroom, proceed directly to a blank wall and touch a hidden spring. A narrow slit in the wall slid back. The killer seemed satisfied as he reclosed the door. He turned around to hurry back to the others, but he didn't get far. A figure, as eerie as his own weird form, stood before him.

"Take off that outfit," the Black Bat ordered in a whisper. "Don't make any noise and no stalling, or I'll shoot." The hunchback shivered and obeyed promptly. The Black Bat opened the secret room, forced his prisoner inside and tied him up securely.

"I'll let the police know you're here," he comforted the man. "No danger of your starving to death. Thanks for the outfit, and pleasant dreams."

He closed the door, removed his cape and stuffed it under his clothing. Then he drew on the disguise of the killer, fastened the false hump in place and pulled down the broad-brimmed hat to conceal his hood. He wrapped the black scarf around the lower part of his face and then hurried to the first floor.

"Took you long enough," the hunchbacked leader snarled. "Come on. The boys dug up a couple of hot cars. They're waiting."

The Black Bat followed the leader, got into a sleek, fast-looking sedan and they rolled away. There were three others of the disguised killers in the car. No one spoke. The driver headed downtown, carefully avoiding the busier streets. The man who sat beside him held a sub-machine gun across his lap and kept his eyes peeled for trouble.

HOWEVER, THERE were no mishaps and the car turned into a modern, well equipped garage. The doors closed behind it and the sedan went into low to negotiate the climb up the winding, steep ramp. It came to a stop on the top floor and everyone piled out. A man, garbed as a mechanic, stood by examining the sedan.

"Wait half an hour," the leader snapped. "Then have one of the boys roll her into the river."

The Black Bat kept to the rear as much as possible and he was already laying out his plans for a fast escape in the event of trouble. He was in a dangerous situation. Capture now would inevitably mean unmasking, being identified as Tony Quinn, ex-district attorney—and then death.

He followed the others into a spacious room fitted up with makeshift furniture. There were two doors leading off it. The wounded men were already taken away, probably to some gangster physician. The Black Bat counted fourteen of the hunchbacked killers assembled here. The very size of this mob indicated that the loot would run well into the millions, because these men would have to be well paid even after the mysterious figurehead who guided them had his huge slice.

The leader took the center of the floor. No one unmasked, no one spoke a word.

"Well boys," the leader said, "we rubbed out White just in time. Too bad we didn't get the Black Bat, but this time White was most important. He was all ready to spill the dope. We now have five of the articles. We know where the sixth is located—unless the man I put on Dr. Norden's trial has slipped.

"Before morning, we'll have the last one and then you get your cut. We break up and the job is finished. There can't be any failure, because you men have been carefully chosen and you do not know one another. It is impossible for anyone to squeal.

"Now, for the details of our last job. It's a ticklish one, but it must be done. By this time tomorrow we'll have disbanded. Each one of you will have more money than you've ever seen in your lives before. We have until two A.M. to get the job finished, so listen closely."

The Black Bat held his breath. It was coming now. In half a minute he'd know everything with which this bizarre case was concerned.

But the leader didn't start talking again. Instead, he seemed to have gone into a trance. Suddenly, he turned on his heel and walked toward one of the closed doors. He opened it and then turned around.

"I'll give the instructions individually. Line up. One at a time you'll file into this next room and get the dope."

The men obediently got into line. The Black Bat found himself near the tail end. They filed in, singly and spent about one minute inside before one of their number opened the door to summon the next man. The Black Bat's heart was pounding. There was an idea growing within his brain that all this was being done because the leader suspected a spy might be in their midst. Someone might have noticed that the Bat hadn't left Downing's house. This fact was further confirmed when two of the garage mechanics came into the large room and stood near the door with drawn weapons.

ONLY ONE man was in front of the Black Bat now and there seemed to be no escape. He had to enter that room and face the consequences. But how had that leader learned of a spy? How had word come to him and decided him on this course of action?

"Okay," one of the killers summoned the Black Bat. "Come on in, pal."

The Black Bat entered a much smaller room. The hunchbacked leader sat behind a desk. An automatic lay on top of it and his hand was within easy reach of the weapon. Two other men stood behind him, on either side. They held guns and eyed the Black Bat narrowly. A third man was directly behind him. The leader began to speak.

"I have received information that the Black Bat is among us, disguised as one of our number. I know all the men in the gang. I'm the only person who does. You'll remove your hat and scarf. When I am sure you're no spy, I'll outline our next move."

The Black Bat's hand moved up to obey, but hesitated. He turned his head and looked at the man behind him, stared at the two guards beside the leader.

"With three mugs watchin' me?" he asked. "I figured nobody except you was to know what we looked like."

"The men will turn around and I'll be the only person to see you," the leader said. "Now, let's see your face." The three guards obediently turned their backs on the Black Bat. He raised one hand toward his face, whipped off the scarf and the hat with one gesture and his other hand streaked for a gun.

The leader let out a yelp of astonishment, made a grab for the weapon on his desk and the Black Bat's gun sang a deadly song. A bullet slammed into the leader's shoulder, sending him squirming out of his chair. The guards spun around and faced a pair of guns.

"Drop your weapons," the Bat warned, "or I'll drop you. Line up against the wall. You—" he indicated a man of about his own build— "Pick up the disguise I just dropped. Put it on and walk out of here. Hurry!"

The man gulped and obeyed, hardly realizing the significance of the Black Bat's commands. He went to the door which led into the garage proper, opened it and darted out. Instantly, three men pounced upon him. As the Black Bat had hoped, that shot was heard and the guards outside were warned to expect trouble in the form of a quick getaway. The hunchbacked killers were nowhere in sight, probably escorted to some other room.

The three guards and their victim were a tangle of arms and legs on the floor. The Black Bat suddenly sprinted through the door, across the cement floor and headed straight for the stolen car in which he had ridden in on his way to the garage. As he opened the door, the guards realized their mistake. Guns opened fire. The hunchbacked leader staggered out of his private quarters and howled orders.

The Black Bat slid behind the wheel. There was no time to start the motor, but the car was headed straight for the ramp. He released the brake and it began moving. Bullets spattered against the machine, but its windows were shatter-proofed against revolver and automatic slugs.

Then, one of the thugs raised a sub-machine gun and sighted it. The Black Bat rolled down the window and fired twice. The man with the rifle curled up and dropped the weapon.

Another man scooped it up, but he was too late. When he fired his slugs only pounded into the rear of the sedan.

THE BLACK BAT gripped the wheel with both hands now. If he tried to brake the machine in order to negotiate the sharp curves at a slower and safer rate of speed, he'd let himself wide open to the guns of men who must be planted somewhere below. The sedan was heavy and gained speed with every turn of its wheels.

Tires screeched as the Black Bat brought the machine around and pointed its nose into the next section of the ramp. His arms ached from holding the car in line. Two more stories to negotiate and then the last and most dangerous part of his escape would loom up. By now, word would surely have been flashed below and the garage doors closed.

He made the last turn, crumpling a fender badly as he did so. Then he shot out of the mouth of the ramp, across the ground floor and straight toward the big doors. There were armed men waiting for him and they opened fire, making a curtain of lead through which he had to drive.

The windshield cobwebbed until he could hardly see out of it. Then the doors grew larger and larger. The sedan was rolling at a very fast clip and it hit the doors with all its weight and speed. They crashed and the car plunged its way through.

Instantly the Black Bat's fingers found the ignition key, turned it and shoved the gear into second. The motor caught and the sedan pulled away with a roar of power.

But the Black Bat wasn't safe yet. Three cars full of crooks darted out after him. They had to open the garage doors first however, and the minute's delay gave the Black Bat an edge which he needed.

Sirens were screeching all around him. He was far more worried about encountering the police than shooting it out with the crooks. Blasting at those killers would be self-defense, but no matter what happened, he couldn't risk the life of a single officer.

A radio car swung around the corner. The Black Bat yanked the wheel of his sedan, careened crazily and avoided a head-on collision with the police car by inches. Behind him streaked the three cars loaded with crooks. The first two got by the radio car, but the last one had a driver of less skill than the others. He tried to avoid the radio car and lost control of his own machine. It climbed the curb, struck the side of a building and before the four men it contained could get out, the radio patrolmen had them covered.

The Black Bat was heading for the suburbs. He flashed along a side street, turned sharply into an avenue and pushed his foot down level with the floorboards. There was a steep hill to negotiate. Halfway up, he lost speed, but so did the pursuing cars. The Black Bat rounded the top of the grade and an even steeper hill loomed up.

Then he opened the door beside him. He clambered out on the running board, made sure the cars loaded with the hunchback killers were still out of sight and then he gave the wheel a mighty tug. The car rocked wildly, headed straight for the soft shoulders and, at that instant, the Black Bat jumped off. He landed lightly, rolled over a couple of times and then darted for the cover of underbrush.

HE SAW the two cars come racing down the steep hill. Brakes squealed when the drivers spotted the stalled car, but they were traveling too fast to make a quick stop. There they turned around and came back as fast as possible.

The two cars were parked about twenty feet from where the Black Bat lay hidden. Everyone in them jumped out to rush across the highway and into the darkness of the marshy land beside the road. All were eager to be the first to drag out what was left of the Black Bat and unmask him. They played right into the Black Bat's hands.

There was a daring plan in his mind. He moved quietly toward the two cars. He took the keys from the ignition switch of one and hurled them far into the night. Then, to make doubly sure he wouldn't be pursued again, he raised the hood and dismantled the distributor by wrenching wires loose. Next, he stealthily crept toward the second car, opened the door very quietly and got behind the wheel.

He stepped on the starter, put the car into second and turned around in the middle of the hill. He gave her the gun and the sedan roared away. On the seat, he found one of the black hats and a scarf.

The men who had pursued him were not the hunchbacks. Apparently they were reserved for the more important business of robbery and murder. Ordinary riff-raff among the gang world was recruited for the necessary strong-arm work.

The only hunchback who had accompanied the chase was the squat leader. The Black Bat knew now that this man was nothing more than a lieutenant, working under the orders of some mysterious higher up. He had removed his hat and scarf so he'd be less conspicuous.

At the base of the hill, the Black Bat turned east and headed straight back to town. He still had the floppy brimmed hat and the black scarf affected by the hunchbacks and the false deformation of the hunch was still in place on his own spine.

CHAPTER XVI

A SECRET FROM BAHAWAL

HE REACHED the same garage which had so nearly proved a death trap. Now came the most difficult part of his plan. He was depending on the fact that the real hunchbacked leader was too far away from a phone or a ride back to town to make contact with his men. The Black Bat had chosen the place to wreck his car very carefully.

He drove into the garage. Half a dozen mechanics swarmed around the car. The Black Bat didn't get out. He couldn't risk that because the real leader of the mob was shorter and stockier than the Black Bat's tall, lean frame.

"Did you nail him, boss?" one of the men asked eagerly.

"He escaped into the woods," the Black Bat gave a fairly good imitation of the leader's voice. "I left the others to search for him. Summon the men here at once. You're sure no police are nearby?"

The mechanic laughed.

"Naw! We told 'em it was a gang fight. They think this garage is on the up-and-up. I'll have the boys down here pronto, boss."

The hunchbacked killers assembled on the ground floor. They were out of sight of the street and if anyone should happen to drive in unexpectedly, two vast trucks would conceal the men.

"You all have your instructions," the Black Bat said, still imitating the leader's voice as best he could. The men were on edge and excited. They noticed no change in the tone. "Some of you may not have received the new orders because the appearance of the Black Bat broke up our meeting. Those of you who do know them will acquaint the others with all the information necessary. We strike at once. There isn't a moment to lose. Get going!"

The men split into groups and filled three cars. These rolled out of the garage about three minutes apart but the Black Bat, in the last car, followed close on the heels of the one before him.

He hadn't the vaguest notion as to where they were headed. He did notice that the three cars took different routes to avoid attracting any attention, but he hung onto the tail of the one he had chosen to lead him. They proceeded downtown.

Suddenly the car he followed slowed. Then the car turned into a driveway between two towering buildings. The Black Bat rolled in right behind it. The other two cars were there waiting. Four of the hunchback killers had already been dispersed to places of vantage from which they could keep a sharp watch.

"Get it over with," the Black Bat snapped at the men who approached him. "I won't be able to help you much. Wrenched my ankle chasing that damned Black Bat. Hurry!"

They nodded and he saw them quietly scale a fence. His eyes scanned the building on the other side of it and his uncanny sight enabled him to read the rather faded letters on a sign fastened high up above the rear entrance.

"Security Bank," he whistled softly. "It remains open until midnight. Dr. Norden had plenty of time to reach it. Now I know what that leader meant when he said he knew where the last article was. Norden put something in that bank and these men are going after it."

THE BLACK BAT blinked the parking lights on his car. One of the guards came running over to him.

"Follow the others," the Black Bat ordered. "Tell them not to forget that this job must be done quietly, and there is to be no killing. We don't want the cops on our heels now, when everything is practically finished. Beat it!"

The weird-looking figure with its hunched spine sped away. Minutes passed and the Black Bat realized that with the passing of time his danger grew by leaps and bounds. The real leader was bound to contact the garage as soon as he could. Once he was told that an imposter had led his men out on this job, he'd rush straight down to the bank.

Then the vanguard of the hunchbacked crooks came swarming over the fence. One of them rushed straight up to where the Black Bat sat in his car.

"A pipe, boss," he gloated. "We had the joint cased right. We just busted in without setting off any alarms, conked the watchman on the head and blasted open the safe deposit box. A sweet job if I say so."

"Well, did you get what you went after?" the Black Bat snapped. "Hand it over. I haven't got all night. The sooner I place this article in the proper hands, the faster we collect our dough."

The hunchback shoved his hand into his pocket, brought out a cotton-wrapped object and placed it in the Black Bat's proffered hand.

"There she is, boss. When do we meet for the big cut? Boy, we sure pulled off these jobs neat. Not even the Black Bat stopped us."

The Black Bat didn't examine the cotton-wrapped object. He merely shoved it into his pocket, shifted into reverse and began backing up preparatory to negotiating the driveway. The thugs watched him and the Black Bat had an idea they were somewhat suspicious of his actions.

He had to back far around. Once, he thought he felt the rear door of the car open and close, but he glanced over his shoulder and saw nothing. He decided it was just a case of nerves.

One of the hunchbacks waved both hands to bring the Black Bat's car to a stop. He looked at the Black Bat with a queer light gleaming in his eyes. "You sure everything is okay, boss? There ain't been no slip-ups?"

The Black Bat shook his head, extended his hand and the thug, in a surprised manner, shook hands with him.

"Everything is perfect," the Black Bat said. "You'll hear from me by the usual channels."

He started the car slowly. Once he hit the street, he'll be safe. Until then he must not give away the trick by undue haste. Then he heard a shout of rage.

"That's the Black Bat," one of the men yelled. "It's the Bat! Get him!"

He tramped hard on the accelerator, turned into the street and gave her the gun. By the time the thugs reached their own cars and got under way, the Black Bat had completely vanished.

"Now how in the world did they know it was the Black Bat?" he asked himself with a puzzled frown. "The real leader didn't show up, not even a messenger."

BUT HE was safe now and for once the victor over this murder mob. When he was well out of town, he pulled off the road, stopped and brought out the cotton-wrapped object. He exposed the largest diamond he'd ever seen. It sparkled like a living thing in his hand.

The Black Bat gave a sharp ejaculation of surprise. He'd expected something like this, but not a diamond so large. He doubted if it could be surpassed by more than two or three gems in the world.

He studied the design of the gem again and counted the sharp points raised in the cutting. There were seven. That number was significant in the ideology of the gods of distant India. *Siva* was supposed to have seven heads. It was very possible that this gem had been cut in this peculiar fashion to honor this goddess of death and destruction in whom every believer paid homage.

The Black Bat relaxed against the cushions of the car, trying to think back and associate this gigantic gem with other facts. Then he stiffened and broke out in a cold sweat. The point of a knife was resting firmly against his neck.

"You will not move," an accented voice warned. "Simply reach back and hand me the diamond. You are an exceedingly clever man and I admit that only sheer good fortune guided me to that bank.

"I knew the estimable Dr. Norden had placed the gem in a safe deposit vault there and I realized the thieves would attempt to gain possession of it as quickly as possible. I was hidden beneath a platform and when you backed close by it, I slipped into the car most quietly."

The Black Bat didn't make the mistake of reaching for his guns. That knife was too firm. When he spoke, his voice was quite calm.

"It seems that you win. You are not one of that murder mob because if you were, the knife would have slit my throat minutes ago. I am very curious. If I give you my word that I shall not resort to violence, will you come around into the front seat? I like to see people with whom I do business."

The man in the tonneau hesitated a moment and then he laughed softly.

"I have heard that you keep your word so we shall declare an armistice, eh? But do not misjudge me. I hold a gun, with the hammer cocked and my finger on the trigger quite firmly. I suggest you place your hands on the wheel and keep them there."

A short, dark-featured little man got into the front seat. His face was the color of bronze and he displayed a row of perfectly white teeth in a wide grin. Then he held out his hand for the diamond. The Black Bat sighed deeply and dropped the gem into the mystery man's palm.

"I owe you an apology," his visitor smiled again. "You see, I was the one who dragged you out of that gas-filled house. You were quite un-conscious and—I meant to have a look at your features. I am sorry for that. I would never have forgiven myself."

"Nor would I have forgiven you, Rajah," the Black Bat inclined his head.

THE LITTLE man gasped.

"Then you—know?"

"I know. You are the Rajah of Bahawal. This diamond belongs to you. I am returning it willingly and you have my promise that the rest of the gems will be in your hands as quickly as I can get them. Now I'd be interested in learning the whole story."

The Rajah stuffed his gun into his pocket and his smile was wider than ever.

"Even in far off Bahawal I had heard of the Black Bat and envied the life he led. Yet the stones are mine. There are seven of them. Two diamonds, two of the largest black pearls ever brought up, two emeralds and a ruby. Singly they are worth a quarter of a million apiece, amounting to a million and a half in all. Together, properly assembled into the garland of *Siva,* they are worth three times that figure.

"My little country has been wavering on the brink of rebellion for months. Spies brought me news that violence was ripe. I am one of the wealthiest men in the world, but I am a strange ruler, too. It is my idea that much of my wealth belongs to the State of Bahawal. All except this necklace which was purchased with my personal income.

"To let it get into the hands of revolutionists would have broken my heart. Therefore I separated the gems and concealed them in apparently worthless bric-a-brac. These articles I mailed to friends in the United States."

The Black Bat turned slightly and faced the Rajah.

"You sent them to Grant Hollis, Robert Kilpatrick, Elmer White, Ed Johnson, Geoffrey Thomas, Dr. Hugo Norden and Alex Pierce. These men were all friends of yours, and had been your guests on hunting expeditions in India. You trusted them, but in order not to place their lives in jeopardy, you concealed the gems so that they wouldn't know the real worth of the articles you sent."

"Exactly," the Rajah nodded. "I wrote each man a letter indicating that I would consider it a favor if those worthless little objects were safely held for me until I called for them in person.

"When I reached the United States, the hunchbacked killers were already in action and it was too late for me to rescue any of the gems. I tried to contact some of the men but they weren't in. Dr. Norden was the only one left who hadn't been robbed, so I was on the lookout for this raid. I could not go to the police because of the publicity. I fled my land, and the usurper of my throne has sent spies to kill me. I could do nothing to help."

For a full minute, the Black Bat said nothing. His mind worked furiously and cleared up several important points.

"Hollis and Kilpatrick were murdered," he said slowly. "None of the others suffered that fate. I've wondered why and now I know. Hollis and Kilpatrick must have accidentally discovered that those objects contained the gems. Somehow the man behind this murder and robbery knew it.

"He had to kill them or the whole game would have been given away. His men robbed the others and the theft of those pieces of bric-a-brac looked merely accidental—as if the thieves hoped they'd bring some revenue. Elmer White guessed what was up when I mentioned the 'garland.' He was murdered before he could talk. Rajah, have you the least idea as to who might have hired those killers?"

"None," the Rajah declared with a groan. "I have tried very hard to figure it out. There is only Mr. Johnson, Mr. Thomas, Mr. Pierce and Dr. Norden left. Thomas never even saw the article I sent him for he has been away for weeks."

"Did you ever hear of an attorney named Fenner, or of Kilpatrick's cousin, James Downing?"

"I have never heard the names before," the Rajah answered promptly. "It may interest you to know that I managed to take considerable money with me. I am willing to offer half a million dollars reward for the return of all the gems."

"Sorry," the Black Bat said slowly. "I don't work for a reward. Breaking up this mob, convicting those behind them, and exacting judgment for the murders they have committed is reward enough for me. The diamond is quite safe with you, Rajah. No one realizes you are in this country. My advice is to keep under cover. Where can I contact you?"

"At the Netherlands Hotel. Under the name of Raj Hanan. If I can be of any help...."

"Drive this car back to town. I'll tell you where to drop me. Then get rid of the car as quickly as possible. Do nothing else until you hear from me."

CHAPTER XVII

EDUCATED FINGERS

NOT LONG after the Rajah dropped him off, the Black Bat was in the privacy of his laboratory. Silk, Butch and Carol listened to his revelations with great interest.

"So six of the gems are in the hands of whoever planned this series of crimes and murders. Without the seventh stone, our mysterious bandit cannot cash in on the full value of the garland. He will go to all ends to get this stone back.

"While he interests himself in this manner, we'll have to concentrate on getting from him, the six other gems. I have theories and ideas, yet none are concrete. I shall need your help from now on and it's going to be a risky business."

"Then you know who is behind it all?" Carol asked tensely.

"No, my dear," Tony Quinn answered. "I have only suspicions and they point in several directions. Our list of suspects includes Edward Johnson and Dr. Norden, and Alex Pierce, all of whom received stones. Then there is Attorney Jay Fenner, a man I wouldn't trust with a one-dollar Confederate piece of currency. He knows crooks and could assemble a dangerous mob, exactly the type of which the hunchbacked killers are composed.

"Lastly, we have Jim Downing. He was in an undue hurry to move into his cousin's home. There is a possibility that he knew about a certain secret room in that house which the hunchbacks used as a hiding place to get clear of the police. Downing vanished rather mysteriously when the shooting began."

Carol's hand rested lightly on Tony Quinn's arm.

"This Rajah, Tony. You are quite certain he couldn't have hired these men to get his gems back? Perhaps he discovered that Hollis and Kilpatrick had uncovered the real worth of the articles he sent to them. Perhaps they refused to give them up, and he killed them for it."

Tony Quinn pressed both hands against his temples.

"Almost anything is possible. The Rajah is smooth, all right. But talking will get us nowhere. Silk, I want you to go to the Netherlands

Hotel and watch the Rajah. Better fix yourself up in that disguise which makes you look like a polished banker. Try to get the next suite to the Rajah. He's registered under the name of Raj Hanan. Keep your eye on him."

"Do I get something to do?" Butch queried petulantly.

"You watch Attorney Fenner. Never let him out of your sight. Carol, Alex Pierce is your assignment. Watch his house. Take your car and park nearby. We'll be out of contact with one another temporarily because I'll be busy, too, later on. We have just a short time before morning. Report back here at six o'clock. Now, on your way."

Silk went immediately to his room, dusted off an expensive suit of clothes which had paid him dividends in those days when he lived by his wits.

When he finished and drew on his clothes, he looked exactly like a typical banker. Pompous, stern and gray-haired. A white-edged vest and ribboned glasses added to the picture. He drew on a black Homburg, surveyed himself in the mirror and nodded in satisfaction.

THEN HE slipped out of the house, walked to the next corner and took a cab. He was driven to a section where stores remained open all night. There he purchased two used suitcases and some second-hand clothing. He filled the suitcases and noted with satisfaction that they were plastered with labels of foreign countries.

He registered under an assumed name, hemmed and hawed at the desk until he had a chance to learn the number of the Rajah's suite and then began making a nuisance of himself by rejecting the quarters offered to him until finally he was deposited in the suite next to the Rajah's.

Silk lost no time in getting into action. He was an old hand at this sort of thing. He opened the window and slipped out on the ten-inch ledge which circled the building far above the ground. Slowly he moved over toward the windows of the Rajah's suite. He reached the window, secured a grip on the frame and took a quick look inside.

The Rajah was just replacing the phone in its cradle and there was a grimace of quandary on his dark face. He seemed to be waiting for someone. Silk had never seen Jim Downing, but he had a good description of him and the man who finally entered the room was certainly the strange-acting cousin and heir of Robert Kilpatrick.

Downing accepted a chair and began talking. Silk gave the lower sash a gentle push upward and opened the window half an inch. He could hear Downing speak now.

"…and therefore I feel that I should be rewarded for my work. You can readily realize that I've risked my life to get this gem back for you."

"Indeed I can," the Rajah agreed. "Of course, you have the stone with you. After I am very certain there can be no mistake I shall be quite willing to talk business."

Downing smiled, reached into his pocket and produced a small leather pouch. He opened it and spilled a flashing stone into the palm of his hand. The Rajah reached for it. Instantly Downing pulled the stone away. He whipped a gun out of his pocket.

"Now you can handle the stone," he smiled coldly. "Not that I don't trust you, Your Excellency, but I can't quite forget the danger I put around myself to get this gem. Have a look, satisfy yourself it's genuine and then—talk business."

The Rajah shrugged, paid no attention to the gun and held the diamond in the light. He asked if he might use a jeweler's glass on it and Downing acquiesced. The Rajah had a glass in his pocket. Downing's finger tightened on the trigger of his gun as the Rajah reached for it. Then he relaxed and the potentate from far away India studied the gem intently. He handed it back with a slight bow.

"Congratulations. This is the real stone. I am willing to pay you fifty thousand dollars for its return. I shall not even ask your identity."

"It's a deal," Downing answered quickly. "Hand me the dough and you get the rock."

The Rajah spread his hands in an eloquent gesture.

"But it is three o'clock in the morning and you cannot expect me to carry such a sum on my person. Tomorrow, at nine-thirty I shall have it. You may meet me here."

SILK DIDN'T wait to hear any more. When Downing arrived at the elevators, he found an important looking man also standing waiting there. Downing nodded affably for he was in high humor. They rode down together, walked across the lobby and Downing stepped into one section of the revolving doors. Unexpectedly he discovered he had company. The wealthy, portly looking man was crammed into the small space also.

"I'm terribly sorry," this man said. "Big deal on in the morning. Couldn't sleep. Can't even think, I guess. That's why I didn't look at what I was doing. Money, my boy, can divert the human mind more than alcohol."

Half a minute later, Silk was in a taxi. He held a five-dollar bill under the driver's nose.

"I've got to make a train. Five minutes is all the time I have. This is yours if you reach the station."

In the darkness of the tonneau Silk was grinning. In the palm of one hand lay the shimmering diamond which had been in Jim Downing's pocket only a few minutes before. Silk entered the railroad station by one door, emerged through another and changed cabs twice again before he reached the vicinity of Tony Quinn's home. He found Tony Quinn, in his role of a blind man, sitting in his usual chair before the fireplace.

Silk drew himself up, lifted Quinn's hand and deposited the stone in his palm.

"Easy work, sir. A positive cinch. Jim Downing probably hasn't missed this stone yet. How did I land it? With my educated fingers, sir."

"Jim Downing?" Quinn asked with a frown. "Did he have this stone?"

"Offered to turn it over to the Rajah for fifty thousand dollars, sir. Looks as if the case has been broken wide open. Downing knows the stones may become very hot before he can get rid of them so he's posing as a private investigator and 'recovering' the gems one by one and selling them back to the Rajah."

Tony Quinn shifted the diamond from one hand to the other.

"It's real because the Rajah would have detected a phony in half a minute. This throws my case off balance, Silk. It blows the whole works into little pieces. Downing profited by his cousin's death and he is un-questionably a rat, but—he came into a considerable fortune from Kilpatrick's estate. His motivation isn't strong enough."

Silk began counting in his fingers.

"Seven stones, sir, at fifty thousand dollars each runs into a consider-able fortune. Downing may have inherited wealth, but you can't tell me he'd turn his nose up at a sum like that. He's just profiting two ways—by killing his cousin to inherit, and getting these stones to sell back to the Rajah. What else can it be?"

Quinn's fingers closed around the stone and he looked steadily into space. Silk was venturing a rather concrete case. Of all the suspects, Downing was the most typical man whose characteristics would run to robbery and violence if the reward was large enough.

Then the phone rang, startling both men. Silk answered it and sum-moned Quinn.

"It's Butch and he sounds very excited, sir."

CHAPTER XVIII

McGRATH GETS
A PRESENT

MORE THAN impatient at the none-too-exciting assignment which the Black Bat gave him, Butch made his way to Attorney Fenner's house. His disgust was supreme when he discovered the place shrouded in darkness. But he secured a dark spot in which to conceal himself and took up the vigil.

He waited only a matter of an hour before things began to happen. A car pulled up with squealing brakes and a young man jumped out, raced up the path to Fenner's porch and pressed the doorbell incessantly. Lights were turned on and, from his hiding place, Butch saw Fenner open the door. The light from the hallway illuminated the caller and Butch's lower jaw stuck out aggressively. The visitor could be none other than Jim Downing.

He was excited and worried. He kept looking over his shoulder as he stepped into the house. Fenner closed the door and Butch followed the movements of the two men by watching the drawn window shades.

They went immediately to a room on the side of the house facing Butch. He began crawling forward very carefully. He was crouched beneath the window when he gave a soft gasp and beat a hasty retreat.

For a bare fraction of a second, he had caught a glimpse of an eerie form flitting through the darkness. The hunchbacked killers had arrived!

Butch's big hands curled into mighty fists. This was rapidly becoming a situation to his liking. Once, one of the hunchbacks passed within ten feet of him, but Butch didn't stir. He wanted to find out what these men sought here. Was it Downing or Fenner? Were they on the prowl, or was this house their headquarters?

Butch couldn't figure it out, but he decided he'd better do something about it. His memory flashed back to the hours during which these men had held him prisoner.

Apparently the hunchbacked men weren't intent on raiding the house yet. They seemed to have vanished completely. Then Butch spotted one of them slipping toward the same window under which he had crouched.

The figure raised his head slightly, took a quick look inside and then returned to the darkness where his friends were concealed.

Butch began wriggling forward, his goal a certain lilac bush close by the path from Fenner's estate. He reached it and lay prone, waiting and hoping. Finally Fenner opened the door of his house and Jim Downing emerged. He muttered a good night and went down the steps.

Downing walked rapidly toward the street. Then, suddenly, two of the hunchbacked men rose up out of the darkness and fell into step with him. Downing made no sound and Butch couldn't see the expression on his face. By his silence, Butch guessed that Downing hadn't been particularly surprised.

There were two cars parked at the curb. Downing climbed into one of them. Four other hunchbacked men arose from the gloom and hurried toward the cars. One lagged behind a bit. He was in plain sight one moment and the next he had vanished as completely as if the night had swallowed him up.

THE OTHERS missed him, started back to search, but a sharp command from one of the cars called it off.

"Let him get away himself," someone growled. "The orders were to stay near the exit."

Both cars drove off. Butch arose carefully. So did another figure, but not of its own will. Butch had a stranglehold on the man's neck, preventing any possibility of an outcry.

Butch held his man by the throat, a foot off the ground, and regarded him thoughtfully. It was one of the hunchbacked killers.

"Remember me, pal?" Butch asked with a wide grin. "Now listen, I'm puttin' you down, but if you make one peep, I'll push your nose outa the back of your neck."

Butch set his prisoner down, but the man's legs had turned to rubber and he wilted like a tired balloon. A hoarse, low cry came from his throat and his eyes glazed. Butch snorted in contempt, hoisted the man to one shoulder and headed away from the house.

When he reached the street, he stopped to consider things. He couldn't very well walk along with an unconscious hunchback draped over one shoulder. Butch's methods were primitive, but highly effective. He merely picked the man up, held him at arm's length and drove a hard right to the chin.

"That'll hold you for a little while," he snickered.

Butch pulled his clothes into some semblance of order, stepped out on the sidewalk and strolled nonchalantly away. He needed a telephone and he recalled that a drugstore about three blocks north had been open when he passed it an hour before. It was still open. He made sure he was unobserved, stepped into the phone booth and called Tony Quinn's home.

"Yeah," he chortled. "Sure it's one of them boobs. How could I be wrong? He's got a hump on his back and I just hung another hump on his chin. What'll I do with him?"

"Hold him right there. I'll be over," Quinn promised. "Be careful that Fenner doesn't spot you and watch out for the rest of the mob."

Butch was sitting on the stomach of his prisoner when the almost invisible form of the Black Bat suddenly appeared.

"Nice work," the Black Bat said. "I need this man. He's unconscious yet, eh? If things work out, you'll have those knuckles of yours in splints before morning. Silk is in a car at the next corner. Join him and wait for orders."

AS BUTCH slipped away, the Black Bat knelt beside the prisoner and quickly peeled off his outer clothing. He exposed the fake hump attached to his spine—and something else that made the Bat's lips come together in a tight line. He shook the man hard and awakened him. The killer opened his eyes, oriented his senses and then caught a glimpse of the Black Bat's hooded head and his ribbed cape. He gave a little sigh and fainted.

"Odd," the Black Bat thought, "how tough these babies can be when they outnumber their victims and hold guns. When the tables are turned, they're like jelly. Fools with ambitions to become criminals would profit by seeing this half-minute egg right now."

HE SET to work bringing the man back to consciousness, jealous of every minute that slipped by. Things were beginning to break. Certain features of the case, previously jumbled in the Black Bat's mind, were starkly clear now. He had work to do and the Black Bat only flew by night.

The prisoner awoke again, shuddered until his teeth chattered and talked. He talked a blue streak between pleading for his life and cajoling the Black Bat with a string of lies about his being forced into the dirty business.

"Then you don't know who is behind the crimes," the Black Bat said slowly. "I'm sure you don't or you'd have sung his name by now. The only contact with this higher-up is through Monk Brady, the short man who leads you on these raids. You and your hoodlum pals stole six gems. Where are they?"

"I don't know. Honest, I don't. Monk took 'em, see? He turned 'em over to the big shot. We was to get our cut tonight but somethin' happened. We got orders to come down here and meet this Jim Downing chump."

"To meet him or take him prisoner?" the Bat queried.

"I don't know. Look, me, I'm nothin' but a little guy. They don't tell me things."

"Where are they taking Downing?" the Black Bat asked.

"Monk has got a hideaway in the cellar of a warehouse down by the river. It's at the end of Elizabeth Street. That's the only place we got left. You busted up the rest of 'em."

"All right," the Black Bat said. "Get up and walk ahead of me. This is a gun drilling into your back and I wouldn't mind in the least saving the state some money by exterminating you."

LIEUTENANT McGRATH was living in a dream world wherein he had the Black Bat at bay and was ready to unmask him. Then the buzzing of his front doorbell brought him back to reality. He jumped out of bed, donned a robe and seized his service pistol. He raced down the stairs, heard a car start away and approached the door warily. He peered through the curtains. There was a man standing on his front porch. A man dressed all in black—with a prominent hump on his shoulders.

McGrath yanked the door open, stepped out onto the porch with his gun extended. His face was hard and uncompromising.

"If this is a trap, you'll get it before your pals start shooting," he warned. "Lift 'em!"

The figure swayed slightly forward, seemed to lose its balance and came headlong toward McGrath. He jumped back with a hoarse shout of alarm and very nearly emptied his gun into the hunchback's chest. The only thing that prevented this action was a glimpse of something white pinned to the man's coat.

McGrath was still wary as he turned the man over. He noticed the swollen jaw, the half-glazed eyes. The hunchback had been rapped on the chin and when he was on the point of recovering his wits, someone had stood him on the front porch. McGrath didn't need a description of the person responsible for all this.

Plastered between the eyes of the half-conscious crook was a Black Bat sticker!

McGrath pulled the note off the coat and read it while his face flushed scarlet.

The note said:

You are slipping, McGrath. I have to go out and nail your killers for you. This will introduce one Billy the Barber. He told me, quite confidentially, that he derived his name because he was employed to shave the throats of certain gentlemen very, very close. His knowledge of the hunchbacked killers' activities are on the same high plane as your own. He knows nothing.

CHAPTER XIX

THE FINGER OF SUSPICION

KEEPING SILK at the wheel as chauffeur, Butch and the Black Bat roared away from McGrath's home. Butch was doubled up with laughter.

"Some day," he opined, "McGrath is gonna get so mad, he's just gonna walk in the house, boss, and blast away to prove that when Tony Quinn is rubbed out, the Black Bat don't show no more."

"Are we on the way home, sir?" Silk queried from the front of the car.

"Not quite yet. Drive to Elizabeth Street and park three-quarters of the way down it. Butch, polish up your knuckles. I'm not exactly certain what we'll find at our destination, but I rather think one of the things will be trouble."

"Boy!"—Butch straightened up quickly—"Oh boy!"

Silk maneuvered the car into a driveway between two abandoned buildings. They all got out and listened to quiet instructions from the Black Bat. Butch and Silk slipped away in the darkness. The Black Bat gave them a couple of minutes and then he made his own stealthy way toward the old warehouse the captured hunchback mobster had described.

Inside, deep within the cellar, there was activity, however, of a somewhat gruesome nature. Jim Downing occupied a chair, not because he particularly wanted to be sitting there, but coils of wire fastened him. He was covered with sweat and the veins in his forehead stood out starkly blue. Four of the hunchbacks were gathered around him and in the center of the room, striding up and down was—Attorney Jay Fenner.

He looked more like a shyster now than ever before. His collar was opened at the throat. A cigarette dangled from his lips. The usual immaculateness of his clothing was gone. He looked like a man considerably harassed. He stopped in front of Downing and faced him squarely.

"Listen, you double-crossing little fool, what happened to that diamond? You had it, because that's why you went to call on the Rajah. The sum of money you were bound to demand must have been too large to consummate the transaction at that hour of the morning. Therefore you had it when you left. Where did you hide it?"

"Somebody picked my pocket," Downing wailed. "I told you that ten times already. Can't you see I'm speaking the truth? And I thought you were my friend, that I could trust you!"

"Friend?" Fenner scowled. "In this business, with the stakes running into the millions, there's no such thing as friendship. It's every man for himself. If I don't make you tell where that stone is hidden, you won't be the only man to die. They'll kill me too."

DOWNING MADE a wry face. "Don't tell me that, Fenner. I went to your house for advice. You left me long enough to make a phone call, and then, when I left, these—these devils took me."

Downing looked askance at the hunchbacked, partially masked men. He shivered and quickly averted his gaze. There was murder written in their eyes.

Fenner threw up both hands.

"One more chance, Downing. Only one more. Without that rock the rest of the stuff is worth little in comparison to its value when assembled.

"I can promise you dying won't be easy. These men will lose a great deal of money by your reluctance to talk. They won't like it and they're very apt to take it out of your hide. Now for the last time—where did you hide that diamond?"

"Somebody picked my pocket," Downing said wearily. "I can't tell you anything else because that's the truth. And even if it weren't, you'd never dare to let me go because I know now that you're the man behind this gang. If I lived, you'd go to the chair. I've been a fool and I admit it, but I'm a little smarter now by experience."

Fenner motioned to the hunchbacked men.

"You see? I can't make him talk, not even when my own life hangs in the balance. Kill him!"

Downing grew deathly pale and he chewed on his lip for a moment. Then words burst from him.

"Kill me! Yes, kill me! So I'll never tell anyone how you looted my cousin's estate. He trusted you. So did I, until I checked the books. You tried to change them around, but you were too late.

"You've been a crook all your life, Fenner. You knew about that secret room in the house. My cousin used to keep his books there and he did sculpturing as a hobby there. You saw me clearing it out. You told those men to hide there while the police searched the house. You're the leader of these men and I'll die anyway."

Fenner's face grew crimson with rage. He advanced on Downing with his fists clenched. Then he gave a derisive snarl and waved his hand to the four hunchbacks.

They didn't need any other command. One of them secured a rope, threw it toward the ceiling and looped it around one of the supporting beams. Another man fashioned a noose out of one end. Downing's wire bonds were removed and he was led into the middle of the floor.

Two of the killers tripped him and he fell with a terrific jar. They pounced on him, looped the rope around his ankles and pulled him two feet off the floor. He hung there, head down and the blood turned his pallid face to a violent red.

Fenner looked at him coldly.

"You'll live a little while like that, but the longer you keep silent, the worse it will be. Better talk, Downing. Better tell us where you hid that diamond. Your story of having your pockets picked is a little too thin for me."

The hunchbacks separated, each one taking up a position at the various sides of the cellar. One stood near the door, enjoying this spectacle of a tortured man's writhings. Everyone knew he was there. Everyone saw him—and then they didn't. The hunchback had completely vanished.

Fenner's eyes grew hard with fear.

"See what happened to him," he cried. "He wasn't supposed to leave the room."

TWO OF the men rushed out. Five minutes went by and neither of them returned. Fenner became paler than Downing had been. He turned on his heel and stalked across the room. There was a door on the opposite side and he vanished through it.

He kicked aside a small packing case and revealed a telephone of the type used to tap wires with. He dialed a number. When he finished talking, he started back into the other room. He took two or three steps beyond the door and stopped in his tracks.

The four hunchbacked men were all there now. They sat in a row against the further wall, their heads lolling limply against their shoulders and the scarfs torn away from their faces. On the forehead of each one was the brand of the Black Bat!

Fenner realized something else was wrong. The form of Downing, which had hung head down, was gone. Only the severed rope swung gently. He gave vent to a bellow of mixed anguish and despair, looked around wildly and finally his eyes came back to the vicinity of the door.

A man stood there—a man clad in black with a hood over his head and from his shoulders were draped wings like those of a bat. There was a gun in his fist.

"Did you finish your call for help, Mr. Fenner?" the Black Bat asked pleasantly. "I'm hoping that certain people will respond. Now just see how high you can stretch your arms and keep them there."

"I—I—you got me wrong," Fenner managed. All the courtroom and office suaveness had vanished.

"Don't talk," the Black Bat said. "I'm not a jury susceptible to your smooth lying. You've played a dirty game and lost. I...."

From deep within the cellar came a hoarse cry of warning.

"Bat! Look out!"

The Black Bat spun around. Two hunchbacked men were advancing toward him with guns ready in their fists. The Black Bat's weapon spoke first. One of the men slithered to the floor. The other opened fire, but things had happened so fast that his nerves were on edge and he missed. Killers never missed the Black Bat twice. The second man dropped and didn't move again. The Black Bat turned back. Fenner was gone.

The attorney seized his advantage, bolted into the other room, cut through it and began racing along the cellar toward an exit—any exit so long as it led him away from the Black Bat. He saw an open door ahead of him, saw the night sky through it and increased his speed. He flashed through the door.

A figure moved out to intercept him. Fenner gave a wild yelp and tried to evade the man, but that was impossible. Two strong hands grabbed him, yanked his arms behind his back and pinned them there.

SILK WAS panting hard. This exertion was usually left to Butch, but he was busy inside rounding up more of those weirdly garbed monsters.

"Walk toward that car," Silk snapped. "Walk fast because I've got things to do and I'd rather lay you out cold anyhow."

Fenner walked—faster than he'd ever walked in his life despite the restraining grasp on his arms. He got into the car, started to turn around to sit down and a wrench smashed against his skull. Silk whirled and headed back toward the warehouse.

Then he gasped in horror. There were cars coming down the street, four or five of them, with sirens screaming. The police were arriving in force. Silk reached the doorway.

"The cops are here—four cars full of them."

In a moment, Butch came racing out.

"The Black Bat says we're to scram and take Fenner and Downing with us. He'll hold the cops until we get clear."

Silk hesitated, but orders were orders. Butch opened the cover of an ash box at the rear of the warehouse, reached into its depths and hauled out Downing. He draped the man over his shoulder and sprinted for the car. Silk was behind the wheel, but he didn't start the motor.

The police cars stopped and rifle-armed men jumped out. Silk groaned when he saw that Lieutenant McGrath was in charge of them. Two patrolmen were advancing belligerently toward the car. Silk had a low feeling in his heart that this was the end of the Black Bat and his associates.

Then a series of shots came from within the warehouse. Bullets sang over the heads of the advancing patrolmen. They spun around, heard a mocking laugh and looked up. On the roof of the warehouse stood an unmistakable figure—the Black Bat!

"Into the place," McGrath yelled. "He's alone and we've got him now."

Silk stepped on the starter during the answering burst of fire from the police guns. He eased the car into low and slid away without being seen.

"He risked his own safety to let us get clear," Silk said with a gulp. "If I didn't think he had a chance of getting out, I wouldn't go. But he gave us orders. There's nothing else to do. He let Fenner make the phone call to see who he'd contact but Fenner was too smart. He called the cops instead to come and get the Black Bat."

Butch was looking through the rear window. Fenner groaned and stirred. Without glancing at him, Butch doubled his fist and smacked him on top of the head. Fenner passed out again.

"Chance?" Butch said stonily. "What chance has he got now, with twenty cops and McGrath all around?"

CHAPTER XX

McGRATH
HEARS VOICES

VIGILANTLY THE BAT watched them get away. Then he rushed across the roof, leaped through the skylight which he had already opened, and landed on the floor inside. He was up in a flash and streaking for the stairway. If he could only reach the first floor, hide himself and wait until the police investigated the upper regions of the big warehouse, he'd have a ghost of a chance.

He did reach the second floor before the police stormed up the stairs. The Black Bat dived into a small anteroom. Unlike the police, he wasn't handicapped by the darkness. His eyes saw that there were stout rafters at the ceiling, like those in the basement.

He gave a running leap and missed. The impact of his weight against the floor brought the police outside to a standstill.

"Don't turn on your flashlights," McGrath warned. "He'll use them for targets."

"But that noise came from over there," someone said in a low voice.

"It came from upstairs," McGrath yelled. "What kind of a dope do you think I am? Up there, all of you. He's probably still on the roof. I'll cover what's left of this floor, but he isn't here."

Pounding of many feet told the Black Bat that McGrath's orders were being obeyed. McGrath broke his own orders however and sprayed the walls with his flash. He sent the ray floorward, grunted and began walking very slowly toward the anteroom in which the Black Bat was hidden. Because of the necessity for haste, the Black Bat hadn't noticed his feet had created a trail on the dusty floor.

McGrath pushed open the door and stepped inside. The Black Bat, in a far corner, could have sent a dozen bullets smashing through McGrath's body, but he would far rather have faced a life term in prison than hurt any officer of the law. His throat was dry. When McGrath turned on that flash, he was done. The end of the trail had come at last. The Black Bat's only consolation lay in the fact that McGrath would be the one to effect the capture. He really deserved the honor.

The Black Bat stepped forward without trying to be quiet.

"I'm over here, Lieutenant," he said calmly. "There's no need to shoot. I'll throw my guns on the floor."

McGrath's head turned and he looked over his shoulder.

"I'm daft," he said aloud. "I could have sworn I heard a voice. This darkness must be getting me—and me with a busted flashlight, too! If the Black Bat is around, he'll only have to slip out of the cellar and swipe a police car. Seems to me I even left the motor running in mine."

"Thanks, Lieutenant," the Black Bat said. "You'll be well repaid. Before dawn I'll put the whole hunchbacked mob right in your lap with the brains behind them ready for a cell. I know why you're doing this. I saved your life back at Downing's house. This is your way of repaying me. I'll not forget it."

BY HIS actions McGrath seemed to have heard nothing. He still talked in a low voice as if to himself.

"I'd hate to land him at that. He saved my neck not many hours ago and I owe him a break, but after that we're even again. Well, guess I'd better go up and see if they cornered him on the roof. Anyway we've got six of the hunchbacks downstairs. That's something."

McGrath walked out of the room, headed for the stairs and climbed them slowly. There was a peculiar smile on his face. He wiped it off before he stepped onto the roof.

The Black Bat found his exit cleared of all danger. He reached McGrath's car and rolled away. There wasn't even an alarm. McGrath had deliberately drawn all his men to the opposite side of the building.

The Black Bat selected the darkest streets possible. He glanced at his watch. In an hour and a half, it would be daylight and he had many things to do. He proceeded straight to the home of Alex Pierce, the jeweler, rolled on by it and saw Carol's car parked nearby. He signaled her, kept on driving until he was two miles away from the vicinity and then he abandoned the police car. He transferred himself to Carol's coupé and sank wearily into the seat beside her.

"You're all right?" she asked anxiously.

"Quite. Rather a few bad moments though, but everything is all right now. What about Pierce?"

"Never stirred out of the house all evening," Carol declared flatly. "I can swear to that. What's happened to Butch and Silk?"

"Having the time of their lives," the Black Bat laughed. "Butch went to town on a few of those disguised hoodlums and was in his glory. He doesn't know it yet, but he isn't through."

"We rounded up six of the killers. There are about eight more of them and I especially want to land this gentle creature who calls himself Monk. He's the brainiest of the lot and therefore the greatest menace to society. Drive home, darling. We'll spend a few minutes there and then hit the road again. That is, I will. You've finished your work on this case."

"Tony," Carol gasped. "You know who is behind all this then? I've been thinking. You know I checked up on the suspicious characters. I'd say it was Attorney Fenner because he had contact with more of those murdered and robbed men than anyone else. He handled some of their legal matters. His reputation indicates that he'd stoop to any level to gain his own ends. It is Fenner, isn't it?"

The Black Bat grinned. "Fenner is in it all right, my dear—in it up to his rotten neck, but he became mixed up in the deal more by accident than anything else. Downing discovered that Fenner had looted the estate of Kilpatrick. He held that over Fenner's head, but someone else also knew that Fenner was a crook.

"That man compelled Fenner to question Downing about a missing diamond. He even submitted Downing to some rather drastic physical torment to make him talk because Fenner had to get that stone. If he failed, his own life was in jeopardy. It was a peculiar turn of events for Fenner also was endangered no matter what happened. If Downing got free, he'd have accused Fenner of leading the hunchbacked men and had a strong case against him, too."

CAROL PARKED the car and followed the Black Bat through the hidden entrance to the house. There, Tony Quinn went directly into the library and dialed the number of Attorney Fenner's home.

Silk answered and his voice carried a worried note which disappeared when he heard Tony Quinn's voice.

"Yes, I made it," Quinn said. "No time to talk about it now. Tell Butch I've some more strong-arm work. Be certain that Fenner and Downing can't get away. Take Downing's keys away from him. Then go with Butch to Downing's house. Post yourselves inside in convenient positions and wait.

"In a little while, the hunchbacked mob will appear. They'll come in force but they'll enter the house two at a time. Just right for Butch to handle. I want them all. Not one must get away. Is that clear?"

"It's not only clear," Silk grunted, "but it's a pleasure, sir. What'll we do with the remains, sir?"

"Bring along something to tie them up with. Make certain they can't help one another escape and, after you've finished, leave the house and report immediately to the laboratory."

Silk hung up at the other end. Butch heard the news and gave a lusty shout. Then his face grew serious.

"When do we start for Downing's house? I was just gettin' practice back there at the warehouse."

Silk paid brief visits to Fenner and Downing. Both were tied up, one on the second floor and the other in the cellar. They were efficiently gagged and restrained from moving at all by ropes.

Silk and Butch piled into the car and pointed its nose toward Jim Downing's home.

Neither spoke a word during the ride. Silk was busy thinking things out, trying to pin down the real brains behind all this. Butch was occupied with more primitive ideas. He massaged his knuckles and kept grinning broadly. They concealed the car, entered Downing's home and Silk looked around.

"I haven't the least idea as to how the Black Bat expects to make these men enter the house two at a time," he said. "Yet, that's what he told me. If they all come at once, we'll be in a bad spot. Suppose you just step into that doorway, Butch. As they pass by, you can get your hands on them. Work fast and don't make any noise."

Silk grew more and more worried as time went by. It would be daylight in an hour now. The Black Bat had to finish the case before then or suspend operations. The gang was badly broken up now. The leader might decide to take what loot he already had and run for it.

Then two cars stopped outside. One by one, hunchbacked killers emerged, ran lightly into the darkness of the estate and waited until they were all congregated in one body. Monk, the squat leader, seemed to be talking. To Silk's horror, they all headed for the house in one group. Even Butch couldn't handle them all. They were confirmed killers, well armed and prepared to shoot it out with anyone.

SUDDENLY THE squat leader held up his hand. He stood rigid and silent for fully two minutes. Then he summoned the others by jerking his head toward a huge, overhanging tree.

"When are they comin'?" Butch asked hoarsely. "My fingers is goin' to sleep waitin'."

"I don't know," Silk replied. "I just witnessed one of the most amazing things I've ever seen. They intended to enter as a group, but something stopped them, just as the Black Bat prophesied. Butch, get set! Yes they are—they're going to enter two by two."

Outside the house, Monk gave his final orders to the mob.

"The big shot pays off tonight," he told the others. "In cold cash, twenty-five grand for each one of you lugs. More dough than you ever saw before. He says we are to enter the house for the payoff, but only two at a time. There's to be an interval of three minutes and then the second pair goes in. That's so you mugs can't see each other even after the job is all finished.

"You take your dough and leave by the back door. When you get to the street, take off the humps, the hats and scarfs and scram. Any mug who don't travel alone gets plugged. Okay, you two start."

He tapped a pair of his men on their arms. They started for the house eagerly. They climbed the steps, crossed the porch and found the front door slightly ajar. They walked in boldly, tried to penetrate the darkness within and hesitated.

"Just follow the corridor," a voice came out of the gloom. "Straight ahead."

Both men gave grunts of approval and headed for the direction of the voice. They never did know just what happened after that.

Each man realized that something which felt like the scoop of a steam shovel, closed around their necks, choking off any attempt to scream a warning. Then their heads came together with a thump.

Three minutes passed and another pair entered to meet the same fate. The third set was dispatched quietly. Then Monk squared his shoulders and spoke to his companion as they headed for the porch.

"I said if you stuck with me, you'd roll in dough. Now it's comin' true, see? The big shot will count twenty-five grand right in your hand and it's all over. You don't know nothin'. If the cops pick up any of the other boys, what'll they say? Not one damn word because they don't know what it's all about any more than you. Let's go!"

Monk knew that his companion walked beside him down the hall and then, he suddenly realized that he was quite alone.

Monk gave a savage growl and reached for his gun. Then he was hurled against a wall. Out of the darkness, stalked a form which loomed up like a giant. A low, growling voice made Monk's blood run thin and cold.

"You're the mug who is the boss, huh? I got some special treatment for you. Here's a sample."

A fist cracked against Monk's cheek and sent him reeling into a corner. He made a grab for his hip pocket, but the giant was on him before he could get the weapon free. Monk was seized by the throat and held dangling off the floor.

Very suddenly he discovered that he had been turned upside down. The gun fell out of his pocket. So did various possessions including a pair of brass knuckles and a deadly looking blackjack.

"Lemme go," Monk yelled. "I give up! I'll talk! Don't sock me again!"

Monk sailed through the air for a short space, landed against the wall again and cowered near the floor, blubbering pleas for mercy. He was yanked to his feet once more, pressed against the wall and then a fist came out of the darkness to smash squarely against his jaw. His head bobbed back under the impact, struck the wall and Monk went to sleep.

Butch let him slump to the floor and rubbed his hands.

"Tough guy, wasn't he?" he said contemptuously. "Tough as cream cheese! I figured he'd put up a scrap and give me some fun. 'Stead of that he turned yellow. Oh well, maybe he'll come to before the Black Bat tells us what to do with him. Then I can mess him up a little more."

CHAPTER XXI

THE BAT TURNS BURGLAR

RAPIDLY TONY QUINN donned the Black Bat's outfit again, cautioned Carol to watch out for Lieutenant McGrath and then he opened a locked cabinet and removed a small bottle of white liquid. He wrapped this in cotton, put it in his pocket and departed.

Carol's car was still parked near the estate. He drove it straight toward the center of the city. Without a wasted motion, he left the car, ran down an alley and reached the back door of a store.

There was no time to cut burglar alarm systems. He withdrew the bottle of liquid, replaced the cork with another that had two fine wires strung from it. He hooked these to a small board which had a pair of batteries attached.

Then he simply raised one foot and kicked in the glass part of the back door. He unlocked it, heard the burglar alarm system go into action and as he raced through the spacious store, he swept stock from counters, smashed in display cases with the butt of his gun and only stopped when he reached the big safe.

He thrust the bottle beneath it, strung the fine wires out as he retreated toward the back door and paid no attention to the shrill sound of a police whistle that rose above the din of the clanging alarm.

On the rear platform he stopped long enough to touch two wires together. Inside the store there was a terrific explosion, a blinding sheet of white fire and then a grim silence broken only by an occasional crackle of broken glass as it fell to the floor.

His eyes twinkled knowingly.

A patrolman swept around the back of the building, gun in hand. He saw nothing for it was still very dark and the Black Bat's black-clad form was not to be distinguished. He vaulted over a fence, streaked madly through other rear courtyards and finally reached his parked car. By the time radio police and protective agency guards showed up, he was ten blocks away and there was a grin on his face.

He whipped around a corner, fighting time now, for everything had to be finished before dawn would make his movements difficult. When he reached the other side of town he stopped the car, got out and merged with the gloom once more. He advanced toward a stately looking house, alert for any signs of guards or traps. Reaching a spot four feet from the driveway, he crouched behind a thick bush and waited. The Black Bat's work was almost finished.

While this went on, another man received startling news over the phone. Alex Pierce awoke with a start, grabbed the instrument and heard a police sergeant describe the bad news.

"Your store was just busted open. Somebody blasted the safe, but he didn't have time to pry the door open so your stock is okay. You better come down. The store is an awful mess, Mr. Pierce."

"I'll be there in ten minutes," Pierce answered.

He hung up, slipped out of his pajamas and threw on his clothes as he hurried downstairs.

He wrung his hands at the destruction in his store, but the police sergeant was right. The burglar seemed to have hoped that one blast of explosive would blow the safe wide open. Pierce had spent a lot of money on that safe. Now it seemed as though his investment had been wise.

"I don't know what's missing yet," he told the sergeant. "The most valuable part of the stock was in the safe so that's okay. I'll arrange with the protective agency to throw a cordon of men around the store. In the morning, I'll have my clerks check carefully and submit a list of what is missing. I'm grateful for your fast work, Sergeant. You probably saved me a tremendous loss."

PIERCE WORE a very puzzled look as he got back into his car. He broke every speed law to get back home and he didn't wait to roll the car in the garage. Instead, he nosed it in to the curb, jumped out and raced madly for the front door. It was locked and he heaved a sigh as he inserted the key.

But when he stepped into the living room he began cursing, slowly and steadily. The havoc wrought at his store was nothing compared to the cyclone which had swept through this room. Chairs were overturned and their cushions slit open. Rugs were rolled up. Pictures hung askew. The contents of his bookcase was dumped on the floor.

Pierce didn't hurry to the telephone. He never thought of summoning the police. Instead, he headed directly toward the fireplace. His finger slid beneath the mantelpiece, found a hidden switch and pressed it. A section of bricks swung back to reveal the shiny surface of a hidden safe.

Pierce reached for the dial, hesitated and looked around carefully. Then he turned the combination with fingers that shook so badly that he missed one of the numbers and had to start over again. At last, the door opened. He reached into the safe and removed a thick, plush-covered box. He snapped the spring and the lid flew back with a soft click.

"Much obliged," someone said with quiet satisfaction. "Now let's have a look at the five stones of the Rajah's garland."

Pierce turned around very slowly. Commissioner Warner and Lieutenant McGrath had quietly stepped across the hallway and entered the room. McGrath had a service pistol trained on Pierce.

"The Rajah's garland?" Pierce asked in awe. "What—what in the world do you mean? This is no time for jokes, gentlemen. My store was looted a few moments ago. During my absence from the house someone entered and—well, you can see for yourselves what happened."

"What's in the box?" McGrath asked as he advanced toward Pierce.

"A necklace," Pierce answered promptly. "It is worth a hundred thousand dollars and belongs to one of my best clients. I had it restrung and took it home to make a careful examination of the pearls. That's what worried me so when I came back to find my house invaded. Loss of this would have floored me financially."

Pierce walked over to his desk and placed the box on it. Warner and McGrath approached, looked at the pearl necklace it contained and then looked at one another. McGrath reached out to pick up the box. There was mingled surprise and confusion on his face. McGrath forgot that he might be facing a very dangerous man.

"Don't touch it," Pierce snapped. "Drop your gun, you stupid lummox. Drop it or I'll drill you."

While Warner and McGrath had concentrated their attention on the plush box and the necklace, Pierce had found an opportunity to lift a heavy automatic out of his desk drawer. He had both police officers covered.

"So you thought you'd land me with a trick like this. Hasn't it occurred to you that I'm a man with brains, that I can outwit any police officer in the world? I'm making no admissions. I don't know why you resorted to this trickery, but it really makes no difference because I'm going to kill both of you.

"Your bodies will be hidden and never found. I have a perfect alibi. Just a few moments ago, I left a score of your own men. The moment you are dead, I shall report this burglary. I drove here very fast, suspecting there was something up. Under ordinary circumstances I should be just arriving. You'll be dead, your own men will back up my story if I am suspected of killing you—which I won't be.

"So, gentlemen, I'm afraid this is the finish. By permitting you to live I place my own neck in a hangman's noose and I'm very susceptible to things like that."

"Or like this?" a voice breathed into his ear.

There was a gun muzzle pressed gently, but firmly against the back of his neck.

CHAPTER XXII

FINAL RECKONING

GUN HAND shaking, his eyes wide in fear, Pierce froze. McGrath made a lunge and, with one blow, knocked the weapon out of Pierce's palsied grip. Pierce turned around, gulped and found that he couldn't even protest his innocence.

The Black Bat stood directly behind him. He motioned toward McGrath. "Open the rest of that plush jewelry case," he suggested. "It's the thickest jewelry box I've ever seen."

McGrath fumbled with the box and six stones rolled out on the desk, throwing rainbow hues all over the room. The Black Bat nodded in satisfaction.

"Looks like the evidence will convict you, Pierce," he said.

"I—I don't know anything about it," Pierce wailed. "I never saw those stones before in my life. Wait! I know how they got there. The hunch-backed killers! They robbed me! They hid them there."

"Your trend of thought is so fast it's crude," the Black Bat said. "Sit down, Pierce, and listen to the story which spells your finish. Hollis and Kilpatrick received certain articles from the Rajah of Bahawal. So did you and the other men victimized in this case. Hollis and Kilpatrick, purely by accident, discovered that the articles contained jewels which, when assembled form the garland of *Siva,* probably the most valuable collection of gems in the world."

"But—but I didn't know that," Pierce cried. "How could I know?"

"You could have found out by accident the way Hollis and Kilpatrick did. But actually you learned through the treachery of Jim Downing. Kilpatrick made his discovery and promptly hid the diamond he found in the secret room of his house where protection was better. Then he told Downing about it. Kilpatrick had been shown the Garland when he visited Bahawal and he recognized the single stone. Downing knew about the secret room and removed the stone.

"He took it to your jewelry store and asked you to have a copy made. He told you that Kilpatrick had been presented with the gem and real-ized it was too valuable for show. Therefore he wanted a copy to display. That was when you first realized what had happened. You found one of the gems in the trinket the Rajah had sent you. Then you set about getting all the gems for yourself. You found it very easy to hire men who would carry out your orders, even when they involved murder."

"Can't you see how foolish all this is?" Pierce asked McGrath and Warner. "I'm a respectable jeweler. I have nothing in common with murderers and thieves."

"Nothing except the fact that you are probably the biggest fence in the country," the Black Bat said. "You arranged that your men would disguise themselves as hunchbacks to be certain everyone would know that one gang was committing the crimes. You killed Hollis and Kil-patrick because they knew what you were after.

"The others, without knowledge as to what the Rajah's gifts contained, only believed that these articles were stolen along with a lot of other things. You wanted this series of crimes to look like the work of a mob intent simply on getting loot."

PIERCE JUMPED to his feet. The Black Bat's gun swung around significantly and he sat down again.

"Dr. Norden grew suspicious," the Black Bat went on. "He examined the article which the Rajah had sent, found the stone it contained and became so frightened that he hurried to a bank and put it in a safe deposit vault. Your men had him under observation and you ordered a raid on the bank. You intended to rob his house but you delayed too long. You then planned to murder him but things got too hot."

"But I have an alibi for the time when Hollis and Kilpatrick were murdered," Pierce protested wildly. "Why, I was even menaced by those hunchbacked men myself."

"Faked," the Black Bat answered. "Your identity wasn't known to any of the killers except Monk. You merely gave orders that they were to rob you and the job did look real. You let Downing live because he looked like a good fall guy."

"And you still haven't evidence against me," Pierce yelled belligerently. "I can prove I was at home when those robberies were committed. You can't tie me up with that gang."

"Yes I can," the Black Bat said softly. "Upstairs, in one of your rooms, you have a short-wave radio transmitter. You used this to direct the movements of your men. The humps on their backs served another purpose than simply to identify them. Certain of the crooks had receiving sets concealed in their humps. They used a small earphone which was hidden by the big hat and the scarf you provided them with.

"When you attended the meeting at Downing's house, you got away from the hunchbacked killers very smoothly, because Monk, the leader, knew you and permitted you to get away. All of you forgot that I can see quite well in darkness. I watched Monk signal you to escape. You rushed home, contacted your men by radio and told them of the secret room which others of your men learned of from Kilpatrick. They made him tell that his stone was hidden there. Of course that stone was only the copy Downing had made. Yet I still had no concrete evidence."

Warner stepped forward. "Have you any now? The radio set will help, but it's not enough to convince a jury."

The Black Bat laughed. "At the home of Jim Downing you will find all of what's left of Pierce's gang. Some of them have the receiving sets, tuned in to the wave length which corresponds to the set upstairs. That was how those killers knew in advance when police were on the march. Pierce simply listened to police broadcasts and relayed the information to his men.

"The hunchbacks always operated in pairs. One of the pair had a receiving set. The other was to hold off anyone who tried to effect a capture so that his pal could get free and the receiving set would never be found. That's why, when we managed to grab some of the killers, they never wore a set."

"That's enough," Warner grated. "We have Pierce right where we want him."

"Wait," the Black Bat interrupted. "One more little detail. Among the gems on the desk is a diamond. It's phony! That stone was taken out of Kilpatrick's secret room. Downing put it there and appropriated the real one. The Rajah has this stone now.

"The fake one was made in Pierce's store, by one of his trusted aides. I've already examined it while Pierce was busy at his store a few moments ago. Every gem craftsman marks phony stones. Pierce's man did too. You can pick him up any time. You will also find Downing tied up in Fenner's home and more than willing to talk. Downing's testimony will easily convict Pierce. Fenner is there also.

"Pierce knew Fenner was shady and through Monk forced Fenner to help. But Fenner still doesn't know that Pierce is behind it. Monk, the leader of the hunchbacks, handled Fenner. I imagine that Pierce was holding Fenner as a fall guy to take the blame if things went sour just as he kept Downing in reserve, for the same reason."

McGrath snapped handcuffs on Pierce's wrists. He yanked the man to his feet.

"About Downing," the Black Bat said, "don't handle him too roughly. At heart, he's not so bad. He tried to sell the diamond back to the Rajah and he knew of his arrival by some rather good checking of incoming ships. As for Pierce, he deserves no breaks of any kind. He ordered his men to torture Kilpatrick when they couldn't find the diamond. He has displayed animal ruthlessness all through the case. Lieutenant, have you a very firm grasp on your prisoner?"

"He couldn't get away if he was Tarzan," McGrath grunted.

Suddenly the lights winked out. No one moved. Three minutes passed and Warner turned the lights on again. The Black Bat was gone!

IT WAS broad daylight when Tony Quinn sat in his study and puffed on his pipe. Carol and Butch were gone. Silk bustled about as though the day was just beginning for him. Neither he nor Quinn showed the slightest trace of weariness.

McGrath and Warner arrived at ten o'clock. Quinn listened to Warner describe what had happened. McGrath was strangely silent until he was ready to leave. Then he faced Quinn, looking down into those dead eyes.

"I'm a soft sap," he said with a strange grin. "I had the Black Bat cornered and I let him go. Of course, it paid dividends because we have the whole gang and I'm getting credit for it all. Have a squint at this."

He held out a shiny gold badge. Quinn's expression never changed, his eyes didn't focus on the badge. McGrath blinked and put the badge back into his pocket.

"Sorry, I forgot you can't see. But it's Captain McGrath now. What do you think of that?"

Quinn extended his hand.

"I think it's great. Much more comforting to be accused of being the Black Bat by a captain of detectives instead of a lieutenant."

"Yeah?" McGrath barked. "Catching the Black Bat will make me an inspector and don't forget that."

As they filed out of the room, Warner looked over his shoulder and winked deliberately at Quinn. But there was no response from the blind man.

Both police officers were helped into their coats by Silk. They walked out to the car. McGrath got behind the wheel.

McGrath cleared his throat.

"Say, Commissioner, I haven't had time to thank you for the promotion. Gosh, I only made those mugs talk. The Black Bat really got them."

"I know," Warner said. "The promotion was not for your work in extracting confessions. You became a captain because you used your brains for once—by letting the Black Bat escape."

Silk watched them drive away. He seemed to droop as the car vanished from sight. Tony Quinn too had relaxed.

"We'd better get some rest," he said.

"Yes, sir," Silk agreed. "But really, sir, a few hours rest will suffice if there is something else going on—"

"There is," Quinn answered as he walked slowly across the room. "We don't know what it is yet, but crime is everlastingly brewing. When it boils over, the Black Bat will have to awaken." He yawned. "I hope it just simmers for two whole days."

THE BLACK BAT AND THE TROJAN HORSE

CHAPTER I

FREEDOM
OF SPEECH

THE MAN was a skinny, crafty-faced individual, utterly unprepossessing in his worn and dirty brown suit. But some strange whim of nature had blessed him with a ready tongue. He went into action first by striking up a conversation with a passerby, and his loud voice brought other listeners. They were mostly young men without jobs, who spent a great deal of their time watching the war bulletins in front of the newspaper office.

The stranger dropped his voice when policemen strolled by and his audience never grew to more than half a dozen. But from his lips dropped poison—the venom of a serpent coiled hidden in the grass, waiting to strike from ambush.

"So what happens?" he asked the group around him. "We grow up and we got no jobs. That's the trouble with this kind of government they call a democracy. They oughta make jobs for us, and pay us good, too. We're just as smart as the birds who make a million bucks while we don't get enough to eat. Now they're going to make us train and maybe fight for them.

"Why should we fight? So these damned millionaires can eat their caviar and drink champagne? Yeah, while we'll be lucky if we get beans. Any sucker who lugs a gun and fights for millionaires is crazy. There's a better living in Germany and in Italy today. That's where these rich guys work for people like us, see?"

A boy, no more than seventeen, elbowed his way closer.

"Mister, are you telling us not to fight if this country gets into war? Is that what you mean?"

"You bet, kid. That's just what I'm trying to drive home. I'm as broke as the rest of you fellows. I don't even know where I'm going to sleep tonight, or get my next meal. But pick up a gun and dodge bullets for a country that don't care? Not me! And you guys oughta get wise, too.

Next thing you know, they'll heave what's left of you into a grave, like a lot of plowed-under cotton.

"Don't fight! Don't even work in munitions plants. Don't listen to the speeches of the war-mongers. All they want are profits from selling guns and bullets to shoot down other saps like us."

While the stranger talked and, to his credit, swayed the small group of young men, a seedy-looking coupé backed to the curb, almost close enough to knock the speaker off his feet. Knowing he held his audience, the speaker only glared at the driver of the car and kept on talking. He preached what amounted to revolution and backed it up with arguments that were corrupt, but nonetheless readily understandable to the young men gathered around him.

THE DOOR of the coupé opened. The whole left side of the car dipped, close to the gutter as its driver got out. He was a hulking brute of a man with fists as huge as boxing gloves. Sometime in the past, his nose had suffered a collision with an irresistible object, which had flattened the bridge. He had a wide, usually placid face, but now there were troubled wrinkles on his forehead.

As he stood listening to the speaker, those wrinkles grew deeper and deeper. Gradually his eyes narrowed and his thick fingers worked convulsively. Finally, as if he could stand no more, the big man moved forward. With a sweep of his arm he pushed some of the group aside and planted himself directly in front of the speaker.

"Listen, mister," he said slowly. "I ain't no college man, see? I don't know much either, but I don't like the way you're talkin'. There's a lot of trouble goin' on in the world and you ain't helping matters much. So why don't you close that trap of yours and beat it, huh?"

The speaker gave vent to a string of curses and shook his fist as close to the big man's face as he could reach.

"I will say what I like. This stupid country allows free speech. No one can stop me. Not you, nor the police, nor the Army, nor the Navy—"

"Yeah?" the big man growled. "Maybe not even the Marines, huh? But I can, you squawkin' skunk. One more yap outa you and I'll use you to clean up the sidewalk. You'll be the broom, see?"

"I shall have you arrested," the speaker yelled. "No one can talk to me this way. Find me a policeman, somebody!"

He couldn't say any more because one of those enormous fists shot out. The fingers seized his necktie and he felt himself being lifted completely off the sidewalk. He began flailing his arms and screaming for help. Those who had been listening to him backed away. They wanted no trouble with this giant who was doing exactly what they had inwardly wanted to do themselves.

The huge man suddenly turned his prisoner upside down, grabbed him by the ankles as if he were no more than a ventriloquist's dummy, and shook him hard. A stream of silver fell out of the speaker's pocket, then several other small objects, and finally a roll of bills fastened together. The silver clip dropped off as the money bounced on the sidewalk, and the bills fluttered around—five of them hundred-dollar bills, a dozen were fifties, and there were twenties, tens and fives in profusion.

"Hey!" one of the youths shouted. "That guy said he was out of a job like us. Look at the dough he's got! He was handing us a line, talking about millionaires, saying we shouldn't fight for them. He's a millionaire himself. Boy, look at that big guy mop the sidewalk with him."

"Yeah," another boy said coldly. "Serves him right. We were a bunch of saps for listening to him. I hope he gets his neck busted."

A POLICE whistle shrilled. Four patrolmen rushed up, and a sergeant joined them. He took one look at the big man and reached for his blackjack. But the big man ceased shaking his victim as the police closed in.

"Put him down, Atlas," the sergeant ordered. "Make one funny play and I'll slug you."

The big man still gripped his victim by one ankle. He held him over the gutter and let go. Then he spread his hands in a gesture of dismay.

"But look, Sarge, this guy was talkin' against the United States. He was sayin' it ain't no good and that nobody should fight for it. He said he'd rather live in Europe. Now I ain't a smart guy, but I don't like what he said, so I just figured I'd show him how I felt."

"That's right, Sergeant." Several of the youths gathered closer. "He was saying we shouldn't fight even if we're drafted. I felt like slugging him myself."

"Who are you?" the sergeant asked the big man.

"Butch—Butch O'Leary. I didn't mean no harm, but a guy can listen to just so much...."

"Hey," the sergeant yelled suddenly. "Grab that fifth columnist! He's crawling along the gutter to make a break for it."

Two patrolmen pounced on the orator and dragged him back. He drew himself up, glared at Butch O'Leary and tried to use the influence of his voice again.

"I am Hans Hofer, a citizen of the United States. I can say what I please, where I please. This ape assaulted me. I demand that he be arrested."

"Okay, sweetheart," the sergeant said. "Murphy, call the wagon. As for you, Mr. Hofer, you better come along, too. With my own eyes I saw you trying to kick that big guy. That amounts to assault, so you're pinched, too."

Ten minutes and six arguments later, a patrol wagon pulled up. Butch gulped as he looked at it, leaped when a patrolman touched his arm.

"Let's go, pal. What's the matter, don't you like to ride in the wagon? Say, I'll tell you what. You ride up front with the driver and everybody'll think you're a plainclothesman."

"Gosh, thanks!" Butch smiled for the first time. "But ain't that against the rules or somethin'?"

"Maybe it is. But if we have to pinch a guy like you, we do it polite. Anyway, that skinny mug is a dangerous guy. If we put you in back with · him, he might get tough and hurt you. Get up on the front seat and don't argue."

A craning, shoving crowd had collected. The dispersing audience of the arrested speaker passed through the crush explaining what had happened. A low hum of angry voices made the sergeant look around worriedly. He hustled his prisoner to the back of the wagon.

"No!" Hofer screamed. "I will not ride in that thing like a common criminal. You cannot make me do this."

The sergeant didn't say a word. He merely grabbed Hofer by the back of the neck and the seat of the pants. Hofer came into violent contact with the front panel of the truck and began to blubber. As the wire doors closed and the wagon rolled away, derisive shouts followed it.

ONE HOUR later Butch O'Leary faced a night court magistrate and tried to tell what had happened.

"I'm guilty, I guess, but I didn't slug him. I just kinda shook him a little. I don't like to hear guys sayin' this country ain't no good, Judge, and that's just what he was doin'. Maybe I shoulda minded my own business, but I ain't smart like you or everybody else in here. I ain't sorry for what I did and I won't promise not to do it again. So I guess maybe I oughta go to jail."

The judge adjusted his glasses, cleared his throat and looked questioningly at the sergeant who had made the arrest.

"Did you take the fingerprints of these two men? You did! Any record of that nature pertaining to Mr. Butch O'Leary is to be destroyed forthwith. He is not a criminal."

"Your Honor," Hofer shouted angrily. "My fingerprint records must also be destroyed. I am here as the complaining witness. I have my rights. It is not a crime to say what you think in this country. The Constitution guarantees me the right of saying what I like. I am a citizen...."

"Your fingerprint record and personal history," the judge interrupted, "are to be sent to Washington. I want to be certain that you are a citizen, as you claim, and that you have no criminal record. Until word is sent back, I hold you in ten thousand dollars bail, on the charge of felonious assault upon the person of one Butch O'Leary."

"Then you must hold him, too!" Hofer shrieked. "He is the guilty one. I am a peaceable citizen. He attacked me. I did not hit him."

"Butch O'Leary, step forward for sentence," the judge announced. "You have pleaded guilty. You had no legal right to strike or touch this man. It is the sentence of this court that you be fined one dollar—without costs—and the execution of the sentence is suspended. You are free to go."

Butch's wide face lit up. He stumbled to the bench, extended his vast hand to the judge and looked a little ashamed even though it was accepted.

"You," the judge said acidly, turning to Hofer, "claim to be a naturalized citizen. Which means that, without coercion on the part of anyone, you elected to adopt this nation as your own. Now, with four-fifths of the world gone mad, you preach the theory that the poor people should not fight for the benefit of the rich. But you had three thousand, four hundred and eighty dollars in cash in your pockets. That doesn't exactly make you a pauper and it refutes any theories you have to offer.

"You have been asked where you got that money and you refused to say. That is within your rights, but we're going to find out just where that money did come from. I have fined a man, given him a court record because he chose to act, instead of listening to your words as so many indifferent citizens do.

"When he laid hands on you, he committed a crime because anyone has the privilege of saying what he wishes in our country. Abroad, you would probably have been shot. Freedom of speech is one of the blessings of the United States, but let me tell you—it will not be blasphemed. You were clever in speaking to only a small group, as though it were nothing more than a friendly street conversation. It shows the way men like you operate.

"Fortunately I can hold you for a short time, and I remand you to jail in default of bail. Take him away, Bailiff, and bring up some of those respectable drunks I see in the prisoners' cage. They'll make the atmosphere of the room smell sweet after what has just passed before the nose of this court."

CHAPTER II

BUTCH HAS A PROBLEM

BUTCH O'LEARY walked out of night court. Somebody had thrust a fat cigar between his teeth. He felt elated, and just a little proud. Yet deep within him lurked doubts. What would Tony Quinn think of this escapade? Quinn had given definite instruction that those who worked with him must keep out of trouble.

Butch was glad everything had happened too fast for the newspaper photographers. If they had taken his picture, it would have been catastrophic. He had to avoid the limelight as much as possible, for Butch O'Leary was one of the three living persons who worked with the eerie being known as the Black Bat.

Butch possessed no supreme confidence in his own powers of thinking. He could fight like a tiger, and he possessed the strength of three ordinary men, but he needed guidance for his peace of mind. Therefore, instead of returning to his own modest boarding house room, he went immediately to an apartment house only a couple of blocks from where he lived. He rang the bell under the name card labeled "Carol Baldwin." She was another of the Black Bat's operatives.

Carol was an extraordinarily pretty girl and as clever as she was good looking. Blonde, with blue eyes and a trim figure, she exacted many admiring glances. As the Black Bat's trusted agent, she had use for her wits. Now they served her well as she listened to Butch's story.

"It was swell of you, Butch," she approved whole-heartedly. "That man deserved to be shaken up a bit. It's all over now, and you have nothing to worry about. They can't connect Butch O'Leary, the man who stood up for his country, and Butch O'Leary, the agent of the Black Bat. Just forget all about it."

Butch dug into his pocket and drew out a thin strand of silvery chain. It was a bracelet of some sort, in the center of which was what seemed to be a flat locket.

"I been wonderin' about this," he said. "When I shook that guy, I musta loosened this and it fell to the sidewalk. I picked it up. Nobody saw me do it. So I pry open the funny lookin' thing, and look—it's got a paper inside, sure enough. What do you think of this, Carol?"

BUTCH'S FINGERS secured a leverage on the locket and forced it open. Carol removed the tiny bit of tissue paper, unfolded it and looked at the picture and the words printed beneath it. She arose abruptly and went into the bedroom for her hat.

"Butch, we're going to see the Black Bat now—at once! You may have uncovered something of great importance."

Carol and Butch left the apartment house, turned down a side street. Making certain that they were not observed, they quietly slipped through a gate into the spacious grounds behind Tony Quinn's house. They walked directly to a small garden house and entered it.

Butch opened a cleverly concealed trap door and helped Carol into a well constructed tunnel. After following her in, he pulled down the trap door. They proceeded along the tunnel until they reached a ladder which brought them up to the white-tiled laboratory inside the home the Black Bat maintained as Tony Quinn.

By this means the Black Bat and his aides could come and go at will, without fear of detection. It had often provided Tony Quinn with a good alibi.

He was seated before the fireplace of his rich study when Carol and Butch were making their way along the tunnel. Dressed in tweeds and a smoking jacket, he held a cane between his knees as he stared blankly into space. For Tony Quinn was stone-blind, the surgeons had said, and with no hope of recovery. His face, particularly around the eyes, was so horribly seared that the scars made a mockery of his former handsome features.

Tony Quinn had been a crusading district attorney of a great city, a fearless man who had fought crime and criminals ruthlessly. One day, in open court, he was preparing to show evidence which would put a killer behind bars. Hirelings of that criminal sought to obliterate the evidence with a powerful acid. Tony Quinn had battled to prevent them, and in the fight the acid had been flung into his face. He was instantly blinded, scarred for the rest of his life when his burned flesh healed.

He had been a broken man, refusing to see anyone and becoming a virtual recluse. Though he was independently wealthy, all his money couldn't find an eye surgeon able to restore his sight.

Then, during a night of darkest despair, Carol Baldwin had come, blonde and lovely, to offer him the corneas of her dying father's eyes. A law officer, he had been shot by a bandit. She brought Quinn to a skilful and unknown country doctor, who performed the phenomenal operation—and Tony Quinn again could see and battle crime.

As his sight returned, Quinn discovered that he had been amply rewarded for his suffering in darkness. He was able to see in the dark almost as well as in daylight. Objects that were invisible to ordinary sight were as clear to him as if he carried a flashlight. He could even distinguish colors that were mere blots to other human beings. But besides that, his other senses had developed to an extraordinary extent while he was blind. His hearing had grown abnormally acute, his sense of touch extremely keen.

Thus had the Black Bat been born. When Quinn returned home, he kept the recovery of his sight a secret. He still pretended to be totally blind, for nobody could suspect a blind man of being the Black Bat. He assumed the name as a gesture of derision for those who were happy when the district attorney had become blind as a bat.

He sallied forth at night, garbed in a hood that covered his scarred face, and cape fashioned like the ribbed wings of a bat. This symbol quickly terrorized the underworld enough to make them offer a huge price to anyone who could prove he killed the Black Bat.

Even the police were instructed to arrest him at the first opportunity, for some of the Black Bat's methods were not entirely legal. He had killed men, though only in self-defense. But when a man dies by violence, the police are required to arrest the killer. They had come close several times, particularly a detective-captain named McGrath. Because of his excitable nature, McGrath had sworn to run down the Black Bat no matter what the danger nor how much time it required.

A SLENDER, almost bald-headed man walked quietly into the study. Quinn didn't turn his head. He played the part of a blind man to the hilt, for there was no telling when someone might be looking in through a window. The newcomer was Silk Kirby, Tony Quinn's combination valet, butler and friend. Silk had once been a slick confidence man, but he had given up this life to aid Tony Quinn and the Black Bat. As smooth as his name, Silk could worm his way into the confidence of even a man who didn't trust himself.

Carrying several newspaper clippings in his hand, he walked over and stood by Quinn's side.

"I've clipped more of those articles you wanted, sir," he said quietly. "Seems as though your hunch was right. There are too many Army officials, Navy officers and even Marine Corps men dying by accident. Major Rolfe is the latest. He was retired about seven years ago from the Coast Guard. Night before last, he was attacked by three or four criminals who wanted to rob him. In the scuffle he received a broken head and died instantly."

"Before Major Rolfe, there were Captain Nelson, Colonel Hickman, Lieutenant-commander Hall," Quinn said thoughtfully. "Rolfe makes the toll four, Silk. All of these victims were retired military men, specialists in their own fields, mostly defense. In case of war they would become invaluable, and now they're dead.

"Two were killed by criminal violence, and in each case it seemed as though robbers had murdered them for their possessions. The other two died as the result of auto accidents. I don't like it. The police and the Federal authorities haven't become suspicious yet, but to me those four deaths came too close to be coincidental. I think those men were murdered."

"Yes, sir," Silk agreed. "So do I, but how can we prove it if the police see nothing suspicious in their deaths? Retired men aren't expected to live long. Because of their advanced age, they are more prone to accidents and to the results of injuries imposed by robbers."

Quinn suddenly made a sharp yet almost imperceptible motion for silence.

"Silk, there's someone in the laboratory! Pull down the window shades quickly."

Silk obeyed the order. Quinn arose and thrust his cane under one arm. Walking swiftly to one wall, he opened a secret door by means of a hidden control. Silk followed him into the spacious room and the door closed behind them. Tony Quinn smiled happily into Carol's eyes and then noticed that hers were serious. Butch, too, seemed worried.

"Something has happened," Carol said. "Not about the Black Bat, or you, Tony. Butch happened to overhear some fifth columnist making a speech about pacifism and revolution. He didn't like it so he manhandled this person. Butch was arrested along with the orator. The judge practically praised Butch in open court and let him go. The speech-maker is being held temporarily."

"Good work, Butch," Quinn said. "I wish I'd been there to help you. There are too many of those subversive elements active right now. I hope you satisfied that sadistic urge you possess."

Butch grinned. "I dunno what sadistic means, Boss, but I sure tossed the guy around till his teeth clicked. I made a sucker out of him, all right. He'd been tellin' everybody he was poor and not workin', but three thousand bucks fell outa his pocket. And I kinda got to like cops. They even let me ride on the front seat of the patrol wagon—and what do you think? I blew the siren all the way to the station house!"

"That's nice," Quinn said and faced Carol. "But what has that to do with me?"

CAROL UNFOLDED her hand and showed the wristlet of silvery metal.

"In the scuffle, Butch must have broken the chain of this bracelet, Tony. It has a locket attached. Remember telling me how suspicious you were of several deaths recently, of ex-Army and Navy officers? Take a look at this."

Quinn took the folded piece of paper. When he spread it out on the laboratory bench, he gave a sharp explanation. He bent closer and studied the paper intently. The picture printed on it was easily recognizable as the well known features of Lieutenant-colonel Catlin. Until his retirement five years before, Catlin had been one of the most able officers attached to the Chemical Warfare Service.

Below the picture, words were printed in extremely fine type. Cryptically they related that Lieutenant-colonel Catlin was in the habit of dining at the Army and Navy Officers' Club each Tuesday night. He attended all piano concerts that were available. He lived in a suite which had the stairway running close to it, and he retired promptly at midnight. According to this document, he was in the habit of walking through parks, even at night. He drank sparingly and made few friends because of his quiet nature.

"Explicit, to say the least," Tony Quinn remarked. "Now look here, all of you. This little record was printed on a hand press, judging by the smudges. It means that a limited number of copies have been circulated. I believe that the men who were given these copies were instructed to kill Colonel Catlin at some time when conditions favored the murder. That's why the habits of Catlin were so carefully outlined. We've got to act—this time, not against crooks and ordinary killers, but against a Trojan Horse!"

"Yuh mean one of them things the Nazis beat Norway with?" Butch asked. "That's a wooden horse, ain't it?"

"It was a wooden horse in the days when it originated," Tony Quinn answered. "Now it has changed its characteristics to those of a slimy serpent that burrows underground and occasionally raises its head to strike. When the opportune moment comes, it will sneak out of its hole and create havoc. Before that day arrives it must be crushed underfoot like the crawling thing it is."

"Show me where I can put my foot on it!" Butch howled furiously. "Just show me."

Tony Quinn leaned back on the high stool in front of the bench.

"But it's not as easy as that. Foreign agents have been living here for years, plotting and planning for just this moment. They are all around us, some of them in high offices. Our job is to rout out as many as possible. Here's our course of action. Butch, I want you to go back to the police station and tell them you're sorry about what happened, that maybe this man you threw around isn't as bad as he seems to be. Ask to see him. He won't be there, for the forces behind him will have furnished bail by now.

"Find out who posted the bail. Find out, if you can, all the facts contained in his record. Determine the name of his attorney, because it would take a clever one to get him out if he is gone. Then report to Carol."

"Do I get in on this, sir?" Silk asked with restrained eagerness.

"When Butch gets his information, it's your turn," Tony Quinn said. "You will watch the man, find out whom he contacts. Carol, you are to stand by your phone for the present. I'm going to see Colonel Catlin. Perhaps he knows some reason why these spies are trying to kill off the ex-service men. Silk, get out my paraphernalia. The Black Bat will spread his wings...."

CHAPTER III

POLICY OF RUTHLESSNESS

J UST BEFORE he donned the robe and hood of the Black Bat, Tony Quinn made a neat parcel of certain instruments he thought would be necessary. Fighting spies that would resort to Trojan Horse activities required the same kind of stealth they used. The Black Bat intended to work against them with their own brand of ruthlessness and slyness.

He put two loaded automatics into special holsters on his person, removed the hood temporarily and replaced it with a wide-brimmed hat. Whenever the Black Bat worked more or less openly, he had to shield his features as well as he could. Those hideous scars around his eyes revealed his identity, with which practically every police officer in the city was familiar.

Carol put a hand on his shoulder and looked anxiously into his eyes.

"Tony, this is probably the most dangerous job you've ever under-taken. Ordinary thugs and killers aren't as clever. They don't have the tremendous resources behind them, nor the number of men a spy ring can control. Please be careful—for my sake. I know just how necessary this work is, and I hope I get into it actively, too. But there's so much danger...."

"In a way," Tony Quinn admitted slowly. "But remember that these rats will be just as afraid of me as I'll probably be of them. If I can, I'll put them on the defensive, make them look to their own wits. It it's necessary, I'll wear them down, one by one. This is a game without mercy. They'll certainly extend none and I'm not inclined to be soft-hearted with termites who undermined so many European democracies by boring from below—and above. Perhaps by morning I'll know more about what we face. Meanwhile we can't let them get to Colonel Catlin. At exactly nine o'clock, you are to phone Catlin's apartment."

Tony Quinn dropped into the tunnel and made his way to the garden house. Within a few seconds he was seated behind the wheel of Butch's old coupé. This car was something like a Q-Boat, for though it looked like a wreck, there was plenty of speed in her smoothly running motor. Recently the Black Bat had installed cleverly hidden compartments which held a rifle with telescopic sights and a sub-machine gun with plenty of ammunition.

He wondered now, as he drove toward the apartment house where Colonel Catlin lived, if some premonition had caused him to make those arrangements. Dealing with Trojan Horse activities might easily require the use of fast-firing automatic rifles or some careful sniping with the assistance of telescopic sights.

It was blindingly dark in the vicinity of the colonel's home. High, heavily branched shade trees gave the street a gloomy touch, but for the Black Bat this was perfect. He parked the car, faded into the darkness of an adjoining building and drew on his hood. Under one arm he carried the package he had made up in the laboratory.

The Black Bat strode rapidly through the night. An ordinary man pursuing this particular course would have stumbled over an oil tank intake that jutted out of the ground. But the Black Bat saw it as plainly as though it were bathed in sunlight. Everything which would have been an obstacle to any other person was easily avoided by the Black Bat.

HE REACHED the rear of the apartment house, which was not a large one. There were no lights in the cellar, indicating that the superintendent was not on duty all the time. This exactly suited the Black Bat's plans. He slipped up to the basement door, examined the lock in the intense darkness and then inserted a key he selected from the ring he carried. The lock slid back on the first attempt.

He slipped into the cellar, closed the door and quietly placed an empty pail about a foot away from it. If anyone tried to sneak in, there would be a terrific clatter.

The Black Bat searched through the gloom of the cellar until he spotted the telephone system. Striding to it, he examined the tiny identifying tags hooked to the various wires from the different apartments. Since he had looked up Colonel Catlin's phone number, he found the proper wire in less than a minute. Swiftly he unwrapped his package, revealing a compact device for tapping wires. He hooked this up, found an old chair and sat down.

From time to time, he glanced at his wrist-watch. When the hands were almost on the hour, he finally heard a buzz. Colonel Catlin's booming voice answered. The Black Bat smiled contentedly, for the caller was Carol, pretending that she had obtained the wrong number. The Black Bat knew now that Catlin was home and that his wire was successfully tapped. If Catlin was lured anywhere, the Black Bat would know that, too.

The spy ring was bound to strike against him soon. Probably the man Butch had mussed up was assigned to this work, if he had obtained his freedom. They would, of course, want to make it seem like an accident, and therefore the Black Bat saw little danger of any attempt at murder while Catlin was home. A hit-and-run driver, or a band of fake robbers who slugged their victim too hard—that would be the best means of accomplishing their designs.

Thirty minutes crawled by before the line buzzed again. The Black Bat listened intently.

"Colonel," the caller said, "this is Anton Morino. I must see you on a matter of vital importance. I cannot leave my home, nor can I explain over the phone. Will you come out here, please? Believe me, I wouldn't call if this were not an extremely serious matter. And please tell no one I called."

"Why, of course I'll come, Anton," Colonel Catlin said. "If I can help you in any way at all, don't hesitate to ask me. Where do you live?"

The man called Anton Morino gave specific directions, which Catlin had to write down to remember. They involved many turns at certain streets. Morino was giving anything but idle directions. This was a trap—a death trap for Catlin! If he followed that route, as he certainly would, death would be waiting somewhere along the roads!

The Black Bat quickly unhooked his instrument and returned to where his car was parked.

Five minutes later Catlin hurriedly emerged. He crossed the street, backed his car out of a garage and headed north. The Black Bat followed, far enough behind to avoid detection, yet close enough to act quickly when things would start happening. Exactly how the killers would operate he didn't know. Most of the section Catlin had been told to traverse was unfrequented. Shots could be fired or even a bomb thrown. But the Black Bat doubted that the killers would resort to such obvious means.

THE CHASE led to the outskirts of the city. Carefully as the Black Bat had watched before, now he searched everything ahead with his incredible eyes. He saw an intersection and—what an ordinary man wouldn't see—a car parked at the junction of each cross artery. Instantly the Black Bat stamped heavily on the gas pedal, making it hit the floor. The old car spurted forward.

But Catlin had already reached the intersection. As he crossed it, both cars shot out. Catlin must have seen one of them coming, for he yanked the wheel hard, veering to the right. The other car was coming from that direction. There was a deafening crash of smashed metal, splintered glass and exploding tires.

The Black Bat was traveling without lights, so he knew his car wouldn't be seen in the intense darkness. Besides, the killers had selected a spot where there would be little traffic. They didn't want to be found at their bloody work.

As the Black Bat turned off the road, he saw four men emerge from the two heavy sedans. One held a short length of iron pipe. Rushing up to Catlin's sedan, they pulled open the battered door and reached in to yank Catlin out. After they stretched him alongside the wreck, three of the men drew back. The actual killer raised the short iron bar. His lips parted in a snarl of hatred as his breath came in savage hisses—until he stopped breathing.

From the darkness beside the road, a jet of flame and the roar of a gun startled the killers. The man with the iron pipe moaned and collapsed across Catlin's sprawled form. The other three whipped out guns and started shooting in the direction of the gun flame. But as the Black Bat pulled the trigger of his weapon, he tensed, moved fast. Every bullet of the spies missed him by yards. They couldn't see him, but they could not know that they presented perfect targets to the super-sensitive eyes of the Black Bat.

One leaped toward Catlin and aimed his gun at the helpless man's head. But he did not shoot. He was dead before he had finished raising his gun.

The other two gave a single bleat of alarm and raced for their undamaged car. As they got in, three bullets smashed through the windows. The whine and crash only served to lend wings to their flight. The car started off with a grinding of hastily shifted gears. Carefully the Black Bat steadied his gun on one arm and sent another slug through the rear window. It had shatter-proof glass, but the Black Bat was using steel-jacketed, high-powered forty-fives in this fight. He was answering terrorism with ruthlessness.

The sedan disappeared into the night while the Black Bat ran over to Catlin. Brutally he hauled the dead spy off, and gently raised the colonel's head. Catlin opened his eyes and stared blankly. He could just make out the outline of the hooded head, though the Black Bat could see every line of his pain-contorted face.

"DON'T BE alarmed," the Black Bat said softly. "You have not been badly hurt. The accident knocked you out and a quartette of playboys tried to make a real job of it by bashing your head in or putting a slug through it. The two men who actually tried to wipe you off the face of the earth were killed. I had to shoot them to save you."

"But I don't understand," Catlin protested weakly. "Please help me up. I—I feel fairly strong now. You killed these two men because they were trying to murder me? Nonsense! Who would want to kill me? I haven't an enemy in the world."

The Black Bat laughed without mirth.

"I'm sorry to contradict you, Colonel. You have several million enemies. Two are dead, but two others got away. They may get help and return. Lean on me, and don't be afraid of me because of the outfit I'm wearing."

"I'm not," Catlin answered. "I know you are the Black Bat and that you saved my life. But why in the world should anybody want to kill me?"

"I'll explain later," the Black Bat said.

He helped Catlin into his old coupé and then ran back to where the two spies lay dead. This was one of the few times that there was no remorse in the Black Bat's heart. He had been forced to kill before. More than once his victim had been some wild-eyed crook who, with a different childhood environment, might not have turned to crime. That kind the Black Bat had never wanted to destroy. But these two men—spies and saboteurs who lived for the day when they might hurl destruction on the entire nation—their deaths didn't bother his conscience.

He knelt beside them. In the center of their foreheads he pasted stickers fashioned after the image of a bat in flight, with wings outspread, dark and mysterious. Then he returned to the coupé and drove several miles away.

CHAPTER IV

HUMAN TARGET

PARKING IN a dark spot, the Black Bat shut off the motor and extracted a pack of cigarettes from a pocket beneath his robe. He handed one to Catlin, lit it and then touched flame to his own. In the glare of the match Catlin saw sharp, cold eyes gleaming from behind the mask. He shivered, praying that he would never be on the wrong side of the game with the Black Bat hunting him down.

"You've been to several military funerals lately, eh, Colonel?"

Catlin frowned. "Why, yes. But what has that to do with a plot to murder me?"

"The men whose funerals you attended also thought they had no enemies, but they were murdered. I can't prove that, of course, yet I know it to be true. By a stroke of good fortune, I discovered you were on the list and I took steps to prevent your murder. Enemies, Colonel? You have millions of them! This nation is rearming. We don't want war, but we want to be ready for it if it comes to our shores.

"Besides our defense preparations, we're supplying the nations that hate and distrust the explosive forces of might. We're trying to keep the world a decent place to live in. At this moment, we're free men, and we'll fight to maintain that freedom. But we're being fought, too, by shadowy figures who work in the dark with underhanded methods.

"Other nations have had tragic experiences with the Trojan Horse, the spies who make countries defenseless by confusing and sabotaging preparations. Those men we must stop."

"Yes, of course," Catlin agreed. "But I still don't see how I'm involved."

"You're in it up to your ears. We're training men, thousands upon thousands of them. More are being brought into the service every day. They need instruction from experienced men to teach them how to fight. If the spies can prevent that, it will be as great a disaster as the sinking of our battleships or the blowing up of our munitions factories. You and those four officers who were murdered—all of you were retired, but you can still be called to active service at any time.

"That call must be coming soon or those spies wouldn't act so quickly. I'm betting everything on the fact that Washington intends to recall you experts to train the green troops. We are under-officered and that condition can be remedied only by having men like you train your successors. The spies want to prevent that and they are willing to resort to murder to do it. Now can you see that there are enemies who can't allow your existence?"

CATLIN WIPED his sweating forehead, took an immense drag on his cigarette.

"Of course I see, and I'm grateful that you showed me the light. Yes, I am about to be called back, just as you say. Those devils certainly are working cleverly. They intend to murder us old men, and we are easy prey. Then, when our ranks are so badly depleted, they'll tackle the younger officers. No one will realize what is happening till it's too late. We'll make them know! Take me home. I'm going to call Washington and, if you don't mind, I'll mention your name."

"You have my permission," the Black Bat said. "I want those slinking spies to know I'm fighting them. That's why I left souvenirs on the two men I killed. But before we start back, I want to know about this Anton Morino who lured you into this trap with a phone call."

"Anton?" Catlin gasped. "Great heavens, he can't be involved! That isn't possible. He hates everything those spies represent. He hates them with all the malevolence of a man who has actually seen their work of destruction. Anton Morino came here from Tyrolean Austria, just after Hitler invaded it. He had to flee for his life."

The Black Bat started his car and pulled onto the road.

"Perhaps, Colonel. Norway accepted many people like that—men who presumably fled from the Nazi wrath. And what happened? Those the Norwegians befriended turned traitor, dug knives into their backs.

They were sent to smooth and prepare a field of action for armed forces that would eventually arrive.

"Don't forget that those monsters don't adhere to the rules of the game—only when someone else pulls the same trick on them. Then they squawk to high heaven and protest that they've been fouled. Anton Morino may be wholly innocent, but until I'm convinced, he stays on my list of suspects. I must insist that you do not let him know what happened."

BUTCH O'LEARY, in response to the Black Bat's orders, paid a short visit to Police Headquarters and then phoned Carol's apartment.

"They thought I was nuts because I wanted to tell that bum I was sorry. But anyhow he's free. Guy named Anton Morino put up ten grand in cash and the bum walked out. What do I do now?"

"Go back to your room and wait," Carol said. "I'll tell Silk what happened."

Silk Kirby was seated before a mirror in one of the upstairs rooms when the phone rang. His appearance was undergoing a radical change. In the past, Silk had learned to adapt himself to two disguises that used to be of great assistance when he pried spare cash from the bankrolls of people with more larceny than honesty in their hearts. Now, as the Black Bat's right-hand man, these disguises often proved invaluable. There could be no connection between the operation of the Black Bat's aide and Silk Kirby, or the whole secret might be exposed. Silk was becoming almost as well known as his master.

He widened his face, changed the contour of his lips and created a couple of sacks under his eyes. A wig, cleverly fastened to his bald pate, made him look years younger.

Silk answered the phone, using the upstairs connection. He listened to Carol's instruction, then hung up. Hastily he completed his disguise with a suit of clothes that Silk Kirby, gentleman's gentleman, would never have worn even to an masquerade.

He locked the house from the inside, slipped out through the tunnel and hailed a taxi two blocks from the house. He had already checked Anton Morino's address, and before long he was studying the place from a safe distance.

It was an old, rambling house, without close neighbors and well isolated from the road by big trees and plenty of shrubbery. Silk was grateful for the protection that these natural barriers offered. He sneaked into the grounds, fumbled around and picked up a small stone, which he threw toward the back of the house. When no dogs set up a clamor, he breathed a sigh of genuine relief.

Silk knew plenty of ways of entering a house without those inside being aware. Many of his former associates had been crooks of high caliber—in their professions, if not in their characters. When he crept to the rear of the house, he blinked in amazement. Four big cars were parked in one of the gloomier spots, yet the house itself was darkened.

Silk straightened up from a crouching position just beneath a window. He failed to raise it, and resorted to the use of a thin piece of metal that he carried on these expeditions. Forcing back the latch successfully, he clambered through the open window and stood listening.

He could hear muffled voices that seemed to come from near the floor, directly across the room. Silk stepped forward warily, moving his hand cautiously in front of him to locate furniture. If he stumbled now, there was no telling what the result might be. He found that the voices came from an old-fashioned hot air vent. Apparently this house was no more up-to-date than its outward appearance suggested. Silk knelt on the floor and listened.

A MAN with a loud, authoritative voice was speaking. With each word, Silk's blood ran one degree colder. The Black Bat's hunch had certainly paid off! This must be one of the chief hideaways of the spy ring.

"And so," the voice went on, "we are this day almost prepared. Yet we must not relax in our vigilance, nor in our constant training. You men gathered here have shown poor results in target practice. When the time comes, I will need men who can shoot fast and straight. Therefore you will report to Hans at the old farm, where no one can hear your practice shots. Prepare yourselves, my lieutenants, for our day is coming soon!

"You will remain at the farm until your aim is true and your firing rapid. Then, and only then, will you be ready. We are strong, yes, but do not let these Americans fool you by their apparent lassitude. Once aroused, they will fight back like demons. We must arrange it so they will have no leaders. Even now we are in the process of wiping out another man who might prove harmful to our mission. He is number five, but there will be more—many mote—and these fools here will go on placidly, never suspecting murder."

"That is right," another voice broke in. "I, Erik Wolfram, say it is so. You have been sent here from the mighty Gestapo to direct our efforts. We are cleverer than any of the fools who oppose us. Even though we have never seen you, our Director, we obey you implicitly. Our cause cannot fail."

"Good," the booming voice approved. "It is well. Now you will stand at attention. About-face, all of you. Do not turn back for five minutes.

Any further orders will come over the usual channels. You have but to keep your eyes open."

A moment later Silk heard a car door slam shut. He scurried across the floor toward the window. Undoubtedly the man leaving the place was the spy leader, unknown even to his own men. Silk knew that if he could seize and identify him, half the battle would be won. But as he reached the window, a car flashed by, turned into the street, and vanished.

He cursed softly and determined to satisfy his frustration by exposing these rats who characteristically used a cellar as their meeting place. The man they called their Director had spoken of a target range where his legions could learn how to kill effectively. More than anything else, he had to find the location of that farm.

Silk looked around for a hiding place, for the men in the cellar would be coming up soon. He headed toward the hallway, moving with absolute silence. He was halfway down the hall when the front door opened and the hall lights were turned on. Silk's hand darted toward the gun in his pocket. But he was a fraction of a second too slow. One of the two men in the hall had him covered.

"What's the idea of using a gun, copper?" Silk snarled, though the men wore civilian clothes. "I ain't robbin' the joint. I'm just lookin' for a place to hole up for the night."

Silk's voice attracted those in the cellar. He swallowed with difficulty when he counted eleven burly men as they filed into the spacious hallway.

"HOLY SMOKE!" Silk carried on his act. "I figured this joint was vacant. Say, all you mugs can't be cops. What is this—a stag party?"

A broad-shouldered man moved ominously toward Silk. When he spoke, his voice identified him as Erik Wolfram.

"Who are you? What are you doing in this house? How long have you been here?"

Silk jerked his head in the direction of the living room.

"I just opened a window about a minute ago and came in. I'm on the lam. The cops are after me and I figured this was one swell spot to hide. So—"

"He lies," one of the men ground out. "A minute ago we stood at attention as our Director's car left here. We turned our backs on it according to orders. We therefore faced the house, and we did not see this man going through any window. He is a spy—an accursed Government-man!"

Silk started forward until a gun, pressed against his chest, stopped him.

"I don't know what kind of an outfit I ran into," he snapped, "but don't call me no G-man. I hate their guts. Search me if you want to. I'm heeled, but you won't find nothin' that'll make you think I'm a G-man or any other kind of a cop. You mugs got me all wrong."

One of the two men who had entered through the front door departed after whispering to Wolfram. When he returned, he carried a corpse over his shoulder. He dropped it and went out after the second body. As the dead men were turned on their backs, Silk gave an involuntary start. Between the eyes of each man was pasted a Black Bat sticker!

"So, perhaps you are not of the police," Wolfram snarled. "But those two men belonged to my organization, and the man who killed them branded his work. We all have heard of the Black Bat. You are the Black Bat!"

"Me?" Silk howled. "Say, if that guy ever caught up with me, I'd be laying there right between your two boys. Listen, if the Black Bat is on your trail, run for cover. I'm tellin' you he's poison."

Wolfram allowed an enigmatic smile to cross his face.

"But perhaps I have the antidote for that poison, eh? You are the Black Bat. You killed my men and spoiled certain plans of mine. Somehow, you learned of this place and sneaked in to watch and listen. But you will never profit by it. A short time ago we received orders to improve our shooting. Even now, we are ready to go to a certain spot where we may shoot as often as we like, without interference. Yet we were desolate because we would have nothing but inanimate targets to shoot at.

"Now all that is changed. We have you—the Black Bat! We can indeed become proficient with you standing before us as a target. You will not mind a little fun like that, eh?"

Silk's eyes flashed across the group of sinisterly grinning killers. Suddenly he lunged forward, slapping down Wolfram's gun as he did so. He managed to bury one fist into Wolfram's stomach and another in a blow that glanced off the cheek. The rest of the mob closed in, eager for blood.

Half a dozen pistol butts slashed at Silk, and most of them collided with his head.

He fell to one knee, wound his arms around the legs of the nearest man and pulled him to the floor. Then a savage tattoo of gun butts all but split his skull apart. He fell face forward and lay utterly still.

CHAPTER V

DESPERATION

SILK AWOKE to the pitching of a car traveling over a rough road. He groaned and tried to move, but his hands and legs were firmly tied. When he attempted to open his mouth, he found that a gag choked back everything more articulate than a groan. A hefty foot struck him on the back of the neck, forced his face into the filthy carpet on the floor. He had to stay that way, half strangling, until the car finally stopped. Then the foot was removed.

Before Silk could even gain a normal breath, his ankles were grabbed and he was dragged out of the car. His head struck the running board so hard that he almost lapsed back into unconsciousness. Bitterly he wished that had happened. It might have lasted long enough to spare him the terror of the grisly end they planned for him.

Two other cars without lights pulled up, and laughing, highly elated men clambered out. Silk was dragged on his back to an old barn, where his legs were dropped. Two men stood guard over him while the others disappeared into the house. For a few moments there was nothing but silence, until the frogs in some nearby swamp lost their sudden fear. Silk shuddered. That was where they would throw what was left of him. In this forsaken spot, his body would never be found.

At last the men filed out again. Silk was hoisted to his feet and the rope around his ankles severed. The gag was also removed before Wolfram confronted him.

"This," he waved an arm expansively, "is theoretically the property of the Fatherland, for it was bought with our money. Here, on the soil of our real country, we accuse you of being a spy. The sentence is death by gunfire—immediately! Walk ahead of me to that tree, the one near the foot of that hill."

Silk fought down his impulse to shudder. He was going to die, but he would not give these murderers the pleasure of seeing a man yap and beg to save his life. He knew that was what they were anticipating, because genuine disappointment showed in Wolfram's eyes.

"Well, thanks for the fast trail, anyway," Silk grunted. "It was stream-lined, all right, but you went too quick for justice to catch up. It doesn't matter. I'll be seeing all of you when the Black Bat goes to town. You can't laugh him off, Nazi. He just doesn't scare. Let's go. You boys want your fun, and I wouldn't spoil....

Wolfram struck viciously, a backhand blow across the mouth.

"You will not speak those brave words when we begin shooting. How can the Black Bat harm us after we kill him? You are the Black Bat, so what is the use of pretending? Walk before me. The slightest trick will mean a bullet through your leg."

Two men seized Silk's arms, half carried, half dragged him toward the tree. He closed his eyes in misery as he stumbled along. Not only had he sacrificed his own life, but he had failed the Black Bat as well! The only comfort he could find was the two Black Bat stickers that had been pasted to the foreheads of Wolfram's men. The Black Bat had already collected a fifty percent profit on what was going to happen now.

THEY LASHED Silk to the tree. A car was driven close enough for the high beam of its headlights to make Silk close his eyes wearily.

"So, it is ready," Wolfram gloated. "We are miles from the nearest dwelling, still farther from any highway. There is no one to hear our shots nor the screams of the spy. Aim for the legs and arms first. We must learn to cripple as well as kill. There may be some we shall wish to take alive, eh? Max, you caught this man. Your reward is that you may have the first shot. Aim well, for the right arm."

Max bared his teeth in a murderous smile as he strode forward importantly. He cocked his revolver and spread his big feet apart to balance himself. Raising the pistol, he sighted Silk's right shoulder along the barrel. A hush fell over the others who waited their turns. This was a supreme moment in their lives. Before their eyes, a man was to die.

Silk didn't brace himself for the impact of the first slug, nor even open his eyes. Nothing seemed to matter now. But when he heard a shot, his eyes widened involuntarily. He waited for the terrific blow and agonizing heat of a bullet smashing through his body. But he had not been hit! Instead, Max was slowly rocking back and forth, the weapon sagging in his hand. Even through the blinding glare of headlights, Silk could see the bluish hole directly through the forehead of the ex-gunner.

A man shouted a hoarse Teutonic curse, ran frenziedly to the still twitching body of his dead friend. He raised his gun savagely. A shot blasted the frightful stillness—and his gun dropped out of his hand!

This time Silk realized that the shot had come from the darkness behind him. Hope surged through his heart, but not for long. As the second victim of that uncanny marksman dropped, Wolfram screeched orders. "Kill him—no matter what happens!"

The men started forward. Instantly unholy bedlam burst loose. An automatic rifle sent whining chunks of steel just above the heads of the charging men. They broke in terror and spread wildly in all directions.

The rapid shooting followed them as they headed for their cars, did not stop even when they piled into two black sedans. A few snapped shots back at Silk, but they were fired on the run and the bullets missed by yards.

Abruptly a weird form broke from the thick woods behind Silk. The gun poised at his shoulder was still firing a challenge at the fleeing men. Then, as the mysterious rifleman came into the scope of the headlights from the abandoned car, Silk gave a shout. There was no mistaking the simulated wings and the hood of the Black Bat!

SILK WAS so weak on his legs after his ghastly ordeal that the Black Bat helped him into the coupé, which had been well hidden off the lane. He grinned at Silk.

"Those rifles certainly came in handy. I reached Anton Morino's house just as they were carrying you out, so I followed the parade. While they held a conference in the farmhouse, I found myself a good spot for some neat shooting. Two of them are dead. If the others hadn't run, there would have been a slaughter. You see, Silk, you're worth a thousand of those lice. Now if you feel well enough, we'll see what those dead men have on them. I'd also like to take a look inside the farmhouse."

As they searched the dead spies, they piled up a small heap of junk. The men were well supplied with cash, which the Black Bat appropriated.

"We'll send it to the Red Cross," he smiled. "Silk, look at this. It's a plain heavy card with a series of small holes punched in it. See the way those holes are arranged? Three with short spaces, then a large space and two more. In some places there are as many as five of the holes in a group."

"Code?" Silk asked promptly.

"I don't know. A code of this kind, depending on sets of symbols, wouldn't necessarily have to consist of holes. It would be easier to make a few dots. Anyhow, we'll take these with us. If it is a code, I'll study it as soon as I have time. Let's head for the farmhouse."

The Black Bat picked up the automatic rifle in his crooked arm, and Silk held the repeater rifle equipped with telescopic sights.

"They've got a leader they call the Director," Silk said. "I overheard that much before they grabbed me. Whatever they are up to is about ready, so they'll strike soon. This Director isn't even known to them. He makes them turn their backs when he leaves the place. Maybe he puts a screen in front of him while he talks. Anyway, I heard him tell those skunks that more orders would follow and all they had to do was merely to keep their eyes open."

"Odd," the Black Bat said puzzledly. "Keep their eyes open for orders? They usually come by mouth. He should have told them to keep their ears cocked instead. This is no haphazard organization, Silk. It's headed by a man specially trained for this kind of work. Either he or his lieutenants must be in the confidence of certain high officials. That's what makes it difficult. You can't clean up a snake's nest until you know where it is. Watch out now. We may run into some trouble in this house."

The Black Bat found that only an unlocked screen door barred his way. He opened it, dodged with cautious swiftness into a big kitchen. He and Silk grew rigid. From one of the distant rooms came a low moan. Holding their rifles ready, they searched the place. In the living room they found a gray-haired man lying in a pool of his own blood. He was still alive, but dying fast. A knife had been thrust through his throat, and another wound close to his heart was pumping a scarlet stream.

PAINFULLY THE dying man lifted one hand off the floor. Between his shaking fingers he held a card that had been punched with a series of holes exactly like those they had taken from the two dead spies. The gray-haired victim seemed to be trying to tell them something with his eyes, for the knife in his throat prevented speech. When the Black Bat took the card, the man attempted a wan smile before his head dropped with a bang on the floor.

"They killed him because he probably knew too much and they thought he wasn't trustworthy," the Black Bat said grimly. "We'll pay them back for this murder. Search the house, Silk. Look especially for letters and papers."

While Silk busied himself, the Black Bat compared the three cards. The two that had been taken from the dead spies were identical. The holes matched up exactly when he placed one over the other. But the third, which was still wet with the murdered man's blood, didn't compare at all. The holes were in radically different series. That these cards meant something vitally important was absolutely plain, but the Black Bat could find no answer.

Silk came hurrying down from the second floor with a bunch of letters tied with a piece of rough cord. The Black Bat opened several of them, found they were written in German. He knew enough of the language to make a rough translation.

"Damn them," he cried. "Silk, this man died trying to help us! He was in league with the spy ring, but not because he wanted to be. These letters are from his wife and two daughters, who are interned in Germany. The letters plead with him to obey the orders of the Gestapo and to keep a close mouth about everything. Now, probably, those three help-less women will be killed or forced to work themselves to death for a cause they hate. This isn't new. They've done it before, in several parts of the world, but it's the first time I've come into actual contact with it. Silk, I wish I'd cut down every one of those men. Come on, we're going back to town. I want to see a Tyrolean Austrian named Anton Morino."

CHAPTER VI

TWO SICK MEN

CAUTIOUSLY THE BLACK BAT parked his car near Anton Morino's home.

"I'll take the rear," he told Silk. "You tackle the front. Use that auto-matic rifle if necessary. If Morino was warned that you are still alive, he has probably run away. But I have a hunch those rats we dispersed are too busy hunting their own cover to help anyone else."

Silk approached the house carefully, and in silence climbed over the east railing of the porch. He bent low for a quick look inside. A man, about fifty years old, was pacing the floor, nervously running his hand through his thick shock of pure white hair. He was heavily built, though not tall, and clad in expensive clothing. He looked clever and meticulous about his appearance.

Silk didn't wait. There might be others in the house, but by now the Black Bat would be ready for action. Silk stood erect, smashed the window with the barrel of his gun.

"Lift 'em high!" he snapped. "That's right. Now walk over here and unlatch this window. Open it wide. Move back ten paces and keep turned toward me. Don't forget that this is a Tommy-gun. It shoots fast and straight."

Silk climbed through the window. Anton Morino sat down heavily and covered his eyes, moaning.

"So it has come at last! For all that I have done, the reward is death. Yet I have expected it." He looked up and his face was agonized. "Shoot—go ahead and shoot me! That's what they sent you here for. I know that one failure is repaid with execution. I have failed, somehow. I don't know how. I don't even care. It will be heaven's blessing when I am dead. Shoot, damn you! Why do you look at me like that?"

A curtain at the far end of the room moved aside and the Black Bat emerged. When he stepped up to Anton Morino, the Nazi's harrowed look changed to awe and terror. He started from his chair, but Silk pushed him back.

"You are the Black Bat!" Morino screamed. "They killed you! You are dead! They told me they were taking you away to kill you—and they never fail...."

"They fail more often than they admit," the Black Bat answered grimly. "Morino, you deliberately lured Colonel Catlin out of his apartment tonight, and sent him over a route along that you knew would mean his death. You are involved in this spy ring. Unless you tell me everything about it, you really will die. First of all, why did you think this man with the machine gun was sent here to kill you?"

"Because I failed them," Morino groaned. "They do not tolerate failure, even when it is not my fault. Colonel Catlin is my friend. I didn't want to help in his murder, but what else could I do? They forced me into it. When he did not die, they said my arrangements were not satisfactory and I would hear from the Director. We men in the ranks hear from him only by bullets or knives. You must believe me."

"Just keep on talking," the Black Bat said. "Who is this Director? Where is the headquarters of the ring? What are they up to?"

"I don't know who he is," Morino cried hysterically. "No one knows his name nor what he looks like. He never permits himself to be seen. But he must be an important man, high in the confidence of officials, because he seems to know everything. There are no headquarters. The Director designates a certain place, and those who receive the orders assemble there. Tonight it was in my own home.

"His intentions are to disrupt the preparedness plans of the United States by any methods necessary. He cares nothing for human lives. He also wishes to prevent supplies from reaching his military enemies. I tell you, he is not human. He is a monster from the depths of hell!"

"What hold does he have on you?" the Black Bat suddenly demanded.

MORINO STAGGERED to his feet, clenching his hands.

"There is no use in being silent now. I am to be killed in any case. Let me open the safe hidden in the farther wall. I can show you things that will make your eyes open wide!"

He didn't wait for permission to cross the room. As he headed toward the farther wall, Silk and the Black Bat followed more slowly. But when he neared a wide rear window, he broke into a wild run and dived recklessly through the glass. Landing in a flower bed outside, he sprang up instantly and streaked away into the darkness.

Silk jerked the machine gun to his shoulder, but the Black Bat pushed the barrel down.

"We'll get him later, alive," he said. "Morino is desperate, Silk. He took a mighty long chance just now and he must have had some terrific reason for it. Keep your eyes open while I search the place."

Morino's home revealed none of the mysteriously punched cards. In fact, it seemed to have been stripped of anything which might have damaged Morino or the spy ring. The Black Bat wondered if he shouldn't have let Silk fire a withering hail of lead after the fleeing man. There was a chance that Morino had put on a good act. Was he the Director, the cunning spy leader who guided every movement along the path to death and destruction?

"Morino put up the bail for Hans Hofer's release," the Black Bat said later, as he and Silk were driving toward Tony Quinn's home. "Ten thousand dollars is a lot of cash to sacrifice, which means there's a paymaster, Silk. He may be this man known as the Director, but I'm sure this cash comes from Berlin and in quantities that are amazing. Imagine it! While their own people are half starved and go around in *ersatz* clothes, or barely any at all, the Nazi Government sends millions over here to keep their Gestapo busy. If we could stop that source of income, we'd break the spy ring wide open. They're faithful to the Fatherland, all right—as long as the money flows freely."

"Butch said there was another man with Morino," Silk informed. "A lawyer named Tolly obtained a *habeas* when the police refused to release Hofer even on bond. He also must know something. Why not pay him a visit?"

The Black Bat looked into the rear view mirror of the coupé. He wasn't being trailed, and no pedestrian was in sight. He pulled over to the curb.

"It's almost morning, Silk. We need rest and time to outline our plans. Tolly can wait. Let's go through the garden gate now. Hurry."

LATE THE next morning, Tony Quinn, holding his cane, tapped along the paths through his estate. His eyes were blank, staring straight ahead, as he walked with the characteristic caution of a blind man. A few people in the neighborhood saw him, which was exactly what he wanted. Not even for an instant did he wish Tony Quinn to be considered anything but hopelessly stone-blind. His former affliction now provided him with an excellent alibi.

Shortly after noon he entered the secret laboratory where he could work unobserved. Placing the three cards in front of him, he studied them with puzzled, brooding eyes. The cards were about the size of ordinary post cards, and the holes punched in them were perhaps a sixteenth of an inch in diameter. When he measured the distance between them, he found that even though several of the holes were grouped together, they were irregularly spaced. Obviously some kind of machine had punched those holes, yet why was there a discrepancy in the spaces?

The Black Bat had access to several master codes. For two hours he vainly tried to associate those holes with a code, but it just couldn't be done. He realized that each recipient of these cards might have a key in the form of a letter or book. By placing the card in a certain position, the holes would bring out certain letters.

"But if that's it," Quinn muttered, "this message must consist of about three small words. These holes wouldn't reveal entire words of ordinary print. There must be something else, some other way of using these cards. Here I probably have the solution to the whole mystery in my hands, and I can't even use it!"

Carol came through the tunnel, soon after dark. She listened intently as Tony Quinn described the events of the night before, and with each word her pretty face became more worried.

"They're such desperate men," she cried, "ready and eager to kill anyone! Fighting them here is worse than fighting them on an actual battleground. There you can recognize the enemy—the one in front, anyhow. But the enemy doesn't wear any uniform here, and he doesn't attack in the open. His weapon is a knife in the back. I wish there were no wars, no world troubles. Why can't we be fighting some nice gentlemanly band of murderers, or maybe some pleasant orphan asylum arsonists instead of these treacherous wolves?"

Quinn chuckled and sat down beside her.

"So far the score is in our favor, and I hope it stays that way. If I only knew where they'd strike next—what their main objectives are—but I'm temporarily stuck. I can't even find any members of that band to argue with."

CAROL LOOKED down at her well manicured nails and said:

"A week ago you told me about the various travel agencies in town, the ones that specialize in arranging trips to Germany, Austria, Holland, and Italy. I've checked them. Since the war started, they have done no business whatsoever, yet they are still in business. Their staffs remain the same, though no customer ever enters the offices. They haven't sold a steamship ticket in months, and still they pay rent on time."

"That's great news, Carol," Quinn exclaimed, his eyes glowing. "You've done fine work. Those agencies can legally, and without arousing suspicion, obtain money grants from their home offices. I suspect the whole business is controlled by the Gestapo. Through these travel agencies the spies must be supervised and paid off. That is the answer, I think."

"There is one group of German agencies," Carol went on. "They're headed by a man called Fritz von Elkin, and if I ever saw a true Nazi, he is it. He lives like a prince and keeps an office like the late Ziegfeld's, just above his travel agency on West Boulevard. I went in, asked for a job and did they snow on me! My accent wasn't so good, I guess."

"Well, that's something to start on," Quinn said thoughtfully. "Fritz von Elkin, eh? That hero used to lecture some years ago on German submarine warfare. I remember that when he told about sailors and passengers swimming hopelessly fifty miles from shore, he actually glowed all over. His attitude was so obvious that nobody would attend any more of his lectures. Von Elkin was an efficient submarine commander, and now he's probably a good spy. So we'll try to scuttle Herr von Elkin. Perhaps, if we get too close, he'll scuttle himself. We'll enter von Elkin's name in my mythical black book. Anton Morino heads it just now, and a lawyer named Tolly also seems to warrant being included."

"Can't I help you, Tony?" Carol asked. "About von Elkin, I mean."

Quinn shook his head. "I'm going to give von Elkin the benefit of my personal attention, Carol. You're much too pretty to be a burglar, and that's exactly what the Black Bat will become tonight. I'm going to perform a one man raid on the headquarters of the travel agency chain, as soon as I can get there.

"See if you can comfort Butch. He mopes around gloomily like a St. Bernard with his tail hanging down and swears I'm neglecting him. But there just isn't an opening for strong-arm work yet. Be a good girl and find Silk for me—without exhibiting yourself around the windows too much. Tony Quinn has no interest in girls, you know."

Carol doubled her fist and playfully tapped Quinn's chin with it.

"In other girls, you mean. I'll find Silk for you."

Quinn was donning his black clothing when Silk hurried in.

"Silk, get the big car out of the garage," he ordered. "I've got to visit the business section—as Tony Quinn. I want you to drive."

SILK PARKED across the street from a big business building. Across the full width of a huge window on the second floor ran a lurid neon sign, proclaiming that the Elkin Travel Service maintained its headquarters there. Above that were the windows of professional men's offices, mostly attorneys and doctors.

"I'm not feeling well," Quinn told Silk. "Something in the pit of my stomach makes me quite ill at times, so I think I'll pay Dr. Norton a visit. His offices are only one flight above the travel agency. There's a tow rope in the back of the car. Please take it out and help me coil it under my coat."

"You're not really sick, are you?" Silk asked with a worried frown.

Quinn pursed his lips. "Yes, but it's not incurable. It has something to do with a spy ring. Their methods are a bit nauseating, but the good Dr. Norton may be able to help. Here is where you come in. You're sick, too—headaches often bother you, and you want a complete physical examination. You'll see Norton first. He doesn't know you, and neither do I. Understand? Get that rope."

Silk took Tony Quinn's arm after he helped him out of the car. Quinn looked straight ahead with the blank stare of a blind man. As he tapped his cane, Silk led him across the street and into the building. They separated in the lobby and Silk went up first.

Quinn gave him five full minutes before he entered the elevator and had the attendant lead him to Dr. Norton's offices. When he went in, the most careful observer would have sworn that those eyes saw nothing. But Quinn noticed with satisfaction that there were no other patients. Dr. Norton came out, helped him into a chair.

"Tony, I haven't seen you in weeks! There's nothing seriously wrong, I hope?"

"Not at all," Quinn smiled. "Shall I go in?"

"If you don't mind, I have a patient in there now. It will take about half an hour, possibly a little longer. I'll ask him to wait if you're in a hurry."

"Did you ever know a blind man to be in a hurry?" Quinn countered. "I'll just sit here. Give your patient all the time he needs."

CHAPTER VII

BLIND MAN'S BLUFF

THE INSTANT Dr. Norton closed his door, Quinn swiftly went into action. He removed the gray tweed trousers he always wore, revealing beneath them the clothes of the Black Bat. From under his coat he took the robe and hood. After donning them, he hid his tweeds under the cushions of the sofa. Hastily he uncoiled the rope Silk had given him, opened the window and looked down. The rear windows of von Elkin's tourist agency were just below. He anchored the rope in such a way that it would hardly be noticed. Letting himself out the window, he lowered the sash so there would be no draft to puzzle Dr. Norton.

As he dangled just outside one of the agency windows, he opened the lock without much trouble and climbed into von Elkin's private suite. He listened carefully, heard nothing.

He examined the contents of the desk, though the place was dark. That didn't trouble him, for the Black Bat needed no light. When he found nothing of importance in the desk, he tackled the locked files standing against a wall. None of his keys would open them, and even a small pick he frequently used proved to be ineffectual.

"Well," he muttered, "von Elkin must have something mighty private in these drawers to have special tumbler locks installed on them." He sighed wearily. "I can't open it like a Jimmy Valentine, so I'll have to do the job as Butch would handle it."

For work of this kind, he always carried a compact kit of the finest tools. A special chisel, hit noiselessly with a padded hammer, cut a small hole in the steel paneling. As he inserted another instrument and twisted it, a large section of the cabinet ripped open like a sardine can. His sensitive fingers manipulated the lock through this hole and the drawer slid open easily.

The Black Bat saw a portfolio lying at the bottom of the drawer. He removed it and glanced sharply at the contents. They consisted of several maps of New York Harbor, showing particularly the placements of the shockingly few anti-aircraft batteries. Before he could search farther, he heard a key being inserted into a lock somewhere outside the office.

The Black Bat replaced the portfolio, stepped quietly to the door and moved with amazing speed to the window where his rope dangled. He gripped it, launched himself into space. But he didn't climb back to Dr. Norton's office. Instead, he began swinging in long arcs until he could look into the window of von Elkin's private quarters. When he reached it, his soft-soled shoes stopped the swing. Balancing himself precariously, he risked a quick glance into the now lighted offices.

Von Elkin, a towering man with a square face and a completely bald head, was cursing luridly at the sight of his burglarized steel drawer. There was one other man in the room—Anton Morino! But he didn't act the craven, terrorized victim of the spy ring's vengeance now. He appeared utterly confident of himself.

"I have long suspected something like this would happen," von Elkin grated. "No matter what the orders are, we go now! I cannot see why the orders were countermanded, anyway—nor why they sent you to tell me I should come back and make doubly sure I left nothing."

Morino was facing von Elkin, with his back toward the office door. As the Black Bat watched, the door opened slowly, silently, and a gloved hand holding a Luger pistol came into view. Before the Black Bat could give any kind of warning, the gun fired twice. Morino threw up his hands convulsively. He fell on the top of the desk and slid off it slowly, leaving a trail of dripping blood.

Five seconds later, a police whistle blasted the quiet outside the building. Loud voices shouted orders. The Black Bat took one more quick glance through the window. Von Elkin was running wildly toward the door.

THE BLACK BAT put the soles of both feet against the wall. Rapidly he climbed back to the window of Dr. Norton's waiting room, and was relieved when he saw that no other patients had entered. He closed the window quickly and coiled the rope around his middle, after he had removed the Black Bat's hood and cape. He slipped into the tweeds he had hidden under the sofa cushions, replaced his jacket and sat down hastily. Perhaps twenty minutes had elapsed since he had invaded von Elkin's offices.

Quinn's abnormally sensitive ears could hear the sound of confusion in the building and on the street. His hands, clasped on the curved handle of his cane, worked nervously. What was going on? Who had killed Morino? Why? What had von Elkin meant when he wondered why Morino had arrived with countermanded orders?

Ten minutes went by while Tony Quinn fidgeted and tried to puzzle out the meaning of all the excitement. Then Silk and Dr. Norton emerged from the consultation rooms. Silk glanced casually at Quinn and walked out. Dr. Norton helped Quinn to his feet and guided him into the other room. Dragging up a chair, he listened as Quinn described some symptoms indicative of an abused stomach. With a smile, the doctor wrote out a prescription, and they talked for a few minutes before Quinn left.

It took a long time for the elevator to reach his floor. When it finally arrived, the operator was shaking with excitement.

"Know what happened?" he yelped. "A G-man raid! Yes, sir— they just raided a tourist place, one of them German agencies! Boy, I never seen so many cops and G-men!"

Quinn left the elevator and entered a crowded lobby. Two men in plainclothes stepped up to him.

"Where did you come from?" one demanded. "Did you see a bald-headed, fat-faced man anywhere in the building?'

Quinn shook his head sadly. "I've been visiting Dr. Norton on the third floor. I didn't see anyone. I'm blind." A uniformed police lieutenant approached and recognized Quinn instantly.

He saw the gun fire twice.

"It's okay, boys," he said. This is Tony Quinn. He's blind, all right. Used to be D.A. before some rats threw acid in his eyes. How are you, Mr. Quinn?"

"Pretty fair," Quinn answered. "What in the world is happening?"

"We just raided a spy nest, sir. Got evidence enough, but no rat. He must have been tipped off. Can I help you outside?"

"Thanks, I'd appreciate it," Quinn said. "My car and the driver are across the street."

Silk elbowed his way to Quinn's side. As he reached for his employer's arm, Quinn was suddenly jerked around. Silk's face went grim, but Tony Quinn only looked blankly over the head of the man who held him. It was Detective-captain McGrath, self-appointed tracker of the Black Bat.

"Wait a minute, Quinn," McGrath snapped. "There's been a murder in this building. In the past few hours there were four others. Two of them were branded with the Black Bat's insignia. Get what I mean?"

"I gather the significance, McGrath," Quinn replied tiredly. "You think I'm the Black Bat. You believe I killed five men and stamped the murders as the work of the Black Bat. Then why don't you arrest me, Captain?"

McGrath flushed. "You know damned well why. Twenty doctors would swear you're blind. I'd make a fool out of myself."

"Don't flatter your creative ability," Silk put in with smooth irony. "You were a fool even before they threw you out of the second grade. Listen, Sherlock. Mr. Quinn is sick. He came here to visit Dr. Norton. Dr. Norton's office is upstairs. Now that Dr. Norton has examined him, I am going to take Mr. Quinn home. Is that simple enough for you to understand?"

"Try leaving here and I'll jug both of you," McGrath threatened. "Stay where you are till I see this Dr. Norton, if there is such a guy. Maybe this is one time you tripped on your own smartness, Quinn."

AS McGRATH disappeared into the building, an official car pulled up and two men emerged. Although the most careful observer would never have noticed his quick glance, Quinn recognized both men. One was Police Commissioner Warner, a slender, distinguished looking man. Beside him was Philip Trent, whom Quinn had known for ten years.

At one time, he had sympathized with Trent for the whole side of the man's face was deeply scarred, his hair was perfectly white, and he walked with a decided limp.

Quinn knew what had caused that. Trent had been a captain in the A.E.F. in 1918, when he led his men in a savage attack. Shrapnel and machine-gun bullets had almost torn him to shreds. Plastic surgery was crude in those days, and it hadn't helped his appearance much, although it had probably saved his life. Since he had also been badly scarred, Tony Quinn knew just how Trent must feel, yet the man worked prodigiously and was well on the way to becoming a power in politics.

Warner spotted Quinn and hurried up to him.

"Tony! What are you doing here?"

"He's waiting for a genius to make sure he didn't murder five guys," Silk explained witheringly. "Five, no less!"

Warner frowned. "McGrath again, eh? Well, Tony, you're free to go any time you wish. McGrath's suspicions are becoming a nuisance. Do you know Phil Trent? Oh, yes—of course you do."

Trent took Quinn's hand and clasped it firmly.

"Glad to see you again, Tony. It's too bad you're not the D.A. these days. We could use a man like you to fight these fifth columnists."

"He's right," Warner agreed warmly. "In conjunction with Federal men, we just raided a German tourist agency. I understand some evidence has been found, but the birds we hoped to trap left their nest. Trent is working with us and with the Federal authorities, helping to run down these influences. Wait. Here comes McGrath. I can tell by his face that the news he learned isn't at all satisfying."

McGrath saluted Warner and then looked at Quinn.

"You can go now, I guess. Doc Norton alibis you okay. The dead man upstairs hasn't got a Black Bat sticker on him, either."

"Ah," Quinn smiled. "Then my wrists are not going to be handcuffed. That's a distinct relief, Captain, although I sympathize with your disappointment. I know just how much you want to find the Black Bat. I'm particularly honored that you think I might be he."

"You?" Trent exploded. "How can any man in his right senses think you— Oh, I'm sorry, Tony. I know just how it feels to be—well, unable to take part in any activity. But McGrath's accusation was so absurd...."

Quinn was looking directly at Warner as he answered Trent.

"Forget it. A thing like this makes life interesting for a blind man. It gives me a great deal to think about. Good luck with your spy hunt, gentlemen. Silk, let's go back to the car."

SILK LED him through the crowd. As they reached the outer fringe of it, the driver spoke softly.

"When you get into the car, take a look at the entrance of the building, sir. There's a short, loudly dressed man there. It's Tolly, the lawyer who bailed out Hans Hofer! I overheard the cops questioning him. He's got an office on the seventh floor."

Quinn glanced across the street for a fraction of a second. McGrath was talking to the man Silk had described. Apparently everyone in the building was being questioned. Quinn leaned back against the cushions and lit a cigarette while Silk wormed his way through the slowly moving traffic.

"I saw the murder McGrath described," he stated quietly. "The victim was Anton Morino, but I don't know who killed him. Von Elkin was in there, too, only he got away. I can't figure out how he escaped. There was evidence in his offices that he was engaged in spy work, but you know that von Elkin is no fool. I can't believe that he'd be careless enough to leave such evidence lying around."

Silk picked up a newspaper and handed it to Quinn.

"I bought it while I was waiting for you, sir. There's an item on the front page that looks interesting."

Quinn put the paper on his lap in such a position that no one could possibly notice that he was reading it. The boxed item certainly was interesting.

ARMY OFFICER THWARTS BANDITS

Major Oliver Rankin, retired, successfully routed two robbers in the secluded sections of Bryant Park late this afternoon. They attempted to use blackjacks on him, but they did not realize that Major Rankin at one time was runner-up for the Army boxing championship. The major seems to have lost none of his prowess. Police are making an investigation. Major Rankin provided them with detailed descriptions of his assailants.

Quinn let the newspaper drop to the floor.

"So Rankin is on their list," he said. "Except for the attempt on Colonel Catlin's life, it's the first time the spy ring's executioners bungled their job. But Rankin is pretty fast with his fists even if he is nearly sixty years old. It's our break, Silk—the one I've been hoping for! They'll try to get Rankin again. Through the men assigned to kill him, I can contact the gang once more. Step on it!"

CHAPTER VIII

MEN WITHOUT MERCY

WHILE POLICE and G-men searched for more evidence of the spy ring's activities at von Elkin's offices, and Tony Quinn returned to his home, a factory on the outskirts of the city became an extremely busy place for so late at night.

It was a fairly large building, run by a man named Aranoff, and engaged in the manufacture of metal barrels and tanks. The factory closed promptly at five. But now—though the hour was close to ten—one whole section was lighted up and a number of cars stood inside the locked yard gates.

Word had gone out that the sales department was holding an important meeting, so the families living nearby thought nothing of it. Perhaps some of the employees wondered why business wasn't better with so large a sales force and all the meetings they held lately. But that was as far as their suspicions went.

Inside the plant, with every window and door carefully guarded, eighteen men were drawn up in two precise lines, standing at rigid attention. At the front of the large room was a five-inch dais, like a miniature stage. The face of it was studded with a battery of powerful lights that were equipped with reflectors.

Suddenly all the other lights in the room died away and the stronger ones were turned on. They blazed straight into the eyes of that strange audience, but no man moved even a muscle. When a harsh voice gave an order, the two rows of men pivoted completely around in military formation. The harsh voice spoke again and they faced the lights. If anyone stood on that stage now, he was completely invisible to his audience, for those lights defied any eyes to penetrate their glare.

"This will be one of our final meetings," a man's voice announced from somewhere behind the lights. "Soon now you will see my face. When you do, you will laugh, my lieutenants, at the way we have tricked these gullible Americans. Now listen to orders. Each of you controls a certain section of this country. Under you are the *Gauleiters* who strut like peacocks—and rightly so, for they are the backbone of our organization. Under them are the privates—the men who will do the fighting. Some of them will do so willingly, because they believe. Others will do so because they are ordered, and know that if they fail, someone dear to them will find life most miserable in Europe. For those who are not citizens, we have arranged that upon a given word they are to be arrested and deported. They will be useful, and upon completion of our mission, we can cast them aside. For, mind you, my lieutenants, there will be no room here for other men who crave power. That lies in our hands, and ours alone!"

A gruff shout went up from the two ranks and their right hands shot stiffly outward in a salute.

"We are almost ready to strike," the unknown leader went on. "All over the nation our groups have their guns, their ammunition and bombs—even gasses, if necessary. Every man knows his job. When you leave here, cards will be distributed. You will forward, one to each of the *Gauleiters* and warn them to stand ready. Bauer, step forward."

ONE OF the men in the front rank took two steps ahead of the others and stood at rigid attention.

"Your squads will concentrate on the submarine factories and bases in New England. They are to be blown to pieces beyond any hope of quick repair. Vogt and Schmidt, step forward."

Another pair moved out of ranks. The unknown spoke again, his voice venomous as he described their duties.

"You are in charge of the New York area. You will see to it that all transportation ceases, that officials who have spoken against us die. Confusion must reign throughout the city. The waterfront is to receive particular attention. No ship can remain intact nor any dock left useful. Our ships at sea will receive radio orders that will be taken care of.

"When we finish, this nation will be in such confusion that we can rapidly consolidate our positions. We shall create panic such as these fools have never before known. All their preparations for war will be demoralized. The help they are sending our enemies abroad will be cut off. We shall show them that we are the masters of the world!"

There were further explicit orders, all calculated to create panic and death. Great shouts went up, accompanied by the stiff-armed salutes. Then Max von Elkin stepped forward and received permission to speak.

"I have bad news. My travel agency was raided tonight. Anton Morino, one of our own kind, managed it! He lured me back to the office so I would be arrested, by stating that he had orders for me to take all my papers, even the non-incriminating ones. I escaped with the aid of the man who leads us so well. Once again he has proved beyond doubt that he is cut from the same great pattern as he who will eventually rule the world."

"And Morino is dead," the unknown's voice stated with a dry laugh. "I dislike only the fact that he died too quickly, for it was his scheme to have himself arrested with von Elkin. Then, safely in a cell, he would tell all he knew, how he was forced to help against his own will and judgment. But he was not quite clever enough, and his fate shall be a lesson to any of you men who may have the same idea.

"There is one other extremely important thing. We have not only the Federal authorities and the police to contend with, but also—the Black Bat! I see by your faces that you fear him. He is as aggressive as we, and he does not adhere to the silly laws of this country. Yes, he is a dangerous enemy, but not for long. Already I have set into motion a scheme which will trap him, and then—he dies!

"When I gave orders that Major Rankin was to be attacked without being injured, I knew just how the Black Bat would act. He has guessed our little scheme far ahead of the police. He knows we seek to eliminate as many trained officers as possible so the preparedness plans of this country will not go forward swiftly.

"The Black Bat will try to protect Major Rankin. Then we shall lure Rankin away, to a place of our own choosing. The Black Bat will follow. Rankin can be easily disposed of, and then we close in on the Black Bat. All is arranged. There cannot possibly be failure. By morning, the menace he constitutes will be no more."

MAJOR RANKIN, brittle-eyed disciplinarian and military tactician, adjusted his top hat while a doorman whistled for a cab.

"Nice evening, Major." The doorman touched the peak of his cap in salute. "Stepping out, eh?"

Rankin didn't smile in return, for he never smiled. Prior to his retirement two years before, he had been known as Sphinx Face.

"I'm making the rounds of my clubs," he stated. "Tomorrow I go back into active service. It seems they cannot do without me. Good night, Grogan."

Rankin climbed into the taxi and sat stiffly erect as it pulled away. The driver headed toward the Officer's Club, wondering unhappily if his tip would be the usual dime that Major Rankin dispensed. He cut over to an avenue and turned north, humming to himself, until another cab came alongside. The driver had his cap pulled so low that his features could not be seen. He blew a blast on his horn and yelled to Rankin's driver.

"Hey, buddy, the boys at the corner asked me to look for you. Your wife's been hurt. Better call your house quick."

The driver straightened up with a gasp, sought a hole in the traffic and pulled over to the curb. He got out and stuck his head in the door of the tonneau.

"Sorry, Boss, but it's my wife— She's been hurt. I'll call and see how bad she is. Won't take a minute and then I'll finish driving you to the club."

Rankin didn't like the idea, but he assented with a curt nod of his head. The driver vanished inside a drugstore.

Two men sidled up to the cab. One of them suddenly yanked open the door, jumped in and shoved a gun against Rankin's side. The other walked around the cab and slid behind the wheel.

"Quiet!" the man with the gun warned Rankin. "If you would live, do not utter one word."

The cab pulled away while Rankin turned scarlet with rage. Once he opened his mouth to speak, but the gun jabbed him painfully and he subsided. The gunman raised his head and peered out of the rear window.

"It goes well, Hugo. He comes."

Completely unaware that he was walking straight into a well laid trap, the Black Bat trailed Rankin's taxi. He had witnessed the clever change of drivers and blessed the hunch that warned him the killers might strike quickly.

When the taxi reached the outskirts and picked up speed, he drew one of his automatics and laid it on the seat beside him. Apparently Rankin was being taken to some spy nest. The Black Bat determined not to strike until he could really damage the spy ring.

THE TAXI driver tooted his horn as he drove up to the gates of a medium-sized factory. A man hurried across the yard to open the gates. They closed after the cab passed through. It drove directly into a garage.

The Black Bat also stopped. Getting out and holding his gun ready, he made a half circle of the factory until he reached the rear. The high fence was made of steel, which made him approach it warily. He knelt, gently tossed his gun against the steel wire. When no electric spark leaped out, he knew it was safe to climb the fence. He went over it with the agility of a monkey.

On the other side, he stopped to study the place. There was a loading platform at the back of the three story building. He made that his goal. The night was to his liking—dark and sultry, with storm clouds gathering ominously in the sky. With the unerring help of eyes that could see as well in darkness as in light, the Black Bat reached the loading platform. He climbed up and glanced at the big sliding door. It was ajar about a quarter of an inch. He frowned, for it was almost an open invitation to enter.

Yet, he asked himself, how could the spies possibly know he was on their trail? If they had somehow become suspicious, certainly they would never have brought Major Rankin to this place. The Black Bat gently shoved aside the door enough to squeeze himself through....

CHAPTER IX

BLACK BATTLE

DESOLATE SILENCE greeted him. He knew he was in some kind of large shipping room, for tiers of steel drums were neatly stacked up. His eyes darted around. Not only could he feel the presence of hidden men—there was an almost indiscernible change in the darkness of the room.

Without turning, the Black Bat knew that the big door had slid shut silently, excluding the faint light from outside. In the pitch darkness he drew his second gun, slipped the safety off and began moving along close to the wall. The advantage of the darkness lay in his favor. Anyone concealed in the rows of steel drums couldn't see him, but he was not handicapped by the absence of light.

When he passed the fourth tier, he suddenly tensed. Two men were crouching low, both holding drawn revolvers. One of them motioned with his free hand. As he crawled down the alley between the barrels, three others followed.

The Black Bat didn't wait for the attack to come. That would be fatal, because these men would open fire the instant they had a target. He began running lightly, without making a single sound. He selected the alley next to the one along which the killers were approaching. Halfway up it, he stopped and listened. They were separated from him only by the steel drums that towered high above.

The Black Bat placed both hands against the drums and pushed hard. They rocked dangerously. Someone let out a screech of warning, but it came too late. The row of barrels tipped over, crashed down on the men who were maneuvering to get the Black Bat from the rear.

In the unholy din, the Black Bat went streaking toward the door that led into the factory. But two men came rushing through it. At the same instant, someone abruptly got sense enough to throw on the light switch. Instantly the Black Bat's advantage disappeared.

His guns blasted. The two spies coming through the door were hurled aside by the force of the forty-five slugs. The Black Bat's cape billowed out behind him, casting a weird shadow against the wall. How he left so quickly, the survivors of the battle never knew. They swore afterward that he simply left the ground and flew away.

Actually he went through the door with the speed of a flash. Others would be waiting, and he had to protect himself. He reached a machine shop, spotted the switch panel just inside the door. He raced toward it, but he saw a gun in the hand of a spy who had suddenly appeared.

The Black Bat ducked behind a work-bench. Coming out on the other side, he snapped a single lightning shot. When the gunmen went down, he reached the switch panel, seized the wires and ripped them loose. Instantly the whole place was shrouded in darkness again.

But flashlights went into action. One picked out the Black Bat as he raced through the machine room. He fired in the direction of the beam. Answering bullets whizzed past his ear as he dodged out of the room.

He was at the front of the building, with four men challenging his attempt to escape through the door. Though they couldn't see the Black Bat, he could see them. Glimpsing a staircase, he went up the steps three at a time. No one was at the landing to intercept him.

As he headed down another long workroom, though, four men came swarming in his direction. Apparently they had been covering the rear windows and the yard in case he tried to escape through the shipping room door.

THE BLACK BAT whirled and raced to the third floor, where the offices were situated. Other men pounded up the stairs in pursuit and harsh voices were giving orders. He had a brief moment to wonder what had become of Major Rankin. The man seemed to have disappeared completely.

Looking straight through the darkness, the Black Bat saw that office space occupied only about one-third of the floor, and factory space the rest. The office was a poor place to stand them off. They might have another way of getting to this floor, perhaps even come at him from behind.

The Black Bat darted between the desks. Closing and locking a door behind him, he emerged into a spacious room filled with half completed steel drums. There were several oxy-acetylene torches on small hand trucks, by which they could easily be moved around. Half a dozen shots rang out. The Black Bat ducked, realized that for a second he had been standing in front of a window. His form had been darkly silhouetted as a target.

"No more shooting—for the moment!" someone called out authoritatively. "He is trapped. There is no way out for him now. If he goes through the windows, he must jump three stories, right into the hands of the men we have waiting there. We have the Black Bat cornered and we can take our own time in exterminating him. There is no use exposing ourselves. We shall force him into that small room at the back, where we can fix him with gas—a quiet, certain and pleasant way.

"One of you go downstairs to the chemical laboratory. You will find a large and well equipped one there. Two others dismantle the big exhaust fan in the rolling room and bring it here, while another repairs the electric light system. Hurry!"

The Black Bat crept toward a window and cautiously peered out. His escape really was cut off. Two men armed with rifles stood behind cover, looking up and watching continuously. The man who headed this particular unit of the spy ring knew that the Black Bat was powerless. He planned to release some deadly gas and blow it in the Black Bat's direction with a huge fan! There was no possibility of help. If the shots had attracted any attention, the men planted outside the factory could say a small night shift was engaged in some special work which happened to be unusually noisy.

The Black Bat took advantage of the temporary lull to wonder just how he was going to get out of this trap. If he were wounded, or if the gas knocked him out, they'd unmask him and the Black Bat would be exposed as Tony Quinn. That would finish his activities and place his life in constant danger even if he did worm his way from the net now thrown around him.

There seemed to be nothing he could do but put his back against the wall and go down with as much company as possible. He still had a few slugs in his guns and an extra clip for each weapon. By making every shot count, he might wear his enemies down. But nobody could intimidate gas with bullets. The spies seemed complacently aware of that, so they were in no hurry to risk their lives in actual combat.

A score of oxy-acetylene tanks were piled up, making a barrier behind which he crouched. Nothing short of a field-gun could break that down.

Abruptly the Black Bat heard the preparations that were being made to smoke him out. He heard them set up the big fan, heard the clink of heavy bottles and the splashing of liquid. The spies kept well out of the range of the Black Bat's guns, for they didn't have to take risks now.

The enormous fan suddenly whirred to life. The mighty breeze it created blew the first cloud of gas toward the Black Bat. His nostrils quivered with dread. Beneath the hood he turned pale, for they weren't intent on simply knocking him out. This was chlorine—one of the deadly gasses used in the First World War! They had easily manufactured it out of chemicals that were common to any laboratory.

ONLY ONE thing lay in the Black Bat's favor. The room in which he was trapped was large. It would require several minutes before a sufficient concentration of the gas could be manufactured to kill him. But what good could that do him? Even several hours wouldn't help much, unless the morning shift of employees arrived immediately after dawn.

He fingered his guns and pondered the chances of making a sweeping charge, shooting down as many of the spies as he could, and trying to make a fierce, swift escape. The odds were probably a thousand to one against success. But by staying here—waiting for the gas to take effect—he had no chance at all. The Black Bat was rapidly understanding how Silk must have felt, tied to a tree and bracing himself for inevitable death.

The Black Bat suddenly coughed—hard, racking coughs. Instantly he heard the derisive laughter of the spies clustered somewhere behind the big fan. The Black Bat realized that they must have located some independent source of electrical power—batteries perhaps, or an emergency switch to operate the fan. The lights hadn't gone on yet, and he knew he had ruined the switch panel beyond hope of quick repair.

More and more of the gas came sweeping his way. In less than fifteen minutes, he realized, he would be dead. Even if he managed to get clear by some miracle, his lungs would be permanently damaged. Of all the ghastly ways to kill, poison gas was the worst.

Gas! The Black Bat gave a start of hope. Perhaps he was not finished, after all....

Working furiously, protected by the darkness, he managed to lift one of the heavy tanks of oxy-acetylene gas to the floor. He rolled it slowly, making no noise at all, toward the middle of the big room. With two huge packing cases that he had seen earlier, he blocked the view from the doorway. Rapidly he turned the valves of the tank, heard the hissing of another gas. If his plans didn't go awry, this gas would grant him life—

He scraped a match, touched it to the nozzle of the tank. Blue, almost colorless, the light of the burning gas made a dull glow in the room. He twisted the nozzle around, keeping the searing flame away from the hose connection to the tank. He deliberately placed the blazing jet two inches from the middle of the tank and waited long enough to see the metal start to melt under the terrific heat. Then he ran lightly toward the rear of the factory. In a corner as far away from the hissing jet as possible, he lay down and covered his head with his hands. He muttered a prayer as he waited.

It might bring a death as hideous as the one the spies intended for him. But it also would show what this factory really was—a hideout and meeting place for spies. Some of them might even be injured badly enough for them to be captured. At any rate, it was better than merely waiting like a docile animal for the slaughter.

Apparently the bluish glow from over the tops of the packing cases had attracted the spies. The Black Bat's eyes penetrated the darkness, saw two of them approach cautiously, with handkerchiefs over their noses and mouths. One gave a sudden yelp of alarm. They sped back—about four steps.

THE OXY-ACETYLENE gas, under high compression in the tank, abruptly let go. The heat from the jet had penetrated the steel sides of the container. The explosion blew the spies back, lifted a section of the building's roof. It tore down one wall, gouged a hole through the floor, sent machinery and stack of tanks rolling wildly. Debris smashed against every wall. Dirt, bricks and pieces of metal struck the Black Bat, although he had tried to protect himself.

A horrible silence clamped down as soon as the blast of the explosion died away. The Black Bat raised his head cautiously. Somewhere outside, automobile motors were roaring into life. He glanced out of the shattered window. Four cars were speeding through the open gate.

The Black Bat drew his guns and limped slightly across the floor, avoiding the weakened section around the spot where the tank of gas had rested. There was still plenty of chlorine to burn his eyes and lungs, but with all the windows blown out, enough fresh air rushed in to dilute the deadly gas.

The Black Bat reached the stairway. He realized that neighbors would put in an alarm, for part of the building was now on fire and thick columns of smoke were beginning to rise.

He saw one of the spies lying against a wall sprawled in death. Two others lay less than ten feet away.

He knelt beside one and made a swift, thorough search. There was nothing of significance in the pockets, but a bulge in the lining of the coat attracted his attention. He ripped the lining away, lifted out a neatly stacked sheaf of the mysteriously perforated cards.

Suddenly a siren warned him of the danger of capture. The Black Bat raced down the stairs, ran like a streak across the first floor and through the shipping room door. He jumped off the loading platform, scurried toward the fence and was over it in a single motion.

All at once, he had disappeared into the night.

CHAPTER X

SET-UP FOR MURDER

AS THE BLACK BAT drove back to town, he realized that at no time during the battle had he seen Major Rankin nor heard his voice. Unless they had concealed him somewhere in the factory, he was either still in their hands or had escaped in the confusion.

The Black Bat was puzzled by that, for he imagined the spies would have killed Rankin the moment trouble started. They had orders to murder Rankin to slow up the preparedness program. They had less than no use for him alive—he might prove a decided hazard. Why, then, had he been permitted to escape or been taken with them in flight?

The Black Bat was still somewhat shaken by his nearness to death. His nerves were on edge, his muscle sore from the tenseness. But worse than that, he felt he had failed his job by not rounding up the spies.

He eased up on the gas. Turning into the street near his home, he pulled to the curb not far from Butch's boarding house. A troubling thought struck him as he shut off the motor. How had those spies known he was coming to the factory? They couldn't possibly have spotted him on their trail unless they had been warned to expect his presence.

In the factory, though, everything had been set to surprise and capture him. They knew he was coming. But how? Major Rankin hadn't known he was under the observation of the Black Bat. Even he couldn't have set any trap.

With his hood and cape stowed under his coat, Quinn walked briskly toward the garden gate. A thousand questions were pounding insistently at his brain. Now, more than ever, he realized that he was fighting the brains and physical strength of a sinisterly clever, fiendishly powerful horde. This was no blundering gang group, but a highly developed organization that was skilled in murder, trained in all the forms of sabotage that existed, well paid, supplied with an abundance of money, and shockingly well shielded. To break down this spy ring, he would have to get at the leader, the baffling man who addressed his audience and then commanded them to turn their backs when he departed.

Nothing short of the leader's capture and the obliteration of his first lieutenants would suffice.

To make matters worse, they might be set to strike at any moment of the day or night. When it came, it would involve the entire nation, Quinn was sure. Death and destruction would follow in their wake. With the element of surprise on their side, they might even gain control of parts of the country and hold them! What was it, if not war?

Tony Quinn slipped through the garden gate. After peering through the intense darkness, he disappeared into the garden house. As he hurried along the tunnel, he removed the floppy-brimmed hat that concealed his features. Silk was waiting for him with a rye and soda, in the spacious living room. Before doing anything else, Quinn downed the drink, instantly felt his tense nerves relax.

"I fell for one of their tricks," he stated bitterly as he donned his tweeds and smoking jacket. "It almost cost me my life. Did anyone call?"

"Only Carol, sir," Silk replied. "She's worried."

"Risk phoning her that I'm all right," Quinn ordered. "Tell her to check up on Major Rankin if she can. Then keep watch while I do some work in the lab. Remember those perforated cards? I managed to get quite a few of them this time. Maybe now we can get some results."

IN THE privacy of his lab, Tony Quinn carefully examined the stack of cards. All of them were perforated like the first ones. Unlike the others, though, the holes of three were all over the card, like some fantastic design.

He set up an infra-red machine, placed one of the cards under it and made a long, careful study of it. The rays brought into relief one corner section of each card, which seemed to have been treated. Quinn consulted a volume on secret ink preparations. Then he spent an hour mixing various solutions and trying to develop whatever was on the cards.

Finally a light gray series of lines came into view, gradually forming into words. But even though he had overcome the secret of the ink, the words meant nothing. They read:

SECT. 10   No. 161

Every card showed the same meticulously hand-printed words. If they had indicated a volume and a page, his lead might have materialized, but with merely a numbered section and just a plain number, they meant nothing. The ink with which the cards were treated was one that had been developed in German laboratories not ten months before. In other words, the spy ring was in constant communication with the Fatherland, and worked with only the most modern devices of espionage.

Quinn straightened up from his exacting work. Silk had placed all the late editions of the newspapers on the bench. Going through them quickly, Quinn found nothing new. The raid on von Elkin's travel office was described, but no tangible results had been obtained, so the article rated only half a column. Maps had been found which incriminated von Elkin. The German travel expert had vanished, however.

On an inner page, Quinn spotted a brief item that made him whistle in amazement. A public meeting at the Officers' Club was in progress right now! Several prominent men were to make speeches endorsing the preparedness program and denouncing the aggression of Europe's most savage invader. A list of notables who would be present was given. They included a great number of active and retired Army, Navy and Marine officers, some with the highest ranks.

Quinn folded the newspaper thoughtfully. It was only a few minutes after ten o'clock, and the meeting had been scheduled to begin at nine-thirty. But those affairs usually started late. The real business would certainly not come up for at least an hour after the meeting opened.

He picked up his cane and strode toward the door which led into his study. Instantly his eyes went blankly staring, and his head assumed the rigid position of a blind man. He called to Silk as he entered the study.

"I'm going to attend a meeting at the Officers' Club," he said. "If those spies are intent on wiping out all the military experts they can, that meeting will be the best opportunity they'll ever have. Drive me there, Silk, and hurry."

"But if you're going as Tony Quinn, what can you do if anything starts?" Silk asked.

"I don't know. Probably nothing. But at least I'll be there and I'll be able to see what happens. Even the Black Bat couldn't invade a meeting hall that size, and it's too late to stop the spy ring's plans, I imagine."

THE COMMITTEE arranging the meeting had selected a spacious auditorium in the center of the city. People were still streaming in when Silk stopped the car and helped Tony Quinn fumble out. He led him up the steps. Forcing a way through the crowd around the door, he managed to reach the entrance of the center aisle.

"I see Commissioner Warner, sir," Silk said. "He's down ahead of us. Shall I call him?"

"Yes, ask him if he can make room for me," Tony Quinn said. Several people approached, identifying themselves. He shook his head with a sad, gentle smile. He smiled in their general direction, yet never looked squarely at them. Suddenly Commissioner Warner took his arm.

"Tony, why didn't you tell me you were coming here? I'd have arranged a better spot."

"I came on the spur of the moment, Commissioner," Quinn said. "Silk was driving by. I heard the sound of many people and asked him what was going on. He read me the banners and placards, so I decided to come in. A blind man appreciates things like lectures, you know. He has to amuse himself by emphasizing the medium of the ear rather than the eye."

Warner led him down the aisle to a good seat about halfway to the platform. Speeches were going on, all concerned with the armaments program. Quinn, sitting erect in his chair, stared straight ahead. His starkly blank eyes, however, saw everything all around him.

Major Rankin was seated in the first row and in full uniform. He certainly seemed to be calm, despite his recent danger. How had he escaped? Why did he appear so unmoved by his near murder? Attorney Tolly was there, too, about five rows in front of Quinn. His oily, bland face kept turning around to study everyone in the audience.

Someone came down the aisle and passed close to Quinn. It was Colonel Catlin, whom the Black Bat had rescued from the spy ring's assassins only a few hour before. Catlin also was in full uniform.

Without moving his head, Quinn counted more than thirty ranking officers of the various military divisions. He squirmed around in his chair. Turning his head in the general direction of Commissioner Warner, he spoke softly, asking who was present. But that was only a pretext, for Quinn' eyes ranged over the entire south section of the auditorium. They missed nothing—not even the tall, square-shouldered man with the black beard and thick shock of black hair.

Trained to penetrate disguises, Quinn knew that Fritz von Elkin, sought by G-men and the police, must have an urgent reason for attending this meeting. He had no doubt at all that it was von Elkin. Now he was sure that things were ready to happen!

He groaned inwardly because he knew he would be helpless to act. Tony Quinn, a blind man, could not rise up to stem a sinisterly furtive attack. He racked his brain for some method of giving a warning. There was none that he could use successfully. Bitterly he resented the pose of blindness he had unwillingly been forced to assume.

"Phil Trent is going to speak," Warner said softly. "Be ready to hear spies and saboteurs get their ears battened down. Trent is plenty upset about them. He's doing all he can to run down the vermin."

A ripple of applause went up as Trent mounted the speaker's platform. Quinn listened carefully, but he also watched everyone seated in front of him. They couldn't fail to strike, especially with von Elkin here. Though von Elkin certainly was not the mysterious leader of the ring, he was unquestionably a capable adjutant and a clever spy. It was more than possible that he would give the signal when the right time came.

Quinn's hands curled into fists. He had to check an urge to rise up and denounce von Elkin, queer the whole set-up, stop any possibility of murder. If he did—then what? Exposure, arrest, the inevitable end of the Black Bat. He relaxed unwillingly and forced all such thoughts out of his mind.

CHAPTER XI

FOG OF DEATH

VEHEMENTLY TRENT was speaking, with all the fire of true conviction for a just cause. His voice was passionate, his gestures perfectly timed. Everyone in the audience forgot his scarred face, his limping walk and the completely white hair that made him look much older than he was.

"We have among us, on every side, men who have been trained for years in sabotage. As head of the Officers' Club, I have done all within my power to combat these subversive influences, but I cannot do this alone. It requires the vigilance and courage of every red-blooded American who wants to go on living life as he knows it. We do not want the slavery which foreign legions would impose upon us if they gained control of this land of ours. The freedom we enjoy is worth fighting for—worth dying for ten times over!

"We do not want the glory of the world, not even the glory of our own nation—but a simple, small thing called honor. Without it, we will become slave legions under the thumb of a malignant power that will spread until we are completely squashed."

Tony Quinn joined in the round of applause that followed. Trent took a drink of water and sailed furiously into the rest of his speech.

"We are arming as fast as the might and resources of this nation can allow us. We are preparing to defend our rights and our own shores in this war-mad world. Yet, while we do this, there are thousands of men concentrated on one task—to slow up and eventually disrupt our defense preparations. To them, human life means nothing. They would no more hesitate to demolish a huge factory filled with workers, than they would shrink from blowing up some small trestle along a rural railroad siding.

"Those are the elements we must battle first. We must wipe them out, expose them for what they really are—treacherous, murderous, ruthless bandits with an insatiable desire for power. The organization which gives this series of lectures has not been idle. Not many hours ago we accumulated evidence against a travel agency which proved to be a spy nest. We found proof of that, even if the man who operated it managed to escape.

"There will be other raids, as fast as we can accumulate the necessary evidence. But we cannot do everything alone. Every citizen of the United States must watch for treachery, must expose it wherever it appears—in high places as well as low!"

Trent went on while his audience remained hushed, drinking in absorbedly every word he uttered. There was something so persuasive about his voice that his convictions reached every man who listened.

Tony Quinn kept staring straight ahead, though he knew that with every passing second the danger mounted higher and higher. His anxiety increased in the same proportion, until he felt as though he could not stand it any longer.

Abruptly, while Trent was still talking, Colonel Catlin jumped to his feet and leaped from his seat into the aisle. He took two or three steps in the direction of the platform.

Quinn saw ten men rise simultaneously on what must have been a prearranged signal. They hurled something against the walls, toward the platform, against the floor almost at their own feet. In no more than two seconds, the auditorium was shrouded in a white fog which even the Black Bat's eyes couldn't penetrate!

HOARSE SHOUTS went up. Men milled about. Someone screamed. Tony Quinn felt, rather than saw, Commissioner Warner leave his chair to take command of the situation. Quinn stretched out both arms. There was no one on either side of him. He knew that his seat was located halfway between the aisles, which meant that the others in the auditorium would be pressed close to the aisles, leaving the center sections empty.

Quinn restrained himself no longer. He climbed on his chair, leaped over the row before his. He repeated this as fast as he could, and no one impeded him until he came to the first row. There two men were struggling furiously. He could see only the vague shapes of their bodies and hear their gasps for breath.

Two others suddenly found their way into the battle. Quinn saw one shadowy arm spring upward, plunge down viciously. With a strangled moan, one of the fighters dropped to the floor. Quinn hurdled over the last row of seats. He could make out the form of the fallen man and one who was bent over him. The remaining two seemed to have fled.

Quinn surged forward. As he did so, the stooped figure straightened up. Holding a knife above his head, he had been about to sink it deep into his victim's body for the second time. But now he aimed it at Tony Quinn. The knife started down. It traveled only a few inches before a hand shot upward, grasped the wrist and gave it a savage wrench. The bone snapped and the knife fell to the floor.

The killer screamed in pain, fought loose and tried to escape through the chemical fog that blanketed the auditorium. Tony Quinn raced close behind, seized his shoulder and spun him around. He snapped a hard fist to the killer's jaw. When the man staggered back, he followed up the blow, putting into it all the power he could muster. The killer crashed to the floor.

Quinn's face remained grim, though at least one of the spies wouldn't squirm through a rat hole to escape. The man would be unconscious for at least an hour, judging by the pain in Quinn's knuckles. It wasn't possible that he had recognized Quinn, either, for the fog seemed thicker than ever.

Quinn turned back and found his way to the injured man's side. As he turned the man over, he muttered a curse. It was Colonel Catlin! The stamp of death was already written on his features, although his lips moved and his eyelids trembled.

"Colonel!" Quinn said softly. "You know who did this. Tell me why you jumped out of your seat. Listen to me. It's the Black Bat, Colonel!"

That name seemed to penetrate Catlin's dying brain. He opened his eyes. Doubt shone in them until Quinn thrust his face close to Catlin's.

"Yes, I'm the Black Bat. I'm also Tony Quinn. You're the one man who knows my secret and I'm telling you only because you must trust me. Who stabbed you? What's behind all this?"

"I... was... fool. Complete fool... should have... known. I wanted... to...."

Catlin's body gave a shudder and his eyes began to glaze. Quinn's shoulders drooped as he let Catlin's body ease to the floor. For the first time in the existence of the Black Bat, Quinn had revealed his identity, but that secret was now locked in the brain of a dead man.

What had Catlin meant by branding himself as a fool? Why had he jumped up so suddenly? There was no question in Quinn's mind but that Catlin himself set off the fire-works. The spies had acted to stop him. Quinn wondered how many more of the assembled officers had died. There was still a great deal of confusion, but someone had smashed windows and cold air was sweeping in to disperse the man-made fog.

QUINN VAULTED the rows of chairs and returned to his original seat.

He sprang into it, making sure there was no blood on his hands or clothing. Swiftly he dropped the mask of blindness over his eyes again.

Two minutes later, Commissioner Warner came fumbling back. When he found Quinn, he heaved a great sigh of relief.

"I'm sorry I had to leave you, Tony. Something happened. The whole audience must have been matched man for man with spies. They threw some kind of glass bombs, which released a smoke that was so dense, nobody could penetrate it. We don't know if anyone has been killed yet, nor if the spies got clear. The fog is beginning to break up now."

Quinn looked anxious. "I should never have come here. I'm only in the way."

"Nonsense," Warner soothed. "If you had your eyes, Tony, you'd have been in there, battling away. I'm afraid I'll have to leave you again. I must see if those damned spies got away, or if they are still in the audience. You just sit tight and don't move for anyone. I'll be back."

The atmosphere had cleared now and Quinn's apparently sightless eyes watched the confusion. He could see Colonel Catlin's body near the platform, with Warner beside it. Quinn moved his head slowly, barely preventing himself from gasping in astonishment.

There had been over a hundred potential victims for the spies—yet Catlin was the only man who had been attacked! In the confusion, a dozen ranking officers could easily have been murdered. Why hadn't that happened? Could all of this have been done with only the death of Colonel Catlin in mind?

Quinn gazed steadily in the direction of the platform, wondering why nobody noticed the spy he had knocked out. Certainly the man couldn't have recovered his wits even sufficiently to crawl to some hiding place. Quinn knew perfectly well the power that lay behind his fists. That spy should still be there, sprawled out and surrounded by Warner's men.

Trent climbed up on the platform and shouted for order. The command in his voice stopped the panic near the exits, which were now completely blocked off by police.

"Gentlemen, please return to your seats! No one is permitted to leave until we have searched for the spies who instigated and carried out this murder. Yes, it is murder! Colonel Catlin is dead—knifed in the back. You can be certain that he will be avenged, gentlemen. From now on my association and I will actively campaign against these murderers who must obscure themselves in a fog to carry out their killings.

"All of you, please sit down! Look through your pockets for identification of some kind, and I warn you, it must be good. Those who cannot furnish it will be held until they are identified. It is an inconvenience, but it may trap some of the killers."

The audience returned to its seats. Warner, in full control of the situation now, posted his men at advantageous positions, Quinn noticed that they were all armed with sub-machine guns. Row by row, detectives studied the identifications presented to them by the people in the auditorium. Some were escorted out of the place, others were lined up against one wall for further questioning.

HE SAW that Captain McGrath was there, working hard. The detective spotted Quinn and came over, dropping into the chair which Warner had previously occupied.

"I know just what happened here," McGrath said grimly. "It's enough to make an Eskimo's blood boil. Remember that I accused you of killing five men? Well, I take it back—not the fact that I think you're the Black Bat, mind you! But if you are, and you did kill those damned spies, I'd like to shake your hand."

"I don't mind shaking hands with you, Captain, but I insist that I am not the Black Bat."

McGrath's eyes narrowed as he came half out of his chair.

"Then how did you know it was me, if you can't see? Answer that one!"

Quinn allowed a faint smile to cross his lips.

"But Captain, you asked me that question under similar circumstances before. It so happens that a blind man learns to distinguish voices. I'd know yours at least a block away."

"Oh!" McGrath said, rather weakly, and dropped back into his seat. "Well, if you are the Black Bat, I'm telling you that all curbs are off. You're fighting these spies and I won't try to interfere. Understand? While this goes on, the Black Bat has a free hand, as far as I'm concerned. He can fight these rats the way they ought to be fought—with bullets!"

"I think you're perfectly right," Quinn said, "even if you persist in barking up the wrong tree. This is a time for all the forces of justice to band closely together. Trent was right. Everyone must fight this menace! Believe me, if I could use my eyes—if I weren't the crippled, helpless man that I am—I'd get into it, too. Good luck Captain. I hope you round up these killers."

"I don't know, Quinn," McGrath sighed. "Sometimes I'd swear that you're the Black Bat. But other times, like now, I begin to think I'm nuts. Anyway, you know how I feel about this. Just sit tight. I'll send a couple of men to escort you out of here."

"I'll stay," Quinn countered. "I'm no different from anyone else here. I'll show my identification. Besides, this is all quite exciting for a blind man. I can't see, but I can hear and guess just what's going on. Thanks for trying to help me, Captain."

McGrath went back to work. Quinn turned his apparently sightless eyes around the large auditorium every few moments, searching for von Elkin. The Nazi spy would never get by with his faked beard and wig. He was trapped, might make a desperate attempt to get away.

Exactly what Quinn could do about that wasn't clear, even to himself. Without the masking fog of smoke, he was completely stymied.

CHAPTER XII

FACE IN THE WINDOW

GRADUALLY THE members of the audience were whisked out, for not one suspicious person had been found. Every man had either identified himself satisfactorily or sent for trustworthy citizens who could make the identification for him.

All the spies, including von Elkin, had made good their escape! But how? The front entrance of the building was crammed with an overflow audience. They certainly would not have permitted anyone to leave after those smoke bombs were set off. Warner, tired and hot, sat down beside Quinn.

"Well, they beat us to it again, Tony. Colonel Catlin is dead, and we haven't a single clue to his murderers. They created a fog of smoke and escaped through it. Of course, everything was set—exits prearranged skillfully. But you'd think one of those spies would have tripped up somewhere. I wish the Black Bat had been here. He has a way of handling situations of this kind. We can't hope for miracles, though, I suppose."

Quinn smiled. "You're hinting, Commissioner. Like McGrath, you have a vague idea that I'm the Black Bat, and now you're offering me a chance to operate. McGrath just did the same thing. I wish I were the Black Bat—not because I would then have the ability to see once more. That would be only a minor item now. I really could help in battling these spies, if I were the Black Bat.

"They're getting more daring every day. Victories in Europe make them more aggressive than ever over here. Triumph has undoubtedly brought additional members to their ranks. I'd like to go home now, if I may."

"Of course." Warner helped Quinn to his feet. "Silk has been clamoring like a madman outside. We couldn't let him in, obviously, and I sent word that I'd take you home. You have a good man there, Tony."

Warner led Quinn along the aisle, through the cordon of police thrown around the building, and down the stairs to the sidewalk. Warner's official car was parked across the street. As they stepped off the curb, Philip Trent joined them, linking his arm under Quinn's free one.

"There's only one thing by which that murder may benefit us," he said earnestly. "It shows the people exactly what the whole nation is up against. All of us have been more or less tolerant of these openly foreign organizations. We've let them have their petty drills and rifle practise. We've passed some minor legislation against their uniforms and laughed at the crooks who usually led them into absurd mischief. But it's not mischief now. We must stop laughing and turn from the defensive to the offensive.

"It's my fervent hope that everybody begins to realize what is going on. They'll be wise in not trying to interfere personally, however, because they can take what just happened as a good example of the ruthlessness these men exhibit. I think...."

Directly across the street stood Attorney Tolly, watching the trio approach Warner's car. Suddenly Tolly gave a shout of alarm and pointed up the street. Warner and Trent looked swiftly, saw a heavy car bearing down on them with its throttle wide open!

QUINN ALMOST visibly restrained the impulse to look. He heard Warner's cry of fear and knew what was happening. Then Tolly came scooting across the highway. As he neared the trio, he went into a wild dive. His arms grabbed Quinn's legs and sent him crashing back. Warner and Trent, now freed of Quinn, made a mad surge out of the way. Careening crazily, the big car passed within six inches of the spot where Quinn lay, with Tolly sprawled at his feet.

Quinn had secured a brief glimpse of the driver of that murder car. He recognized the black wig and beard. Fritz von Elkin had made a deliberate attempt to run down the three of them. Just whom he meant to kill wasn't clear. Trent, perhaps, because of the savage manner in which he had attacked von Elkin's principles. It might also have been Warner, because he represented an organized fight against spies.

"What—what happened?" Quinn gasped as Tolly got up.

Warner and Trent rushed over and helped Quinn to his feet. Warner pumped Tolly's hand.

"That was a brave thing you did, sir. Trent and I were squarely in the path of that car, just a little fuddled, I think. You acted promptly and efficiently. You saved the life of a man who couldn't help himself. This is Tony Quinn. He's blind."

Quinn's hand was proffered, but only in the general direction of Tolly. The lawyer took it.

"I wondered why you didn't try to jump. And believe me, Mr. Quinn, you've got a couple of mighty good friends by your side. They seemed to be willing to risk their lives to protect your own. What I did was nothing, but I'm glad I happened to be around, anyway. My name is Tolly. I'm an attorney."

Warner led Quinn to his car after Tolly and Trent left. The police commissioner was obviously shaken by the episode, and a little disgusted when the police cars returned. No trace of the murder vehicle had been found.

"I've got to stick around," he told Quinn. "Things are happening so fast, I don't dare leave until the whole mess is cleaned up. I'm sorry that you were exposed to such danger. And, Tony, remember what I said about the Black Bat? If you should bump into him, I'd like to have him know just how I feel."

Quinn sank back against the cushions of the sedan.

"I'll keep my nose out of this, from now on," he said sadly. "I'm just in the way. Oh, don't try to tell me that's not the truth. What good can a blind man be? From what I heard, you nearly lost your life—you and Trent—trying to protect me. As for the Black Bat, I'd sell my soul to be in his shoes for just a few hours. I'm sorry to say that I doubt if he'll meet me or that I'll run across him. But if I do, I'll give him your message."

AS WARNER watched the car disappear down the street, he stood stroking his chin thoughtfully. There was a fixed notion in his mind that Tony Quinn really was the Black Bat. Warner had known Quinn for years, knew just how aggressive he'd been as district attorney. The Black Bat fought exactly same way, and the touch of this mysterious marauder of crime sometimes seemed identical with Quinn's former efforts.

Against those theories, though, was the word of a dozen competent eye specialists who had stated firmly that Quinn would never see again. Warner also recalled how that searing acid had burned so deep and so fast. He had been present at the scene, had witnessed the entire horrible affair. If money could have cured Quinn's sight, he would now have the use of his eyes, for Quinn was wealthy enough to spend almost any amount. He had spent a small fortune, too, but without an iota of success.

Warner shrugged his shoulders and decided that he and Captain McGrath were a pair of fools even to suspect that Quinn was the Black Bat.

In Warner's large car, Quinn sat rigid, holding his cane firmly. His face was without expression, but his brain worked furiously. For one of the few times in his life, he felt the unmerciful assault of doubt.

Had that careening car been meant to kill Trent, Warner or—Tony Quinn? Did someone suspect that he was the Black Bat? Was the spy ring going to concentrate on him as their greatest menace? Yet he knew that he had given himself away in no manner. His dual identity was just as secret as ever. He had never relaxed his pose of a blind man while he was Tony Quinn, and as the Black Bat he had worked under cover at all times.

Still, those doubts kept crawling around miserably in his mind. He didn't worry only for himself. There were Silk, Butch and Carol to be concerned about. Any man cunning enough to have determined the identity of the Black Bat, would also have run down those three people as the Black Bat's aides.

He thought of Major Rankin, too. He had been in the audience, yet apparently no attempt had been made on his life. Why? The spies had certainly tried to murder him before, and he had been at their mercy during that meeting. And how had von Elkin managed to get out of that building without detection? How had the ten or twelve spies accomplished the same thing?

Quinn kept tapping his cane gently on the floor of the car. That was the only betraying sign of his justifiable nervousness.

Silk was waiting at the house. Quinn had never seen him so worried. He drank the rye and soda which Silk had prepared and spoke in a low voice.

"We've got to watch our step, Silk. It's possible that someone knows I'm the Black Bat. I'm not sure, of course, but things happened to give me that idea. Perhaps I'm just growing too suspicious, but it won't hurt if we're careful. Later on, I want you to slip out and contact Carol and Butch directly. We can't trust the phone any longer."

Quinn shuffled slowly across the floor of his study, using his cane to make certain the path was clear. He sank into his accustomed chair in front of the fireplace. Silk dragged over a straight-backed chair, sat down and picked up the newspapers which he had placed on a small table.

"I'll carry on as usual, sir. I've already looked over the papers, and I'll tell you what I've learned from them. Early tonight, G-men conducted raids all over the country in a search for fifth columnists. They found nothing—nothing at all, sir! While the items don't mention this, I can read between the lines. The spies were tipped off, somehow!"

TONY QUINN nodded. "That's what makes it so difficult. They have people who are trusted in various high circles. They pick up information you or I could never hear. That's transmitted to their headquarters, where the little items from all over the land are assembled. Some especially clever mind goes over these and arranges the items to organize a concrete picture of what is to happen.

"But I promise you, we won't be idle any longer. I have one hope—Fritz von Elkin. He's a fugitive, so he must be holed up somewhere. I think I know where he is. You'd imagine that his taking refuge in the section where his kind of people live would be dangerous for him. It wouldn't. He'd be less conspicuous there than among those who don't speak as he does. So I'm going to invade that section and find him."

"But how?" Silk asked. "You can't travel around as the Black Bat and ask a lot of questions. Those people won't talk, even if they wanted to."

"I know, and that's where you come in, Silk. I'm going to take one of the biggest chances of my life. I'm going into that area without the hood and cape. It's up to you to find some way of covering these scars on my face. A pair of colored glasses, an old suit, a tin cup and cane will be my disguise. Dangerous? Yes, but there is no alternative. We can't just wait for those spies to hit again. Next time they may pull whatever big coup they have in mind. I want you to—

"Silk, be careful now! Someone just ducked past the window in the east wall. Fold the newspapers and don't show any sign of haste. Walk to the kitchen, pick up a gun on your way, and go out. If you see anyone, grab him. Shoot if you have to."

Silk licked his lips nervously, but that was his only unusual reaction.

"What if they take a shot at you through the window?"

"I'll have to accept that chance. Now get going."

Silk obeyed the orders explicitly. When he returned twenty minutes later, he had nothing to report.

"I searched the whole estate, sir, but there's no sign of anyone. Are you positive it wasn't a mistake? Some shadow or a branch of a tree—"

"There was no mistake, Silk. You know how my eyes function. Whoever it was, he took only a fleeting glimpse into the room. I had no chance to see his features, but I did hear his clothes catch on a bush. We're under observation, and not by a gang of small-time crooks. Slip through the tunnel and get Butch and Carol."

Silk nodded, stepped close to Quinn and unobtrusively slipped a gun into the pocket of the smoking jacket.

"If you see anyone else, let him have it," he advised.

Silk had a sudden thought.

"Say, McGrath must be prowling around again!"

Quinn tamped tobacco into his pipe, keeping his eyes fixed before him.

"I thought of that. I'll just make sure."

Quinn arose, walked sightlessly toward the telephone and slowly dialed McGrath's home by counting the holes with his finger. The detective-captain answered almost at once.

"This is Tony Quinn. I am calling because I want to warn you that I informed Commissioner Warner of your ideas concerning the Black Bat. He might ask why a respectable member of the detective bureau should agree to consort with a criminal like the Black Bat. Good night, Captain."

Quinn hung up slowly, shaking his head.

"It couldn't have been McGrath," he said softly. "Now hurry along, Silk. We've got to go into action immediately, before these spies really manage to put us out of action."

CHAPTER XIII

CHANGED FACES

F ORTY-FIVE MINUTES later, when Silk returned, Carol and Butch were already in the laboratory. Quinn had been seated in front of the fireplace all that time. Now he slowly arose, yawned hugely and stretched with great weariness.

"I think I'll go to bed," he told Silk. "You may lock up."

Silk examined each window, making sure the latch was secure, and pulled the shades almost all the way down. After Quinn had made his way up the stairs to the second floor, Silk extinguished all the lights.

Then, in the darkness, Tony Quinn retraced his path. He avoided the furniture, kept as close to the wall as possible. Opening the secret door, he slipped inside. Silk remained upstairs, watching and listening. Carol ran into Quinn's arms, as Butch watched.

"Tony, Silk told us you're under suspicion! I had a feeling something like this would happen. Oh, Tony, what are you going to do? Can't we help you?"

"I'm going to war," Quinn said grimly. "And you can help, both of you as well as Silk. Here's the idea. I'm forced to resort to a disguise— a simple one, but it ought to work. As a blind beggar, I'm going to look for von Elkin. You and Butch must keep me in sight at every second. If anything happens, Butch, you can wade in. I don't care how many heads you break or how many jaws you dislocate. Silk is ready to act the same way. He's getting the disguise material ready now. Meanwhile, Carol, did you learn anything about Major Rankin?"

"Plenty! I studied all the newspaper files on him and I asked a few questions in the right places. Major Rankin once served as military attache to the United States Embassy in Berlin. He was constantly exposed to Nazi *Kultur.* Maybe some of it soaked in. Secretly he might have renounced his allegiance to our country and joined the Nazis. It's happened before—in Norway, Denmark, Belgium, and even France."

Quinn whistled softly for a moment before he spoke.

"It does build up suspicion against the major. I never knew any of that before. Anything else?"

Carol nodded. "In checking up on Rankin, I discovered that one of his closest friends is a man named Roscoe Bell. He used to be an international economics expert before Hitler blew the continent wide open. Bell was in constant contact with the aggressive powers over there. He sold, or negotiated the sale of more oil and machine tools to Italy than any one in the United States.

"He's welcome at the embassies of the Axis nations, and he's an exceptionally clever man. I had a look at him." She shuddered. "He's got the kind of face that curdles milk—reminds you of a death's-head."

When Butch stirred angrily in his chair, it groaned under his immense weight.

"Say, Boss, lemme have a crack at him, huh? Ever since I shook that bag of bones who had me pinched, I been achin' to slug one of the big rats. I'll make him talk."

"I think you could, at that." Quinn laughed. "But the time isn't ripe yet. Don't worry, you'll have a chance with those fists of yours. Here are my orders. Our lives might hinge on the way you follow them, so don't miss anything. It's after midnight now, but we can't afford to wait. Our plans go into action immediately. They may require some time before things hatch out.

"Butch, loaf around the section I will indicate. Silk will follow me. Carol, have a fast car ready, and also keep Silk in view. In that way, we will never be out of sight of one another. If any of us disappear, the others will immediately start things humming.

"We're to look particularly for Fritz von Elkin, but if we run across anyone else connected with the spy ring, that person will serve us just as well. What I'm aiming for is to locate their main hideout or meeting place. Sooner or later the leader will put in an appearance to give his orders. Then we shall have him."

CAROL AND Butch hurried away, to keep a rendezvous at the appointed spot. Quinn slipped back into the house, made his way to the second floor and found Silk getting the disguise material ready. As he sat down, Silk went to work.

"It won't be such a good job, sir," he said unhappily. "I'm no expert at this, but I think I can fill in those scars around your eyes. Maybe I can even turn you into a sallow-complexioned, glum sort of a man. Will that do?"

"Yes, I think so."

Fifteen minutes later, Quinn looked at himself in a mirror and decided it certainly would do. Silk had used a light plastic material to fill in the acid scars, and then colored it to match the slightly dull complexion he had given Quinn's face. A deft application of another substance gave the impression of a week's growth of beard.

"I've been studying up, sir, so maybe it isn't as bad as I thought," Silk explained. "Got myself a few odds and ends for experiments, too. But I never thought I'd use them on you."

Quinn removed his tweeds and donned an old black suit, which Silk had carefully rumpled and soiled in spots. A wrinkled shirt and an old, narrow tie completed the illusion. When he donned dark glasses and put on a battered hat, he nodded approval.

I COULD face Captain McGrath and get away with it," he said. "There's no doubt that I'll fool men like von Elkin. You know, Silk, he cannot possibly be the leader of this group. I think Morino was killed by the real leader while von Elkin stood by. Then you heard von Elkin ask his master certain questions, which also eliminated him.

"I don't like the way Major Rankin has acted. First of all, he was kidnaped quite smoothly, and a neat trap was set for me. They knew I was watching him. That means they deliberately failed to kill him the first time, knowing I'd read the newspaper accounts, and get on Rankin's trail. But Rankin was the prisoner of at least eight or ten men. Yet he got away, and as far as I know, he never even made a report of the snatch.

"He was once subjected to Nazi influence, and no matter how I hate to suspect an officer of our Army, Rankin must fall under that classification. Then there's Attorney Tolly, who bailed out Butch's friend, Hofer. He had an office in the building where Morino was killed. He could easy have committed the crime and then given himself an alibi by going back to his office."

"But if he was the leader of the spies, and he also suspected that you were the Black Bat," Silk asked after a moment, "Why should he risk his life to save you?"

"That I don't know. Perhaps it wasn't a serious attempt on my life. It may have been aimed at Warner or Trent. Or it may have been a ruse to find out if Tony Quinn really was blind. I almost gave myself away, Silk. Tolly shouted a warning, and he put plenty of expression in his voice. If I had turned my head and seen the car coming, I would have jumped for it. Then they'd have known I wasn't as blind as I pretended to be. So Tolly saved my life, or thought he did. Why? Was it to throw all suspicion off himself?"

Silk was putting on a disguise of his own while they talked. He changed his appearance to that of a much younger man, and his skin took on a healthy, tanned color. Silk was completely at home in this disguise. During the lush days of his confidence work, he had used it often, pretending to be a new arrival in a big city and wide open as prey for other slick confidence artists.

Quinn slipped back to the laboratory, stuffed a pair of guns in special holsters that gave no indication of a bulge. His hood and cape went into another prepared pocket. Then he went through the tunnel, reached the street and walked away briskly.

It was long after midnight when he saw Butch patrolling his assigned area. Carol was driving her car slowly over the section he had indicated. Silk appeared, too, after a short time. They continued operations until the hour became so late that they might have aroused suspicion. The Black Bat called off the hunt for that night, but he was glad of the experience he and his troupe had undergone. They had proved they could keep one another constantly in sight.

Late the following afternoon, Tony Quinn had two visitors—Commissioner Warner and Philip Trent.

"Glad you dropped in, gentlemen," Quinn said sincerely. "A blind man finds time heavy on his hands. All I can do is listen to the radio, and even the war news seems to lose its horror, eventually."

Trent laughed. "This isn't just a social call. We dropped in to see how you felt after that terrible experience last night. But we also want to solicit your help. Financially, I mean."

Quinn looked puzzled as he stared straight ahead.

"I don't get your point, but if you are seeking funds to combat this spy ring, name your own figure."

Warner looked questioningly at Trent.

"Remember what I said? Quinn may be blind as far as his eyes are concerned, but he can see and understand the menace that faces this nation. You've hit it on the head as usual, Tony. Trent has been raising funds from members of the Officers' Club and certain other important men. But even though they have been more than generous, he needs all he can get."

"We're going after that spy mob with every bit of power we can muster," Trent said. "But we don't intend to interfere with the Federal authorities. What we learn will be turned over to them for action. You see, some of the foreign people here have relatives in Europe, and they are under the control of the Gestapo or whatever other secret police agency those various nations operate. Those unfortunate people are compelled to obey orders from the spy ring.

"By providing sufficient money to get those relatives either to the United States or some other land where they can breathe in peace, we hope to break up this compulsion of unwilling aides to the spy group. It will take large sums, and I'm going on the air tonight in a plea for cash. It won't come in fast enough to suit our purposes, so I hope to interest fifty or more men who are willing to donate a thousand dollars each."

"Silk, my checkbook and a pen," Quinn called.

Silk brought them. After he guided Quinn's shaky pen onto the proper lines, he handed Trent the check.

"This will take a few people to safety," Trent said gratefully. "I'll let you know later just what happens. Thanks again."

Warner lingered a few seconds and spoke in a low voice.

"In your dreams you didn't see the Black Bat by any chance, did you, Tony?"

Quinn chuckled. "I'm afraid not, nor in my limited travels either. Anything new on the murder of Colonel Catlin, Commissioner?"

"Not a thing," Warner sighed. "I'd like to know how those men got out of that auditorium, but mostly I want to know why Catlin was knifed. My best men haven't been able to figure it out. It's keeping me busy, too, and I only took time out because Trent felt a little hesitant about coming to see you for a donation. He's got a smart idea there. It ought to help some. Don't miss his broadcast tonight, because he certainly intends to make the fur fly."

CAROL AND Butch hadn't been idle. They reported before dinner, which Silk managed to serve in the laboratory. He had carefully drawn all the window shades before carrying the trays from the kitchen.

"I've worked on this man, Bell," Carol said. "Everything confirms my first suspicions. He's a sympathizer with those alien interests because United State neutrality laws have practically put him out of business. He can't export anything that's worth real money, like munitions. He visited Major Rankin at three-twenty, stayed in the suite for almost an hour, and then went directly to the section we were patrolling last night.

"He owns considerable real estate there, including several meeting halls used by Bunds and certain athletic societies that are patronized by men who have a real need for calisthenics."

"It ain't that," Butch put in with a broad grin. "They drink too much beer. I been around that section all day myself. Boy, they sure got good beer! Like you said I was to do, I followed Tolly around. That guy's business is plenty dead, if you ask me. But he spends a lot of time around the beer joints up there. They think he's a big shot. Everybody knows him. I even seen a couple of gents slip him that funny salute they tire out their arms with in Europe."

"All right," Quinn said. "We'll invade their stamping grounds again. Butch, as soon as you've eaten your usual three meals in one, go back there and wait for us. Carol, keep your car tank filled, and have it ready for a quick getaway. We may need it. Silk, you'd better get the stuff set for our disguises. I have a feeling we'll see action tonight."

CHAPTER XIV

THE DISAPPEARING MAN

IN HIS disguise as a blind beggar, Tony Quinn lapped his cane noisily to add to the sum of thirteen cents he had obtained during the first two hours. He worked mostly around a big hall which had been prepared for a meeting.

At nine o'clock a few men began entering it, but some of them looked around furtively before they climbed the steps. Others walked in boldly, boastful of the fact that they had been invited. Quinn frowned. This was going to be a big meeting, with well over two hundred in attendance. Certainly the clever leader of the spy ring wouldn't risk anything quite so open, even in a section inhabited by people of his own nationality.

As he passed the place for the fifth time in less than an hour, Quinn saw, through his dark glasses, something which aroused his interest. Men were going into the hall, but these made a sharp turn just inside the door and seemed to vanish.

A car pulled up and two men climbed out. The Black Bat recognized them instantly as some of the spies who had been in the auditorium where Colonel Catlin had met his violent death. Now he was certain an important meeting was to be held. He reasoned also that the assembly in the main hall was merely meant to quell any suspicion that a far more dangerous meeting was to be held elsewhere in the building. This area was well policed these days. Uniformed men and detectives constantly kept their eyes open for trouble.

The Black Bat kept tapping his cane and softly calling for alms. He saw two bulky, square-faced men emerge from the hall, descend the steps and start what seemed to be a patrol in front of the place. They saw the Black Bat, whispered to one another and then approached him. He recognized their type immediately. These were Gestapo agents, selected for their ability to keep cruel hands clamped around the throats of those who hated what they stood for.

One of them grabbed Quinn's shoulder. The other struck a match, whipped off Quinn's dark glasses and almost shoved the flaming match into his face. Quinn's eyes never flickered, for they had that dead stare of the blind. When the Gestapo agent blew out the match, Quinn began feeling around the sidewalk for his glasses.

"I ain't done nobody no harm," he whimpered. "Please don't take me in, Officer."

The two men looked at one another and winked. One of them kicked the dark glasses toward Quinn's hand. He picked them up fumblingly and put them on.

"Get away from here!" one of the agents warned harshly. "If I see you again, I'll break those glasses—and your arm! You are not wanted around here. Is that understood?"

"I—I'll go," Quinn whined. "But I got to eat. A blind man can't do no work to make money. He's got to depend on kind people, but I'll go. I don't want no trouble with the police."

Quinn turned around. Tapping his cane, he obediently went off. One of the agents nudged the other, stepped quietly behind Quinn and delivered a hard kick that struck Quinn's ankle. With a choked sob, he tapped his way painfully to the next corner and rounded it.

SILK WAS waiting in a doorway, his face livid with rage.

"I saw them do that, sir. With your permission, I'd like to take a crack at the rats."

"I'll take care of them myself," Quinn said grimly, "and in just a couple of minutes. They seem to think this is Berlin. Now listen carefully. The meeting upstairs in that hall is a blind. I think the real business will take place in the basement. There's an alley beside the building, and a side entrance which leads to the basement.

"My theory is that when the proper moment arrives, our mysterious spy leader will come in person to deliver his speech. If that happens, we'll have him. Contact Butch. Take him with you and slip down that alley. Warn Carol to be ready, because this will have to be worked with blinding speed."

Silk looked puzzled.

"But those thick-necked mugs who chased you away— They'll pounce on us like a pack of dogs."

"I'll clear the way for you," Quinn laughed. "Once inside the place, let Butch go to work on anyone who is in your path. Wait for me. I'll follow shortly, but when I enter, it will be on the heels of the spy master.

"So, you cannot follow orders!" the Gestapo agents grated.

Find Butch and Carol, and then watch me do a little angling. I'm really going to enjoy this."

Quinn waited until Silk gave him a covert signal that all was ready. Then he adjusted his glasses, tapped the cane briskly and turned the corner, heading straight toward the two Gestapo agents. When they saw him coming, they gaped in surprise. Quinn kept on until he started to pass them. But they seized him, dragged him across the sidewalk and shoved him against a brick wall.

"So, you are stupid, eh? You cannot follow orders. Well, one of these days, you and all your kind will be wiped off the streets. If I had my way, you would get death. You are an impediment to the rule that is to follow here. But because you have disobeyed, we shall teach you a lesson—a good lesson, *ja*."

The agent doubled his fist, stepped back a pace and swung hard. As the fist streaked toward his face, Quinn ducked. It struck the brick wall instead, drawing a cry of anguish from the Gestapo agent.

Quinn suddenly moved fast. He thrust out one arm that sent the second agent flying toward the gutter. Then he ripped off the smoked glasses and began running swiftly down the street. The two agents came rushing after him, but Quinn knew they'd never risk shooting at him. They would capture him, if possible, and then silently make sure he'd never talk. By deliberately exposing himself as a fake blind beggar, Quinn knew they'd leave their posts and clear the way for Butch and Silk.

He skidded to a stop near the mouth of an alley two blocks away. Veering sharply, he picked up speed as he headed into its dark maw. Now the advantage was in his favor, for he could see perfectly in the gloom. The two agents followed down the alley, but they had to slow up, trying to find Quinn's shadowy form.

"A spy he is, and he dies!" one of them said in a hoarse whisper. *"Mein Gott,* if the Director knew how close he was to the meeting tonight! There must be a leak, eh?"

The agent turned his head. Instead of seeing his partner standing beside him, he saw an eerie form, made all the weirder in the darkness. For a moment he thought he had gone mad. He was staring at a huge figure with wings. Then recognition dawned, and one hand shot to his hip pocket.

"The Black Bat!" he whispered in horror.

HE GOT his gun half out of the pocket when the Black Bat's fist smashed him full on the nose. The blow hurled him back against the wall. Before he could shake the blood out of his mouth and eyes, the gun was wrenched from his hand, thrown far into the alley.

"You asked for this," the Black Bat said stonily. "Anybody who kicks a blind man around deserves the beating of his life, but you're doubly deserving of harsh treatment. Your kind is not wanted in this country. You gained admittance here by subterfuge. You threaten those who want to stay here and enjoy the freedom your own land does not provide. Get your fists up! You boast about physical prowess and 'strength through joy.' Enjoy this for a starter."

The Black Bat's gloved fist hit the Gestapo agent a slashing blow across the cheek. The agent stumbled and fell. The Black Bat grabbed his necktie and hauled him back to his feet.

"No! Do not strike me!" the agent whimpered. "I will give you money. I will go back to my own land. I will do anything you...."

"Yellow!" the Black Bat said harshly. "Unless you've got some poor, half-starved victim under your whip, you're only half a man. You can hand it out, but you can't take it. Your kind never can, but you get it, anyway."

He held the agent at arm's length and drove a mighty punch straight to the chin. The agent went limp. Letting him drop, the Black Bat walked into the alley and found the second agent, who was beginning to moan and stir. The Black Bat slammed home another blow, wiped his hands as though they'd touched filth. Then he pushed both men into a small alcove used for garbage and ash cans. He propped them up and shielded them from view with the cans.

Then he hastily stripped off his hood and cape, put them away, and donned his dark glasses and worn hat. After picking up his cane, he returned to the sidewalk and tapped along the street. As he neared the meeting hall, he saw the big doors close. A moment later a sedan turned sharply and crawled down the driveway beside the meeting hall.

It stopped, the headlights winked out, and the door beside the driver's seat opened. A man stepped out. In the gloom he was just a shadowy blur, but the Black Bat's eyes saw that he was heavily shrouded in some kind of cape. He disappeared through the side entrance.

The Black Bat was after him quickly. Making sure no other guards were posted nearby, he changed to his hood and cape, and then entered a huge, faintly lighted room. He saw an electrical switchboard, curtains and ropes, and realized that he was behind a stage. Apparently the basement of the building was used as a theater.

Then his eyes made out a form lying prone on the floor, near one corner. The Black Bat made only a cursory examination of the unconscious man. The lopsided jaw gave silent proof that Butch had been at work. Abruptly a hiss attracted his attention, and Silk came from behind a stage prop. When the Black Bat joined him, Silk whispered in his ear.

"We've got him. They're ready to hold a meeting and the big boy himself just stepped onto the stage. The only man on duty here is over in the corner. I think Butch all but killed him when he started to draw a gun. What shall we do now?"

"Butch is to take the left wing of the stage," the Black Bat replied softly. "You take the right wing, and I'll slide under the curtain in the middle. His nibs wore a big cloak. We've got to get that over his head so he can't see you or Butch. Then, after he's properly silenced, we'll perform a neat job of kidnaping. All set?"

"I've been set for days, sir. You give the signal."

THE BLACK BAT hurried to the center of the curtain. Dropping flat, he raised the curtain an inch and saw the feet of the mystery man. Gruff commands came from the small theater out front and then the intense lights were turned on. The Black Bat raised his hand, saw Butch and Silk waiting. He brought it down, sliding under the curtain at the same instant. All three of them converged on the cloaked leader. Butch's huge paw clamped across the man's mouth. Silk tripped him silently, and the Black Bat whipped the cloak over his head. He nodded to Butch. The big man rammed home a knockout blow, picked up the limp victim and retreated toward the wings, with Silk following.

The Black Bat slid beneath the curtain again. He ran to Butch's first victim and quickly slung him over one shoulder. He carried him onstage, propped him up against the curtain and plastered a Black Bat sticker on his forehead. Then he darted off the stage and out of the building.

As he left, he could hear the eager spies hailing the expected appearance of their leader. The Black Bat slipped off his hood and cloak as he raced up the driveway. Carol was waiting in the car, with the motor humming. Silk sat beside her and Butch was in back. Their victim was huddled in a heap on the floor. When the Black Bat got in, Carol quickly drove off.

"Head for Logan Park," he ordered. "It isn't patrolled, and it's dark there—just right for my interview with the big shot. And, Carol, that was slick work. You too, Silk—and you, Butch."

"Aw," Butch replied modestly, "that was nothin'. I never even made my knuckles tingle. That guy's jaw musta been cut outa putty. Say, Boss, do I get a crack at this baby? Just a little two-minute round?"

The Black Bat chuckled. "He's my meat, Butch, and I'll handle him with kid gloves until he talks. This has been one grand night's work. Silk, jump out at the next corner. Phone the F.B.I. and tell them where they can round up those spies in a hurry."

Carol turned into the park and stopped at the darkest spot she could find. As he got out, the Black Bat hauled his prisoner with him and spoke softly to his aides.

"Keep cruising around. When our pal wakes up, I don't want him to see your faces or hear your voices."

He carried the cloaked figure deep into the park, laid him down on the grass and knelt beside him. When he wrenched the cloak open, he groaned in disappointment.

The man they had kidnaped was Fritz von Elkin—the one man who couldn't possibly be the leader of the spy ring!

CHAPTER XV

WAVE OF TERROR

O **PENING HIS** eyes, von Elkin stared, then instantly closed them and shivered violently. That hooded head and the cape told him exactly who had negotiated this kidnaping.

"I have done nothing," he moaned. "There is no reason why you should kill me."

"There won't be—if you talk." Von Elkin's eyes showed that he understood the quiet threat. "First of all, I want to know just why you were assigned to address that meeting. Isn't that the job for your leader?"

"I know nothing." Von Elkin sat up, rubbing his swollen jaw. "I received orders only an hour ago, and I obeyed them. I was to put on a cloak, Cover my face and go to the meeting. I was not told what to say, and under no circumstances was I to reveal myself to anyone. I swear that is everything I can tell you."

"Then let's take it from another angle," Quinn said. "When Morino was killed, you were in the same room. The man who murdered him fired through the doorway of your office. Who was the man who handled that gun?"

"*Himmel!*" Von Elkin's eyes popped wide. "How do you know that? Even the police have not found out about it yet. You will not believe me. Anyway, if I talk any more, I will be killed. There is no difference, whether my death is at your hands or by the orders of my leader."

"I'm afraid you've got us all wrong over here, von Elkin. We don't torture or murder people to make them talk. Those customs we leave to barbarians. We'll let the law take its course. You may be convicted of murdering Morino. If you are not, then the worst possible punishment you can expect is deportation. We could send you back home by way of Japan, and even pay your fare."

"Send me—back—there?" von Elkin gasped in terror. "No! In the name of humanity, do not deport me! I will be killed at once for having failed. They will show no mercy. I'll tell you everything I know. Everything! The man who leads us is unknown to the entire organization. Whenever he addresses us, lights are thrown into our eyes, so we cannot see his face, though he can see us. His orders come by letter, by phone and by messenger.

"Yes, he did kill Morino. The poor fool had lost his nerve and was ready to confess to the police. Yet I did not see his face even that night. After killing Morino, he told me I could gain my freedom by going to the roof, jumping to the next building and using the side door to escape. A car was waiting for me. He had disappeared before I went to the roof."

"What are your leader's plans? What does he intend to sabotage and when?"

Von Elkin dry-washed his hands nervously.

"By answering that, I forfeit my life. Yet what can I do? The plans are ready. When the signal is given, our men will strike in every part of the country. They have machine guns, grenades—everything with which to kill and create terror. Sympathizers will feed them and store ammunition. Shipyards, factories, public buildings—all are to be destroyed. The plan is so huge that sometimes it makes me shiver."

"When does all this happen?"

"No one but the Director knows. He alone can give the signal. I swear that is the truth."

THE BLACK BAT reached under his cape and placed one of the perforated cards on von Elkin's knee.

"Read that. Tell me what it means."

Von Elkin had only to glance at the card to recognize it.

"Through these cards will come the signal. No one knows what they mean, but when the time comes, we will learn how to use them. The lieutenants distribute one to every member of the organization. I also have one."

Von Elkin reached toward his pocket, but the Black Bat gripped his wrist hard. From the spy's inner pocket, he brought out the card. Clumsily von Elkin knelt, bent over the Black Bat's shoulder and pointed to the perforations.

"You see, that is what I mean."

Suddenly he gave the Black Bat a vicious shove, sent him rolling over on the grass. The spy was on his feet in a flash, racing away into the darkness. He plunged headlong into tall shrubbery and kept running. He was shaking badly and sweating with fear, but he had escaped the Black Bat. Naturally he could no longer return to the spy ring after what he had told. There was plenty of room to hide in this big country, though....

"All right, von Elkin. Put your hands up and come out of there. If you try to duck, I'll put a bullet through you."

Terrified, von Elkin saw the Black Bat standing ten feet away.

"Ach!" he cried. "You are not human! You found me in this darkness. It is not possible!"

A gun that pressed against his ribs told him it was indeed a fact. He offered no resistance. He was thoroughly beaten, and he knew it. This black-garbed figure was even more frightful than the Gestapo, or the sinister voice of the Director.

Von Elkin was quickly bound with his own necktie and belt. The Black Bat slung him across one shoulder and marched back toward the car. As he neared it, he threw the cape over the spy's head. Butch was waiting to stow the prisoner into the car.

DETECTIVE-CAPTAIN McGRATH came home late. His wife was away and he preferred to work overtime rather than sit home all alone. After he put his car away, he walked around to the front of the house and let himself in. The instant he snapped on the living room lights, he jerked erect in surprise.

Strapped to one of his big chairs was Fritz von Elkin, his mouth gagged. A note had been pinned to his vest. McGrath read it in amazement.

> Compliments of the Black Bat, Captain. Here is Fritz von Elkin, in whom you and the F.B.I. are greatly interested. He doesn't know much and I've already milked him dry of all the information he could give. He did not murder Anton Morino, but he is a self-confessed spy and his name will look good on your records.

McGrath went to the phone and called the local offices of the Federal Bureau of Investigation. Twenty minutes later, two G-men were clamping handcuffs on von Elkin.

"Nice work, Captain," one of them said. "We certainly wanted this man badly."

Dismally McGrath shoved the Black Bat's note toward the two G-men.

"Don't thank me. The Black Bat did it. I'm just a go-between."

"Honestly and sincerely spoken," a voice stated from the back of the room.

Everyone whirled. The Black Bat stood just inside the door, an automatic gripped in his hand.

"I'm sorry I had to startle you," the Black Bat apologized. "I wasn't sure McGrath would listen to me, and I really needed a representative of the F.B.I. to hear what I have to say. Sit down, gentlemen. Shall we declare a truce for the moment? After all, we all work on the same side of the fence in this particular case."

"You've got my word that I won't try to nab you," McGrath grumbled.

"And ours," one of the G-men added quickly. "In fact, we have orders to give you a free hand. Before Colonel Catlin died, he notified the Department that you were at work on the case. He was a little proud that even you didn't know he was in active service again. Catlin had been assigned to Military Intelligence several months before. I think they killed him because he had learned too much."

The Black Bat walked over to von Elkin and stripped off the gag.

"How about it? You were in the meeting hall when Catlin died. You may even have been the man who killed him. Why was he murdered? What was he trying desperately to say?"

"I did not kill him! None of us knows who did it. We had orders to capture him, but not to kill. I do not know why he was murdered. You must believe me! I am telling the truth."

"SO CATLIN was on active service with the Military Intelligence." The Black Bat balanced himself on the corner of McGrath's living room table. "That puts a new light on the subject. Those others who died—apparently by accident, or in the course of a hoodlum robbery—what about them? Were they on active service, too?"

"We don't know," the G-man answered. "This is the first time anybody claimed those men were murdered."

"Well, they were. Here is what I want to say. The spy ring is big—far more enormous than you probably believe. Its tentacles stretch into every city in the nation. They are well armed, and already have sympathizers prepared to hide them and to secrete ammunition. In effect, they intend to perform as the parachute troops did in Belgium and Holland—to destroy and terrorize.

"Contact your Washington office and prepare them against this shock. Men must be ready twenty-four hours a day to operate from every branch office you have. They are to be completely armed and augmented, if necessary, by regular Army men. This is no crackpot scheme. It's war on a modern scale.

"If the spies succeed, the whole program of the United States is bound to be delayed, with disastrous results. If my plans carry through, I shall flash word to your Washington offices when and where to strike. We may be able to gather the whole ring into one net."

"As far as we're concerned," one of the G-men said, "those are orders. We'll hike von Elkin to our local office and grill him. He may spill something he forgot to tell you. I'll get in touch with Washington and have the arrangements made. Nothing will be left undone. You can depend on us."

"I am," the Black Bat said grimly. "So are a hundred and thirty million other people." He arose and backed toward the door. "Do you know anything about the raid I ordered on the spy meeting?"

"It was a fizzle," a G-man said. "We found nothing but two hundred men all singing the 'Star Spangled Banner' and getting ready to close their meeting. They had resolved to fight for democracy."

"I was afraid of that," the Black Bat said. "Did you search the basement?"

"Yes. All we found was a stage-hand who said some burglar had slugged him. But there was a short-wave radio on the stage, too. We looked it over. It couldn't get messages from any great distance and all the sending apparatus had been removed."

The Black Bat nodded. "Take good care of von Elkin. You might give him a drink. He looks as though he needs one. Good night, gentlemen."

The door closed softly, and he was gone.

CHAPTER XVI

ATTACK IN THE DARK

RETURNING TO the car, the Black Bat got in beside Carol. "Drive back to the house," he ordered. "Butch, you get your wreck of a car over to the corner of White and Damon Streets. Park it there, and then go back to your boarding house."

After Butch was dropped off, Carol drove to the neighborhood of the address the Black Bat had given Butch. She parked on a lonely side street.

"Can I help, Tony? I feel as though I'm just an ordinary chauffeur."

"Not at the moment. But I'm working on an idea, and you'll be more than useful in it. Right now I'm going to pay Fritz von Elkin's hideout a visit. I learned the address from some papers he had on him. Von Elkin may have been holding back. I'm not sure, but I think he may have been one of the men who fought Colonel Catlin just before he was stabbed.

"The smoke was pretty thick, yet I'm reasonably certain he was hanging onto Catlin. He'd deny that, not because of his vast faith in the totalitarian regime which controls his life, but as a matter of self-preservation. He doesn't want to be suspected of murder. Go back to the house and wait for me in the lab. Silk should be home by now, and we can have a council of war."

She turned toward the hooded and caped figure at her side.

"Tony, this is the greatest thing you've ever done. It's more important than running down crooks and murderers. I'm proud that I had something to do with the origination of the Black Bat."

"I'm just grateful," the Black Bat held her hands, "for a kind Providence that turned you my way—not because you brought back my sight. That's incidental. But it allowed me to know you. Some day our task will be completed and the Black Bat will retire. That day will mean that you and I can be together as long as we live. Providing, of course, that you want it that way."

"I do, Tony. I do! That's why I worry so much when you're prowling around, especially when you work against these monsters. Even if they only suspect that Tony Quinn is the Black Bat, they may think it necessary to murder you. I—I've never really been afraid before, but I am now."

"I know," the Black Bat said softly. "It has affected me the same way. But, Carol, if we fail, a great number of people will die. There's no telling what will happen if that gang gets the upper hand. I'd willingly lay down my life to prevent it, yet you can rest assured I'm not going to take foolish chances. Those men will give no mercy, and they can expect none in return. I'm beginning to understand all that has happened so far. The chase may be nearly ended. Now, go back and wait for me. This particular job is plain routine."

The Black Bat left the car, darted across the sidewalk and invaded the spacious yard of a large house. He watched Carol disappear around the corner before going on. Through the inky darkness, he crossed other yards without blundering into anything that might give an alarm.

Scrutinizing the house in which von Elkin had been hiding, he wondered how the spy had ever managed to afford to live there. The house was an old-fashioned affair, with gables and turrets, and there were even blinds outside the windows. Some of these had been shut.

Warily the Black Bat approached the rear door. For all he knew, a dangerous number of spies might be holed up there. The ordinary lock on the door gave to his skill in less than a minute.

HE WALKED across a kitchen, saw opened tin cans strewn around, and dirty dishes and pans in the sink. He opened a cupboard and looked at the supply of food. There wasn't much—certainly not enough to feed many men.

In the middle of the dining room, he stopped and listened. His sensitive ears heard a faint creak, but no other sound. The creak might have originated in the structure of the house itself, for the place was old. The Black Bat walked noiselessly into the huge living room, drawing a gun as he entered. His search of the room revealed nothing of interest. A study and a library at the rear of the house were just as unproductive of evidence.

Returning to the reception hall, he climbed the wide staircase cautiously, grateful for the silence which his crepe-soled shoes insured. There were several bedrooms and a sewing room on the second floor. Only one door was closed, apparently leading into one of the bed chambers. He turned the knob swiftly, flung the door wide. His gun came up, ready for battle. But nothing happened. The same grim silence still gripped the whole house.

When the Black Bat stepped into the room, he knew it held what he sought. On a small dressing table was von Elkin's disguise—the black wig and the beard.

He saw a desk in one gloomy corner and approached it. Before he started to examine the contents of the drawers, he looked down at the waste-basket. It was half full of crumpled papers, among which were the yellow pieces of a torn telegram form.

The Black Bat bent down and picked up a scrap of the yellow paper. It contained only the date of the wire, stated that it had originated in Washington, D.C., and following this was the telegraph company's code numbers. He impressed them on his mind, for the wire might be important, especially since it came from the nation's Capital. There was a chance that it might reveal some spy with his nose stuck deeply into Government business.

For one brief instant, the Black Bat was not on guard. All his attention was centered on picking the scraps of the ripped telegram out of the basket and assembling them.

When he heard a soft step behind him, he started to arise. Abruptly his cloak was thrown over his head. The Black Bat was really blinded. A hard blow knocked the gun out of his hand before he could pull the trigger. He moved away quickly, trying to drag his engulfing cape down so he could see. There was no chance of accomplishing this, for the mysterious marauder worked fast.

He rocked the Black Bat with a hard punch to the chest, directly above the heart. Another slammed painfully into the pit of his stomach. The Black Bat had to give way under the attack. Each time he tried to remove the cape, another blow landed.

Suddenly he realized that the attacker was deliberately forcing him back in a certain direction. That instant, he felt an open window behind him. He made one last frantic effort to land a wild punch, but it missed. That was his last chance. Two strong arms lifted him and thrust him through the window.

THE BLACK BAT felt himself slipping, sensed that his attacker had stepped back for a kick or a final punch. The Black Bat suddenly relaxed, but his two hands shot out. One of them seized the top of a sturdy blind.

When the last attack came, he was shoved completely through the window. He managed to hang onto the blind with one hand, and reach for his second gun with the other. Whipping it out, he fired two quick shots through the window.

He heard a snarled curse, the sound of furniture being tipped over. Again he fired, and then hastily removed the cape from around his head. He could see now, but the room was empty. The door was closed and a fire burned furiously in the waste-basket.

The Black Bat swung onto the sill and dropped back into the room. The papers were already almost consumed by the fire, but he turned the waste-basket upside down to smother the flames. Snatching up the gun that had been knocked out of his hand, he darted toward the door. He flung it open and leaped out onto the balcony overlooking the reception hall.

Three guns burned a deadly greeting. The Black Bat leaped aside, saw a trio of spies half hidden by doorways on the floor below. His automatic spat once. A spy fell out of the doorway like a log of wood. The other two were shooting fast, but the darkness impeded their aim. It had no effect on the Black Bat's marksmanship, however. He nailed another with a bullet between the eyes. The third man gave a startling scream. He ducked out of sight, and the Black Bat heard him racing toward the back door.

None of those three had been his attacker, the Black Bat felt certain. The man who had seized him had owned thick arms and the great strength of a powerful body. For some reason he was sure that he had tangled with the real leader of the spy ring. Therefore, that telegram must have been vitally important. The Black Bat raced down the steps. As he neared the bottom, the front door opened. His gun came up with the speed of lightning.

He let it sag, for Butch was standing in the hall, trying to penetrate the darkness. Under one arm he carried a limp figure. The Black Bat's hopes surged high when he saw that. Butch may have accidentally nailed the leader.

"Butch!" the Black Bat called softly. "Put him down. Where'd you get him?"

"I was just parkin' the car when I heard shots," Butch explained. "So I kept on drivin', and I saw this baby runnin' like mad. I jumped out, and he argued with me a little, so I conked him. Did I do wrong, Boss?"

"Put him on the floor," the Black Bat said. "I want to take a look."

Butch obeyed by simply letting his burden fall. The Black Bat turned the man over, saw a piggish face, a partially bald head, and a thick neck. The Black Bat had never seen this man before, as far as he knew.

He heard tires grit along the driveway, raced to a window, A sedan was turning crazily out of the drive and onto the road.

"Butch, get in your car and trail that sedan. Don't lose it! Phone Silk just as soon as you find out where it's going. Step on it!"

"Okay, Boss." Butch started for the door. "But if I was you, I'd lam outa here. Boy, them shots were louder'n bombs."

LEAVING BUTCH'S victim on the floor, the Black Bat hurried back to the room where he had fought for his life. Hastily he turned the waste-basket over. He groaned, for every scrap of paper had been consumed by the flames. But he didn't waste time in searching the desk. If it had contained anything of value, the unknown attacker would have destroyed or taken it.

The Black Bat rushed down to the thick-necked man, who was beginning to come out of unconsciousness. After looking out the front door to make sure no police cars were pulling up, the Black Bat lifted the heavy man. Without too much exertion, he carried him through the house, out the back door and behind the garage. He let the man down and slapped his face gently until he fully awakened.

"Don't make a sound," the Black Bat warned. "When you talk, speak in a whisper and speak fast. I'm in no mood to argue, either. Who are you? What were you doing in that house?"

"It's my house," the man answered, with a frightened look in his eyes. "I'm Roscoe Bell. I own it. I was just coming home when some giant jumped out of the darkness and that's all I remember. I suppose that must have been you. What's the idea of a mask and— Wait a minute. You're the Black Bat! What do you want with me? I can't tell you anything about crooks."

The Black Bat started. Butch had captured Rankin's friend—the salesman of death weapons!

Sirens were howling in the distance. The Black Bat was in an uncomfortable spot, for he had no car, and the police were bound to throw out cordons as soon as they found two dead men in Bell's house. Even though he might be allowed his freedom and not be unmasked, there would be dangerous delays.

"This time I'm not interested in crooks—of the average kind," he stated. "I'll be back. Don't forget that, and if I were you, I wouldn't try to leave town."

The Black Bat stepped away and faded into the darkness. Instantly Bell began yowling for help. He saw radio cars pull up and disgorge uniformed men. "It's the Black Bat!" he yelled. "He went this way."

Bell pointed frantically, but the sergeant who stepped up didn't even look in the direction Bell indicated. Two of his men ran into the house. An instant later, they shouted their finding of the two dead men.

"So the Black Bat was here, eh?" the sergeant said. "That's okay, but not for you. My hunch is that he came here to run down some evidence you have. So we'll all go down to Headquarters and have a little talk with the commissioner. Maybe you can explain those two stiffs in the house, huh? Don't start yapping right now. Stick out your mitts, brother, and find out what bracelets feel like."

Bell's eyes glittered in hatred.

"You have no right to arrest me. I know nothing about any dead men in my house. I was on my way home when the Black Bat knocked me out. I warn you, there'll be a civil action if I'm taken to Police Headquarters."

"Yeah, I've heard that before," the sergeant said wearily. "Now, are you coming quietly or must I see if my gun butt is as good as the Black Bat's fist?"

CHAPTER XVII

STEALTHY VISIT

N O MORE than a minute was needed for the Black Bat to find a dark spot and remove his cape and hood. He took the soft, floppy-brimmed hat out of an inner pocket and donned it. Then he started for home by devious routes which would not take him near too much traffic. He had to risk the possibility of being detected only because he was forced to.

In a quiet section of the city, he drew down the brim of his hat and walked into a drugstore. He bought a package of cigarettes and then went to the phone booth. Quickly he dialed Captain McGrath's home.

"This is the Black Bat," he said. "I need your help badly. A telegram from Washington was in the possession of certain people neither of us likes. I'll give you the office and the code number. Maybe you can get a copy. Can you get it in twenty minutes?"

"I'll get it, if I have to blow open the doors of that telegraph office," McGrath promised. "The truce we agreed on is still effective. Call me back. Don't worry about my tracing the call."

"I won't," the Black Bat chuckled. "You tried that often enough before and never succeeded. But I'll take your word, Captain. Here are the numbers."

He gave them and then left the drugstore without attracting attention. Long ago, he had learned never to be conspicuous by acting furtive. He held his head high, though that revealed his scars. Twenty minutes later—from a cafeteria phone booth—he called McGrath again.

"I had them read the wire to me over the phone," McGrath said. "It's addressed to Colonel Catlin and it says: 'Nests closing before net is drawn. Look for leak. Has word spread around about this?'"

"Thanks," the Black Bat said. "It helps a lot. Maybe we'll have a neat little package of spies wrapped up for you in a few hours. Did von Elkin talk?"

"He clammed up the minute you left. The only thing that guy is scared of is the Black Bat. Good luck on your hunting. I wish you'd take me along."

"And have you break every law on the rule books?" the Black Bat laughed. "You'd never live it down, Captain. I admit you really would be helpful, but it just can't be done,"

The Black Bat slipped through the garden gate of his home without being seen. As he entered the tunnel, he breathed easily for the first time in what seemed to be hours. He had noticed that Butch's car was parked in its usual place. Butch, therefore, had returned. The Black Bat was eager to find out where the spy had driven.

They were all waiting anxiously for him. Silk prepared a quick lunch while Butch reported what he had done.

"I follow the guy out of the city. He turns up a road like the kind they have on farms. I park and go up, too. I see this guy drive through a big gate. When I sneak closer, I see a lot of guys in funny looking uniforms, and they keep sticking their arms out at one another. Then I scrammed. The road he turned off on is just past a big billboard and a heap of sand that's gonna be used when the roads get slippery. It's a pipe to find."

"Carol," Quinn said, "you and Silk go to work. I want that place completely investigated, it sounds like one of the Bund camps, so be careful. Find out how many men are there. See if you can determine whether they are armed, and if they intend to stay there all night. This business is getting ready to break and we must blow it to pieces before they have a chance to act. At exactly one o'clock in the morning, either be back here or phone. I'll wait until then. If I don't hear from you, I will assume you need help."

SILK WAITED only long enough to put on the disguise he had used when the spy ring captured him in Morino's house. After he and Carol left, Quinn finished a sandwich in two bites. He replaced the guns in his holsters with fresh weapons and handed one to Butch.

"You may need it. Sometimes fists and strength aren't enough. Bring your coupé to the garden gate and wait there for me."

Quinn spent about ten minutes looking over the sheaf of perforated cards again. Here in his hands lay the possible means of unmasking every spy nest, preventing them from opening a murder drive all over the country. Did they really mean what he was beginning to suspect? He shrugged. That was a question that only time could answer. He put them away.

Glancing at his watch, he saw he had plenty of time before the deadline he had set for Carol and Silk.

When he came through the tunnel, Butch was parked and waiting. Quinn climbed in and gave several precise directions that brought them to one of the best parts of the city. Not quite a suburb, nor actually a section of town, it offered the prospective tenant the choice of an apartment or a whole house—both at remarkably high prices.

"We're going into that brick house," Quinn said. "I want you to come just in case my opinion is wrong."

"Are we gonna grab the big shot?" Butch asked hopefully.

"I hope not. Capturing him would only bring the day of attack closer. He'd find some way of sending out word and then all hell would break loose. Follow me. I'll warn you when there is anything in your path."

"Okay," Butch agreed. "Say, it sure must be somethin' to see in the dark. Just like a cat, huh?"

"That's exactly how we must work—like cats," Quinn warned. "If anyone is in the house, we must leave without making a sound. There are to be no heads broken this trip."

Ten minutes later, the Black Bat and Butch stood in a small study. The walls were lined with books, most of them concerning military tactics. The Black Bat quietly searched the place before he did any actual investigating. When he knew the house was empty, he returned to the study where Butch waited.

Seeing a glass trophy case on the mantelpiece, he stepped up to it. Butch could only see a blur, while the Black Bat's eyes made out everything as clearly as though it were day. The trophy case contained a forty-five Army automatic and an officer's sword. Mounted on a velvet background were the shoulder insignia of a major of the United States Army.

"Stay near the door," the Black Bat whispered. "If anyone comes near, be ready to go through the rear window. I'll open it now."

Butch nodded and moved to obey the orders. The Black Bat walked to the rear wall of the room, raised a window and swiftly peered around outside. He frowned deeply under his black hood. Just outside the window was a projection of wall about two feet thick. In the room itself, though, there was nothing like an alcove to account for that bulge. He stepped up to the wall and removed his black silk gloves. Slowly he passed his extremely sensitive fingers over the wall.

He spent fifteen minutes at this painstaking task, but it brought results.

Suddenly his fingertips encountered a slight lump in the wall. He manipulated it experimentally. With a whir, an electric motor went into operation and a four-foot section of wall silently slid back.

Revealed clearly before him was a closetlike room, not more than two feet deep. A shelf occupied part of this space, and a number of leather-bound volumes were neatly stacked on it.

He removed one, saw that it was a diary, almost twenty-eight years old. As he glanced at a few of the pages, he gave vent to a whispered exclamation. Then he deliberately tore one of the pages out of the book.

After he replaced the volume, he studied a number of maps that were tacked to the hidden wall. They were ordinary route maps given away by filling stations, but there was one for each state. They had been carefully drawn into oblong sections, so that each entire map was divided.

The Black Bat stepped back, made the door slide into place again. Then he went directly to the desk in the middle of the room. Sitting down, he opened the drawers and removed a number of hand-written documents. As he studied these, he was comparing them with the page he had ripped out of the old diary. His eyes could follow every word, every stroke of the pen or pencil, even though the room was so dark that Butch was blinking blindly.

Carefully he replaced the papers he had taken from the desk. He arose and strode without hesitation to where Butch stood guard.

"I'm going upstairs, so keep your eyes and ears open. I'll be gone only a couple of minutes."

He headed straight for the master bedroom, which was easily identified by the lavish furniture it contained. He appropriated a towel from the bathroom, using it to wrap around certain objects. Then he hurried down and closed the window in the study. With Butch closely following him, he left the house. The only evidence of their visit was the absence of a towel. That was hardly apt to be noticed, and the objects he had taken had not often been used.

Butch drove him to another part of the city, where the Black Bat ducked into a yard. He unloosened the knot in the towel-wrapped bundle he carried. Lashing this to his wrist, he climbed a rear porch pillar. He reached the sloping roof and crawled over it to a partially opened window. It was no difficult trick for him to open it without making a sound. Then he slipped into a bedroom and turned on a lamp.

Commissioner Warner jumped erect, grabbing wildly under his pillow for a gun. Then his sleep-laden eyes made out the black-caped figure that stood beside his bed. He relaxed with a sigh of relief.

"Sometimes I think I ought to hang a badge on you and let you work openly," he complained. "Then you won't scare the wits out of me on your midnight visits. What's up? Did you get anything on the spy ring?"

THE BLACK BAT placed his towel-wrapped bundle on Warner's bed.

"Inside this package you will find certain articles which should be covered with fingerprints. They are things that my suspect won't miss immediately. Have those prints brought out and then take a plane to Washington. Check the prints with every bureau available, although I think that perhaps the Military Intelligence will have some information on them. Get back here as quickly as possible and wait for me to contact you."

Warner placed a hand exploringly on the bundle.

"So you've rounded him up, eh? I wish I knew how you managed to do it. I've got over eighteen thousand men working for me, and not even one of them could get anything on this spy case."

"They must adhere to laws," the Black Bat laughed. "I don't. I have no rule book to consult every time I want to go into action. It gives me an advantage, you see. Now, I think you'll be back by mid-morning, or early afternoon at the latest. Those prints must be checked, so happy hunting in the fingerprint files in Washington."

The Black Bat moved toward the window and abruptly vanished as Warner rubbed his eyes. Swiftly he swung his feet over the edge of the bed and started to get dressed. The Black Bat rarely called for help, but when he did, that aid was always of vital importance. No one knew this more than Warner.

An hour later, a Police Department plane was carrying him quickly toward the nation's Capital.

CHAPTER XVIII

ZERO HOUR

E VEN AS the Black Bat was prowling the darkness, Carol and Silk reached the camp which Butch had described. They left their car hidden in the brush and walked beside the narrow lane until they saw an arch and a high wire fence surrounding the whole camp. The sign on the arch was intended to identify the place as an outdoor trap shooting club. There were two men standing just inside the gates. Each casually held a rifle in the crook of his arm. Carol tugged at Silk's sleeve.

"Butch was right," she whispered. "It's nothing more than a blind for an armed training camp. Silk, we've got to get inside somehow, and find out how many men are assembled here and why they are gathered at this time of night. I understand a little German. If they talk, I may be able to translate enough to help us. It's your job to find out how to get in."

Lying flat on his stomach beside Carol, Silk looked at the high mesh fence and shook his head.

"There's only one way to get inside. We've got to circle the place until we find a tree with a branch that hangs over the fence. And watch yourself, Carol. Those steel wires may be charged. I'd be willing to bet on it."

They crept back into the protection of the forest that surrounded the camp. Silk climbed a tree. Using its uppermost branches as a lookout station, he studied the area as well as he could in the dark. The Black Bat's eyes were badly needed just then. But Silk managed to sight the outline of a tall tree a few hundred feet to the left. Its thick boughs hung far over the fence.

Silk noticed patrols pacing alertly just inside the camp. Entering the place might not be so difficult, but getting out would be another story. It was certainly too dangerous for Carol. Silk crawled down to rejoin her.

"I see a way in, and I'm going to take a chance. Let's suppose I were the Black Bat. Would I let you go along?"

"You wouldn't, but I'd go, anyway," Carol stated. "Don't think you can talk me out of going."

Silk shook his head. "If we're both caught, how will we let the Black Bat know? Look, you stay here. Be ready to run for the car at the first sign of trouble. If they get me, I'll make plenty of noise. Can't you see that's the only way we can do it?"

Carol gave in to Silk's persuasion, but with bitter reluctance. She followed him to the large tree, watched him crawl out over the limb and finally drop safely on the ground within the fence.

Silk was now on extremely dangerous ground. If they caught him, he'd be killed just as surely as dawn would come in a few hours. He glanced over his shoulder at the big tree which had offered him entrance.

Silk made a wry face, cursing himself for being a fool. There were dozens of other trees that were just as tall and almost as near. But the overhanging branches of those trees had carefully been lopped off— leaving only the limb by which he had entered. Had that been done deliberately? Was this particular section specially patrolled? Were the members of this devil's organization all around him now?

SILK DREW a gun and kept on going. There was nothing else he could do. He saw a clearing with a dozen long, low barracks arranged to form a rude circle, with their entrances all facing a large drill grounds. Enough light came through the windows to let him see the uniformed men who strutted around, saluting one another.

He wondered uneasily when camps like these would be outlawed and their members closely questioned. In almost any European country, such a Bund would have been smashed with bullets. Those who survived would have been granted the privilege of dying more slowly in a concentration camp. That must not happen here, he swore.

Silk did not have the hearing of the Black Bat, nor those uncanny eyes that could penetrate the most intense darkness. He could only keep constantly on the alert.

He reached a spot as close to the parade grounds as he dared, when suddenly a car came swiftly through the gates. Two men stepped out. Barked commands brought the camp members into straight, precise lines. They stood at attention while a man in civilian clothes gravely marched along the ranks, holding in his hands a small package of perforated cards. He handed one to each man, then stepped back a few paces and drew himself up as erect as a protruding stomach would let him.

"So," he said sternly, "we are ready. The day has come. By this time tomorrow, we shall be in control of great areas of this stupid country. There will be blood spilled. Some of you may die, but that is a glorious death, and you should court it. Show no mercy. Those are the orders of our Director. The cards have been distributed all over the nation.

"Those who receive them know what to do. You, too, have received those same instructions, but they are not to be acted upon until the zero hour—nine-thirty tomorrow night. Before then, you must strip the secret arsenal. The job has to be complete when you leave here at dawn. Munitions will be available in large quantities elsewhere, but we will need every bit of it we can find. Refuge has been arranged for us, if we do not succeed. But we shall, of course."

Silk gulped and broke out in a cold sweat. This information was absolutely vital to the Black Bat's plans. Silk wanted only one more thing—to identify beyond question the man who had issued those orders.

Taking a desperate chance, he crawled behind one of the barracks. As the pompous leader went back to his car, he crossed directly in front of the headlights. Silk got a good look. He didn't recognize the man, but he memorized every detail of his features and build.

Silk retreated slowly and cautiously. The ranks had broken up, and the men were probably spreading out all over the camp. If he ran into a patrol, the whole game would be lost. He neared the section of fence over which he had crawled. It was possible that all the guards had been temporarily withdrawn so every man would be in ranks when the final orders were given. Now they'd be coming back.

He crouched, looked around, and then started to sprint toward the fence. He wasn't worried so much about his own safety. He had to deliver to Carol the message he had for the Black Bat. Silk realized that devastation would scorch the whole nation if he failed.

FOUR MEN suddenly came running to intercept him. Silk's gun roared. One of the men stumbled, fell, and didn't move again. The other three ducked for cover, began shooting at the same time. Silk risked everything on a dash to the fence. There he knelt to hold them off. Carol was just outside, well concealed by the darkness.

"Never mind me," he panted in a low voice. "Tell the Black Bat that zero hour is nine-thirty tomorrow night. Those cards were handed out. Run!"

Silk fired his last two bullets into the darkness. The guards wouldn't charge immediately. They would wait until they were sure Silk was at their mercy. By then Carol would have reached the car and escaped with the all-important message.

He waited five minutes. Then he arose, stretched his hands high and watched five men approach him cautiously. Two of them made a lunge for him. Silk went down under the impact, but he didn't try to fight. There was an odd kind of peace in his heart, for nothing they could do mattered now.

One of the men punched him brutally in the face. Holding his arms, they forced him back to the drill grounds. The word must have passed around quickly, for every man in the camp was already assembled there.

"We caught him just in time," one of Silk's captors reported to a tall, stern-faced man. "A moment before, he had come over the fence. It was good that he did not come sooner, eh?"

"It makes little difference," the camp commander growled. "We should not permit him to leave, anyway, but I have no time for him right now. Lock him in one of the barracks and maintain a strong guard. Double the patrols at once and shoot to kill if anyone else appears."

Silk was dragged to one of the smaller barracks and thrown inside. When the door slammed shut, Silk grabbed a table and pulled himself erect. He wiped the blood off his face, found a chair and sat down wearily. It might be the end of the game for him. But once the Black Bat had the information which Carol carried in her alert brain, he'd know what to do.

Ten minutes passed, and then Silk heard the sounds of a commotion outside. Within a few moments, the door of his temporary prison opened

Carol was shoved inside! As the light suddenly went on in the barracks Silk saw that her clothes were soiled. There were scratches on her face and an unholy determination in her eyes. Silk sprang half out of his chair, but he sank back defeatedly.

One of the men who had shoved Carol inside saw Silk and gave a yelp of recognition. He had been part of the band that had previously tried to use Silk as a human target.

"It is the man whom the Black Bat saved! These are the Black Bat's spies. Guard them carefully. Pass the word about that the Black Bat may be nearby."

Carol sat down beside Silk.

"I'm sorry," she said in a low voice. "There were more of them coming to the camp. They spotted me and—here I am. What are we going to do? How can we get the message through?"

"Quiet!" Silk whispered. "They don't know yet that I overheard the orders. They think I had just come over the fence when they grabbed me. We've got only one chance, even though it may mean our lives. I hate to think about it. It's after the deadline now. The Black Bat will know we're in trouble and he'll ride through hell to get us free. But what if he fails?

"This damned pack of lunatics will hit hard in every part of the country tomorrow night. They'll have the advantage of surprise. While I think they won't make any headway, there will be lives lost, factories and shipyards will be blown up. It will put back the rearmament program at least six months, and that might be fatal."

CAROL DRAGGED her chair close to Silk's.

"The Black Bat hasn't failed us yet, Silk. You know how he works. These strutting, saluting maniacs won't think fast enough for him. You'll see."

Silk got up and shuffled unhappily around the prison. At each window a guard was posted. Two more stood at the single door. Escape was impossible. But Silk happened to glance across the parade grounds, attracted by a sudden confusion. Two uniformed men were dragging someone from the direction of the main gate. Silk pressed his face against the glass. Abruptly his world blew up into fragments.

The man who was trying to wriggle out of the clutches of his captors wore a black, ribbed cape and a black hood over his face. The Black Bat had fallen into a trap!

CHAPTER XIX

TRICK AGAINST TRICK

Q**UICKLY BUTCH** drove the Black Bat back to Tony Quinn's house. He parked the car, and they walked briskly toward the garden gate. Before they reached it, the Black Bat seized his arm and held him back. Signaling for Butch to remain quiet, he crept forward until he could look around the gate.

As his eyes swept through the darkness, he made out three shadowy figures that were furtively approaching the windows of the living room. Careful as they had been, the Black Bat's acute hearing had detected the sound of their feet on the grass.

"I was afraid this might happen," he returned and whispered to Butch. "They suspect I'm the Black Bat, and those men are here to do a neat job of murder. We've got to get them, Butch. I'll slip down the tunnel and sneak into the house. The rest is up to you. Just be sure that not one of those men escapes."

Butch's face was grim as his big hands curled into lethal trip-hammer fists.

The Black Bat slipped through the gate, reached the garden house without being seen. Two minutes later, he was in the laboratory, hurriedly removing all traces of the Black Bat's identity. He thrust an automatic into the pocket of his smoking jacket and opened the hidden door. Stepping into the study, he walked directly to his accustomed chair in front of the fireplace.

He didn't turn on the lights.

The trio of killers was still prowling, looking through windows. Soon they'd reach the study.

Tony Quinn reached for a newspaper, slid the gun between its folds and kept his finger on the trigger. He kept the newspaper on his lap. Just then, he heard stealthy sounds outside the study window, saw a face rise up and glance quickly inside. Quinn's finger grew tense on the trigger. He'd give Butch every chance to do all the work, but if he saw a gun turned his way, he'd shoot.

Suddenly Quinn saw a man's whole form flash by the window. The sound of a fist crashing against bone reached his ears. He leaped up and hurried to the window. Outside, neatly arranged in a row, lay three unconscious men. Butch stood over them, nursing his right fist and grinning broadly. Quinn opened the window.

"Butch, pile all three of them into the coupé. I know it will be crowded, but never mind how you stack them. Drive somewhere and dump them. Then hurry back. It's after the time I allotted Silk and Carol. They may be in trouble."

"You gonna turn 'em loose, Boss?" Butch blurted. "They'll keep on thinking you're the Black Bat, won't they? Maybe I oughta wring their necks a little, huh?"

"No. Follow my orders. We're not murderers, Butch. These poor fools know nothing. The leader of the spy ring gives his orders, and they are carried out by men who have no idea what they're doing. Anyway, as soon as they wake up, they'll run for it as far as they can travel. Get going, and step on it!"

Quinn sat down again, forcing himself to be patient until Butch would return. Carol and Silk were thirty minutes overtime. Were they trapped—or dead? He had a violent urge to take the sleek sedan in his garage, cast aside all pretense of not being the Black Bat, and go after them. But he resolutely put this wild idea aside. To keep it from tormenting him, he made his mind review the case, considering each suspected person.

TOLLY, THE lawyer whose clientele consisted mostly of people of the same nationality as the spy ring. He had saved Quinn's life when von Elkin tried to run him down. Von Elkin might know the solution to everything, but blind Tony Quinn couldn't testify that he had seen von Elkin driving the murder car.

Then there was Roscoe Bell, who so far had hardly entered into the case at all. But his background made him seem the logical one to run the spy system. He had lost a fortune when war conditions ruined his export business. He had practically worked for the regimes now interested in disrupting the United States as much as possible. Bell looked powerful enough to have been the man who had tackled the Black Bat in the darkened room. He might have lied about being on his way home rather than leaving, when Butch seized him. He looked powerful enough to be that man.

Major Rankin also seemed to require considerable thought. It was more than possible that he had absorbed Nazi ideology, returned to the United States and become one of their spies. Treason like that had often happened all over the world recently. Quinn knew that military secrets had found their way into the hands of the spy ring—secrets which only someone close to the Army and Navy could obtain.

Yet far back in his mind lay clues which almost sewed up the right man in a net from which he could never extricate himself. Quinn hesitated to use those clues, however. The arrest of the spy leader now would serve only to fan high the smoldering fire in the hearts of his followers. The only way to stop this fiendish attack was to gather in the whole spy ring first. Every branch, every man prepared to attack, must be captured!

There had never been any doubt in Quinn's mind that the perforated cards were the key to the entire puzzle. How they fitted it had been the only problem, but in the past few hours he had found several important hints.

From his desk in the study, he took a stack of ordinary road maps and brought them to the laboratory. Laying them on the bench, he picked up one of the punched cards. He placed it in the upper left-hand corner of the map, traced its outline, and repeated the process until the whole map had been marked off.

For a long moment, he pondered his next step, switching his eyes anxiously from the cards to the map. When he flipped through the cards, turning them on their reverse sides, he suddenly drew in his breath. The faint gray numbers of one corresponded to the number of the highway map!

He had suspected that before. Now he merely had to find out which part of the map the card fitted, and that was only a matter of patient experimentation. Starting at the upper left-hand corner, he slid the card along. He discarded each section until the tiny holes suddenly blended with a number of highways and intersections....

Quinn's first impulse was to shout with triumph. But that would only waste valuable time, and he hadn't really solved the complete riddle.

After marking the highways and intersections with a pencil, he stared at the cards and maps, trying to figure out the significance of the whole puzzle. What did it mean? He had an important clue, but did the rest of the cards substantiate it?

Taking a deep, hopeful breath, Quinn searched through the perforated cards for the first two he had found. Then he checked through his stack of road maps until he came across one that corresponded with the number written in secret ink on the back of a card.

"If this works," he whispered anxiously, "I've got the key! If it doesn't...."

He marked off the map in rectangles and, by sliding the card along experimentally, found the proper section. Each perforation marked a road or corner!

QUINN WAS still rushing through his job when Butch came through the tunnel. The huge bruiser was grinning with glee.

"I did like you said, Boss. I threw them over the edge of the city dump. Just for luck, I plastered each guy a couple more times. What's next?"

Quinn donned his black outfit, stuffed his guns in place and hurried out with Butch to the coupé.

"We're going to that camp you found," he explained. "Silk and Carol must be in trouble. This time we'll be invading enemy territory, Butch. It will be dangerous, but no matter what happens, Carol and Silk have to be saved."

Butch drove savagely at a terrific pace through the night. As they slowed at an intersection, the Black Bat's eyes flitted over a group of billboards. He singled out the most interesting. Sponsored by the Officers' Club, it implored the public to rescue American natives who were in danger abroad. The Black Bat nodded thoughtfully.

When Butch found the lane, the Black Bat pierced the darkness, and soon discovered Carol's car hidden in the brush. Now he was sure they had been captured. Stealthily he led Butch toward the camp. There seemed to be no guards posted outside the high fence.

"You can't see them, but there are fifty or more uniformed men in that camp," he told Butch. "There are too many shacks to search quickly. Carol and Silk must be in one of them, but which one? Butch, are you willing to risk your life in this cause? Would you put on my cape and hood, deliberately let yourself be captured and thrown into the same hut with Silk and Carol?"

"Anythin' you say, Boss. But is it okay to slug a few of them mugs before they grab me?"

"Slug away. Here, put on the hood and cape. Stay right where you are until I go back to the coupé and get a duplicate outfit. Butch, I know you've got what it takes. We'll pull through because we have to."

Later, Butch crept toward the main gate. He knew that the hood and cape made him a marked man. The foe might open fire the instant he came into view, yet Butch kept on going. When he saw two men standing just inside the gate, he picked up a stone and hurled it. Then everything happened swiftly, noiselessly, like an old silent picture. Without a sound, one guard sprang into the tiny shack beside the gate. Almost instantly a dozen men with rifles raced out of the woods.

They rushed through the gates, which had suddenly flown open. In his hiding place, Butch held his breath. Two men came closer, beating the underbrush. He waited until they had almost found him. With silent viciousness, he leaped up, grabbed their necks, banged their heads together violently. They collapsed to the ground.

Grinning behind his black hood, he wheeled to face six other men. The only sound was the crack of bones as his fist pulped one man's face. Even when he raised both hands and surrendered, nobody jeered or shouted triumphantly. Capturing the Black Bat was too awe-inspiring a feat for such ordinary emotions....

CHAPTER XX

DEATH BY THE ROPE

UNDER COVER of carefully chosen shadows, the Black Bat was close to the gates when the men charged out to surround Butch. As he hoped, no one remained to watch the gate. Unobserved, he ran through, dived into tall grass just in time, for men were racing from camp to aid the guards.

Still in his hood and cape, Butch was hustled to the drill grounds. The tall camp commander emerged from a barracks with an impatient scowl on his face. He swaggered up to the captive.

"So this is the Black Bat," he sneered, awed despite his attempted sarcasm. "The man police and thieves could never capture. It proves, my followers, that we are much cleverer than the law or even organized crime in this country. Now we shall see who this Black Bat is. Then we shall take care of him and his two comrades."

The hood was wrenched off Butch's face. Then Butch was dragged toward the barracks where Silk and Carol were held.

The Black Bat saw all this with considerable satisfaction. He had hated to risk endangering Butch, but they were almost bound to imprison him with the other two.

The Black Bat ran lightly through the thick woods. Because he could see everything in his path, he made no noise. When he reached the back of the barracks, he spotted the guards beside the windows. Smiling grimly, he dropped to all fours and crawled closer. Then, with inverted gun, he suddenly plunged.

The guard at the rear of the barracks didn't hear nor see him coming. The gun crashed down, muffled by the military cap of the guard.

The Black Bat scratched on the window. Silk sprang to it, opened it quietly.

"They strike at nine-thirty tomorrow night," Silk whispered. "In case we all don't get clear, there are almost a hundred men here. They've got a whole secret arsenal ready."

"Where is it?" the Black Bat asked.

"In a small shed near the drill grounds. I saw them bringing guns out of it."

"Be ready. When that ammunition dump lets go, the whole camp will be in a panic. Scramble through this window and head for the gate. Is Carol all right?"

He saw her smiling confidently at him. The Black Bat waved, then faded away into the darkness.

He found the arsenal easily, for it was the only building that didn't look like a barracks. One man was posted at the door. The Black Bat crept forward, gun ready. All the other Bund members were gathered in small groups on the parade grounds, rehearsing verbally what they'd do when the time came to strike. He had to cross a cleared space before he could reach the arsenal. That entailed considerable danger, but he didn't hesitate.

AS HE approached, the guard shouted an alarm and started to raise his rifle. The Black Bat fired once and the man went down in a heap.

Like a flash, the Black Bat leaped through the door. He saw boxes of ammunition, a heap of grenades and sub-machine guns loaded and ready for action.

He seized one as the uniformed spies closed in ominously on the building. He grinned expectantly. They outnumbered him, but they had given him the whip hand....

His automatic rifle suddenly blasted, spitting flame and lead. Nobody could battle that stuttering death. Even the verbally fearless spies had to break ranks and flee. He could have shot them down, to the last man, but that would have meant shooting them in the back. He held his fire.

Swiftly he grabbed a hand grenade, yanked the pin, dropped it. He raced out, timing every action then to the split-second. Everything had to move on a time-table.

Like a clap of thunder, the ammunition dump went up.

Carol, Silk and Butch were sprinting toward the gate—straight into the muzzles of guards they couldn't see! But the Black Bat saw the rifles aimed. He squeezed the trigger of his machine gun, chopped inevitable death at the guards. As they went down, the men who had fled came charging back, revolvers roaring. He whirled on them, trapped.

Like a clap of thunder, the ammunition dump went up. The terrific concussion hurled the Black Bat to the ground, but he was up before the camp members knew what had happened.

The Black Bat and his aides ran madly down the lane. They piled into Carol's car—all but Butch, who took the wheel of the coupé. In another moment they were streaking back to the city.

"Carol!" the Black Bat ordered crisply. "Stop here. We don't have much time, but there's something I must investigate."

Carol stopped abruptly. The Black Bat knew the danger of delay, yet this was vital enough to risk capture. He hurried toward a billboard at one side of the road, stepped behind it. What he read in the dark on

the reverse of the sign made him whistle in grudging admiration. He returned quickly to the car, signaled Carol to start instantly.

"What an idea!" he said. "But nothing really surprises me, after that last hour at the camp. Carol, I can't let you take chances like that! I swear I'll stop sending you into danger."

"Of course you will, darling," Carol laughed, "when there is no more Black Bat. Are we finished for the night?"

"We're finished," the Black Bat said. "So is the case—except for one more important detail. Butch is right behind us. Signal him to come abreast. I'm taking the coupé. You three go back and get some rest. No questions now. I can see them ready to burst from your lips. Tomorrow afternoon, Silk, I'll have a little job for you. But keep some coffee ready when I get back, will you?"

"Yes, sir," Silk answered. "Don't forget, though, the deadline is nine-thirty. Those cards have been sent out already. Every spy in the country has one by now. And, say—I had a look at one of the big shots of the ring. He was a heavy-set man, with practically no neck at all. Blonde, too, and about five feet eight."

"The Honorable Mr. Bell," the Black Bat mused. "It's a perfect description of him. He's the man who slugged Butch. I'll soon have a little talk with him."

The Black Bat changed cars when Butch stopped. He streaked ahead of Carol's sedan, driving straight toward Bell's home.

WITHOUT AROUSING any attention, the Black Bat entered Bell's house. He hadn't long to work, for with daylight, the Black Bat must fold his wings. Stepping lightly through the kitchen, he suddenly froze into immobility. The front door had suddenly banged shut! Gun in hand, the Black Bat advanced cautiously. There was no one in the hallway. He headed for the library. As he reached it, he holstered his gun and sprinted inside.

A man was hanging from an old-fashioned electric light fixture. An overturned chair lay beneath him. The whole situation spelled suicide, except for the banging of the front door which the Black Bat had heard.

He seized the waist of the victim, quickly loosened the noose and finally extricated the man's neck from it. Carrying the limp form to a sofa, he laid it down gently and made a quick examination.

The victim was Roscoe Bell—the man who had visited the Bund camp only a short time before and issued the final orders for the assault against American civilization! He wasn't dead, for the Black Bat had cut him down before he choked completely. Yet Bell responded to none of the Black Bat's efforts to awaken him.

"Drugged," the Black Bat muttered. "He deserved this, but I wonder if the spy leader wasn't a bit too soon."

He carried Bell out of the house and put him in the coupé. There was a visitor in Tony Quinn's home that night—a visitor who lay unconscious until midday, when a black hood was drawn over his head. He could breathe easily, yet not have the slightest idea where he was nor who nursed him to normal.

BEFORE NINE-FIFTEEN the next night, twelve men slipped down an alley and into a side door which led them to a dimly lighted room. A stage occupied one end of the room. A radio stood against one wall and incongruously played soft dance music. The men entered singly, and about ten minutes apart, so it required two full hours before they were all assembled.

Their faces bore expressions that varied from strain to worry. They wore no uniforms and gave no salutes. Instead they talked in low voices, as if they were afraid some unseen presence might overhear.

"Do you think it will go all right?" one asked. "It will be hard for us if it fails."

"Bah, how can it fail?" another replied. "Tonight is the turning point for us. Tonight we hear how our men can fight and kill. We see, for the first time, the face of our Director—the man who has planned all this."

"But at the camp last night," the first man said uncertainly, "the Black Bat was there. A hundred of our men could not hold him, nor even shoot him down. He is free and I do not like it. What if he comes here?"

"How can he? Who knows of this place with the exception of ourselves and our Director? It is agreed that the Black Bat heard nothing of our plans, nor did those people whom he apparently rescued. He does not know when we strike any more than this silly Government does. Look, it is nine twenty-five! In five minutes, that foolish dance music will stop and something else will come over the air. Music to our ears, eh? But not sweet notes for the others who live in this country."

"It will be over by midnight. We shall hold many of the most important and strategic points. Other men will rally to our banner. There are two million of us in this country—two million who owe allegiance to the Fatherland, whether they believe so or not! Some will join, and the others will feel our vengeance. We cannot be beaten."

As the hands of the clock over the radio reached the half hour, the men drew into one rank. They stood at rigid attention, all gazing expectantly at the small stage.

The already dim lights in the room winked out. Half a second later, the blinding lights on the stage were turned on. The men closed their eyes, made no other movement. Then they heard the voice of the man they called their Director.

"You are all here. Good! In a few moments we shall know the results of our long, careful planning. How can we fail? The radio will carry full reports. When I am assured that victory is ours, I shall come down off this stage and you will know me. You will have a good laugh, too—at the discomfiture certain important officials are going to feel when they realize how they were tricked. Meanwhile, stand at ease. Any moment now it will start."

FIVE MINUTES passed by. Then the dance music was abruptly cut off and the voice of an announcer, vibrant with excitement, broke in.

"We interrupt this program to bring you startling news. Five minutes ago, one of the most important bridges on the West Coast was blown up. A Navy yard in the same region was turned into junk by bombs.

Other reports are constantly coming in. It is our duty to remain calm, though it appears that a Trojan Horse organization has struck at us.

"All transportation in New York City has ceased, due to explosions. A submarine base in New England has been bombed. All through the Middle West, the South—everywhere—there are riots. Men in uniforms, equipped with machine guns and hand grenades, are creating a panic wherever they strike. Stand by! There are orders from the nation's Capital coming through."

The leader's voice gloated over the glaring footlights.

"You see? Some have doubted me. They are the same type who doubted the man we worship, but he fought his way through, and he is now the undisputed leader of the entire world. One of the last strongholds of the weak plutocratic democracies is on the verge of breaking down. These people have wasted too much mercy for their fellow men. The world is well rid of that kind. From this moment on, only the strong will survive, to the greater glory of the man who has urged us on. Listen, does that news not sound pleasant?"

"Military law has been ordered in more than a hundred communities," the announcer cried. "In some places, authority has passed out of the hands of the police and into those of the Trojan Horse killers. The enemy is machine-gunning ruthlessly. Men, women and children have died by the hundreds. Armories have been blown to bits, and with them the equipment needed by the National Guard. The war has crossed the Atlantic so swiftly that none of us is prepared.

"Police insist that no one leave home under any circumstances. If the enemy troops—whether they are parachute men or not, we do not yet know—come into sight, phone the police at once. Do not try to intercept them."

The announcer kept stating incidents that grew more gruesome by the moment. Finally the leader spoke softly.

"It is time. We have won without question. What happens after this achievement will be unimportant. Therefore you will turn the radio down. Gentlemen, you will now meet your leader!"

The overhead lights were turned on and the footlights began to dim. This man, whom they knew only as the Director, liked theatrical effects, for they lent more glamor. The dozen subleaders stood at rigid attention but with gaping mouths. Even the news that still came through the radio was minor. They were about to meet the mysterious figure who had led them to victory.

The footlights grew dimmer and dimmer. Suddenly they were extinguished entirely. The leader moved forward a few steps and he was smiling broadly.

"I have purposely spoken to you in a disguised voice," he explained, "but secrecy is no longer necessary."

The man who faced his audience was Philip Trent! He was the man who headed the Officers' Club and campaigned for funds with which to fight the very organization he directed. Trent's smiling face creased into an angry frown.

"Well," he asked roughly, "why doesn't someone speak? Is your amazement too much? Have you lost your tongues? Come, many of you know me. Can't you see how I have tricked these pigs?"

"Be careful whom you call a pig!"

The voice spoke softly, close to his ear. Trent's face turned pale, making the scarred cheek grow a beet-red. He felt a gun digging into the small of his back as he raised his head and gaped at the windows of the cellar meeting room. Constructed of steel, they were now open. Through each protruded the ugly snout of a machine gun. Trent turned his head slowly, saw a hooded and caped figure standing behind him.

"The Black Bat!" he shrieked.

CHAPTER XXI

END OF A SPY

HASTILY OTHER people walked up on the stage—Commissioner Warner, the Chief Inspector of Police, and men from the Federal Bureau of Identification. Trent glared at them with hate-filled eyes.

"So I have been tricked! Somehow you found this place, but you are too late. I cannot be executed without a trial. Before you can even put me in jail, my men will be here. They have taken over the most important sections of the country. I shall give orders that unless I am released, one thousand civilians will be shot down. No, five thousand—for I am worth that many of your stupid kind. As in everything else, a democracy has acted too late."

"Turn up that radio," the Black Bat ordered crisply. When a G-man obeyed, the radio started playing dance music. At the end of the number, an announcer merely stated the next song on the program. There was certainly no hysteria in his voice. Then the music was cut off again just as it had been before. The same excited announcer rapped out further bulletins.

"The whole country is in the hands of the enemy. Our Army has been smashed. The Navy is thousands of miles away, on fake orders. Officials are even now negotiating terms of peace...."

"Do you see?" Trent sneered. "Now do I go free, or is it your desire to commit suicide? The first stipulation of peace will be your deaths unless I am freed."

"Just keep listening," the Black Bat retorted.

"We're licked!" the radio voice continued. "The White House has just been destroyed." Then the voice changed suddenly, accompanied by a laugh. "How am I doing, boys? Was that realistic, or wasn't it?"

Trent's grin turned to a stare of fear. His men actually cringed.

"The broadcast was faked," the Black Bat explained. "We tapped your wire hours ago and hooked it to a microphone. An accomplished radio announcer brought you the news you wanted to hear, but your whole scheme has collapsed, Trent. Those little perforated cards you sent to help your aides have helped us more. You were much too sure of your-self. The way you requested donations for use in running down spies was a masterpiece of conceit, for you intended to use that money in financing the spy ring.

"You even had billboard posters put up all over the country, but these had a more significant purpose. On the backs of certain sections of the posters were printed maps and full directions for your men. With the aid of these, they could find arms, refuge and sympathizers to lend a hand. The perforated cards were simply placed over the proper maps and each perforation revealed the location of a signboard bearing that ad. Your men had only to visit the billboards."

"But when they did, they ran into police and G-men, who were planted there! Your years of intrigue were useless, Trent. Every person you involved in this scheme has been exposed and arrested. It was clever—we all admit that. Your men knew nothing. If they were picked up, they couldn't talk. Until the day and hour you set, they would remain in ignorance."

TRENT SUDDENLY drew himself up. "All right, gentlemen," he replied suavely. "I only acted the part to see how good I was. Yes, I did head this band of spies, but only to nail them all. I planned to turn the entire group over to the authorities. However, there were some mysterious persons behind it and things got out of hand. At least, that's what I thought. Those broadcasts nearly frightened twenty years from my life."

"A good story," the Black Bat applauded. "But how do you account for the fact that four retired military officers told you—and you alone—certain military secrets, which soon passed into the hands of the powers you represent? You knew those officers would realize that no one but you could have transmitted that information, so you had them destroyed.

"At first I thought you were intent on killing off all capable officers to slow down the defense of this country. I believe your own men thought the same thing. But you failed to kill Colonel Catlin after he informed you that authorities intended to raid certain spy nests. You notified those spies and as a result the raids were fruitless.

"But you didn't know that Catlin had been called back and was an active member of Military Intelligence. He received a wire which informed him that the spies had been tipped off.

"He suspected you, and was going to expose you before the meeting you had called. You beat him to it, but fortunately I found enough of that wire to get a copy."

Trent spread his hands in wild appeal.

"Have you forgotten that I served in the A.E.F., that I was badly wounded? Look at my face, my hair! Do you think I'd turn to the people who almost killed me? Certainly I deserve some benefit of the doubt."

"You got it," the Black Bat said. "I suspected you, but I couldn't make myself believe a man of your standing and history could possibly have turned spy. However, that doubt is gone now, because you are not even Philip Trent. You are the Baron Otto von Dahlke, one of the greatest spies of the First World War! Your fingerprints prove it. You were on the verge of being captured just before the armistice, but you managed to escape. You fled toward the German lines, where you were wounded by your own side.

"You were taken to a German hospital, and there a colossal plan was concocted to get you to the United States as Philip Trent, who had really been killed. You took his identification, pretended a minor case of amnesia and shell-shock for a while. You were sent back to this country. Just before you arrived, Philip Trent's sister was mysteriously killed—by your agents—because she alone could have known you were not Philip Trent.

"A man named Roscoe Bell sponsored you. You moved away from the midwestern city where Trent had lived, and came to this city. Bell set you up in business because he was promised a great deal of export business in return. You kept Trent's diaries well hidden in your home, so that if anything happened which demanded that you recall Trent's past, you had his history for reference."

A pair of G-men brought Roscoe Bell into the room. White-faced, he pointed at Trent.

"Everything the Black Bat said is the truth. I'll swear to it. Von Dahlke came here and established himself as Philip Trent. Later, when another power ruled his Fatherland, he was appointed head of all secret agent activities in the United States. He became a disciple of the new Fatherland. I was in it up to my neck, so they made me hide von Elkin, threatening to kill me if I refused. But now that I'm free of them, I'll talk, all right.

"I heard that broadcast. If van Dahlke's plans had gone through, that's exactly what would have happened. I'm a poor specimen of an American right now, but believe me, I'll do what I can to make up for it!"

"SO YOU see," the Black Bat went on, "a net has closed around you, Trent, alias von Dahlke. You'll be charged with murder first—the murder of Anton Morino. He never wanted to work for your spy ring, but you forced him by threatening to kill his relatives in Austria. But Morino reached a certain point and couldn't go any further. He even refused to trust me, and crashed through a window to escape. Then he made a fatal mistake.

"Knowing that Philip Trent was fighting spies tooth and nail, he went to you. He was afraid to tell the police because he had been involved. You must have asked him to help trap von Elkin, but in reality Morino trapped himself. You were afraid to take any chances that he may have talked to someone else, so you tipped off the G-men to raid von Elkin's travel agency. You killed Morino there.

"I can prove that Morino saw you just before the murder. Commissioner Warner met you only a block away from the building, but I didn't know that. There are apartment houses on either side of your home, too. They have doormen, and those people are incredibly good at remembering faces. They even recall that the murdered officers came to see you often.

"You started the Officers' Club so you'd be in constant contact with men who knew what was going on. Some of them may even have known the real Philip Trent. But the wounds you suffered provided a good alibi for your changed appearance and the fact that you might not remember everything.

"You had the stage set at the meeting so your spies could escape easily. You ordered all the men out front to listen to your speech so the spies could get out by a rear exit unobserved. You sent von Elkin to take your place at a meeting night before last, but von Elkin didn't understand the significance. That night, you were to make a radio broadcast appeal for funds. You did make a recording which was to be short-waved to the meeting while von Elkin appeared as a dummy."

Trent closed his eyes and drew a long breath.

"Very well," he said stiffly. "I cannot deny proof of that kind. But there is one thing I will tell. The Black Bat ruined my plans, and so I shall expose the Black Bat. He is Tony Quinn! Yes, Tony Quinn—the blind man!"

The hooded figure behind Trent jabbed him with the gun.

"Turn your head, von Dahlke. Look toward the door. Detective-captain McGrath happens to be standing there—with Tony Quinn! I did not wish a blind man to be suspected of performing in my role. I knew you suspected him, and I took steps to prove he could not possibly be the Black Bat."

Trent stared at Tony Quinn, who stood beside McGrath. Quinn's eyes stared ahead blankly, apparently seeing nothing.

"Which settles that," the Black Bat said. "Now I think the entire performance is over. I admire your cleverness, von Dahlke. Any man who can pose as another over a period of years is no fool. I suspected everyone but you at first. Attorney Tolly, because he had so many close connections with your kind. But Tolly was only trying to help bring stranded relatives to this country.

"Major Rankin, too, acted oddly. He didn't even report his kidnaping except to his direct superiors, because he detested any form of publicity. He got away from your men in the confusion I started. I should have—"

Von Dahlke suddenly spun around, shot a straight-arm jab at the Black Bat's chin. He streaked toward the door. For an instant he was in a cleared space—until the machine guns at the windows ripped stuttering blasts of death. Von Dahlke hesitated. Staring blindly, he drew erect for a second, and then plunged forward on his face.

TONY QUINN was driven home in McGrath's car. Silk was at the door to let him in.

"Say, I guess I must have been all wrong about you, Quinn," McGrath said contritely. "I'm sorry."

But after McGrath drove away, Silk let out a quiet, victorious laugh.

"I think I did it rather well, sir, but it was nothing like the way you could have handled it. That spy wouldn't have made a break if you were in the hood and cape I wore."

"It's just as well," Quinn said. "Men of his kind are safer dead. You know, I thought it was Trent right after he and Warner were helping me cross the street and that murder car came roaring down on us. Trent didn't make the slightest attempt to push me out of the way. He actually kept such a hard grip on my arm that Warner couldn't get me out of the car's path. I couldn't tell them that, of course, without exposing myself as the Black Bat.

"So, Silk, this calls for a celebration. Carol and Butch will arrive soon. We've defeated a group of men intent on destroying our country. I hope it will arouse our people to the full realization of what a Trojan Horse in our midst is capable of doing. We need to be toughened. We've got to become stronger, harder than those gangsters abroad. I know, from this case, that they must be fought as they fight themselves—without mercy, with absolute relentlessness."

"I think," Silk replied softly, "that with you to fight for us, the Nazi menace will not make another Norway, Holland, Belgium, or France, of America…."